Ireland's Master Storyteller

Published in 1998 by Marino Books
an imprint of Mercier Press

Trade enquiries to CMD Distribution
55A Spruce Avenue
Stillorgan Industrial Park
Blackrock County Dublin
Tel: (01) 294 2556; Fax: (01) 294 2564

© Éamon Kelly 1998

ISBN 1 86023 080 6

A CIP record for this title is available
from the British Library

Cover photograph by Fergus Bourke
Cover design by Penhouse Design
Printed by ColourBooks Baldoyle
Industrial Estate Dublin 13

Ireland's Master Storyteller
The Collected Stories of Éamon Kelly

ÉAMON KELLY

Contents

Introduction

Storytelling is the oldest form of entertainment. It was there before the written word. Storytelling goes back to the time when people lived in caves, and after a hard day's hunting for food the occupants sat in the open air and when supper was over there was one man there who told of the adventures, dangers and escapades of the day. He was the first storyteller.

You can be full sure and certain that when the Red Indians sat around the camp fire at night and smoked their pipe of peace there was one brave who told of the glories of his nation; tales of how his ancestors survived the elements and the hostilities of a neighbouring tribe.

When the Arab train camped in the desert as the sun went down and the camels were arranged in a circle, the fires were lit. When they had partaken of a meal and rested, there was one man there who told the history of his people and of the great men who at one time walked the world. I have heard it said that the Arabs and the Irish are the best storytellers, but where do you leave the Jews? They were good storytellers too and they have two Testaments to prove it.

I always associate storytelling with the fireside, and so it ever was in Ireland. When the day's work was over in the fields the people crowded into that house in the village where the best storyteller was. They sat on chairs, stools and even on the floor. Long before electricity or oil lamps were heard of the only light was from the fire or the spluttering glow of a bog deal splinter. The firelight lit up the faces of the listeners and that of the storyteller as he told tales handed down from father to son –

some tales that went back to Oisín and the Giolla Deachair and some about recent happenings in his own district.

As well as being a good narrator, the storyteller was the local historian and genealogist – a walking library, the repository of folk wisdom and custom. In the days before radio and television the people provided their own entertainment in the long winter nights. After the story was told there was a song or maybe a dance. Many of the kitchen floors in the old days were made of mud but there was always a large stone flag in front of the fire. The stepdancer danced on this and with his iron-tipped shoes knocked sparks out of it. I often heard tell of the front door being taken off its hinges and placed in the middle of the mud floor for two people to dance the challenge hornpipe.

If there were no musical instruments the young people lilted the dance tune and men lit bog deal splinters in the fire and circled the dancers with a ring of light. Mummers were not unknown in country districts then, and in my own place on St Bridget's Eve, boys and girls would dress up in the most outlandish clothes and pull a piece of old lace curtain over their faces as a mask. They used to carve a face on a large turnip with the eyes and mouth deeply incised. They would scoop out the centre of the turnip and put a lighting candle into it.

The sculpted head was fixed to the handle of a broom and a stick put across to hold a coat. With a headscarf this effigy was carried in procession from house to house and the light coming through the eyes and mouth of the head looked eerie in the dark. When the mummers came to the storyteller's house the floor was cleared and they danced a set and sang a song. The effigy was held high and money was collected. Then they all settled down and listened to the storyteller tell of the man who was apprenticed to a doctor or the tale of Dean Swift and his serving man.

In a gathering like this you had all the rude elements of the theatre. The storyteller provided the comedy and sometimes the tragedy because he could bring a tear when he spoke of the death of Naoise and the Sons of Uisneach. The song was there, the music, the dance and the dressing up. I call this form of entertainment 'theatre of the hearthstone' – a diversion having its seed in the time when our forefathers sat at the mouth of a cave and listened to the happenings of a day's hunting.

Éamon Kelly

Beyond the Horizon

My father never took off his hat except when he was going to bed and into Mass, and my mother said he slept in the two places. At that time every man covered his head. There was respect for the brain then.

As well as covering the head the hat is a handy receptacle. If you are caught short you can give a feed of oats to a horse out of a hat. You can gather apples in the orchard or bring in new laid eggs from the hayshed. In fact, you could nearly put a hen hatching in a hat . . . well, a bantam or a guinea hen.

Headgear gives a man authority. The popes and kings and bishops know this. They always cover their heads when they have something important to say. And where would the storyteller be without his hat when he sits at the fireside to tell a story?

In the long winter nights long ago, the talk'd often turn to some great man who was in the world one time. In our house we'd often talk of Aristotle. Of course the old people had a more homely name for him. They used to call him Harry Stottle. He was a great schoolmaster, and the way he used to teach was walking around the fields so the pupils could be thinning turnips or making hay while they were learning their lessons. In those days great store was set by the pupil's knowing the name and the nature of everything that flew and everything that ran, of everything that grew, and everything that swam. But the old people held that despite all his great knowledge, there were three things Harry Stottle could not understand. And these were the ebb and flow of the tide, the work of the honey bee, and the fleetness of a woman's mind, which exceeds the speed of light!

There were these two Kerrywomen. They met on the road one day. One was going to town and the other was coming from town – this now was away back in 1922 when the IRAye were fighting the IRAh. And all the bridges were blown down. So after a heavy day's rain you'd wet more than your toes fording the river!

The woman going to town, who was on the small side, said to the woman coming from town: 'Were you in town what time is it what price are eggs is the flood high?'

As quick as lightning the woman coming from the town said: 'I was three o'clock one and fourpence up to my arse girl!'

Agus ag trácht dúinn ar uisce, as the man said when he got the half of whiskey at the wake, the Ceannaí Fionn used to sail the watery seas between Iveragh and the continent of Europe long before the Danes discovered Ireland. He used to take over what'd keep you warm on the outside and bring back what'd keep you warm on the inside. He used to trade wool for wine. Not a bad swap!

The Ceannaí Fionn's right hand man was Cluasach Ó Fáilbhe, and like Harry Stottle, for they were long headed men, they wondered greatly where the tide went to when it was out and where it came from when it was in. And often on their journeys to and from France and Spain they looked out over the Atlantic Ocean and they wondered too what was behind the horizon, for at that time no one knew. So they went to find out but the horizon always remained the same distance in front of them. After many months they came back nearly demented from hunger and thirst, although 'tis said all great explorers at that time took enough provisions to last them for seven years going, seven years coming and seven years going astray. They came back and this was the story they told.

One day they saw a great hole in the middle of the ocean and the sea on all sides pouring down into it.

'Ah ha,' says the Ceannaí Fionn, 'we know now! That's where the tide goes to when it is out. But where in the devil does it come from when it's in?' He hadn't the words out of his mouth when an almighty pillar of water shot up out of the hole bringing with it broken ships and every kind, class, form and description of wreckage.

'That,' said the Ceannaí Fionn, 'is where the tide comes from when it's in!' A wall of water as high as Mangerton mountain drove the ship westward before it till finally they came to a wall of brass. The sailors hit the wall with their oars and so loud was the report that all the fish stuck their heads up out of the sea. I suppose they thought it was dinner-time!

They sailed along the wall till they came to a breach high up in it. Now as sailors are knacky with ropes, they made a rope ladder, threw it up and the Ceannaí Fionn sent up a sailor to see what was at the other side of the horizon. When the sailor got to the top of the wall he gave a great crow of delight and jumped down the other side. Now they had only three sailors on board the ship, so the third fellow got a tight warning, to come back and tell what was at the other side. *Mo léir!* When the third sailor got to the top of the wall he nearly hopped out of his skin with delight and turning his head he said, '*Críost go deo!* Did I ever think I'd live to see it!'

And giving vent to one father and mother of a great yehoo he jumped down the other side.

Now if the Ceannaí Fionn and Clusach Ó Fáilbhe were ever again to see Iveragh they knew they'd have to pull down the rope. This they did. And what was behind the wall? Nothing would convince the people who heard the tale but what the sailors saw was women. The Ceannaí Fionn said no. That they had plenty of time to reflect on it and his belief was that what the sailors saw was the face of God. His belief was that the world was not made all in one slap, all in one week like we were told. Even the eastern half of it would be too big a job for that.

His belief was that the brass wall was a sort of hoarding the Almighty put up to keep out the sea while he was finishing the western half of the world! And very likely!

If they didn't see what was at the other side of the horizon, Cluasach Ó Fáilbhe got a glimpse of another world and this is how it happened. On their way home they were often hungry and they used to throw out the anchor and do a bit of fishing. One day when they went to pull in the anchor they couldn't, so Cluasach Ó Fáilbhe said he'd go down to see what was holding it. He took a deep breath and down with him along the chain to find that the anchor was hooked under the lintel of a door. He went into the house and there inside was, oh! a beautiful young girl.

'Oh, Cluasach,' she said, 'I'm watching you every day passing above in the ship. I'm out of my mind in love with you and will you marry me?'

'All right,' said Cluasach, 'I will. But I'd like to go home first and talk to my mother.'

'If you go home,' she said, 'you'll have to give me your solemn promise that you'll come back again, and if you break that promise,' she said, 'and if you are ever again on the sea, I'll go up and bring you down myself, for I can't live without you!' She had it bad!

Cluasach gave her his promise and he disentangled the anchor from under the lintel of the door and up the anchor flew bringing him with it. He told the Ceannaí Fionn about the beautiful woman in the house below.

'Don't mind her,' says the Ceannaí Fionn, 'You'd get your death from rheumatics living down in that damp old place.'

'He came home and he told his mother, and the mother wouldn't hear of it either. Marrying foreigners! What did he think! She kept him off the sea, from that out – it was no more ships for Cluasach. Time wore on and he couldn't get the image of this beautiful woman out of his mind. One day the men were playing football below in the strand. One awkward fellow kicked the ball into the tide, and Cluasach, forgetting himself, went in after it. And there she was inside in the waves waiting. She threw her two hands around him and brought him away down with her, down under the sea, down to Tír Fó Thoinn. And he never came back, and I suppose he married her, but he used to send a token. Every May eve for fifty years after, the three burnt sparks used to come into Trá Fraisc. Didn't he live a long time down there with her! Marriage never shortened a man's life if he meets the right woman.

Going to America

We lived in an inland parish and the men sitting around my father's fire talking about the Ceannaí Fionn, well, you could count on the fingers of one hand the number of those that ever saw the salt water, except the man going to America. And as the old woman said, 'God help us he saw enough of it!' And I remember a fierce argument cropped up between Batty O'Brien and Coneen Casey, a thin wiry fellow, as to how long it was since the first Irishman set foot in America. Weren't they caught short for a topic of conversation!

'Well now,' says O'Brien, a man of large proportions and an historian to boot, 'I can answer that question. The first Irishman to set foot in America was St Brendan the Navigator, for of course 'twas he discovered America. Although he kept his mouth shut about it.'

'How long ago would that be so,' says Casey, 'since St Brendan set foot in America?'

'I can tell you that,' says O'Brien, 'St Brendan was born in Fenit, in Kerry around the year AD 500, and he died in Anachuin – I have all this now from the lips of a visiting ecclesiastic – he died in Anachuin about 580. We'll take it now that he did his navigating in his prime, say from 525 to 540. Add all that up and take it from the year we are living in and it will bring you to within a hen's kick of fourteen hundred years since St Brendan set foot in America.'

'Is that all you know?' says Casey, sort of cool, 'Irish people were going to America before that.'

'Can you prove it?' says O'Brien.

'Faith then, I *can* prove it,' says Casey. 'Otherwise I wouldn't have drawn it down. My own granduncle, Thade Flor, was going to America after the famine. In a sailing vessel they were. They were becalmed one evening late, about two hundred miles out from the coast of the County Clare. So they threw out the anchor and went to bed for the night – what did they want up for? In the morning there was a stiff breeze blowing. They pulled in the anchor, and do you know what was caught in the hook of it? The wheel of a horse car!'

'And what does that prove?' says O'Brien.

'It proves,' says Casey, 'that Irish people were going to America by road before the flood!'

I myself saw the tail-end of that great emigration that half-emptied the countryside. Often as a small child going to school I called into a neighbour's house to say goodbye to a son or a daughter that was going to America that morning. One kitchen I went into was so dark inside the poor man couldn't shave himself there. There was only a tiny window. If you threw your hat into it, it would be like an eclipse of the sun.

And I have a clear picture in my mind of Pats Pad Duinnín, barefoot in his thick woollen undershirt and long woollen drawers covering him from his Adam's apple down to his ankles – I'd say he got out of that regalia very quick when he hit New York at ninety in the shade. And there he was outside the open door, where he had plenty of light, shaving himself in a looking glass held up by his small brother. So it was, 'Up a bit, up a bit, up a bit. Will you hold it! Down a bit. Where am I now? Tilt it, but don't crookeden it!'

And you know, make it your own case, it was very hard for small Jer D. to judge where his face'd be.

'Hether a bit, over, down! God in heaven I see the clouds but I don't see myself. Up a bit, down a bit. Blast it! Will you hold it straight. I'll look sweet going into the train with a skelp gone outa the jaw!'

He was lathering himself with Ryan's Keltic soap, and after saying goodbye to him I remember wiping the soap off my hand on the backside of my pants as I went down the road to school. I remember too being taken by a neighbour's daughter to a dance – I was only ten at the time – given in a house in the locality for those going to America. Good fun it was too – the best American wakes they say were in Ireland – and the best Irish wakes in America!

The old people sat around the hearth, drooped and *go brónach*, the red glow of the fire on their faces, their feet keeping time to the music. A set dance was in full swing, the young dancers knocking *fág an bealach* out of the flagged floor, the lamplight throwing their dancing shadows on the whitewashed walls. Down at the butt of the kitchen the musicians were playing. And it was said that these musicians never repeated a tune in the whole run of the night. They had a name for every tune. 'The pigeon on the gate', 'The turkey in the stubbles', 'The cat rambled to the child's saucepan', 'The maid behind the bar', 'Tell her I will'!

If a strange musician didn't know the local names, and the dancers wanted a specific tune, there were rhymes to recall the tune to the fiddler's memory, like, 'When Hannie got up'!

Oh when Hannie got up to admire the cups
She got a stumble and a fall,
Fell on the chair and broke the ware
At Thadeneen Andy's ball!

Or another one was:

Take her away down the quay
I won't marry her at all today
She's too tall I'm too small
I won't marry her at all at all.

In some places those dances were outlawed. They used be raided. In fact a well-known Kerry footballer, the first time he saw a flashlamp – carbine they used to have before that, the stink of it! – he told me that he was sitting behind the door on a half-sack of bran, a girl on his knee, when the curate flashed a light into his face. And coming at him as it did, all of a sudden out of the dark – especially when he had something else on his mind, he thought it was the end of the world. The effect it had on that man. Put his heart sideways. He never scored after!

All dancing was banned, even in the daylight! Didn't I myself hear Father Walsh saying off the altar: 'I'll put an end to the ball nights. I'll put an end to the porter balls and the Biddy Balls! While there are wheels under my trap I'll go into every corner of the parish . . . I don't care how far in from the public road these . . . balls are held to evade ecclesiastical detection. I'll bring 'em down out of the haysheds! It has come to my ears that young women of marriageable age in this parish have remarked "How can we get men if we don't go to the balls?" I'll tell 'em how they can get men. I'll tell 'em how! They have only to come round to the sacristy to me any Sunday after Mass and I'll get plenty of men for 'em without any balls!'

Sentries used have to be posted outside the dance house to raise the alarm when they heard the wheels of Father Walsh's trap – that was before he got the rubber tyres!

One night is gone down in history. Around twelve when the hilarity was at its peak, high jinks in the kitchen and capers in the room, the front door burst open and a sentry rushed in shouting, '*Tanam an diúcs*! He's down on top of us. He's coming in the *bóthairín*!' Well the back door wasn't wide enough to take the traffic. That for terror! The women's coats and shawls were thrown on the bed below in the room, and in the fuss and fooster to get these, two big women got stuck in the room door. Couldn't go'p or down! Until one clever man put his hand on one of their heads, pushed her down till their girths de-coincided and they were free.

Moll Sweeney was the last one out of the house, pulling her shawl around her. Of course when she left the light she was as blind as a bat and who did she run straight into – head-on collision – but the parish priest, who was coming in the back way – look at that for strategy to catch 'em all. And Father Walsh to keep himself from falling in the dirty yard, and ruining his new top coat that he had bought that day in Hilliard's Chape Sale, had to put his two hands around Moll to maintain any relationship with the perpendicular. Moll was trying her level best to disentangle herself.

'Will you leave go of me! Will you stop I said! Stop I'm telling you. Take your two hands off me whoever you are, and isn't it hard up you are for your hoult and the priest coming in the front door!'

The Gobán Saor

But to come back to the American wake. Between the dances there'd be a song. It would be hard enough to get some of those fellows to sing. One man might be so shy he'd want two or three more standing in front of him, 'Shade me lads!' Or he might run down below the dresser or over to the back door where the coats'd be hanging and before he'd sing he'd draw a coat in front of his face.

As the night wore on there would be many young faces, as the man said, with hunger paling, around the kitchen. That way down in the room refreshments were being served. When it came to my turn to go down, there I saw and heard my first storyteller. A great liar! A stonemason by trade. There he was with his back to the chimney piece shovelling in currant bread and drinking tea out of borrowed delph. When he was finished he blew the crumbs off his moustache, and fixing his eye on a crack over the room door he began, 'A trade,' says he, 'is as good as an estate. A man that knows his trade well can hold his head high in any community, and such a man was the Gobán Saor. He was in the same line of business as myself, he was a stonemason. No word of a lie he had the gift and this is how he got it.'

'It so happened one day that the Gobán Saor was out walking when who should he see approaching but an old man with a bag on his back and he bent down to the ground with the weight of it.

'"A very good day to you," says the old man, "are you

going far?"

"'To the high field to turn home the cow," says the Gobán, "do you know me?" For the old man was driving the two eyes in through him.

"'I don't," says the old man, "but I knew your father well." With that he left down the bag and sat on top of it.

"'It was ever said," says the old man, "that your father would have a son whose name would be the Gobán Saor and this son would build the round towers in Ireland – monuments that would stand the test of time, and the people in future generations would go out of their minds trying to find out why they were built in the first place. One day the Gobán Saor would meet an old man who would be carrying on his back the makings of his famous monuments. Did your father ever tell you that?"

"'He did not," says the Gobán, "for he is dead with long."

"'I think I'll be soon joining him," says the old man, "but I have one job to do before I go. Where would you like to build your first round tower?"

"'I'm going to the high field to turn home the cow," says the Gobán, "so I might as well build it there."

'They went to the high field and the stranger drew a circle with his heel around where the cow was grazing. He opened the bag and they dug out the foundations. Then he gave the Gobán Saor his traps; trowel, hammer, plumb-rule and bob, and he showed him how to place a stone upon a stone. Where to look for the face of the stone and where to look for the bed, where to break the joint, and where to put in a thorough bond.

'The wall wasn't long rising, and as the wall rose the ground inside the wall rose with 'em, and they were a good bit up before they thought of the door, and they put in a thin window when they felt like it. When they got thirsty they milked the cow and killed the thirst. The tower tapered in as they went up and when they thought they were high enough the Gobán came out of the top window to put the coping on the tower. By this time the field was black with people all marvelling at the wonder. The Gobán's mother was there and she called out, "Who's the young lad on top of the steeple?"

"'That's your own son," they told her.

"'Come down!" says she, "and turn home the cow!"

'On hearing his mother the Gobán Saor climbed in the window. The ground inside the tower lowered down with him. When he was passing the door high up in the wall the Gobán jumped, and the cow jumped, and the old man jumped and that was just the jump that killed him and he is buried where he fell, the first man in Ireland with a round tower as his headstone – Daniel O'Connell was the second!

'The Gobán picked up his bag of tricks, and after he turned home the cow, his mother washed his shirt and baked a cake, and he went off raising round towers up and down the country. He married and we are told he had a big family – all daughters, bad news for a tradesman, except for an only son. The son, as often happens, turned out to be nowhere as clever as his father, so the Gobán said he'd have to get a clever wife for him and this is how he set about it.

'One day he sent the son out to sell a sheepskin, telling him not to come back without the skin and the price of it – *craiceann is a luach*. Everyone laughed at the son when he asked for the pelt and the price of it, except one young woman. She sheared the wool of the pelt, weighed it, paid him for the wool and gave him back the pelt and the price of it.

'The Gobán said to the son: "Go now and bring her here to me." The son did and the Gobán put her to another test to make sure. He sent her out with a thirsty old jennet he had, telling her not to let him drink any water unless it was running up hill. She took the jennet to the nearest stream and let him drink his fill. And it ran up hill – up his neck. She married the son and was the makings of him!

'When the Gobán Saor had finished the round towers in Ireland, he turned his hand to building palaces, and as every palace he built was always finer than the one before, his fame spread until the King of England sent for him to put up a palace for him, for he wasn't satisfied with the one he had.

'This morning the Gobán Saor and his son set out for England and when they were gone awhile the Gobán Saor said to his son, "Shorten the road for me."

'And the son couldn't so they turned home. The following morning they set out for England and when they were gone awhile the Gobán Saor said to his son, "Shorten the road for me."

'The son couldn't so they wheeled around for home a second time. That night the son's wife said to her husband, "*I gcúntas Dé a ghrá ghil*, what's bringing ye home every morning. Sure, at this gait of going ye'll never make England."

'"Such a thing," says he, "every morning when we're gone awhile my father is asking me to shorten the road for him and I can't."

'"Well where were you got," says she, "or what class of a man did I marry! All your father wants is for you to tell him a story and to humour him into it with a skein of a song."

'Oh a fierce capable little woman! *Pé in Éireann é*, the third morning the Gobán Saor and his son set out for England and when they were gone awhile the Gobán Saor said to his son: "Shorten the road for me."

'And the son settled into:

> Doh idle dee nah dee am,
> Nah dee idle dee aye dee am,
> Doh idle dee nah dee am,
> Nah dee ah dee aye doh!

'And with that they set off in earnest. The son humoured the father into the story of the Gadaí Dubh, and they never felt the time going until they landed over in England where the King and Queen were down to the gate to meet 'em.

'"How do I know you're the right man," says the King.

'"Test me," says the Gobán.

'So the King pointed out a flat stone up near the top of the old palace, and told the Gobán to cut out a cat with a tail on him on the face of that stone. The Gobán took his magic hammer and aimed it at the stone and up it flew and of its own accord it cut out a handsome cat and it isn't one tail he had but two – the Gobán's trade-mark, a thing that was widely known throughout Europe at the time.

'"Fine out," says the King. "You're elected", taking the Gobán to one side and showing him the *cnocán* where he wanted the new palace built.

'"And I've the stones drawn and the mortar mixed," says the King.

'So the Gobán Saor and his son fell to work and cut the foundations, and it wasn't long at all till the palace was soaring for high, with a hall door fifteen feet off the ground and a ladder going up to it that the King could pull in after him in case of any scrimmage, for there is no knowing how *trí na céile* things were in England at that time.

'Well, when the King saw the way the palace was shaping, he was rubbing his hands with delight, and he was every day saying to the Gobán, was it true that the last palace he built was always finer than anything he ever built before? The Gobán said that was correct.

"I'm glad to hear it," says the King, "and as sure as you're a foot high the day the palace is finished, there's a surprise in store for you."

'The Gobán was wondering what these words meant and this is how he found out. 'Twas a daughter of Donaleen Dan's that was housekeeping for that King of England at the time his own wife was that way and not able for the work, and every day when the Gobán and his son'd come in to their dinner the two of 'em and Miss Donaleen'd be talking: *Bhí an Ghaeilge go blasta aice siúd, agus is i nGaelige a bheidís ag caint i gcónaí*, and the King of England didn't know no more than a crow what was going on!

"Bad tidings," says Miss Donaleen this day. "That King is stinking with pride, and he's saying now that if the Gobán Saor and his son go off and build another palace for the King of Wales or the King of Belgium, it will be better than his own, and then he won't have the finest palace in the world. So as soon as ever the job is finished he's planning to cut the heads down off the two of ye! That's the surprise you're going to get!"

Wasn't it far back the roguery was breaking out in 'em, eroo!

'The Gobán slept on this piece of information and in the morning he said to his son: "If my plan don't work I can see the two of us pushing *nóiníns* before the hay is tied."

"*Cuir uait an caint*," says the son. "Here's the King coming."

'Along came the King rubbing his hands with delight and he

said to the Gobán, "Is this now the finest palace in the three Kingdoms."

"'It is,' says the Gobán.

"'And tell me," says the King, "is it long until you'll have it finished?"

"'Only to put the coping on the turret," says the Gobán, "but the implement I want for doing that is called the *cor in aghaidh an chaim* . . . "

"'English that for me," says the King.

"''Tis the twist against crookedness," says the Gobán, "but bad manners to it for a story, didn't I forget it at home in Ireland after me, so I'll hare back for it and bring my son to shorten the road for me."

"'You'll do no such thing," says the King, "you'll stand your ground and I'll send my own son for it."

'Well, that was that for as we all know there's no profit in going arguing with a King.

'Now at home in Ireland the Gobán's son's wife, that fierce capable little woman, was baking a cake this day when who walked in the door to her but the King of England's son.

"'Such a thing," says he, "I'm from over."

"'Is that so," says she. "Is it long from the palace?"

"''Tis nearly ready now," he said, "only to put the coping on the turret, but they forgot the implement for doing that, 'tis called 'the twist against crookedness'."

'She tumbled to that: "You'll find it there in the bottom of the bin," she said, "and if you're not too high and mighty in yourself you can stand up on the chair and stoop down for it."

'And if he did, she kicked the chair from under him, knocked him into the bin, banged down the cover and locked it.

"'Ah-ha-dee," says she. "You'll remain a captive in there until my husband and my husband's father'll come home to me, so write out a note to that effect and hand it out through the mousehole!"

'He did, and she gave the note to the Gobán's pet pigeon, and he knew where to go with it – why wouldn't he! And the plan worked and she hadn't long to wait and she knew who was to her coming up the *bóthairín* when she heard:

> Doh iddle dee nah dee am.
> Nah dee iddle dee aye dee am,
> Doh iddle dee nah dee am
> Nah dee ah dee aye do.'

That stonemason had never been a mile from a spring well, but to hear him talking you'd swear he's been to the moon and back. Going away was the topic on the tip of everyone's tongue that night and the storyteller liked it to be known that he was away himself. This is how he acquainted us of it.

'In my father's time things were slack at the stonemasoning and my mother said to me: "Isn't it a fright," says she, "to see a big fosthook like you going around with one hand as long as the next, and why don't you go away and join the DMP's for yourself!"'

'They were the old Dublin police, a fine body of men. So I took her at her word and hit for Dublin and the depot, and joined up, and after a *tamall* of hard careering around the barrack square, a solid grounding in acts of parliament and all that I was put into a new uniform and let loose in the city of Dublin!'

'My first assignment was public house duty in Parnell Square – kind of a swanky place. I tell you I wasn't long there when I

instilled a bit of law and order in them lads with regard to late
closing and that. Things rested so. I was this night going
along . . . it would be well after half eleven I'd say – when I saw
a light coming through the hole in a shutter of a certain
establishment. I went up and put my eye to the hole and what
was it, you devil, but a line of lads up to the counter with loaded
pints! I banged on the knocker and the publican came out.
"What's this?" says I, "what class of carry on is this?"

"'Oh Ned," says he, "sure you won't be hard on me."

"'Ned!" says I, "what Ned! I don't know you my dear
man, or the sky over you!"

"'I'm a cousin of your own twice removed, I'm a boy of the
Connor's from the cove of Sneem!"

"Jer Dan's son," says I.

"'The very man," says he.

"'Well now," says I, "you could have knocked the cover
off my pipe, I never knew you were in Dublin or in the
public house trade."

"'Oh I am," says he, "come on away in till we try and
soften things out."

'Well, seeing that he was a connection and all to that
I went in with him, but I must say this much for him. He
was not a grasping fellow. I was no sooner in than he
cleared the premises, sat me down and landed me out a
healthy *taoscán* from the top bottle in the house and told me I'd
be welcome at any time which I was!'

'I was this night above inside in the cousins with my
shoes off toasting my toes to the fire, a smart *smathán* of punch
in front of me. We were tracing relationships when around half
past twelve the thought was foreshadowed to me that the DI
might be around on a round of inspection, do you see. I stuck
the legs into the shoes, mooched out to the front door and there

he was coming up along, so I pulled the door after me and pretended to be standing in from the rain. Up he came.

"'Night Ned," says he.

"'Night Officer," says I.

"'Be telling," says he.

"'Nothing to tell," says I, "the publicans in this quarter are living up to the letter of the law."

"'Good," says he, "I'm hearing great accounts about you. Come on and we'll bowl down along."

"'Right," says I, and made a move to go, but couldn't stir a leg. What was it but when I pulled the door behind me the tail of my coat got caught in it, and there I was stuck like a spider to the wall. Wasn't that a nice pucker to be in! If it was raining soup it is a fork I'd have!

"'Have you e'er a match?" says I sparring for wind.

'Decent enough he handed me a box of 'em. I began cutting a bit of tobacco to put in the pipe, all the time racking my brains for a way out of the pucker. With that there was an almighty crack of thunder that nearly rent the heavens.

"'It'll make a dirty night," says I, "and your best plan now'd be to run along home to the little woman for she'll be frightened."

'And they do — about the only thing they're frightened of! That put the skids under him and off he went. Up here you want it, down below for dancing! When he was gone I bent down to try to disentangle myself out of the door when I heard a voice behind me. "You didn't give me back my matches." says he.

'Oh a mean man, that same DI. I was back stonemasoning the following week.

Going to the Train

The young people going away to America would contribute too to the general hilarity and I remember that night Mick the fiddler told the story about his father and the three travelling tailors.

At that time poor people could only afford meat once a week. And before that again there was a time in the history of Sliabh Luachra when people could only have meat three times a year, at Christmas, Easter and Shrove Tuesday night.

One Sunday Mick the fiddler's father was sitting by the hearth. The spuds were done and steaming over the fire, and at the side of the fire, nesting in the *gríosach*, was a small pot, the skillet. In the skillet was a piece of imported bacon called American long bottom bubbling away surrounded by some beautiful white cabbage. For a whole week the poor man had been looking forward to this hour. And you wouldn't blame him if his teeth were swimming in his mouth with mind for it. His wife Mary was laying the table when the front door opened and in walked three travelling tailors, ravenous.

D'réir an seana chultúr, 'twas share and share alike. Already Mary was putting out three plates so that the man had to think quick. Mick the fiddler himself was only a small child of about a year and a half running around the floor in petticoats. They wouldn't put any trousers on a little boy at that time until he was five – people were more practical. The father picked him up and began dangling him that way.

'He didn't dance and dance, he didn't dance all day, he didn't . . . ' When the tailors weren't looking he whipped a big spud out of the pot and then attracting the tailors' attention he let the spud fall from under the child's clothing into the cabbage and bacon!

You'd travel from here down to see the look on the tailors' faces.

'I'm afraid,' says he, letting down the child . . . 'I'm afraid it'll be spuds and salt all round . . . Of course Mary and myself could eat the bacon. After all the child is our own!'

It was common at the time to give those going away a little present. Maybe a crown piece or a half-sovereign. Happy indeed'd be the one that'd get a golden guinea. As well as that the girls might get wearables. A pair of gloves or the like, and it was usual to give the men a silk handkerchief. You'd see 'em sqeezing it and on opening their hand if it bounced up it was pure silk. Of they'd throw it at the wall and if it clung to the mortar it was the genuine article. And you'd see those handkerchiefs the following morning waving from the train as it went out of sight under the Countess' bridge.

In the morning the horses'd be tackled, and anyone who could afford it'd go to the station. Often I was there as a child. At that time it would take the young man going to America eight to ten days to get there in rickety old ships – you could feel the motion of the waves under your feet. And then when he landed over in New York he'd have to work very hard to put the passage money together to bring out his brother. That's how 'twas done. John brought out Tim and Tim brought out Mary. Maybe then he'd get married and have responsibilities, so when again would that young man standing there . . . when again would he come back over the great hump of the ocean . . . if ever.

He'd be surrounded on the platform by his friends, and when the time came for him to board the train he'd start saying goodbye to those on the outside of the circle, to his far out relations and neighbours, plenty of gab for everyone, but as he came in in the circle, to his cousins, to his aunts and his uncles, the wit and the words would be deserting him. Then he'd come to his own family, and in only what was a whispering of names, he'd say goodbye to his brothers and sisters. Then he'd say goodbye to his father, and last of all to his mother. She'd throw her two arms around him, a thing she hadn't done since he was a small child going to school, and she'd give vent to a cry, and this cry would be taken up by all the women along the platform. Oh, it was a terrifying thing for a small child like me to hear. It used even have an effect on older people. Nora Kissane told me she saw a man running down the platform after the train so demented he was waving his fist at the engine and shouting, 'May bad luck to you out ole smokey hole taking away my fine daughter from me!'

And there was a widow that worked her fingers to the bone to get the passage money together to send her son to America. A rowdy she wasn't going to be sorry after. A useless yoke, nothing for him but his belly full of whiskey and porter when he could get it, singing in the streets until all hours of the morning. A blackguard that put many a white rib of hair on his mother's head and took three young girls off their road. The devil soften 'em. They were worse to let him.

The woman was not going to go to the station at all to see him off, but when she saw the other women going she said she might as well. And then when she saw how lonely the parents were parting with their children she thought, 'They'll think me very hard-hearted now if I don't show some concern.' And of course when her heart wasn't in it she overdid it. She went over to the window of the train he was standing inside in the carriage, and throwing her hands to heaven she said, 'Oh John, John, John, don't go from your mother! Don't go away, John. Oh you sweet, utter, divine and lovely little God sitting above on the golden cloud why don't you dry up the Atlantic ocean so the ship couldn't sail and take my fine son away from me. John, John, don't go from your mother, John!'

He opened the door and walked out saying, 'I won't go at all, Mother!' He went down the town and into the first public house and drank his passage! You heard the singing in the street that night!

Pegg the Damsel

Choo chit, choo chow, choo chit, choo chow, choo chit, choo chow. Choo, choo, ch . . . ch . . . ow! Ch . . . ch . . . ssssssh! Cork! Glanmire Station. Cork!

Whatever part of Ireland you left that time going to America you'd have to pass through Cork and then down to Queenstown.

Over here for the boat train. Over here all those for Queenstown. All aboard the boat train! Mind your coat in the door there! All aboard! Choo chit, choo chow. Choo chit, choo chow.

In the morning they'd go out in the tender, out the harbour to where the ship was waiting. They'd go on board and sail away, and the last thing they'd see − often I heard those who came back remark on it − the last sight of home was the Skelligs Rock, the half-circle of foam at the base of Sceilig Mhichíl.

Now that they were gone the people at home sat back . . . and waited for the money! The first Christmas cards we as children saw came from New York. They had lovely drawings of St Joseph and the Holy Family, but lovely and all as those drawings were they couldn't hold the candle to the picture of George Washington − and if George Washington or General Grant weren't inside the crib with the Holy Family there wouldn't be much welcome for the Christmas card. Indeed I heard of one man who used cut open the letter, shake it, and if a few dollars didn't fall out he wouldn't bother reading it! What bank would change a Christmas card!

But to be fair the money nearly always came to the mother. It was the indoor and outdoor relief – the dole, grant and subsidy of the time. She would put it to good use. It would go to buy the few luxuries they'd otherwise have to do without at Christmas. It would go to improve the house, to put extra stock on the farm, to educate a child – where did the civil service come from! And as people got old the money'd go to take out the appendix or to put in false teeth!

Anyone that ever went the road to Killarney couldn't miss Pegg the Damsel's slate house. 'Twas at the other side of the level-crossing, and you couldn't miss that either, for any time I ever went that way one gate was open and the other gate was closed – they were always half-expecting a train!

Pegg's house was done up to the veins of nicety. Dormer windows out on the roof, variegated ridge-tiles, walls pebble-dashed – what you could see of 'em – for they were nearly covered with ivy. In the front garden she had ridges of flowers, surrounded by a hedge, beautifully clipped, you may say the barber couldn't do it nicer, and one knob of the hedge left rise up, and trained to give the effect of a woman sitting down playing a concertina – Pegg herself, of course, for she was a dinger on the box! I tell you if you heard her playing the Verse of Vienna, you'd never again want to turn on the wireless. How is this she had it!

> Father Walsh's, Father Walsh's,
> Father Walsh's top coat,
> For he wore it and he tore it
> and he spoiled his top coat.
> Diddle dee ing dee die doe,
> Diddle dee ing dee die dee,

Diddle dee ing dee die dee,
Diddle dee ing dee die doe.

She was brilliant! Of all the posies in Pegg's garden the roses took pride of place, She had 'em there of every hue – June roses, tea roses, ramblers and climbers. Now, at the back of Pegg's house there was a farmer living called Ryan, and he had a goat running with the cows. And a very destructive animal he was too. He came the way and he knocked into the garden and he sampled the roses, and he liked 'em, and he made short work of 'em!

Pegg complained the goat to Ryan. 'And what do you want him for?' says she, 'with ten cows, sure 'tisn't short of milk you are!'

'Ah, 'tisn't that at all,' says Ryan, 'goats are said to be lucky, and another thing they'll ate the injurious herb and the cows'll go their full time – if ye folly me? You needn't be in Macra na Feirme to know that!'

'You'll be doing full time,' says Pegg, 'if that goat don't conduct himself, for I'll have you up before the man in the white wig.'

'Play tough, now,' says Ryan, a man afraid of his life of litigation, for it can lighten the pocket. 'I've a donkey chain there and I'll shorten it down to make a fetters for the goat.'

Which he did! But when the goat got the timing of the chain, like the two lads in the three-legged race, he was able to move as quick with it as without it.

Now, that was the same year Pegg married the returned Yank ... or was it? 'Tis so long 'go now ... everything is gone away back in my poll. 'Twas! A man that went in a fright for fancy shirts – and they do. One day is all he'd keep the shirt on him. Look at that for a caper! The poor woman kept going washing!

This morning she rinsed out his red shirt and put it outside on the hedge to dry. That was all right, no fault until the goat bowled the way, and handicapped and all as he was, he broke into the garden – attracted by the colour, I suppose! And Pegg the Damsel opened the front door just in time to see the white button of the left cuff disappearing down the goat's throttle.

There was no good in calling the Yank. He was in blanket street waiting for the shirt to dry! All night work he had in New York and he used to sleep during the day, but as he had no night work here he used to sleep day and night!

She chased the goat with the broom and he made off up the railway from her. He ran down the slope and when he was crossing over the tracks, well, 'twouldn't happen again during the reign of cats, didn't one link of the chain go down over the square-headed bolt that's pinning the rail chair to the sleeper. He was held there a prisoner, he couldn't lead or drive, and what was more he heard the train whistling – 'twas coming now. Wasn't that a nice pucker for a goat to be in, and if I was there and if ye were there, we'd lose our heads, but the goat didn't. What did he do? He coughed up the red shirt and flagged down the train!

Shrovetime

Pegg's Yank, the man in the red shirt, came home on a trip and made a match with Pegg. Pegg was a monitor – well a junior assistant mistress – so he had jam and jam up on it!

A lot of young people going away at that time looked upon America as a place or state of punishment where some people suffered for a time before they came home and bought a pub, or a farm or married into land or business . . . like Pegg's Yank. A fair amount succeeded. If you walked around the country forty years ago every second house you'd go into either the man or his wife had been to America.

Many is the young woman came back – well she wouldn't be young then after ten years in New York, but young enough! – and married a farmer, bringing with her a fortune of three or four hundred dollars. Then, if the farmer had an idle sister – and by idle there I don't mean out of work! – the fortune was for her. Then she could marry another farmer, or the man of her fancy, that's how the system worked, and that fortune might take another idle sister out of that house and so on! So that the same three hundred dollars earned hard running up and down the steps of high stoop houses in New York city could be the means of getting anything up to a dozen women under the blankets here in Ireland! And all pure legal!

There was no knowing the amount of people that'd get married at that time between Chalk Sunday and Shrove Tuesday. But quare times as the cat said when the clock fell on him, no one at all'd get married during Lent, or the rest of the year. So, if you weren't married by Shrove Tuesday night you could throw your hat at it. You'd have to wait another twelve months, unless you went out to Skelligs where the monks kept old time. Indeed a broadsheet used to come out called the Skelligs List – it used be shoved under the doors Ash Wednesday morning. Oh, a scurrilous document in verse lampooning all those bachelors who should have, but didn't get married during Shrovetime.

> There's Mary the Bridge
> And Johnny her boy friend,
> They are walking out now
> For twenty one springs!
> There's no ditch nor no dyke
> That they haven't rolled in –
> She must know by now
> The nature of things!
> 'Oh, Johnny,' says she,
> 'Do you think we should marry
> And put an end for all time
> To this fooster and fuss?'
> 'Ah, Mary,' says he,
> 'You must be near doting.
> Who do you think
> Would marry either of us!'

Who indeed! But the matchmaker was there to put the skids under 'em. That's one thing we had in common with royalty, matchmaking – of course the dowries weren't as big!

Why then there was a match made for myself one time, and it is so long ago now that I won't be hurting anyone's feelings by telling ye the comical way things turned out.

At that time anyone that had the notion of giving the place to his heir, be it son or daughter, would make that fact known down at the chapel gate and elsewhere coming up to Shrove. And Sylvie na Scolb was among those that gave vent to such a rumour in the year I'm alluding to. Sylvie's way of living was small, the grass of a couple of cows, but as he was a thatcher he wasn't depending on it.

An only daughter is all he had for the place, and clever enough, faith, he was all out to get a tradesman for a *cliamhain isteach*, so he ran an account to our house, and the old people here at the time said nothing could be lost by entering into negotiations. Word was sent back that we'd meet the other party in Coiner's snug the coming Saturday.

Come Saturday, and it was my first glimpse of Sylvie. Oh, a cross little wasp of a fellow! Is it any man that shot his own father-in-law in the leg the time of the moonlighting! But a great warrant to drink you may say! For when my father put the pint in front of him, with the first slug he drove it below the tops of the church windows, wiped the froth off his moustache and said: 'Now then!' So we got down to business. 'No man,' says Sylvie, 'I'll darken my door down to seventy pounds! And there'll be no twenty pounds down and the rest at the first christening! A lump sum or nothing.'

'*Cúis gháire chughainn*,' says my father, ''tisn't a demesne you have – rushes and fellistrums, aren't you getting a man with a trade?'

'And he's getting a good girl!' says Sylvie.

'We didn't see her yet,' says my father. 'Take fifty.'

'I said seventy.'

'Take sixty.'

'Look,' says Sylvie, 'put another five on top of it, and don't anyone hear us haggling here like Sheridans!'

'Twas done and my father called for another round. Sylvie must have got into the wrong trousers coming out in the morning, for he never ventured near the pocket at all. And isn't it the likes of him that'd get on!

'Well,' says Sylvie, viewing me for the first time, 'What night are you coming over to see Béib, Ned?'

'Whatever night ye are eating the gander,' says I.

'Aiting the gander' was a very enjoyable pre-nuptial function that went on to give the parties a chance of getting acquainted.

'The gander', says Sylvie, 'will be Thursday, so let ye come early and walk the land.'

We all sailed over Thursday, walked the land, inspected the stock. 'Twas aisy count 'em, three cows and a jennet! Counted the cow tyings in the stall – extra cow tyings'd be put in during the making of a match. They'd be taken out and more with 'em when the old age pension officer'd come!

Then we went in to see Béib. Well, as nice a girl as you could wish to see, but very shy and distant in herself. She hadn't a word for the priest only 'Yes' and 'No', and inclined to call me 'Sir'!

We all sat in to roast goose and there was dancing after, and when Béib and myself took the floor what did the fiddler strike up, out of pure devilment, but the Mason's Apron. We had the sport of Cork and Béib said she thought she liked me, and I couldn't say anything with the crowd around.

We were in town again the coming Saturday doing the bindings – the marriage agreement. All the signing! You'd think it was the Treaty of Versailles! The double deed came in at the time, and the two of our names were put in the land. The sixty-five pounds was paid down – to the attorney for the time being in case of any crux. A proviso was put in for fear Sylvie and the missus'd take to the room. The usual proviso was that the old couple'd get their full needs of combustibles – milk, turf, butter and eggs, a seat in the car to Sunday Mass, or any other big excursion like going to town to turn the bit of money. And the wedding was to be the coming Tuesday – Shrove Tuesday.

I went to bed early Monday night in the room below the kitchen. Our house was all on the ground in a hollow and it was just as well for the wind was rising, and it was cold enough to snow – and as the man said, it looked as if it might be a white wedding!

I found the night awful long! The cock crew and it never dawned. The old people got up and made tea. They thought the night awful long. I got up. We all went to bed again. Well, between the ups and the downs I woke up in the latter end – I think 'twas the cock woke me – to see a chink of light coming in at the top of the room window. I jumped out, ran down and opened the door. What was it, you diggle, but a wall of snow up to the eaves of the house! The clock was stopped . . . I didn't know where I was. I dolled up in a jiffy and tunnelled my way out through the snow and made every nearway for the chapel. There was no one there, but knowing women I made allowances. I waited on.

'You're getting very devout!' says the parish clerk, coming up behind me. 'Where were you yesterday?'

'Getting ready for today,' says I.

'That you mightn't sin,' says he. 'Isn't *today* Ash Wednesday. Don't you see the women coming in for the ashes!'

That explained it! I knew there was something unnatural in having to get up five times the one night – for a man of my age!

I was in bed since Monday. But when I explained the thing to the injured party that I was snowed under for two nights and a day . . . they wouldn't hear of it.

'Clear,' says Sylvie, 'or I'll make a strainer of you with the double barrel.'

And of course Béib wouldn't look at the same side of the road as me from that out. I was free and she was idle for another year! But it didn't set me back much, for before Lent was out I went building gate piers to a place called the Lots, where I met the little woman that's with me since. If Béib was nice Juil took the cake, and I married her for love and in that way started the fashion in this locality.

But there were plenty of love matches that time too and plenty of love-making. How you'd know that is by the bluebells in the wood and the long grass on the slopes of the railway. They used to come in for a bit of flattening! That was all right in the summer of course, but coming home from a ball night in the middle of winter, you might be conveying home a little pusher and she might say to you, 'I know what you mean but the grass is wet.' Well, there was nothing for it then only to go up on a hayshed. And if you were a clever young lad you'd pick a hayshed where the dog knew you, otherwise the farmer'd be out and leave the print of the four prongs of the dung fork in your backside – that'd bring down your temperature! He wasn't worried about the damage you'd do to the ten commandments, but that you might set fire to his hay.

You'd never think it now, but I spent a few nights in a hayshed myself. The first time I was only fifteen, fair play to me! There was a friend of mine, much older than me conveying this pusher home from a ball night – four o'clock in the morning. She had a sister coming in the way like, so I was only giving him a helping hand. The sister was as young as myself, a pure greenhorn. After a bout of tickling we fell asleep!

But it was always said those made matches worked well. Although I did hear a travelling man say . . . There used to be a bed for the poor in nearly every house that time – *leaba na mbocht* – if it wasn't there the man of the house would go out in the haggard and bring in a number of sheaves of oats and spread 'em on the floor . . . two for a pillow. Then there was an old linen sheet kept for the purpose, to cover the straw. At bedtime the traveller would lie on that, his marshal cloak around him like Sir John Moore, but unlike Sir John Moore he'd be up with the crack of dawn in the morning and he'd have all the straw out in the yard and the floor swept.

These men were always welcome for they were great carriers of news and gossip, and I heard one of them say that he knew for a positive fact that the morning of a wedding a different woman was substituted at the altar steps. I never heard it myself and I remember drawing it down to Master Buckley.

'It never happened,' says he, 'only more of this bla'guarding put out to ruin our reputation!'

I don't know. The travelling man told us of another case which he saw with his own two eyes. And by the same token it was a man home from Springfield Mass. that married into this place where there was an only daughter – oh very well to do. All saddle horses that were in the wedding drag. There was a race back to the house, every man with his woman up behind him – riding *cúlóg*. Very romantic, he said, but awful dangerous over stoney ground. Some of them were thrown off, but I suppose that was part of the fun. He was at the wedding that night. We asked him was he invited. No, he said, he strawed. And that's a thing used to take place – if you weren't invited to a wedding, you could see the inside of the house for a while by strawing it. The straw was a disguise, and this was how it was done. You'd make a straw rope, a *súgán*, a *méaróg*, it was made with the finger. A stretch of the hands would be long enough. Two fellows'd hold that. Then you'd get clean scotched straw, eight or ten laces at a time, attach it to the rope falling to the ground all along until you had a fine curtain of straw. You tied that around your middle and it covered you all the way to the floor.

Then you made a second *méaróg*. You took the laces of straw as before, and there was a very clever knot for fixing the laces to the rope. The way it was done the second knot kept the first one in position and so on. When the curtain of straw was ready you lifted it up tied it on like a cape and it covered you from the shoulders down as far as it would go. Now you made a third straw rope, it was a three-piece suit, fixed the straw along it, and when it was complete you brought the rope around, put a knot on it leaving a circle just big enough to go down over your head. Then bringing all the straw into a point you made a tall cone-shaped hat. When you tied the straw six or eight inches down from the top the hat looked like a small stook of oats, or maybe more like an indian's wigwam, only they'd be the *suarachy* indians that'd go into it! Then you'd lift it up, let it fall down over your head and you were completely covered in straw, except, as the man said, you could see out but you couldn't be seen in.

There was a damn nice cuck on top of the hat, and the captain of the strawboys would part that in two places making three cucks on top of his hat. This was so it would be easy to pick him out in the crowded wedding house. He gave the orders. He had his men numbered, there might be ten of 'em in a batch, because if he called out their names in the house they'd be known. You'd have to be very wary inside there and keep an eye on your comrade in front and hope the fellow behind kept an eye on you. The danger was that some blackguard with the signs of drink on him might redden a splinter in the fire and set fire to the straw!

After the batch of strawboys was admitted to the wedding house the captain, altering his voice, would wish the newly married couple joy. He and his men'd be given a drink, and in return they'd dance a set. This payment they gave with a heart and a half. Idle women'd be mad to go out dancing with the strawboys. The great fun for them'd be trying to find out who the men were, poking their fingers through the straw masks to see who was behind them. When the music was in full swing there was nothing as lovely as all that whirling straw under the light of the lamp.

In the old days of the mud floor the door'd be taken off the *bacáns* and two strawboys'd dance the challenge hornpipe on top of it. That was before the oil lamp, and to brighten things up the other strawboys would redden bogdale splinters in the fire and ring the dancers with a blaze of light. As well as dancing, a man whose number was called out by the captain might give a bit of a dust-up on the box, or play the flute. The travelling man said when his number was called he told the story of Bláthnaid, the daughter of the King of the Isle of Man. The story was so well received, and he was a dinger to tell one, that the bridegroom asked the storyteller to remain on for the rest of the night as his special guest. This he did, and when his comrades went out he took off his straw suit and, as he said himself, sat with the select.

It was a great wedding. The man home from Springfield Mass. spared no expense in food or drink. At that time it was a great boast to have it to say 'we danced till daylight' and weddings'd last the night and maybe into the following day. Now, it was only natural to expect that the newly married couple might like to be alone for a while. What they used to do in some places was to go down in the room and put the press to the door, or run upstairs.

Upstairs they went in this place for it was a slate house, They'd be gone for a while, but the hilarity'd be kept up, no notice taken. People had enough upbringing at the time not to remark on what was natural. About an hour after, the man from Springfield Mass. walked down the stairs, his face as white as chalk, a wild *sceón* in his eyes and he cursing under his breath the day he ever put foot inside the door. He walked out, his brother had to go up and get his clothes, for it seems the one he married was not a proper woman!

God bless the mark! 'What would you do if the kettle boiled over? What would you do but to fill it again. What would you do if you married a soldier? What would you do but to marry again.' But that man never married again, and people in authority who couldn't be without knowing, never lifted as much as a little finger to dissolve that unnatural union. And the money he brought into that house as *cliamhain isteach* was never paid back to him, and his people and her people used to belt each other black and blue over it every fair day. The old people always said that God could knock you sideways for laughing at a man in misfortune, but we couldn't help smiling in our minds for we knew that the man from Springfield Mass. would never have found himself in that pucker if he gave a few nights up on a hayshed with her!

Mick the Fiddler Comes Home

There were also those who came back from America – those who only went over to see the time. Such a man was Mick the Fiddler. He said the climate over didn't agree with him. He got a crick in his neck from looking up at the tall buildings.

The day before he sailed for America Mick helped his brother and his brother's wife Moll Phil to set the barley in the high field – he was home again in time to cut it! His brother went to the railway station to meet him, and when Mick the Fiddler got off the sidecar above at the gable of his own house, he looked around at the countryside and said, 'So this is Ireland!' Only gone six months! He had a crease in his trousers that'd shave a gooseberry for you, and the tie he had around his neck I wouldn't like any bull to see it! He didn't know anyone that came to meet him, even those who were in the same book as him going to school. He went straight into the kitchen, and very taken aback by the way at what he saw sitting up on the hob by the fire. He said to his brother's wife, 'Say, Moll, what's this longtailed bugger in the corner?'

'Wisha, Mick,' says she, 'is it how you don't know the cat!'

But of all the people ever to come back from America, Mick the Fiddler gave the best of value, for he answered all questions appertaining to the nature of New York. Signs by, the house used to be packed every night and the brother and the brother's wife, Moll Phil, pusses on 'em, for they usedn't get to bed until all hours. Another thing,

Moll Phil was very house-proud. Her kitchen was shining. You could eat off the floor, and it killed her to see all of us streaming in every night, bringing the mud of the locality on our shoes.

Mick's first night home he was telling us about the boat going over. He said they must have saved the company a fortune on food. It was four days before they could keep anything down. In those days all emigrant boats had to pull in to Ellis Island in New York Harbour, where they had to undergo a very strict medical examination.

A newspaper would be held up in front of you, and you'd be expected to read a skein out of it. They were all good scholars going over that time, but again there might be the occasional man that wouldn't know B from a bull's foot up on the gable of a house. He'd be questioned to see how the talk was by him. He'd be asked what is a cloud? Or to explain a mountain. Mick said one of the Hanna Finns up there near Loo Bridge made an awful bad fist of the reading. Poor fellow, I suppose he got excited, so the American said to him, 'Say, can you tell me what a lake is?'

Finn said, 'I can and will tell you what a lake is. 'Tis a hole in the arse of a kettle!'

Mick told us when it came to the medical examination you'd be prodded and poked the same as if you were a bullock at the fair. The way the doctor'd look through the hair of your head and under your finger nails, you wouldn't be one bit surprised if he looked up a certain place to see was your backbone straight!

All the clothes, Mick said, had to be taken off, even the socks, and put in a little *cábúis* and you walked in naked to the doctor. When Mick was walking in naked, who should he meet charging out against him but one of the Caseys of Túirneóinneach making a fig leaf with two hands. '*Fo fó thíona,*' says he, mad with fright, 'Where's my trousers, 'tis a lady doctor that's inside!' The Caseys were ever virtuous! Mick said he'd be better off if he covered his face instead. She mightn't know him when he went in again!

Mick's first job over was working in a shoe store where a beautiful lady came in one day for a pair of shoes. Like many beautiful women, according to Mick, she had one small fault – she had an awful big *spág* of a foot. And nothing'd satisfy that girl, Mick said, only the fanciest pair of shoes in the house, and of course the shoes refused to go on her. Mick was trying to be of all the help he could. She'd find it hard to get a more attentive assitant. Down with him on one knee, and in an effort to get her heel into the shoe, he took the liberty of taking her by the leg. Looking down at him she said, 'Have you a horn?'

Mick's next job was drawing water in a big barrel in a four-horse car for baptising black and white babies. They weren't piebald, Mick told us, a handful black and a handful white. At this time it seems the population of New York was mounting. In the chapel where Mick was working there were four curates, their sleeves folded up to their elbows, baptising away all day and the water flowing out the front door.

The same as here, those babies were baptised in the bottom of the church, but wakes were held in a funeral parlour. Mick was at one of these wakes. He told us the man was laid out in a coffin with the lid off, and he dressed up in a new suit – no habit – the same as if he was going to a dance. Mick thought it a shame burying the new suit with him, until someone called him aside and told him there was no back to the suit! I tell you, the Yanks'd learn you how to live!

The wake he was at . . . he was a Dannehy boy from the butt of the Paps. He fell under a train at Penn Station. Mick took the day off to go to the wake, and on the way he called into a speakeasy, it was during prohibition, where he struck up a friendship with an American-born Kerryman. They used to call those narrabacks, so the two set out for the wake. The narraback didn't know Dannehy or the sky over him, but he said he'd go along for the fun of it. They called to a few more saloons on the way and when they arrived they were spifflicated, paralytic, and missed the funeral parlour by inches. They went in next door, knelt down and, mustering up all the reverance they could, they began to pray. Where were they kneeling but in front of a piano with a lid up. Luck of God, they didn't put their elbows on the bed. They got up and walking away the narraback said to Mick, 'I did not have the privilege of knowing your friend, but I must say he sure had a fine set of teeth!'

I'll never forget as long as I live one night we were in the house and Mick the Fiddler was on his favourite subject – skyscrapers. There was a man there that had been on an excursion to Cork, and he said, 'Well now, Mick, would those skyscrapers be as tall as one of the spires of St Finbarr's Cathedral in Cork?' Mick looked at him. 'God help your head! They'd go down that far in New York before they'd even think of going up! And they go up so high they had to take a brick off one chimney to let the moon pass!'

And those buildings go up so quick. Mick said when he was going to work one morning they were digging out the foundations for a new skyscraper, and when he was coming home from work that evening the tenants were being evicted for non-payment of rent. That put the Round Towers and the Gobán Saor in the ha'penny place!

There were so many questions to Mick about the topography of New York that he decided he'd draw a map. There was no piece of paper in the house big enough so what did Mick do only put a coating of ashes on the flag of the fire, and with the top of old Din Donovan's walking cane he drew in the ashes the outline of the island of Manhattan. Ten miles long, Mick said, and three miles wide, bought by the Dutch from the Red Indians for less than fifty dollars. 'Don't you think,' says Mick, 'there were bargains going in those days!'

With the top of Din Donovan's walking cane he drew the avenues running north and south and the streets running across, and he said the number of buildings between two streets was called a block, and that there were eight blocks to the mile – if you could believe him. He began to show us places. The names were as well know to us as the townlands of our own parish, the Bowery and Chinatown, and he said there was a Kenmare Street in Chinatown – weren't they caught short for names! Riverside Drive, Hell's Kitchen, Columbus' Circle and Central Park West. Well, there was a simple poor man there and looking at the map he said, 'I'd know where in the middle of all that ashes is my sister Hanna!'

'Do you know her number?' says Mick. 'Two hundred and forty West Eighty-Fourth Street.'

'Right,' says Mick pointing down with the walking cane, 'between Amsterdam and Broadway. There is where she hangs out!' Which was true for him, for she worked in a laundry.

The cat sat up on the hob and began to wash her front, then arching her back she opened her mouth wide – you'd swear she was laughing. The dog was lying on the floor a bit down from the fire. If he only knew half of him was inside in the Hudson. There he was with his snout down on his two front paws a few inches away from the ashes of Mick's map. He was barking in his sleep, and isn't it lovely to hear him 'wuff, wuff, wuff', whatever little images are running through his mind. I suppose that he pictures himself after sheep on the mountain, or maybe mixed up in some other carry-on!

The dog took a deep breath, filled himself up, you could nearly count his ribs. Then of a sudden he let it all down his nose in one snort and demolished three-quarters of an acre of skyscrapers! You could see the little particles of ashes rising up between you and the light of the lamp, and you could see Moll Phil's face, and it was like the map of South America!

Well, there were Breshnihins there who had brothers in the Bronx, Sheehans who had sisters in Staten Island and Keoghs who had cousins in Queens, not to mind those with relations in Brooklyn, Yonkers and the Jersey Shore. 'Twas like a pantomime, they all wanting to know where their people were living. But Mick told 'em, as all these places were outside the island of Manhattan – up the Hudson and down the bay, turn to Coney and Rockaway – the chairs had to be pulled back and more ashes brought out to add to the map!

In the middle of all this activity the cat hopped off the hob and marched down Fifth Avenue – you'd think it was Patrick's Day. We began to call the cat in case she'd bring the ashes on her pads all over the house. And the dog woke up when he heard us talking to the cat, thinking he was being left out of something. Got up and walked over and sat down in the middle of the Bronx and began to wag his tail. Now the ashes began to rise and Mick the Fiddler knew the fat was in the fire so he started to call the dog. Cess! Cess! Nice doggie. Nice doggie! And the dog, a big, soft, half-fool of a sheepdog, to show his friendship sent his tail around like a propeller churning up the ashes until you couldn't see your finger in front of your face. Out of this dense fog came Moll Phil with the sweeping brush, and as I was the nearest to her I got the first crack of it. 'Aha,' says she, 'I'll give ye the Bronx! And I'll give ye Chinatown!' The same as if she was the mounted police, she cleared the kitchen. We all spilled out the front door like dirty water out of a bucket, bringing to an abrupt ending Mick the Fiddler's graphic description of the island of Manhattan in the State of New York in the Continent of America.

Killing the Pig

Mick the Fiddler, like all the returned yanks, when he wore out the clothes he came home in, you wouldn't know him from the man that never stirred out. He sat at my father's fire when his day's work was over, and talked with the other men about the life around us, and the things that mattered most in that life, food, drink and tobaccy, love, marriage and the hereafter!

> Oh God on High that rules the sky come in
> the open door
> And bring us mate that we can ate
> and take away the boar!

That was the prayer of a servant when his master killed a very old gentleman pig! Why then when I was young it'd be the poor man that'd let the winter past without killing a pig. And if you went into a house in November, you'd have to pick your way to keep from banging your head into the flitches of bacon hanging down from the rafters smoking away!

Not everyone could cure a pig. Some'd overdo the salt, others'd be too skimpy with it – you'd hear of those that'd put a dust of brown sugar or a pinch of saltpetre in it for flavouring. No matter! If it was done right 'twas hard to cap the home-cured bacon. Say what you like, *a mhicó*, there was no better dish for the working man.

And wasn't the fresh pork lovely! And the puddings! Oh my! When we were nippers we'd give our two eyes out for the puddings! Puttens we used to call 'em. So there's no harm in saying that it was an event in the house the day the pig was killed.

Although women had no heart for the slaughter. The women in this house used to take to the fields, their fingers in their ears, for the screeching of a stuck pig would curdle the blood! As a child I used to be a bit terrified myself. Of course, I used get very fond of the pig while he was fattening. No day'd pass that I wouldn't give him a call. I found the most agreeable time to visit him in his *áras* was when his belly was full. He'd often sit on his behind, his head to one side, looking at me with his small eyes as he scratched his waistcoat with one of the two toes of his hind leg. He'd always take it as a great favour if I gave a rub of my heel to a place he couldn't get at, and the fatter he got the more places got out of reach.

Passing neighbours'd be brought to have a look at him by my mother. They'd marvel at how he had improved since the last time. You'd think the pig'd be enjoying all this admiration, until he'd get a slap of a hat on the rump to make him walk around, so that the neighbours could guess his weight and compliment my mother on his condition. Poor fellow, if he only knew, every extra pound he put on brought the day nearer when he'd wind up in the pot.

> Green grow the rushes o,
> the blackbird and the thrushes o,
> We'll kill the pig with the curly tail,
> and we'll have mate tomorr-ee-o.

For the purpose of killing the pig, there was in every locality an expert butcher, and the man we had there, credit where credit is due, was quick to dispatch! From the time the pig found himself on the flat of his back on the table in the yard, four men steadying him for the knife, until he was hanging by the hind legs from the ladder, scalded, shaved and emptied out, with three pointed sally rods keeping his waistcoat open, and a big spud in his mouth, everyone worked like lightening and it was all over in a flash.

A few of the neighbours'd be in again the following night for the salting. And how many stone of salt'd cure a pig? I'm told three stone is overdoing it. Two-and-a-half stone is enough! Well I should know it! Many is the time I brought it across the handlebars of the bike from Barraduff!

We used to nail a board around the table to keep the salt from falling on the floor. The salt was rubbed well into the flesh with the fingers and the palm of the hand, and deep pockets'd be made for it to carry the brine to the bone. And when the last piece'd be put in position in the big tub – a wine barrel we'd use – and a weighty *carraig* put on top of it to press it down, the man of the house'd be happy. But of course his worries wouldn't be over till the ninth day when the pickle'd be expected to rise. If it didn't rise'd be a calamity, but if it did, it'd keep rising, and in three weeks' time it'd be up to the top, and your bacon was cured only to hang it up. And once there was york in the garden, swedes in the haggard and spuds in the pit no one in that house'd be hungry for the winter.

But to come back to the puddings! Here is where the women shone. From early morning the day after killing the pig, they'd be down to the river turning what seemed to be miles of intestines inside out and washing 'em in the running stream.

In the house then, in a while's time, they'd be all around this big pot, where they were after mixing Macroom oatenmeal and milk with the pig's blood, added to that'd be rice, onions, breadcrumbs, pepper, salt, allspice and the diggle knows what else.

Then the intestines'd be cut into lengths of up to eighteen inches. One end would be tied with a bit of bageen thread, and the lovely way the women had of keeping the other end open like a funnel with the thumb and first finger of the left hand, and then with the free hand they'd begin ladling in the mixture with a big spoon – and the filling of the puddings was in full swing!

When a pudding was three quarters full – room had to be left for expansion in the cooking – the ends'd be tied together to make a bowlie, it looked for all the world like a small bicycle tube pumped up. Then over the fire'd be another big pot, the handle of a brush across the mouth of it, and the women'd run these hanks of pudding in over the handle of the brush, in a form that the greater bulk of the puddings'd be dipping into the boiling water. Then they'd be turned around as they cooked, getting an occasional prod of the fork to keep 'em from bursting. When they'd be all done there'd be a string of puddings from here down to the dresser, and take it or leave it, there wouldn't be one of 'em left two mornings after. For at that time the custom was when you had the plenty you'd share it with your neighbour and he'd do the same with you when God smiled on him! A plate of porksteak a finger high, and a circle of pudding, maybe two, would find its way to every house in the townland. What a heart the people had then, and if you or me were to put our foot inside the door of any of those houses when that pork or pudding was sizzling in the pan, you'd be invited to sit over to the table and share it. Though it would not be thought proper manners or good rearing to be in a hurry accepting it. 'No, no, no,' you'd say, 'I only left the table after me!'

That was the old way and a person that'd take food or drink in a neighbour's house, or even sing a song at a dance without a little forcing was considered forward!

I had an uncle living at the other side of the mountain, and one morning long before I was confirmed I was sent over to my uncle's to know would himself and Mary come over to us when we were having the stations. I was over the mountain once with my father so I thought I knew the way.

After a while climbing I wasn't so sure for nowhere could I see the little landmarks my father pointed out to me. I made poor headway on rough ground. Times I'd put my head over a knob thinking I was at the top, only to find that I had as far more to go. The day was going and the hunger began to pick me, but I kept going and when I got to the top of the mountain the heart was put across me altogether for the fog fell.

'Don't move in the fog – wait until it lifts,' my father'd say. So I sat down, but the quietness and the queer things I thought I saw in the drifting fog made me afraid, so I began to aise myself with the fall, feeling with my feet and holding on to the heather with my hands, until after ages I heard a small sound of water tinkling. I knew now that I had covered a fair bit of ground, so I kept the little stream company till it brought me out of the fog. And there far below me I could see a house.

Was I divarted! With no bite gone inside my lips since morning the sight of a house was welcome. I belted down the side of the mountain and by the time I got into the yard it was dark. There was a light in the stall. A man came out and I asked him where was Íochtarchúil – where my uncle was living.

'Íochtarchúil,' says he, 'is away to the west of us. But no one in his proper senses would venture that far tonight. Come in and stay with us and I'll point out the way to you in the morning.'

I went in with him, and like the story while ago, I was born the right time for the table was being laid. It seems the old man and the son were at the fair that day, and it was only now they were having the dinner. Wasn't I in luck! The son's wife was there, a returned yank very likely, judging by the speech and the complexion.

The spuds were taken up, strained and put steaming. In a while's time they were turned out on the table and plates full of home-cured bacon and cabbage. Oh Glory, and I was ravenous! Then the woman of the house, give her her due, invited me to sit over, and of course I knowing my manners said – and you'd say it without thinking, 'No! No! No! Look if it killed me I couldn't touch it – I only left the table after me.'

She didn't ask me any more! The old man and the son began to force me. She shut 'em up saying, 'Didn't you hear what the kid said!' And wasn't that the tantalising I got, to have to sit there looking at 'em stowing it away – the big mountain of spuds going down in the middle of the table and small mountains of peels rising at their elbows.

And then to kill me altogether what did they do? Fed the dog within a foot of me! I was going to say let me bring it out in the yard to him so that I could ate it myself. And I'd say he'd let me too for he was a friendly old buffer!

The table was cleared and we all sat up to the fire, and there, so near me, I could put my hand into it, was the pot nearly a quarter full of potatoes. I was praying that nature'd call 'em out, but it didn't, or if it did it didn't call 'em out together!

Bedtime came and I was put down in the room with the old man. There were two fine camp beds below. Well, I thought he'd never doze off. He was so curious! He wanted to know every single thing about everyone belonging to me, but when he found out I wasn't related to anyone important he began to yawn and fell asleep.

I waited till his snoring was nice and regular, and then I crept out of the bed, doing my level best to avoid the chair where my clothes were draped. It was as dark as pitch. I tried opening the door and one of the hinges began to complain. I put my weight on the latch. That worked, and I was in the kitchen. Not knowing what I'd bump into there, I thought it safer to go down on all fours and crawl.

After a time I made an attempt to rise and got an unmerciful wallop on the top of the head. Where was I, you diggle, but under the table, and not alone there for something cold and wet tipped me in the face. I'd have passed out then, only for thinking of the dog. It could be worse if he barked!

From where I was now, I could make out the hearth, so I crept up feeling for the pot. I found it, and with no implements no more than Adam had, I settled in to ate the spuds. I don't remember enjoying any Christmas dinner like it.

When I was full I walked down, my eyes getting used to the dark now, and using the same trick of putting my weights on the latch, I shut the room door without making a sound.

But this time I suppose I was getting too cocksure of myself, for I fell over the chair and woke up the old man!

He cracked a match and when he saw me standing there in my shirt he pointed under the bed, saying, 'You didn't have to go out at all then, perishing yourself!'

I didn't say anything only hopped into bed and dropped off. When I got up in the morning the woman of the house was making a great singsong about the empty pot of spuds.

'Where,' says she, 'could they have gone to?'

'Yerra, I suppose,' her husband said, 'the dog ate 'em!'

'Why then if he did,' she said, 'in the circus he should be, for he peeled 'em as well.'

After Hours

Well, there was this public house I knew of a time. You'd hardly ever see anyone going into it or coming out of it. It was run by three sisters, fairly ancient, I'd say they were behind the door when the good looks were being given out. You'd want to be paid if you were to give any time looking at 'em. One of the sisters'd always be at the entrance, dyddling away to herself, looking up and down the street, the two hands under the apron. By the way, do you see, that it was a gay house.

The time the railways and the roads were cut during the second trouble there was an awful shortage of drink in town, and Ned Connor, when all fruit fails welcome haws, went into the public house I'm talking about. Ned had an awful mind for porter, he'd drink it out of a horse's crupper. The sister that was at the door dyddling the 'Blackbird' backed in before him.

Ned called for a pint, and when after a lot of *taoscing* she put it on the counter, Ned said, 'This pint isn't full.'

'Ah,' says she, 'I left room on top for your moustache.'

Ned had what can only be described as a big straggly growth on the top lip. When he put up the money she found she was a few ha'pence short. The price of the moustache Ned told her. The porter was so flat, little *súilíns* winking on top of it, that it gave Ned enough to do to finish the pint.

When finally he got it down Ned made a move to go, and as she dyddled she kept an eye on him. 'Are you off?' she said.

'Oh I am,' says Ned.

'Of course,' says she, turning as sour as the commodity she was selling, 'only for the shortage of drink in town you wouldn't come into me at all.'

'Well I can tell you one thing,' says Ned, 'you'll have a lot of dyddling done before I'll come into you again!'

Ned was noted, but fierce, for the drink. He took every known pledge in his time including the anti-treating pledge. That was brought in to counteract the habit of standing your round, which is all right if the company is small, but if you have seven or eight in a batch, and maybe, before you know where you are, the man that opened the proceedings is off on the second leg of the course, then there's rough weather ahead. And the man of limited capacity don't he suffer! His wife at home thinking he is enjoying himself.

One of the pledges Ned took only allowed him one drink a day. He settled for a pint. That was all right until he was seen pouring two pints into a quart jug, making one drink of it. He went from the quart to the sweet gallon and finished up worse than ever. And I'll never forget one Whitsun I was going doing the rounds at Gobnet's Well, John Lynch was with me the same day and we got up to Ned going down Sliabh Riabhach.

Whit was late that year and it was very warm so we went into the Mills. I called and when the pints were put on the counter Ned Connor caught his glass and ran out in the yard with it. When he came back 'twas empty. John Lynch called then, and the same thing happened. Ned came back with the empty glass in his hand. T'was his own turn to call then and when he was making for the back door with the third pint 'twas only natural that myself or John

Lynch'd remark on it. Well, for one thing he was playing poo-paw with the conversation, so I said – '*Croí an diabhail*, Ned where are you going with the pints or what class of caper is this?'

'Ah lads,' says he, 'have patience with me. I have a pledge against drinking in public houses.' Of course as the day wore on he forgot to go out and broke that pledge too!

Ned was married. God help the poor children, they were often hungry and the wife was to be pitied. Now it so happened that the wife had an aunt. A pure druidess of a one. She came visiting and she wasn't long in the house when she pointed out to Ned the error of his ways. He had to go down on his knees and promise that he'd give the drink the go-by or she said she'd make a *lúbán* of him, and she would, for she was a fierce major of a woman. She marched him into the convent to Sister Benedict and made him take the teetotaller's pledge.

And to everyone's surprise he kept it – well for a while. One day in town he fell into bad company and broke out. He arrived home paralytic. He had to hold on to the back of a chair in an effort to maintain his relationship with the perpendicular and to make things worse his wife's aunt was there. Did she read him a lesson!

'After all the promises you made,' says she. 'A man with such little respect for his word, not to mind the welfare of his wife and family, could not expect to see the light of heaven! A nice husband! And a nice father. Have you no fear of the hereafter? And what would you do if the Lord called on you this minute.'

'To tell you the truth, auntie,' says Ned. 'I couldn't stir a leg!'

Ned went steady after that – he had to, for the wife's aunt came to live in the house with 'em, but even in time she relented a small bit. Ned was allowed to go back to one of his former pledges, a pint a day – no quarts or sweet gallons – just, as the aunt put it, one imperial pint a day. Ned got into the habit of taking the pint about closing time or a little after it, and there is a bit of history attached to that too, and I might as well tell it while I'm at it.

Ned had a white tom-cat that used folly him everywhere. He'd go up the stairs after him every night when he was going to bed. Ned'd be tricking with him and they'd have a little boxing match through the banisters of the stairs. When Ned'd take his trousers off and put it on the seat of the chair, the cat'd make a hammock of that until morning. He'd cross the street every night after him and sit on the window-sill of the pub until Ned came out.

The cat was as well known as a bad ha'penny. People passing along the village at night and seeing him sitting on the window-sill of Meskill's pub knew that Ned Connor was inside having his daily imperial, which he never went beyond and his temperance brought him a little prosperity. You see he had a fine roomy house and the wife encouraged by the aunt began to keep people – turned it into an aiting house.

Two young guards used to have their dinner there. The force was only in its infancy at the time. The guards weren't long coming to the house when they were like one of the family. Yerra, they'd go in and sit in the kitchen, and throw their caps on top of the dresser. In the kitchen they came to know the cat. They came to know too about Ned's habit of going across the road to Meskill's for his daily pint after closing time, and knowing Ned so well they'd never raid the pub while the cat was sitting outside on the window-sill.

Raiding pubs was almost a nightly occurrence that time, for the licencing laws were not as liberal then as they are now. The weekly paper'd be full of court cases. I saw it given down myself where a guard at twelve o'clock at night after being given an assurance by the publican that there was no one on the premises, went upstairs, opened the door of a wardrobe and a man fell out. People'd go into an auger hole rather than have their names in the paper!

The guard swore that in another room he found three men sound asleep in a small bed with the clothes up to their chins, the picture of innocence. What they didn't know was that their feet were cocking out at the bottom.

'A wonder they didn't feel the cold!' says the Judge.

'How could they,' said the guard, 'and they having their shoes on!'

But to go back to Ned. I was in Meskill's myself one night when he came in. Even though it was gone closing time there was a big crowd inside. There was something on in the village the same day. I think it was a bull inspection. The publican was in no hurry out with 'em and now that Ned was in, and the cat outside he felt safe . . . at least for the length of time it took Ned to down one imperial pint.

The talk was nice and leisurely and Ned'd be no more than half-way down the glass when there was a sharp knock at the front door.

'Open up in the name of the law!'

'*Croí an diabhail*,' says Ned, 'it must be strange guards. Our own lads'd have noticed the cat!'

'Clear,' says the publican, frightened of an endorsement, 'out the back!' as he began to pour drink down the shore. In another second the lights were out, total eclipse, and there was what I can only describe as a stampede towards where we thought the back door should be. We were going into presses and everything. And when we found the door the first of the crowd out were bolting back like a squad of rabbits that'd meet a ferret in the turn of a burrow! There was another guard at the back gate!

Now, we made for the stairs, and some of us got out the upper window on to the roof of a shed, and the plan was, if our geography was correct, to get down into a neighbour's yard and make good our escape. And do you know what I'm going to say! The corrugated-iron roof of a shed on a wet night is an awful slippery place. The legs were taken from under one fellow and he went sliding down and fell ten feet on top of God only knows what! I could not repeat here what he said, and he had hardly himself straightened when another fellow fell on top of him.

Well, there was one huge corporation of a man there – they told me after he was home from South Africa on holidays – and we were all hanging out of him. Blessed hour tonight if the man didn't lose his balance, and crashed on the flat of his back on the roof bringing us all down with him. Such a report! Cows, pigs, geese, all the animals in the vicinity woke up, as we went skeeting down the roof and fell on top of one another into the black hole of Calcutta!

Then you heard the language! Drink lubricates the talking machine – 'twas like Dunkirk! And to make matters worse, whatever way it happened, down into the publican's yard we fell. The guards were there before us, our names were taken, so we had all our work for nothing!

When we came out in the street Ned Connor went straight to the window-sill, but there was no sign of the white cat. He couldn't believe his eyes. Whatever look we gave, there below on the school wall was Ned Connor's white cat holding a loud conversation with a member of his own community, and she seemed to be saying to him 'Not now-ow-ow. Not now-ow-ow.'

'Well bad manners to you anyway, Pangur Bán!' says Ned rubbing his shins. 'I'd have nearly gone without my imperial pint tonight if I knew you had a date!'

Tobacco

There was a man here near us, a cobbler, and he was full sure that John Bull was a certain rich man living in a big mansion over in London. And when the old-age pension came out in 1908, nothing in the world'd convince him but that John Bull was paying it all out of his own pocket! The cobbler was going around saying, 'He must be rotten with money and all of it he's giving away!'

But to go back to 1908. One comical result of the news that a pension was coming in for everyone over seventy was that some women aged ten years in one night! One woman we all heard of, whenever she'd have a row with the husband she'd grig him with, 'The fooleen I was, a young girl like me, to marry an old lad like you, ten years older than me. Wasting my life on you!' As it turned out she was drawing the pension before him. Or can anyone believe daylight from women! They were quick to take the pension!

But joking apart, it is very hard for us to realise how badly-off old people were at that time. You see, they'd have given over their house and land to a son. Of course there used to be an agreement or an understanding that the old couple would remain on in the place and be supported. In return for that support the old man'd work in the fields as long as he was able, and the old woman'd give a hand around the house and mind the children as long as she was able.

Old people could be an asset in the house, and the

generations could get along fine together and they did. The one fly, of course, in the ointment, could be the son's wife. A lot depended on her and on her nature. She'd have her own young children to occupy her and as the old people got older and more helpless they might be coming in her way, and relations, as the man said, could get strained! They'd be strangers in her eyes and if she was hard-hearted she'd begrudge 'em the very bite that went into their mouths.

In one house, not a thousand miles from where I'm sitting, they had a bull in the tub. At dinnertime the daughter-in-law put a bit of beef the size of a half-crown in the old man's plate. God, it looked miserable alongside a mountain of turnips. He called for more. She gave him another bit of beef the size of a shilling and a big scoop of turnips.

'Gi' me more mate!' says he.

'You've enough,' she told him. 'If you ate any more of it the bull'll be roaring inside you.'

'Why then,' says he, 'it won't be for the want of turnips!'

I tell you the pension was a blessing to old people. It made 'em independent, although it was only five shillings in 1908, or maybe only half-a-crown. They were able to contribute towards their support, and the man could invest in a half-quarter of tobaccy, and the woman in an ounce of snuff, if she was that way inclined. Bonar Law or Asquith, or whoever brought in that pension, should be given a medal – there are statues being put up to men that did nothing.

Prior to the pension there was this old man, and like the story a while ago, he was living with his son and daughter-in-law. They had a rising family and because of that, and the poverty of the times and the poorness of the land, they were pulling the devil by the tail. But the daughter-in-law was a big-hearted woman, a good servant, and whatever was going, everyone, including the old man, got his fair share. But she drew the line at that. Not one ha'penny would she spend on tobaccy for him.

And I wouldn't mind but he was a martyr to the pipe. He'd give his right hand from the elbow down for a smoke. Usedn't he try and cure the leaves of the *cupóg* and smoke it – he used! And he'd smoke white turf. Some brands of that were very hot. He'd have to lie on the bed after with his tongue out trying to cool it!

His eyes used to get watery for the want of a smoke. He'd get so blind walking along the road, he'd be saluting gate piers. 'That you John? Have you any bit of tobaccy?'

Even the bush growing out of the side of the ditch, he'd think it was a saddle-horse! *An buile tobac* the old people'd call that form of madness.

The time I'm talking about his eldest grandson was about seven or eight years. He and his grandfather were great friends; they were as thick as a cow and cock of hay. And it used to grieve the little *garsún* to see his granda suffering for the want of a smoke. Often when the two of 'em would be sitting down together minding the cows out of the ryegrass the young lad'd say: 'Granda! Granda! When I'm big I'm going to get an awful lot of money and what am I going to buy for you?'

'An ounce of tobaccy,' the old man 'd say. 'You can keep the rest of it for yourself.'

And short as the legs were under the grandson, you'd often see him belting across the fields if he heard a neighbour was at a wake or a funeral, to know would he have even half a pipeful of tobaccy for his granda.

If ever he succeeded in getting a knob of plug, he'd call his granda behind the car-house where there was a seat in the *cúl ghairdín*, and sitting there, he'd watch the old man cut up the tobaccy, and then break it with his fingers into *brúscar* in the palm of his left hand, very careful not to let the smallest morsel of it fall on the ground.

Then there'd be a big ceremony preparing the pipe, scraping the inside of it with the knife and turning the ashes into the pipe cover, which'd be made out of a blackening tin. A few handy taps with the handle of the knife on the bottom of the upturned pipe to make sure it was empty. Then he'd put it in his mouth and suck the air through it. A thousand pounds to a penny it would be blocked, so the young lad'd have a go and get a *tráithnín* to act as a *réiteoir*.

He'd watch his granda take the pipe apart at the place where the silvery ferrule was, and run the *tráithnín* through the short stem until it disappeared, and when it came out the other side the fox's tail at the end of the sop'd be as black as the ace of spades – the same as if you pulled a bush through a chimney.

Then, after freeing that part of the stem from the ferrule up to the head, his granda'd put the pipe together, put it in his mouth, and this time you could hear air whistling through it. Now to fill it. The mouth of the pipe'd be put under the palm of the left hand, and with the right forefinger his granda'd coax the tobaccy into the pipe, searching the crevices of his palm and in between his fingers for any stray particles of the precious weed. Then the ashes in the cover'd be spread on top and pressed down, not too hard, with the thumb. Nothing now but to redden it!

He'd have no match of course! Only millionaires had

matches that time, so he'd cut a strong twig, bring it to a sharp point with the knife and give it to the grandson. He'd go into the kitchen and spear a half-red coal of fire and bring it out. The old man'd blow the coal to get a little flame. Then he'd put the coal on top of the pipe, maybe shading it with his hat, start to puff and in a few seconds he'd be going like a limekiln. But it would have to get nice and red before he'd put on the cover, and then he was smoking in earnest. A great look of contentment'd come over his face and the *garsún*'d smile to see his oul gran' so happy.

I don't think people lived as long that time as they do now. Anyway it came to the old man's turn and he was called away. The children were put up to bed in the loft earlier than usual that evening. The house had to be readied and provisions got for neighbours and relatives that'd be coming to the wake.

Sometime out in the night the grandson woke up. He thought it strange all that buzz of conversation under him. Then he remembered. It must be the wake. He never saw a wake before. He stole out of the bed and over to the well of the stairs. The kitchen was full. Some people were sitting over to the table drinking tea, a thing he wouldn't get himself only once in a wonder. There was no shortage. Little did the child know that people used to break themselves that time in order to have a good wake.

He could see saucers of snuff going around. Everyone taking a pinch and praying, 'The Lord have mercy on his soul.'

'*Solus na bhflaitheas dúinn go léir.*'

'Amen, *a Thiarna!*'

'He's in heaven anyway.'

'What did he ever do to anyone!'

'All his life trying to make ends meet!'

The next thing he saw was a man going around with a bucket of porter and handing out cups of it. And he said to himself, 'They all liked my granda!'

If he only knew, some of 'em hardly knew him.

The place was full of smoke. The child thought the chimney wasn't pulling. Not at all, 'twas tobaccy smoke. The surprise he got to see every man and some of the old women puffing away to their heart's content!

He came down the stairs and moving in and out through the crowd he made off to the room where his granda was laid out. 'Oh God help us, poor oul gran. He got so small and so pale!'

The room was full of people too, and he couldn't take his eyes off two men that were there cutting tobaccy and filling it into clay pipes. And looking at all the tobaccy he ran over to the bed, 'Oh granda!' he said, 'isn't it an awful pity you didn't live till the stuff got plentiful.'

Love and Marriage

Haley was doing a line with one of the Cormacs. Two girls that were there living with the mother. Big mopseys they were too and very red in the complexions. There wasn't much humour in 'em. They were shy and awkward, very quiet, and would nearly burst out crying if you said goose to 'em.

Nonie was one of their names and I think the other one was called Delia. Oh *Dia linn*, what a family he picked! The mother was cute enough though, and when she heard who Nonie was doing the line with, she urged her to invite Haley into the kitchen. Bring it out in the open like, it mightn't be so easy for him then to back out of it. Anyway, Haley was a good catch as we'll see farther on.

On the slope of the railway he used to be courting Nonie before that, but if the night turned wet they'd go into the car-house. That was handy enough too, with a sop of straw under 'em in the body of the donkey car, though it was a devilish draughty place for there was no door to the front of it.

'Twas warmer in the kitchen. The only drawback there being the mother, and of course Delia. The mother would talk the hind leg off a duck. Conversation is all right if you haven't anything else in mind, and of course Haley had. After a few nights the mother took the hint, Nonie looking daggers at her, so she gathered herself down to bed.

The mother and the two daughters used to sleep in the room below the kitchen. But the devil a sleep the mother would go to until Haley was gone. She would too. The ear cocked. Haley as I said was a good match, a house to himself and a nice holding, so the mother was anxious to find out if he was serious as regards Nonie.

Anyway, it was common knowledge if he was going to marry it wouldn't be altogether out of blackguarding, for with no one in the house he wanted a woman. As we saw, the mother was gone down to bed, but still Haley didn't have Nonie to himself, for Delia was sitting there, two watery eyes on her, looking into the fire. After a while Haley got fed up of this, the night going, so he whispered to Nonie, and Nonie taking the hint gave Delia a nudge saying: 'Wouldn't you get up and go out and give a sop to the cows!'

Poor Delia got up and went out and stayed outside all night in the stall waiting for Haley to go. But when he got the house to himself the devil wouldn't shift him, the settle pulled over in front of the fire by the two of 'em. Haley liked his comfort. But if the silences were too long the mother below in the room would give a 'Hm, hm!' and get a fit of coughing, so that for all the peace Haley got from that quarter he'd be as well off on the slope of the railway.

One night Delia was a bit late going out to throw a sop to the cows. She had a heavy pair of shoes on her, she was digging furrows the same day. And the mother below in the bed, hearing what sounded like a man's footsteps going out, and the clatter of the door closing she shouted up to the kitchen, 'Indeed and it was time for him to go. Come on down now the two of ye, and bring down the vessel before ye!'

Well Nonie was mortified. Her complexion was always high, but she got as red as a turkeycock at the mother's remark. It had no effect on Haley. It would take more than that to embarrass that bucko.

After a year of the mother going to bed early every night and poor Delia going out to throw a sop to the cows, Haley married Nonie. In Haley's house the wedding was, and people who were there told me it was a fine turn-out. No expense spared, this and that there, currany tops and what-not, all kinds of grudles, buns, trifle and that shaky shivery stuff you'd ate with a spoon.

The wedding went on all night, into the following day as long as the drink held out! When all the 'goodbyes' were said, and all the relations gone, Haley and Nonie milked the cows and went to bed!

She was the first up in the morning, and she wasn't long at all gone downstairs to the kitchen when Haley heard her crying below. Down with him, and consoling her he said, 'Now, now, now, what's wrong with my little *circín?*'

'Oh,' says she, looking up the chimney. 'There's a loose flag above there in the flue, and when the little child comes to this house it'll fall down on him and kill him!'

'*Tanam an diúca!*' says Haley getting over the shock at being introduced, so early on, to the contrariness that seems to strike women after marriage. The thought couldn't but cross his mind that women were like little doves until you had 'em in the nest!

'Look now,' says he, all *grá mo chróí*, 'if it'll aise your mind at all, I'll mix a bit of mortar and I'll pin around the flag, and make it as firm as the rock of Gibraltar!'

A thing he did right away, though he was as black as a chimney sweep when it was over. A good job the little child hadn't come to the house. There'd be a hop knocked out of him when he saw the sort of father he had.

The day wore on, no other hitch and they went to bed again that night. She was first up in the morning, and she wasn't long below in the kitchen when he heard her crying again. Down with him and there was Nonie below striking her two hands together and kicking up an awful hullabulloo.

'What's wrong with you, crayther?' says he half- shivering there in his shirt.

'Do you see those banisters there in the stairs?' says she. 'They are so near together that when the little child comes to this house he'll shove his head out between 'em and get choked!'

'If that's all the worry you have, 'tis soon rectified!' So he got a saw and cut out every second banister, saying 'By jamonies, he'll have to have an awful big head on him now to get caught between 'em!'

He was praying that that'd be the end of it. *Mo léir cráite* she wasn't landed down in the kitchen the third morning, when he heard the *olagón*. He ran down and trying to control himself this time, he said, 'What's coming over you now?'

'Look at the cut of that yard,' says she, bringing him over to the back door. 'And look at that big pool of *múnlach* in the middle of it, and when the little child comes to this house what's to prevent him from running down the pavings and falling into the *múnlach,* and getting drowned on me. And if you were a proper man and concerned about the feelings of your wife, you'd put the butt on the car and get a few loads of bog stuff and fill it up.'

'My patience,' says he, 'is worn to a thread, and don't think,' says he , 'that you're going to have me in a *baitín* boy running down the stairs every morning and listening to a cock-and-a-bull story about what's going to happen to the little child when he comes to this house. If he's going to be anything like you, I can see that I have an exciting future ahead of me. I'm going away from you now,' says he, 'for I won't be consoled in my mind until I find out if there is another woman in the barony more contrary than the woman I married!'

And wouldn't you think it would be hard for him! He walked on, and in the course of his travels he met all varieties of women. Some of 'em beautiful, and as the man said, a beautiful woman is a jewel! Haley met these too, and he was beginning to think that if he was to keep his promise not to return home until he met a woman more contrary than his wife, he'd never again see Nonie.

And the love was there, and the longer he was away, the fonder he was getting of her. One day, at noon, he came to a house with no windows facing south, where he saw a woman drawing sunshine in a sieve into the kitchen.

'Give me a sledge,' says he, and he broke a round hole in the south wall of the house and he fitted the sieve into it and made a nice window – a bit draughty maybe, but it left in the sunshine!

Another day he came to a place where he saw a woman blindfolding sheep to prevent 'em from going through a gap into a piece of ryegrass she had.

'Wouldn't it be simpler,' he said to her, 'to build up the gap!'

'Can't you build it up yourself so!' says she. 'And I'll bring you out a bit to ate while you are doing it.'

He set to work and she went into the house, and broke white bread into hot milk and made what we call goody. A spoon of sugar on top that and children'd go mad for it. But it could hardly be considered a fit diet for a working man.

When she was bringing it out of the house, she was walking into the slanting sun, and looking back she saw her shadow.

'Who are you?' she said. 'Maybe it is hungry you are,'

throwing back a spoonful of the goody. And as the shadow kept on with her she said, '*Crymonás* you must be starving.' So she kept throwing back spoonfuls of the goody to the shadow, till by the time she arrived where Haley was building the gap the dish was empty!

Haley gave her a look like a summons and gathered his legs out of the place.

The third day he came to a house, where he heard the farmer inside bawling his head off the same as the poor people used to be roaring long 'go when the quack German doctor used to be going around curing the rheumatics. The only difference being, that the quack German doctor had a musician outside the window blowing the bugle, so that his patients couldn't be heard crying – for that would be bad for business!

Haley ran into the house and there was the farmer's wife with an affair like a big flour bag down over her husband's head, and she belting him away on top of the nut with a beetle. Such treatment! As Haley said, you wouldn't do it to a black Russian!

'You'll kill the man!' says he, 'or what are you doing that for!'

'That's a shirt I'm running up for my husband,' says the woman. 'And I'm making a hole on top of it for his head. I've to make two holes for the hands yet!'

'Give me a scissors,' says Haley. And he cut a hole on top of the bag, and the farmer's head popped out, and I can tell you that the man was relieved.

'My eyes are opened for me now,' says Haley. 'I thought the woman blindfolding the sheep and the woman drawing sunshine in a sieve were bad, but for the height of contrariness you capped all! A person don't know how well off he is in his own house, until he travels out and sees what other women are like.'

So he turned on his heel and went home to Nonie, and I suppose it was only the strangeness of marriage that upset her. In a while's time she gave up the capers and settled down to be a most sensible little *dailc* of a woman, proud and independent, thrifty and industrious, smiling and companionable, in other words, as priceless a little person as ever sat under a cow!

The Hereafter

There's a thing there's no noise about now, and when we were young our hearts'd be up in our mouths if we heard there was one of 'em coming. It would be well published beforehand, you may say, and it would be a very dull man living in a very out of the way place that wouldn't hear of it. Then, when the time'd come the roads'd be black with people going there: men, women and children, although some people'd say it was no place at all for children. Ye think now I'm talking about the circus. I am not then, but about the mission!

Once every five years the mission'd come here, and my neighbours'd be talking about it for three years before and two years after. For, no word of a lie, it did make an impression, and an impression that was needed in certain quarters. Well the vows that'd be made and the pledges that'd be so taken! Line after line of hardened old campaigners facing the altar rails the final Sunday. Everyone'd be so changed you'd swear that from that out judges'd have to hang up their wigs and publicans'd have to go selling shirt buttons.

Two holy fathers that used come here, and even though of saintly appearance, they were well versed you may say in every description of villainy. They'd light the chapel with language, bringing their voices away down very low, and then making a tremendous shout that'd frighten the living daylights out of everyone. People used to be afraid to go up near the altar. And we'll say a shy man sitting there, if the holy father fixed his eye on him, and he in a rage, the poor man'd pass out!

Even down near the door where we used to be, you'd be shivering in your shoes, for each night they'd go from one evil doing to another, from the sins of life to death, from death to judgment, and from judgment, as was only natural, to the place below! Oh glory! The fires of hell'd be described down to the very last detail, the smoke and the steam and the gnashing of teeth! Poor old women sitting there in the chapel, no more sin on 'em than the child in the cradle, only trying to make ends meet, and the tears rolling down their cheeks at the thought of all those people suffering on the hobs of hell for all eternity.

And I'll never forget one night, there was this woman from out the Bower, a hat on her, and there she was as unconcerned as if she was at a football match. Of course the holy father couldn't help but notice her – 'twas the big man that was on the same night. And when she was going out the gate after, 'twas the small man said Benediction, the big man was there before her.

'How is it,' says he, 'my good woman that you were so unmoved by all the suffering in hell's flames?'

'Yerra father,' says she, 'I'm not from this parish at all!'

And they used to travel from parish to parish after the missioners – some people can take an awful hammering!

One night the sermon'd be given over to drink; another night to company-keeping and so on. There'd be some sins mentioned and if the people were given a free hand they wouldn't know how to go about committing 'em! But coming in to the second week we'd all be coming closer to grace, and the final night would be glorious. Old lads there with no more note in 'em no more than a crow trying to sing. 'Never will we sin again!' And the great blaze of light when all the candles were lit for the renouncing of the devil. I can tell you if that bucko put in an appearance that night he'd get a belt of a fist as quick as lightning! Such fervour!

Monday morning we'd all return to normal life. And I'll never forget this Monday morning. I was over here at the forge putting slippers on the mare. There was a big crowd there and the only topic of conversation was the mission. And some people held that after all that was said we were given a very poor inkling as to what heaven was like. Well, they admitted heaven was mentioned earlier on but at that time very little hope was held out for the people. But now that they all expected to go there, they were wondering what sort of place it was. Would they have to work there! What would the weather be like!

And we'll say for instance the man that was married twice here, which one of 'em would he be walking out with in heaven? He couldn't be walking out with two of 'em – or maybe it was all right in heaven to have two – they didn't know!

The blacksmith was wondering would there be a public house there where we could go in and sit down, he said, and talk to the neighbours. Well there was this fellow there, a good footballer in his day, until he got broke in the wind and wound up carrying the *ganseys*. Heaven wouldn't be much in his eyes anyway, unless they had an occasional football match.

'Maybe,' says he, 'we'd get up a team and travel out!'

Another man there used to scrape a bit on the fiddle – he wasn't much good. He'd like heaven to be a place where he'd meet all these musicians and they'd be exchanging tunes.

All the young people said heaven wouldn't be much to write home about if there was no dancing.

Now there was an old lad sitting up on the hob, never opened his mouth during all this, only making curlicues in the ashes with his walking cane. '*Sea*, dance!' says he with a smile, 'from what we heard about heaven in the chapel during the past two weeks, there won't be enough there from this parish to make up a half set!'

And did the people pay heed to the missioners? Oh-h-h they did! It had a very beneficial effect. Although some took it too serious so that it played a bit on their mind. There was this woman and she took the sermons on company-keeping very much to heart. She was married but the husband died and left her with an only son.

She brought up the son very strict. Even from a very early age he wouldn't be allowed talk to girls. He wouldn't be let go anywhere girls'd be. He was never at a dance. He had to keep away from all places of temptation, so that he wouldn't be the cause of bringing disgrace on her or having her named called from the altar. The result of all this was that he grew up backward – going the opposite side of the road when he saw girls coming! John the Shyman people used to call him.

One Sunday after a mission, he was going the near way through a wood with his mother, and they met a young couple linking arms together! 'What are they up to, Mammy?' says he to the mother.

'Don't mind them now!' says she, 'that's only a brother and sister going to the holy well, praying.'

He had his doubts about that, especially when he saw the two lovers fall into a bed of bluebells.

'Look the other way!' says the mother.

'Oh,' says he, 'no wonder the missioner is making tapes on the altar!'

When his mother died he had no one to do anything for him, and this poor man's daughter used to come housekeeping. Now, look we'll be charitable, maybe she was put up to it for he had a fine farm of land! Anyway she got around him and they had to get married. Look at that after all his mother's warning.

He had nearly to be tied to bring him to the altar, afraid of his life of the PP, but nothing was said for the PP didn't know. But six months after, when the wife presented him with a big belter of a baby boy, John the Shyman nearly went out of his mind.

Two days after was the christening, and when he heard he'd have to bring the child to the chapel, rather than confront Father Furnane, he took to the hill. The father-in-law wasn't long bringing him back. The horse was tackled, and when the wife's mother, holding the child, was made comfortable sitting on a *gabháil* of straw in the body of the car, John the Shyman and the two witnesses to the baptism sat in and they drove off to the chapel.

Now the parish priest we had there at the time, Father Furnane, had a strict rule concerning baptism. It would take place at three o'clock on the dot, and if you weren't there at that time you'd have a little pagan in the house for another while. The baptism party were very much aware of this so they were urging John to hurry the horse, for if they were late Father Furnane'd ate the face of 'em. The weather was dry and the band came off the wheel.

By the time it was retrieved, the wife's mother and the child taken out of the car, the horse untackled, the wheel taken off, the band put on it, bits of kippens wedged between the band and the felloes to tighten it, the wheel put back under the car, the horse tackled, and the wife's mother and the child put sitting on the straw, I can tell you a good bit of the day was gone.

Then too because of the precarious condition of the band, speed was out of the question, so that Father Furnane was gone into the sacristy by the time they arrived at the chapel. But the wife's mother, brazen enough, faith, took her place with the child and the two sponsors at the baptismal font. John the Shyman ducked down behind a pillar to hide!

The parish clerk, oh a very officious fellow, with a long black coat buttoned up to his chin and ideas above his station! Sure one time at confirmation he nearly got a parish from the bishop. Of course hearing the baptismal party arriving late, he marched out from the sacristy, looking every bit as furious as Father Furnane, and pointing to where the little child was he said, 'Who is responsible for this?'

And John the Shyman putting his head around the pillar said, 'It won't happen again, Father!'

The First Church

In ancient times in Ireland a man was held in high regard if he could make a verse, build a house or tell a story, and the poet, the stonemason and the seanchaí had permission to sit at the same table as the king. Now the most famous stonemason ever to sit down with a king was the Gobán Saor and he had a contract to build the first church for St Patrick. The bargain was that the saint would pay him the full of the church in grain. Churches were not very big then. When it was finished the Gobán Saor said to St Patrick, 'Fill it with grain for me.'

'I will,' says St Patrick, 'if you can turn the church upside down and make a vessel of it,' thinking he had him flummoxed.

The Gobán Saor and his men got together and in no time they turned the church upside down and made a vessel of it. St Patrick filled it with grain and the Gobán Saor drew it away to his own barn and left the church upside down, and it is that way ever since!

At that time you could hardly throw a stone in Ireland without rising a lump on a king's head, they were that plentiful. St Patrick's idea was to baptise the king and the rank and file would follow. A clever plan too; only a foreigner would think of it. It was at the building of the Tower of Babel the argument arose as to who was the king of the tradesmen, and for peace sake the foreman went around and he said to the mason, 'Who made your tools?' and the mason said, ''Twas the smith.' And he said to the carpenter, 'Who made your tools?' And he said, ''Twas the smith.' And he said to the smith, 'Who made your tools?'

And he said, "Twas myself.' 'That settles it,' says the foreman. 'You're the king of the tradesmen.'

There's no gainsaying it but the smith was an important member of the community and held in such respect that in places when people'd kill a cow for the tub the head would go to the smith to make soup. And prior to the vet, the smith was a horse doctor, and you wouldn't have to dig as deep in the pocket to pay him. What am I talking about, usen't he pull teeth! And 'tis said there was a cure in the water where he cooled the iron. I can't think now what it was a cure for, I don't remember was it taken or applied – if it was a cure for forgetfulness, I'd do with a sup of it myself. When it came to baptising the tradesmen, St Patrick, knowing his history, called to the forge. The smith was working very hard making *cráiníns* for thinning scythes. The day was hot and he was pouring sweat but he gave St Patrick a hearing right away for the saint's first words were, 'Come on and I'll stand to you.'

So they went across the road to the public house. The smith said he'd have a pint. St Patrick called for something temperate, a drop of sherry wine. When the pint came up St Patrick noticed that there was a good finger of froth on top of it so he said to the publican, 'Here, you might as well spill a half-one into it, into the pint.'

The publican did, and when St Patrick was paying for the drink he put only the price of the pint and the cherry wine up on the counter. And the publican said, 'What about the half-one?'

'What about it?' says St Patrick. 'If the pint was full 'twouldn't go into it!'

St Patrick was good enough for him! And turning to the smith the saint said, 'Is this the usual caper, not filling the pint?'

'Oh, 'tis,' says the smith. 'No man coming in here is getting his proper measure.'

St Patrick turned to the publican and talked to him good and stiff and told him, 'Don't think,' says he, 'that you're making any profit on it. By cheating the working man you are only fattening the devil.'

The publican laughed at this. Didn't believe in it, of course, a pure pagan!

'All right so,' says St Patrick. 'Open up that *cábúis* there under the stairs.'

The door was opened and there was the devil inside hardly able to walk with flesh, a gloss on him!

Well, the hop that was knocked out of those there, and because of the hop that was knocked out of the publican he told St Patrick he'd mend his ways.

'We'll see to it,' says the saint. 'I'll be calling around here again. I'm going down the country for a month.'

On his way back St Patrick called to the smith and he had all the tradesmen rounded up for him and a contrary bunch they were too. *Is túisce deoch ná scéal*, they say. So before the baptism they all adjourned to the public house, and St Patrick, throwing his eye along the counter, noticed that the pints were full. Only what you may call a little christian brother's collar on the top of every one of them. He enquired from the smith if this was regular.

'Oh indeed,' says the smith, 'ever since your visit here there's a complete change in parliament. Every man coming in is getting his full measure, and what's more the publican is doing the trade of the place.'

'*Ní nach ionadh*,' says St Patrick. And going over he congratulated the publican.

'Ah, that's all right,' says the publican with a watery smile, 'but I'd like to know what effect all this is having on the quare fella under the stairs!'

'Open the door,' says St Patrick.

He did, and there was the devil inside so thin that only for the two horns you could pull him through an auger hole. If he turned sideways you'd mark him absent.

Well, the outcome of all this was that conversions were taking place with such rapidity that they ran out of salt for making holy water!

But the masons played a dirty trick on St Patrick. He was going along of a Sunday morning, and he saw the masons working. He told 'em they'd have to give up their pagan practice and keep the Sabbath, and why weren't they coming down to Mass? They couldn't, they said, because they had bad shoes, all white and burned from the mortar. He gave 'em the money and told 'em all to go away and buy shoes and that he'd delay the bell so that they'd be in time for Mass. They went off. You could buy shoes on Sunday for the shopkeepers were the last to be converted.

When it came to the sermon St Patrick turned around on the altar. He scanned the congregation. No masons! He was going down the town after and passing the pub he heard a great burst of hilarity. He looked in and there were the masons inside stocious on the price of the shoes. He kept his temper. 'I'll leave 'em to God,' he said. And that's why down to this day you'll never see a good shoe on a mason and another thing they'd drink Lough Erne dry!

Father MacGillacuddy

St Patrick never travelled on a tour of conversion without his crozier, his mitre and his full canonicals. And signs on it, those who followed him are very fond of the finery. When we were small our mouths were open back to our two ears with wonder the first time we saw a bishop on the altar. Such grandeur! Even out in the open at that time the clergy went in for a bit of style. A top hat . . . well, a three-quarter top hat . . . what we used to call a caroline hat. You could nearly bring water from the well in it!

Father MacGillacuddy sported a silk hat over a flowing beard, and a fine dash he cut in a velvet waistket and cutaway coat sitting up on the side of a sidecar knocking sparks out of the road going over to the chapel. Young lads playing pitch and toss or ducks off when they heard the horse they'd shout, 'Inside the ditch, Father Mac's car is coming!' God help any animal or mortal who wouldn't have the agility to get out of his way. The women said he looked very regal with the beard. They said he reminded them of the picture of the king on the side of the tea canister. And he was very fond of royalty! Didn't he go all the ways up to Cork Exhibition and got an introduction to Queen Victoria and to Albert to boot.

'Where are you ministering, Father?' says Albert to him.

'Gloungreeshkeen, my lord,' says Father Mac.

'A thriving town that,' says Albert.

Father Mac did not baptise as many as St Patrick, but then again, he wasn't at it every day, only Sunday after Mass and

Wednesday at three o'clock. He had stricter rules than St Patrick, and if you weren't at the chapel on Wednesday at three o'clock on the dot, you'd have a little pagan in the house for a few more days.

Timeen Sweeney from Abhanasciortán was walking in the chapel door on Wednesday at five mintues past three, and who was walking out against him but Father MacGillacuddy.

'You're late,' says Father Mac and pointing to the little child in a neighbouring woman's *gabhál,* he says to Sweeney, 'Take it home and bring it back again, Sunday.'

'God blast it! It . . . it . . . it. What "it" have you?' Sweeney was a fright for cursing – no control of the tongue.

'Blast it.' He was after coming an awful long journey . . .

'Blast it, splash the holy water on him! He won't take you a minute. He isn't the size of my fist.'

Sweeney wasn't much bigger himself and married to the tallest woman in the parish. After the marriage they were in the sacristy; of course on a morning like that a bit of levity was in order even for Father Mac. 'Well, Tim,' says he, 'when you went about it you got a fine tall woman!'

Sweeney was pure sick of these jokes and turning to Father Mac he said, 'She won't be always standing, Father!'

Baptism or no baptism, Father MacGillacuddy would drive straight into town every Wednesday and straight up to High Street. He'd bring the horse skeeting on his four feet to a sudden halt in front of Thadyess's where he'd get the few commands for the week.

At that time there'd be poor men holding up the corners, only too glad of the opportunity to earn a few pence holding a horse by the head. Wasn't that how Shakespeare started in London! Father Mac would call one of these. 'Flynn! Come here and hold my horse!' Flynn would come and hold him every Wednesday but he'd get nothing for his trouble, although Father Mac would not refuse an offering himself!

Flynn used to grumble but seeing who he was trucking with he didn't have the gumption to demand his rights, but, as the man said, constant dropping wears the stone. This Wednesday when Father MacGillacuddy drove up, Flynn walked away.

'Come here, Flynn,' said Father Mac, 'and hold my horse.'

'I will not, Father.'

'Come here, Flynn!'

'I will not,' says Flynn, 'I'm holding him long enough for you now and you never gave me nothing for it!'

'Flynn, do you hear! Hold my horse or I'll stick you to the ground!'

'Ah ha,' says Flynn. 'Why don't you stick the horse to the ground so!'

He couldn't. And why couldn't he? Because the clergy were given no power over the animal. Over humans and spirits. Yes. They had the power there. When we were small the heart used be driven crossways in us with all the talk about the spirit of Béalnadeaga. No one'd pass that place at night. People used to go up Liosbáibe and over through Meenteogs to Gneeveguilla and Knocknagree out of pure dread.

The spirit was a woman. She was able to pull a man off a galloping horse. When she was finished with him the way she'd kill him was to give him the breast milk into the eyes. *Slán mar a n-ínnstear é!* She was of terrifying appearance, always enveloped in a ball of light, and one man said she came so close to him he could see the little red blood vessels in the whites of her eyes. He was lucky. He was carrying a knife with a black handle. That saved him!

She had to be banished. It wasn't Father MacGillacuddy read over her . . . it was another priest . . . I forget now what's this his name was! God knows then maybe it was a friar. It isn't everyone that can do it. And the penance he put on her was that she would forever be, for all eternity, draining the Dead Sea with a silver spoon!

'Good riddance! Didn't she attack a poor man coming home with a butt of turnips from Gloungreeshkeen! He began pegging the turnips at her in the name of the Father and the Son and the Holy Ghost. It must be the last turnip that turned the tide for she disappeared, and he fell down in a faint in the body of his car. His wife woke up when she heard the horse galloping into the yard. She knew by the crack of the axle, a frosty night, that the car was empty, and, all concern like at the idea of his having an idle journey, she hopped out of the bed and throwing up the window said, 'John, have you the turnips?'

'Only for I having the turnips,' says he, 'I wouldn't be here!'

St Patrick never came to Kerry. How could he when the Cork people stole his donkey. He stood on a hill above Kanturk and lifting his hand he said, *'Beannuím uaim go léir siar sibh.* I bless ye all west from me!'

How well now it was a donkey he had as his mode of conveyance! He knew about the flight into Egypt! And the entry into Jerusalem! But he might as well be idle as to be trying to show the good example to his followers. Henry Ford had no more than invented the automobile when Father MacGillacuddy had one! He was the only one in the parish with a motor car until after the second trouble. The backfiring of that instrument drove all the animals cracked. Distracted farmers hopping off the wings of sidecars taking off their coats and putting them over the horses' heads until Father Mac's car was gone.

Oh, and a reckless driver! Failing to take a turn didn't he go through Coneen Casey's gate, and knocked down a cow inside in the field. When Coneen saw the car, he couldn't get over it. He said for a thing that could run so fast wasn't it a great wonder it couldn't jump as well. He knelt down beside the cow as grief-stricken as if it were his mother. The neighbours came running. in. 'Is the cow dead?' says Larry. 'No,' says Coneen, 'she is not dead, but she doesn't know anyone!' She didn't know what hit her!

There was a girl living over the road here – one of the Killbrains, Norry Killbrain. She was working in Cork for a while and when she came home she was up to the knocker in all the ways of the world. Powdered and painted and a Woodbine hanging out of the lower lip. Norry was mad for cars. She'd be out on the road before every motorcar. She said she loved the smell of the petrol and the lovely creaking of the leather seat when she'd sit on it. And she used be picked up too – Staters and everything passing at the time.

I don't think the peepers were too good by Norry, for one day she ran out before Father MacGillacuddy, the hand up. He came to a halt in a cloud of dust like a sandstorm in the Sahara. When he saw the painted hussy I can tell you she got a reprimanding. For all the notice she took of it. Standing there as brazen as you like, her two cheeks blazing, after she wetting the cover of *The Messenger* and rubbing it into 'em.

'A nice example,' said Father Mac, 'and a nice example you are giving the young women of the parish! Is it there our Blessed Lady is? No fear. No one ever saw her smoking – in public. No. And she hadn't herself raddled with paint!"

'No,' says Norry, 'and her Son didn't have a car under his A--- either!'

Eoghan Rua and the Priest

Eoghan Rua Ó Súilleabháin was mowing hay one day in the County Limerick. Poets used to have to work that time . . . and do you know they were making better songs when they were working. It was a *leaca* field and they were mowing against the rising ground, and when they put their heads over the brow of the hill they saw a big house. So Eoghan said to the local men, 'That looks like a place where a man'd get a good dinner today!'

'You are out of luck there,' the local men said, 'that's the parish priest's house.'

'What'll ye bet now,' says Eoghan, 'I'll get my dinner out of him.'

'You haven't a hope,' they said, 'but try it if you want to.'

They mowed away and when dinnertime came Eoghan hopped out over the ditch, walked up and knocked at the presbytery door. The housekeeper came out.

'I want,' says Eoghan, 'to see the parish priest.'

'You can't see him now,' she said. 'He is just sitting in to the table, and he won't see anyone until his dinner is over and his punch is taken. Is it a sick call?'

'It is far more serious than that,' says Eoghan. 'It is about money found lost.'

Any money found lost at that time was always handed in to the presbytery. The housekeeper went up in the room and told the priest what Eoghan said to her.

'Don't let him go,' says Father John, 'bring him in below to the kitchen. No, no, bring him up here in the room where I can keep an eye on him.'

The housekeeper went down and told Eoghan to come in. In with him and up in the parlour and sat down to the table opposite Father John, and taking off his hat said a very loud grace in Latin. Eoghan could do it! Didn't he open a school at Knocknagree Cross! There was a big platter of laughing potatoes in the middle of the table, and another plate with more comestibles keeping it company.

Now in olden times when a servant man was going out working for a farmer he'd say to his father on the first morning leaving home, 'Da, when it comes to dinnertime how will I make sure that I'll get my full share of potatoes?'

His father would say, '*A mhic ó,* when you are sitting around the table with five or six more *spailpíns,* and when the big *ciseán* of spuds is put in the middle, my advice to you, is to be eating one, to be peeling one, and to have one in the heel of your fist and have your eye on another one!'

So Eoghan, being a *spailpín,* had good training when it came to a snapping match between himself and the parish priest for the potatoes, and he got a fine dinner. When they were finished the parish priest got up, wiping his mouth with a napkin the size of a pillowcase.

'Well now my good man,' says he to Eoghan, 'and how much money did you find lost?'

'Yerra,' says Eoghan, 'I didn't find any money lost, Father. I only came in to ask your advice as to what I should do in case I did find money lost!'

Father John looking at the big pile of potato skins at Eoghan's elbow and thinking of certain remarks made by St Paul about eating and working said to Eoghan, 'There's a hundred of cabbage outside there in the haggard. Go out and set it!'

Then he rang his little bell, the signal for the housekeeper to bring up his punch. Indeed Eoghan could smell it as he went out the kitchen door. Eoghan spat on his palms, took the spade and opened a furrow straight as a die the length of the haggard. He put in the cabbage plants about half a pace apart, and put a forkful of farmyard manure – of course that isn't what they used call it – down to the root of every plant. There was plenty of it there. The parish priest kept a cow, and then there was his own and the curate's horse.

That done, Eoghan cut a sod with the spade, turning it in to fill the furrow, and cover the base of the plant. As he went along he gave each sod a smart tap with the back of the spade to firm it in the ground. He was in great form after the feed, the sun was coming out after a shower, the birds were beginning to sing and he was in humour for composing. He was so taken up trying to get the words to run right for him that he took the spade out of the ground and was swaying from side to side in time with the tune of his new song.

In the presbytery the priest drained his glass, and walked out to see how his labourer was doing in the cabbage patch. He hopped up on a low ditch behind Eoghan. He listened for a while and then taking the note from the poet said:

> *Sclábhaí ag obair go mall*
> *Is buille aige thall's abhus!*

And Eoghan turning capped it with:

> *Sagart is Laidean in a cheann*
> *Is a bholg ag damhsa le puins!*

Roughly translated what they said might sound something like this.

> A labourer swinging the lead
> And the blows go sideways glancing!
> A priest with Latin in his head,
> While the punch in his belly is dancing!

Now, any other clergyman from here to Magherafelt would have let it go at that, but Father John didn't.

Looking at the birds wheeling above him, he said, 'As you are so smart maybe you can tell me when the raven will get his speech.'

'Maybe I can,' says Eoghan, and sticking the spade in the ground and putting his shoe on the treddle, he said:

> When Mount Brandon and Bolus will meet,
> And the whale on the beach takes a walk,
> When the clergy for gold lose their greed,
> It is then the black raven will talk!

The Priest and the People

It is often I heard small farmers laughing as they recited that rhyme of Eoghan's, and if the truth were known it was those very small farmers gave the priests the name of being greedy. When I was young no Sunday would pass without Father Mac having to drop the hint about dues still outstanding. It was true for him when he said that it was like going to the goat's house for wool, to be going to some of those farmers for money. Men that would argue with the devil over a ha'penny on the flagstones of hell for all eternity, according to Father Mac.

When Father MacGillacuddy was enlarging the presbytery he put a levy on the farmers of so much a cow. That was the old system and it was fair. If a man had only one cow he paid a half-a-crown, and if he had ten he paid twenty-five shillings. Father Mac left it to the farmers to say how many cows they had – he wasn't long in the parish at the time.

Two years after, when the farmers were looking to have a creamery built, a cow census was taken and Father Mac was astounded at the sudden jump in the cattle population. 'Oh ho,' he said to himself, 'I'll have to be up earlier in the morning to be a match for these lads!'

When Shrovetime came round a young man from up near the County Bounds was getting married and he and his father came to the presbytery to settle up with Father Mac about the marriage offering.

'Seven pounds, your reverence,' the young man said, giving a bit of *swee-gee* to the cap, 'my place is small,'

'And wet!' his father added.

'How many cows have you?' Father Mac asked him. The poor old cow was the yardstick here too!

'I have ten cows,' says the son.

'But he's only going under seven of 'em,' says the father.

'To be going under as many as seven so early in the spring is good,' Father Mac said, 'and with the help of God in another month he'll be going under all of 'em.'

Then coaxing the conversation away from the subject of money the parish priest talked to the two men about the dexter cow, and wondering what her future was like, he put his hand into the press and brought out a bottle of the hard tack. With his other hand he hauled out two glasses and half filled them, giving the father a tint more than the son, and that was a tint well spent. The father thought the dexter cow a comical animal and said if she drove milk out through her horns he wouldn't have one of 'em on his land. They were all in good humour now and by the time they got around to the bargaining again, Father Mac topped up the glasses which drove the marriage offering up too! Father Mac was as good a warrant to drive a bargain as any man that ever stood in a fair field and before the glasses were drained he had a pound a cow got out of the young farmer.

The following day walking along the village street he said to the publican, 'Well Michael, and how much a glass are you getting for your whiskey?'

'Less than a shilling a glass, Father.'

'Ho, ho, ho!' Father Mac said. 'I got over a pound a glass for mine last night.'

Of course the clergy weren't always in big houses. In the bad times they lived in hovels, and hadn't a shoe to their feet while the parson drove around in his buggy. A man breaking stones at the side of the road said to the parish priest, 'Which of ye is nearer to heaven, Father. Yourself or the minister?'

'Oh, I'm nearer to heaven,' says the parish priest.

'It's hard to credit that,' says the stonebreaker. 'There are you without a shoe to your foot and here comes the minister in his carriage!'

'I'll go in hide now,' says the priest, 'and when the minister's carriage is passing put out your thumb and let it rub along the side of the carriage.'

The priest ducked down and the stonebreaker put his thumb up against the side of the carriage as it went whizzing by.

'Oh!' says he.

'What's wrong with you?' says the priest.

'Oh,' says he, 'my thumb is burned off me!'

'There you are now,' said the priest, 'if it is that hot on the outside of the carriage what must it be like inside!'

'Hell, Father!'

That priest had a curate and at the time they lived in a one-roomed *bothán*. The curate was a pure saint. Every ha'penny he ever got he gave it away to the poor. He would give the coat off his back to a poor man.

One morning he was coming back from an old chapel they had made of sods, and he met a beggarman looking for help.

'My poor man,' the young priest said, 'I can't help you today.' And he couldn't, for he had given away his last cent the evening before to a destitute mother to get food for her child.

'For God's sake, Father, and the sake of the Holy

Angels, put your hand in your pocket,' the beggar implored.

'I'm sorry,' the young priest said, 'I have nothing for you today.'

'You won't deny the Blessed Mother, Father, for God's sake put your hand in your pocket!'

The young priest did, saying, 'Look, I'll show you my pockets are empty. There isn't a . . . ' But there he found a half-crown. He knew he had no money. Not a half-crown. He had not seen one of those since the day of his ordination. There were many uses he could put it to, but he gave it to the beggar.

He came home to the one-roomed shack and told the parish priest the whole story.

'I knew,' he said, 'I had no money. Isn't it wonderful! The age of miracles is not past!'

'Ah! Miracles my hat!' says the parish priest. 'You'd want to watch whose trousers you're putting on in the morning!'

Connor the Carman

Dan Connor was a carman on the road to Cork. He'd be car-ing butter and when butter'd be scarce he'd be car-ing corn. One evening he filled his load and propped up the shafts of the car just high enough that by rising the ridge band he could back in the mare.

He hit the hammock early that night, and was up in the morning before six. He hung down the kettle and while that was coming to the boil, he tackled the mare. That done he wet a cup of scald, and put a fist of oatenmeal into it – it was all he had time for. He didn't rouse the wife, they weren't long married, and he straightened out for Cork.

The mare had no mind for the road, she had a foal that year and like the Christian they'd be lazy parting with their young, so that it took a lot of coaxing to get her into her stride. They were down as far as Mary Lyon's, that's the house with the steps going down to it. There they met the postboy. He had a letter for Dan and Dan didn't look at the letter until he had the grain sold in Cork and the goods in the car for the road home.

When he opened it then, there was a hop knocked out of him, for it was a letter from an attorney in New York saying that a wealthy lady, a connection of his mother's, had died there, and that it would be to Dan's advantage to come over quick as there were others watching the money.

Dan, now, was a man that wouldn't let his right hand know what his left hand was doing, so he tied the mare, giving her eight to ten feet of play, to the back setlock of another car that'd be passing his own house, and told the driver to tell his wife, Nora, that he would be delayed.

He turned then on his heel and went down to Queenstown and boarded the ship for America, and at that time you'd be ages on the ocean.

When, after a few days, Dan didn't come home Nora got panicky. Carmen going the road were told to enquire about him in Cork. They did but there was no news of Dan. At that time anyone returning from the city on foot could take a nice near way across the river at Inchees. You had stepping stones there, but they were the treacherous stepping stones as many a man knew to his cost. There was a flood and a good while after a body was found in the river a mile below the crossing.

Seemingly there was a likeness, as far as a likeness could be made out, to Dan. The Sergeant said everything tallied, there was no one else missing and Dan was buried in the family ground, and his wife killed herself crying at the graveside. That was the tearful face that had many admirers; she was young, only a few months married and had the run of anything from ten to twelve cows. She was like the young widow that was bawling crying the day of her husband's funeral, and a man proposed to her.

'I can't marry you, I can't marry you!' she said. 'I am promised to the man that shaved him!'

Nora Connor had good neighbours, and they came together and saved the harvest, and they came together and did the spring work for her and cut the sod of turf. She came well out of it and so did the mare, no car-ing to Cork, only a bit of work around the farm and she didn't mind that for she was near the foal. *Seadh*, foal! He was a fine lump of a young colt, jet black with four white socks and a white star on his forehead, going mad with *teasbach*, clearing the five-bar gate or any other obstacle until the parish priest put his eye on him.

Certain of the clergy at that time were toffs, riding with the agent and dining with the landlord. I don't know now did Father Mac bid for the colt; anyway, her neighbours told Nora Connor she'd get a better price for the colt at Cahirmee fair. She wasn't short of money, no great demands to meet seeing that Dan left her with no encumbrances. She was a good catch, and signs by, after a respectable time had elapsed accounts of a match were coming to her. One man in particular had it very bad. He was a man that was trucking in cattle; they used to call him The Blocker. If you put me on my oath now I couldn't tell you what was on his baptismal certificate. We knew him only as The Blocker.

Mrs Connor was coming from town one day and she met the parish priest on the road. They were talking and he said that if she had any notion of settling down again The Blocker would make an advisable partner for her. Well, seeing the way it was drawn down and who said it, she let the match go ahead, but the wedding was held over until the twelve months'd be up and she could get out of the black clothes.

After the marriage they were in the sacristy, talking, and Mrs Connor, well Mrs The Blocker as she was now, said to the parish priest, 'I know you have your eye on the colt and seeing you had such a big hand in today's happy event, I'll give him to you in lieu of the marriage offering. The parish clerk will be at the wedding dance tonight and he can bring the colt home with him.' Father Mac was divarted! Out with the party into the wedding drag, and drove out to Dan Connor's where everything was laid on for a right night's jollification.

'Twas dark that night when Dan Connor arrived in the big field in front of his own house. Back from America and the money in the inside pocket with a big safety pin on it. He couldn't but notice the room and kitchen all lit up, music and helooing, and shadows hopping on the screen. The wedding dance was in full swing.

Dan didn't know what to make of it. He sloped around outside lazy to go in. He put his back to the stable door where the light fell on his face. Now, this was the time the priest's clerk decided to go home and bring the colt with him. He made out for the stable, and when he saw who was there, his mouth opened to yell but no sound came out, but I can tell you he put the front door of the presbytery between him and Dan Connor in double quick time. The door of the house opened again and a bunch of strawboys came out.

'Ah, here,' says Dan, 'I'd better see what's up!'

And taking one of the strawboy's hats and letting the disguise fall down over his face he walked in and asked the wife out dancing. Going around in the set he was very free-making, more so than a man should be with a newly married woman.

'Will you stop it!' said she, wriggling away from him. 'Give over! Don't you see my husband is looking! Or who are you?' she said, whipping the hat and high fiddle from his face. And when she saw who was there, she melted in a faint on the floor. The people were dumbfounded but the music kept going for the fiddler was blind.

'What's happening in my house?' says Dan. The fiddler when he heard that took the bow away from the strings and walking in the direction of the sound let his hands run over the face.

'*Croí an diabhail*', he said, 'Dan Connor! He didn't change one iota!'

When the people saw that Dan was solid flesh they were relieved, and they began to hum and haw and God blast it where was he? His body was found and he was buried. That was twelve months ago and what could the woman do but marry!

Nora Connor was helped to her feet and throwing her hands around his neck she said, 'Dan, Dan, Dan, Dan, *a stór*, if you only came home a few days earlier I wouldn't have made such an ape of myself!'

And consoling her he said, 'Nora, do you know what I'm going to tell you, the story could have been a lot worse if I was a couple of hours later!'

And looking at The Blocker, Dan says to him, 'Let me see your back!'

The Blocker went out the door a quiet man, his tail between his legs, and do you know another man who didn't come well out of it? Father Mac, he got no colt!

The Parish Clerk

Now, Father MacGillacuddy's parish clerk was a tall graceful man falling slightly into flesh, with a soft serene countenance like you'd see on a tomcat after drinking a lot of milk. He was slow and stately in his gait as he walked the road, a straight back on him – you'd swear he'd swallowed a crowbar – and a long black coat buttoned up to the chin. Ideas above his station! You could forgive passing strangers for tipping the hat to him. Only for he keeping out of the bishop's way people said he'd have got a parish, for he was very devout.

When the bishop was coming for confirmation, Father Mac put the parish clerk whitewashing the dry wall in front of the house. The parish clerk got his bucket and set into work, making short, lazy brush strokes in time with the slow air of a hymn – you'd know by him that he'd love to give out benediction!

> Hail Queen of Heaven the ocean star,
> Guide of the wanderer here below,
> Thrown on life's surge, we implore,
> Save us from peril and from woe!

Along came Father Mac. 'Very nice,' he said, 'singing at your work and a hymn too. Very laudable, but show me the brush. Don't you think this would be more suitable,' he said as he changed the tempo to:

Father O'Flynn you've a wonderful way with you,
All the old ladies are longing to pray with you.
All the young women are longing to play with you,
You have a way with you Father O'Flynn!

The bishop was very old and didn't even notice the whitewash when he came. The confirmation was held that year in the outside chapel, five miles away from the presbytery, and the bishop, because of his age, was short-taken during the ceremony, and the parish clerk brought him out the sacristy door and ducked into Hannah Maroya's. She had a contraption in the yard; the missioners used to stay there. Hannah Maroya's man that made it. He threw his hat down on the bottom of a tay chest, drew the pencil around it, cut out the hole and propped the chest over the stream in the back garden. But Hannah Maroya thought that a bit draughty for a bishop, so she said, 'Wait a minute my Lord.'

She wasn't long away but the bishop thought it was an eternity.

'This way, your Lordship.' she said and she took him down in the parlour and there, with a good sup of hot water at the bottom to knock the sting out of it, was a big chinaware pot and a blessed candle lighting at each side of it! That was respect!

The Mission

The darkest night that ever came in the history of the universe
Timeen Sweeney went out to catch a jennet. He fell into a hole
in the ground and lifting his eyes to heaven he said, 'Well may
bad luck be to you for a moon, you'd be out all right a bright
night!'

Timeen wanted the jennet to go drawing gravel for his
day's hire the time they were building the new line. It was
in the middle of the winter and the days were short so that
he had the dark with him going to work and the dark with
him home from work. Now, this was the very occasion the
government – over in London they were that time, and
God knows near enough to us! – picked to bring in an act
of parliament compelling the owners of all vehicles, self-
propelled or otherwise, to display a light in a forward
position on all such conveyances on the public highway
after lighting-up time.

That was the law. Timeen had heard of it but like many
country people he thought it didn't apply to himself. He
was soon, as the man said, disemburdened of this idea.
One Saturday night coming home tired and hungry he was
held up by two well-fed RIC men who wanted to know
where his light was. He was in the humour for telling them
that it was next to his liver, but he knew that they weren't
in the humour for hearing it.

He made an excuse, that it was a new law, that he had
only heard about, that he hadn't time to go to town and buy a
new car lamp and that they should be lenient – it was as good-

sounding word as he could think of – with him this time.

They paid a lot of heed to his pleadings! His name was taken and he was told to expect a 'whereas' ordering him to appear before the bench the coming Tuesday. He went home very upset to his wife, but she was inclinded to take the long view of it. She told him to let the bad luck of the year go with it.

'Go out,' she said, 'and untackle the jennet and water him and I'll have the spuds on the table when you'll come in, Timmy boy.'

A small lunch is all he used to take to work, so that he'd have the principal meal of the day when he came home at night. Late dinner, as he used to say himself, like the quality. And a fine dinner it was too. When the wife emptied the pot of potatoes into the *ciseán*, he couldn't see her across the table with the steam rising out of 'em. She came then and landed a big plate of home-cured bason and boiled turnips in front of him, and a basin of buttermilk, a thing you'd seldom see in the winter, to wash it down. No hotel could come up with a meal like that and it would make your mouth water to see him wiring into it, for though the man was small he had a whale of an appetite. He loved the spuds. They were dry that year, balls of flour! He put a little *caipín* of butter on top of every one, which didn't get time to melt before it disappeared into his mouth. A few bulges in his cheeks as the spud came under the grinder and an up-and-down motion of his Adam's apple told you that it was on its way to the glory hole, and his mouth was ready for a scoop of turnips or a tasty bit of bacon. He was the picture of contentment sitting there with the traces of buttermilk leaving a white moustache on him that reached nearly half-way up to his nose.

The dinner over he settled himself by the fire for a little

snooze as was his wont before he'd take a drag at the pipe.

'Timmy,' his wife said to him, 'it isn't going hatching you are there, and it the closing night of the men's mission!'

It must have been the two policemen that put the thought of God out of his head. He began muttering to himself, lazy to leave the fire.

'Saturday night! What a night for closing a mission. They did everything baw-ways in the parish. I'll be late now,' he said to his wife.

'You will not,' she told him, 'if you hurry. Get out of the old duds.'

He gave a rub of the towel to his face, and put on his new coat and hat. 'It'll have to do,' he said, 'it isn't to America I'm going!'

The chapel was near enough and it looked like as if he was late for when he went out there wasn't a sinner in the street. The light in the chapel wasn't very good but he could make out the parish priest standing at the door. He was giving the tongue a rest during the mission and confining himself to ushering the people into the chapel. As you couldn't swing a cat in the porch the parish priest walked Timeen all the ways up to the front of the altar. He hadn't anchored that far up since the day he was married.

The chapel was small, the ceiling very low under the three little galleries, and with the big crowd inside in a while's time the place got awful stuffy. And we'll say now, a man with a big cargo of spuds on board ... a man we'll say that was accustomed to take a snooze at that time every night, well, you wouldn't blame him if his eyelids got a bit heavy.

The rosary started and Timeen survived the first decade, but half way through the second one, in the middle of a response, his tongue stopped working, his backside sagged down looking for his heels, his head dropped sideways and with his mouth open he went off to sleep. There he was lost to God and the world and the people around him wishing they were in some other part of the chapel, for their great dread was that he might commence to snore and unless he could time the snore with the response he'd be heard. A man kneeling behind tapped Timeen on the shoulder. Timeen stirred himself and, half-asleep, sat back in the seat. Thinking he was at home he put his hand in his pocket, took out his pipe and put it in his mouth. Then he took out his penknife and half-quarter of tobacco and began cutting it.

The people in the immediate vicinity went pale at the thought of what the holy father would say if he looked around and saw a man smoking within a hen's kick of the altar. The man behind touched him on the shoulder a second time, and what did Timeen do? Handed him back the penknife! The holy father, whose back was to the congregation, must have noticed some falling off in the fervour of the responses, for he came in with a very loud 'Our Father who art in heaven' which brought Timeen to his senses. I can tell you when he looked up and saw the altar in front of him he wasn't long putting the pipe and the makings of the false incense in his pocket!

After the rosary came the sermon, but on the closing night the sermon is mild. There is plenty of praise in it for the people and the efforts they made to make the mission a success but a warning note is sounded now and again about the occasions of sin. A good bit of excitement is built up during the hymns, one holy father conducting and old lads with no more note in them no more than a crow trying to sing, *'Never will we sin again!'* Then comes the big blaze of candles for the renewal of the baptismal vows.

'Do you renounce the devil and all his works and pomps?'

'Oh, we do.'

'Louder!'

'We do!' And they were never more in earnest than the night we're talking about. I can assure you if the boyo with the horns put in an appearance he'd get a taste of his own medicine, they'd set fire to him with the candles!

Timeen Sweeney was like a hen on a hot griddle in the middle of it all. In his hurry out of the house to be in time for the mission, didn't the poor man forget his blessed candle. He was muttering to himself that the Royal Irish Constabulary put everything out of his head expecting him to have a lamp on his car.

'Here I am,' he said to himself, 'with one hand as long as the next in full view of the missioner.'

Just then the holy father noticed him and said, 'My good man where is your candle?'

And Timeen, half out of his mind with excitement at being spoken to in front of everyone, said, 'Blast it, Father, that's the second time tonight I'm caught without a light!'

Civil and Strange

Ná bí beag ná mór leis an gcléir – be civil and strange with the clergy. Well you'd have to be, for they were a step above the common. When I was young you'd have only the sons of rich farmers, big shopkeepers or professional men ordained for the home diocese – sons of poorer men were sent foreign. People used to remark that you'd know the farmer's son by the way he handled his horse, and the shopkeeper's son by the size of his name over the confessional.

My father remembered the first parish priest to be ordained in our parish. I was often shown the house he came out of. They were big farmers and that ordination added greatly to their respectability. In the shops you'd be left standing at the counter until they were served. I remember the priest's sister fine, everyone called her 'Miss'. At that time herself and the principal teacher's wife were the only two women facing in the chapel with hats. That is not taking into account the tuppenny ha'penny landlord, one of our own, that had a small grandstand built for himself and his family at the right-hand side of the altar, so as to be away from the commonality. His wife wore an enormous hat.

In those days to carry any weight with the people the makings of a priest should be respectable and fairly well to do. In their eyes, riches and authority went hand in hand. Signs by when the bishop had to go dipping a bit lower in the barrel for vocations, and when my neighbours heard that the son of a small boggy farmer had gone to Maynooth, by the dint of his own brains, they shook their heads and said, 'Wisha, God help us then, he'll be the priest without power!'

The old clergy had authority. Apart from a fondness for money you couldn't see any fault in their way of living. And if there was any fault the people'd gloss it over with, 'Don't do as they do but do as they say!'

If we were to do everything they said that time, Ireland would be an open-air monastery! Small children would nearly have to be imported, for the young people'd never get the hang of things. Father Mac with a big blackthorn belting the courting couples out of the bushes and he had the full support and the sympathy of the people in that. The mothers anyway. 'My poor man. All the trouble that young crowd are putting him to. He's worn off the bones aby 'em.' Of course, to my mind there'd never be any religion in this country only for the women. The men never took to it in the same way! The women driving 'em out to confession, up to the altar and down on their knees to say the rosary. Timeen Sweeney, his mind a thousand miles away, doing eleven Hail Marys to the decade and twelve to the decade, and his wife saying, 'Glory, Tim!' That was like a hul-a-hul or tally-ho to him; he'd then do thirteen to the decade!

The men sitting around my father's fire to give you an inkling as to how devout they were. We had a holy picture up on the wall. The picture of a workshop with St Joseph cutting a big plank and our Lord, He was only a young lad at the time, blowing the sawdust off the pencil line out before him. There was a cracked carpenter there from near Macroom, and he'd often look at the picture, being in the same line of business himself. He thought St Joseph was a disgrace to the trade. A man you'd be expecting a headline from, the old traps he had.

He said that saw wouldn't cut butter on a hot flag!

'If you don't give up that talk,' the women told him, 'you'll find yourself on a hot flag for all eternity.'

Eternity, according to the men sitting around my father's fire, was fairly long. If a smith had a pet crow and every day after feeding him the crow wiped his beak on the horn of the anvil, when the horn was worn down to the size of a darning needle that might be the start of eternity. That was one man's idea. A second man put it this way. If you got a rock the size of Ireland and the crow wiped his beak on that every thousand years, when he'd have the rock worn away that'd be the start of eternity. But a third man wouldn't give into it. He thought the crow's droppings would add more to the rock than his beak'd wear off it. More likely he said the crow'd wind up with a big round ball the size of the world and that'd be the start of eternity!

Of course the church one time believed the world was flat! The cracked carpenter from near Macroom would never let us forget that. 'Didn't they shove Galileo into jail for saying it was round! They excommunicated him!' Oh, that was a sore point with the men sitting around my father's fire, for excommunication was taking place nearer home that time. We know that absolution was always refused in the case of a reserved sin – making *poitín* or committing perjury. There was no notice taken of that, but withholding the sacraments from the men out fighting was a different thing. And they'd often tell about this man called King that was very prominent in the Land League, and in jail the time of the Plan of Campaign.

King defied the priest. He would not give up the movement. So when he was refused absolution he walked straight out of the box and out of the chapel and never again darkened the door of it. His wife and family had to put up with hearing his name called from the altar. King couldn't be swayed – blacker he got. When there was a station in his house, he'd shake the green rushes in the yard like the palms on the road to Jerusalem, but when the parish priest walked in over the rushes, King walked out and stayed outside until Mass was over. The only place he was ever seen in the same company as the priest was at the burial of an old comrade. That would be a special day. And I suppose his thoughts would often go forward to when his own time would come, and to the class of a turnout he'd get. Well, his time did come; it will come to all of us, and his family was hoping that at the end he'd make his peace with the church and through the church with the man above. Men of influence came to talk to him. It was all of no avail. He did without 'em up to now and he'd go without 'em!

Coming near the end his two sons used to stay up with him every night. They'd sit in the kitchen and take it in turns to go up in the room and talk to their father. He'd be rambling in his speech and talking about the skirmishes he was in long ago. The son would remind him that those days were gone now and forgotten. 'Will I send for him?' 'No,' his father would say.

One night when the two sons were sitting by the fire, one of 'em said, 'I think I have it.' So he went up in the room and he said to his father, 'Da, what field will we bury you in?'

'What are you saying to me? I'll be buried with my people in Nohevilldaly. You know that,' he said to the son.

'Oh no, Da!' His son brought his voice down a bit because of the effect of what he said had on his father.

'If you die outside the church, Da, you can't be buried in consecrated ground. There'll be no funeral or nothing. Do you hear me?' he said when the old man didn't answer. 'Will I send for him?'

'Do whatever it is you want to do,' his father said, 'and don't be asking me about it.'

The priest came, and King died in the bosom of the church.

> He was buried with all honour,
> It was a glorious sight.
> There were four and four more clergymen,
> And they all dressed up in white.

The custom was at that time that four men of the same surname should shoulder the remains, and the man in charge called out: 'Are there four Kings there to go under the coffin?'

Four Kings? There weren't four kings left in Europe that time not to mind Gloungreeshkeen!

A Quiet Drink

If two funerals are converging on a graveyard it is a common belief in some places, that the last man in will be the other man's servant for all eternity. Now that's exactly what happened the day King was burying. The other procession was seen a good bit off, and they, seeing the Kings, put on a little spurt, and the Kings too increased their pace to the point of comicality, but for all the extra effort the two remains arrived at the graveyard gate almost simultaneously, and it looked like as if the Kings were going to make it. But the widow of the other man , I forget now who is this he was, he wasn't very prominent in this life, his widow took off her shoe and hit the back left-hand King under the coffin on the head. He sagged at the knees, and in the resultant disarray her husband got in first! A man is nowhere without a woman to his back!

I was coming from a funeral in Rockfield and there were three more with me. One was Dan the Dip anyway. It was very late and we coming through the town. We had enough in the same day but, there you are, the devil picked us, so we said we'd have one more *smathán* for old time's sake. It was long after hours and the public houses looked as silent as the grave, the shutters up and the lights out, and it didn't look as if we'd score.

'Well,' says Dan the Dip, 'what did we get tongues for?' and he went around making enquiries and he got the high sign for a certain establishment, so over we went, gave three knocks on the fanlight, left a silence, two knocks, left another silence and one knock.

Oh glory, I only hope the gate of heaven will open as quick for us. There was the publican and he said: 'Don't stir a sop or a ha'port, be as still as statues.' And he let his eye wander up and down the street taking his time until he was full sure and certain there was no one suspicious at large and then he said, 'Come on in!' He shut the door, making it a big compliment and telling us the great favour he was bestowing on us.

He put us into the front snug and as he said himself, because of its proximity to the street he would require us to be awful silent. Which we were. There wasn't a splink of light in the snug, and someone said near me, and I nearly hopped out of my skin, 'Is that you Ned?' And who was there, judging by the voice, but Collins, a man I built a cowhouse for that same spring. I said, 'The devil fly away with you, Collins, and the start you knocked out of me in the dark!'

Well, I don't know, it is next door to impossible to carry on any business in the dark, where money has to change hands and pints of porter have to be filled out. But along came the publican and he had a candle lighting under the mouth of a canteen so that there was only a circle of light going on the floor, the naked flame not exposed, for it could go through a crack in the shutter and the police passing outside'd see it and the fat'd be in the fire.

He brought us the drinks and by then my eyes were getting accustomed to the place and I looked in through the cubby hole to the bar, and there was a fair scattering of people inside. They were talking away very low, a sort of rumble it would remind you, for all the world, of the buzz of bluebottles trying to get out of a butter-box. I introduced, having my manners, Dan the Dip and the two lads that were with me to Collins and he had two fly-by-nights in his own company, and he introduced them to us.

We were putting out our hands in the dark in the

direction the voices were coming from, I know, I nearly got the eye knocked out of me and I wound up shaking hands to myself!

After all the warnings we got to keep quiet you'd forget, and we got a little bit loud and the publican used to come every now and again, as he said himself, to admonish us. He was very precise in his speech and why not he? A brother a doctor over in England, another brother holding down a parish in Nebraska and a son in the police in Singapore. I tell you there's money in drink!

After a couple of jorums – the lubrication can have an effect on the tongue, it will loosen the hinges – we got awful loud and Collins was the loudest for he was a bit of a blackguard.

'Did you ever hear Ned,' says he, 'that this barber next door used to go down to the palace every morning to shave the bishop? This was a regular commitment and the bishop was lucky, for he was a good barber, as good a man as ever learned his trade, until he took to drink and in time it began to show in the hand.'

The bishop saw it, but the barber was so long shaving him that they were used to each other, and he didn't want to be making changes, bringing a new man into the palace, maybe to be taking stories out of it. One morning after a hard night the barber lathered the bishop. The bishop would have his eyes closed for that, and when he opened them he noticed that the shake in the barber's hand was very bad. There was nothing for it now only offer it up! When the job was done the barber held up the looking glass, and the bishop saw small little oozings of blood all over his face, and throwing his eyes to heaven he said, 'Oh, God, isn't drink a fright!'

'That's right, my Lord,' said the barber, 'it makes the

skin very tender!'

There was a loud guffaw. And when you are not supposed to laugh it is the very devil to keep it in. We were shoving the caps in our mouths to hold back the great *tulc* of laughing, and Collins, enjoying the state he had put us in, gave vent to a loud he-haw an ass needn't be ashamed of!

The publican came charging out and said to Collins, 'God, man, you'll be heard in Gullane, and remember you are not a customer in this establishment. I strained a point to let you in here!'

'Well now,' said Collins giving him the glass, 'go away and strain another one!'

Very good why. At this minute the publican's wife came running downstairs. She was on an LOP at the top window and she said that there were two guards passing Hanaffin's. We cocked our ears and sure enough we could hear the pounding of the two pairs of feet good and slow and solid approaching nearer every second, and when they were coming to the door we held our breath waiting to see would they halt. No, they passed on and they were barely out of ear shot when Collins settled into

When the roses bloom again down by the river

'Shut up Collins! Put a sop in it!'

And a robin redbreast sings his heart's refrain!
For a the sake of old langsyne,
I'll be with you sweetheart mine
I'll be with you when the roses bloom again!

With that there was a frightful pounding at the front door. And the publican said, labouring up from the bottom of the throat a nice tone, 'Who is they-ur?' You'd think he was talking to a bishop. 'Who is they-ur?'

'Guards on duty, open up!'

Well, the publican got frightfully excited. He had been caught a few times before and the licence could suffer.

'Look,' he said, 'I am inviting you all up to the parlour. There, take a bottle of stout every man of ye. Say I gave it to ye and remember we are arranging an outing and I am going too. Upstairs quick!'

As himself and the wife cleared the counter of porter-stained glasses we pounded up the stairs. Collins was the slowest for he was almost legless. We got into the parlour where it was fine and bright, but I couldn't get 'em to settle down so that we could prepare what we were going to say to the sergeant. There they were staggering around examining the knick-knacks on the what-not and looking at the photographs on the wall. There was a big photograph of the publican's brother, the doctor, another stylish one of the Nebraska parish priest, not to mind the Singapore policeman in full regalia.

We were only barely sitting down when another uniformed figure appeared at the top of the stairs. It was the Sergeant and looking around he said, 'Can ye account for yeerselves now. Can ye account for being on licenced premises after hours?'

I said, 'We were invited.' Well, we were invited upstairs anyway!

'And what about the refreshments?'

Dan the Dip holding the bottle to his heart told him: 'The publican stood us that.'

'Fair enough,' the sergeant said, 'but explain to me now about this outing!' There was no answer. He looked at me and I said, 'We are going on a pilgrimage.'

Letting his eye ramble around the room and taking in the state of the company, he said: 'I didn't know there was a pilgrimage to a brewery! Where are ye going?'

'To the Reek,' I said. 'We are going to Croagh Patrick.' And I was very sorry after for having said it, for I knew if he questioned the people there some of them wouldn't even know what county the Reek was in. We told him then, and the publican joined in, that we were making plans whether we'd go by train or take the bus, where we'd stay the night before and so on.

Everything was working out fine, and even though it was unusual for people from our locality to go to Croagh Patrick the Sergeant believed it for he shut the book. The relief on the publican's face was plain to see as the Sergeant made for the door. Now all would be hunkey-dorey only the Sergeant paused to have a word with the publican's wife on the landing, and Collins, thinking he was gone gave vent to a drunken guffaw. 'T'was a bloody great plan!' says Collins. 'An outing to Croke Park! He believing we'd go all that way when we could hear the match on the wireless at home!'

Collins never put his leg across the threshold of that establishment again.

The Poor Souls

There was this man Malachi Dhónail and he could read with the priest and out-do him in power. The same Malachi had power over animals too. If he didn't like you he could put a plague of rats on your house the rats'd do his bidding. Some strangers were in Malachi's kitchen one night and down near the dresser they noticed two rats sitting on the edge of a pan and they wiring into the hen's mess. And sitting on the table was this big hoor of a white cat and he blinking at 'em. The strangers couldn't get over the unnaturalness of the cat's behaviour, so one of 'em said to Malachi, 'What's wrong with the cat?'

'Ah,' says Malachi, 'you should see him if a strange rat came in!'

Malachi would never get involved with the clergy only when he had drink taken. He was one day standing in the chapel yard arguing with the priest. There were two pigeons perched on the gable of the chapel.

'Come on now,' says Malachi to the priest, 'which of us will have his bird down first!'

They began to read and in a while's time the two pigeons came tumbling down.

'Now,' says the parish priest, 'my bird was down first.'

'Yes,' says Malachi, 'but mine is fit for the pot.'

There wasn't a feather on Malachi's bird. The priest walked into the bottom of the chapel. Malachi followed him in and bringing his voice down a peg, by the way out of reverence, he said to the priest, 'Come on. I challenge you by the dint of reading to light a candle on the altar from where we are standing.'

'Come on,' says the priest – wouldn't you imagine he'd think more of the cloth. 'Come on then.'

Well they began to read and in a while's time a little flame appeared on the candle on Malachi's side of the altar. It began to flicker but he fed the words on it and it blazed up into a fine strong flame. Over at the priest's side of the altar a little light appeared on the candle. It began to flicker, spluttered up and then went out. There was a little puff of smoke as a red spark died on top of the wick.

'What happened to me?' says the priest.

'You went astray,' says Malachi, 'in the reading of one syllable. It was as tight as that!'

'You are an evil man,' the priest told Malachi, 'and it is by the power of darkness you lit that candle. You'll come to a bad end. You'll die in drink!'

'I won't go unknown to you,' said Malachi.

And sure enough Malachi, in a drunken state, stumbled into a stream. He was found face-down there, and the old people said that the instant the soul left the body the gable of the chapel fell in!

By the same token I was in a public house in Baile Bhúirne. I was stranded there of a night. There must have been five or six of us in the back snug and we were having a discussion as to the size of the human soul. We were fairly far gone! One man said it was so small you could hold it in the cup of your two hands. He made a little cage with his cupped palms, and moving his thumb he put his eye to the opening and began to describe the soul to us. He said it was like a small bright bubble with a little pulse in it, about the size of a little *peidhleachán* with red dots in what looked like wings. If you lifted your thumbs it would fly away.

And he told us about this soul, it was a lost soul, it was in total darkness and was clinging to the back of an ivy leaf. There was no sound ever in the dark except maybe the ivy leaf flapping in the wind.

One time the soul heard someone laughing and it said, 'Who is that?'

And wasn't it another soul at the other side of the ivy leaf.

'How long are you there?' says the first soul, and the second soul said, 'Three times three score years.'

'I'm here far longer than that,' the first soul said, 'I've lost all track of time, but tell me, why were you laughing there now?'

'Because I heard good news,' the second soul said. 'Just now wasn't there a son born to the son of my son's great-grandson, and when he is twenty-two years of age he'll be ordained. And at his first Mass he'll remember all those of his own family gone before him and that morning I'll be free! Did you hear me?' he said, for the first soul didn't answer.

'I did,' he said, 'fine for you. I've no one belonging to me.'

'Have courage,' the second soul said. 'Do you know what I'll do? Whatever good is coming from that first Mass I'll go halves in that with you.'

Our Lord and His Mother were out walking above and she says to Him. 'Did you hear that, hah?'

He said, 'I did, what about it?'

'To think,' she said, 'that that lost soul after waiting so long for his release, and then when the means of his release comes he's willing to share it with a complete stranger. What are you going to do about it?'

'Well I suppose,' says He, 'for peace sake I'll have to do something!'

She went away and put the sheets airing, and that night St Peter had two more Baile Bhúirne men in heaven!

The Severe Penance

There was this man and he had three sons, and when it came to the time for him to settle up his affairs, to his eldest son he gave his house and land, to his second son he have his passage across the sea and to his third son he gave enough money to get him through college to be a priest.

The third son set out – there were no roads or railways in Ireland then – and he kept going, lodging a night here and a night there, until at last he came to the college which was somewhere near Athlone. Five years he gave there until he was turned out a fully ordained priest. He got ready then and he put his books in his bag saying, 'I must go home now and see my mother and my father and thank them for all they have done for me.'

He set out and he walked all through the day, and when darkness was falling he saw a light that way from him. He went towards it and saw that it was a rich man's house. He walked into the yard and he asked for lodgings.

'You can have a bed here and welcome,' the man told him, and indeed that man didn't know what to do for the young priest he had such a high regard for him.

The young priest was a fine figure of a man, and the daughter, as you might say, put her eye on him when she brought him in his supper, and a fine supper he got. When they were all in bed that night the young woman came into the room where the young priest was. She wanted him right go wrong to give up the church and marry herself.

'A handsome man like you,' she said, 'throwing away

your life.' She was an only daughter and she told him that. 'And we'll have this fine house,' she said, 'and all that's going with it if you marry me.'

'Don't be telling me your mind,' he said, 'for it is no good. I have my vows taken. I'm satisfied with that, and I can't ever marry.'

She gave it up then when she saw it was no good for her. But in a while's time she came back again to the room where the young priest was. He was asleep now and she put a gold plate belonging to her father between the books in his bag and out with her.

When the priest got up in the morning he was readying himself for the road. He put his coat hanging that way on the door while he was washing his face. Unknown to him the young woman came and put a piece of cold roast beef in his pocket. Now it was Good Friday and she didn't offer him any breakfast. Even in a rich man's house, at that time, Good Friday was black fast.

When he was a couple of miles from the house, she went and told her father that the man who stayed the night was gone and that the gold plate was missing. Her father saddled his horse and it wasn't long until he overtook the priest.

'You looked like an honest man,' her father said to him. 'Little did I know I was harbouring a thief!'

The young priest was brought before the jury. Her father showed them the bag, they opened it and there sure enough was the gold plate. There was only one punishment for a thief at that time, so he was sentenced to be hanged. When he was up on the stage and before the rope was put around his neck, he was given permission to speak. He told the people who he was, that he was on his way home to see his father and mother, and that was how he came to be in the rich man's house.

'That young woman there,' he said, pointing her out to the people, 'wanted me to marry her, but I couldn't give in to that. I don't know,' he said, 'how the gold plate came to be in my bag or how the fish came to be in my pocket.'

'It wasn't fish I put in your pocket,' she said, 'it was roast beef.'

She should have kept her mouth shut, for the jury began to cross-hackle her and in the end she had to admit that she put the gold plate in his bag. Now in everyone's eyes her crime was as bad as that the young priest was supposed to have done, and the jury said there was no way out of it only hang her. When she was mounting the stage she said to the young priest, 'As sure as there's a God in heaven you'll be the sorry man yet!'

He came home and he saw his people and after a while he was allotted a parish. He was happy and contented and he had the respect of everyone. All was fine until one day he was on a visit to the landlord. The landlord had a fine garden near his house and the young priest was walking there after a good dinner, reading his office, when a young woman came up to him. He didn't know her and thought she was someone connected with the house. She was ever so forward and free-making and began linking him around the garden. Now, that way in a quiet corner there was a sun house. He ran into it to be out of her road but she went in after him. And it seems that by the dint of sweet talk she turned his head and the young priest forgot himself.

When they were parting the young woman said, 'You ought to know me! I'm the woman you hanged. I came back to blacken your soul!'

He was a sorry man now, and he wasn't getting any peace of mind day or night, so he went and made his confession to the bishop and the bishop told him he was damned.

'There's no hope at all for me?' said the young priest.

'There's no hope at all for you,' the bishop said, 'unless you take this bundle of needles and get a boat and put to sea, and as you row away, every hundred spades throw out a needle until the last needle is gone. Then unless you are able to gather up all those needles and bring them back to me you are lost for ever!'

'I'll never see your face again,' the young priest said, 'for that's an impossible thing to do.'

But he got the boat, and he put to sea and as he rowed away, every hundred spades he threw out a needle, and when the last needle was gone so was his strength, for he had no food or no drink. He was three days then under the heat of the sun, and on the evening of the third day he saw land.

He made towards it and put ashore. He walked for a while and when darkness fell he was in a big wood. He saw a light, he drew near it, and there he found a house and around the fire were twelve children. He asked them for something to eat and they gave him his supper.

He told them his story and about the cruel penance that was put on him by the bishop, and he asked them if they could at all, to tell him of any person he could go to that would save him from the terrible consequences of this penance.

'We don't know,' the children said, 'but for the next three mornings at six o'clock a monk is coming here to say Mass. If he can't save you, no one will.'

The young priest went to bed. Every bone in his body

was aching after the long journey, and he fell into a sound sleep. When he woke he asked the children did the monk come yet?

And they said, 'Mass is over and the monk is gone!'

He was so heavy with sleep that day he could hardly keep his eyes open, and so that he'd wake in time for Mass the second morning, he slept that night on the cold flags of the floor. When he woke he asked the children if the monk came yet?

'Mass is over,' they told him, 'and the monk is gone.'

He was in great dread now that he would miss Mass the third morning, so he went to the wood and cut down a thorn tree. He made a bed of it, and when night time came he took off his shirt and lay on the bed and the thorns bit into his flesh and kept him awake until the monk came. When Mass was over the monk was leaving and the young priest went up to him and said, 'Don't go awhile. I have something to tell you.'

And he told the monk all he had been through since the day he was ordained and about the penance put on him by the bishop and what he would have to do if he was ever to see his home again.

'Tomorrow,' the monk said, 'you will go into the nearest town, and go up to such and such a street where you'll see a woman selling fish. Take the first fish you'll lay your hand on; that fish'll be fourpence and here's the money. Open the fish and take out what's inside, but I implore of you put the fish back in its place!'

Next morning the young priest went into the town and kept walking until he came to the place where the woman was. He took the first fish he laid his hand on and paid the woman. He opened the fish and there inside were the needles.

He left the fish with her and came back to the house. The children got some food and drink ready for him, and he turned his face towards home. When he landed he pulled the boat up on the shore and made off to his own house.

When the bishop heard he had returned he came to the young priest.

'I can't believe it,' he said, 'that you are back. Have you the needles?'

'There they are there,' says the young priest, 'you can count 'em.'

Now it was the bishop's turn to be uneasy in his mind and he was getting no peace day or night, so he said he'd go to the Pope. He made his confession and he told the Pope about the penance he put on the young priest and how it turned out. When he had finished the Pope reaching that way above his head took a parcel down from a shelf and giving it to the bishop he said, 'You wronged a good man.'

The bishop opened the parcel and it was full of needles. He went then and he got a boat and put to sea, every hundred spades throwing out a needle.

But the bishop never came back!

Eoghan's School

Eoghan Rua Ó Súilleabháin had a school too, though it was not as big as the one near Athlone. Eoghan's school was at Knocknagree Cross. Father Ned Fitzgerald that opened it and Father Ned Fitzgerald that closed it. I remember enquiring when I was small why Father Ned did that. The old people didn't know, though one man with a glint in his eye wasn't long giving a reason for it.

He said Eoghan was a hard man for the women. Like Diarmuid, Eoghan had the *Ball Seirce*, no load to any man, and the attraction being there the women were mad about him. At wake or wedding or anywhere you'd have good-looking women, Eoghan would be planked down in the middle of 'em. Like that Eoghan was one night at a wake surrounded by a prize bunch of merry women. Whatever caffling was going on one woman made an indelicate sound, a small report, but loud enough to be heard.

Then all the women began to laugh and nudging each other said, 'Ah ha dee, Eoghan!' by the way blaming it on him.

'What's natural,' says Eoghan, 'can't be remarkable, but I'll bet a pound to a ha'penny I'll find out which of ye ruffled the air!'

They had a fine piece of innocent fun blaming each other and blaming Eoghan. The clay pipes were being handed out, at the time the women smoked too, and they were in a circle around the blazing splinter waiting their turns to get up steam. They had to be careful reddening the pipes from that thing or they could set fire to their headgear. Eoghan left 'em alone for a bit and then of a sudden he said, 'The lady that "killed the cat" her dandy cap is on fire.'

A pair of hands went up to a head, giving the game away, and realising the trick Eoghan played on her she went to give him a good- humoured thumping and wound up rolling in his arms – a thing she didn't find any fault with!

But to come back to Eoghan's school, English was making its appearance in Sliabh Luachra at the time and the well-to-do, there weren't many of them there, believed English was the coming thing that you couldn't get on without it. The mothers liked their daughters to be precise in the new language, pronouncing it to a 't', able to given an account of themselves when they went into Killarney, and of course it would also improve their marriage prospects. So they sent their daughters, big grown women down to Eoghan's school at Knocknagree Cross to get a good grounding in grammar. Now, Eoghan's grammar school was a continuation of a hayshed, and it seems Father Ned Fitzgerald paid a surprise visit and found Eoghan on a bench of hay with one of these young women. As the man said that told me the story, 'She could parse but not decline!'

It wasn't the end of the world that time if you lost a job like school-mastering; you could turn your hand to the spade, the reaping hook or the *grafán*. As well, a poet like Eoghan could turn a few bob by making up a praising song for the well-to-do. Eoghan was still a young man when he made a song of praise for one Daniel Cronin, when the same Cronin was made lieutenant of the horse soldiers in Killarney. The song was in English, which was what Eoghan thought might suit in Cronin's case. Cronin never paid Eoghan for the song nor even let on he got it, which was nothing short of an insult.

Eoghan was one night in a public house in College Street

and Cronin's name came down. If it did Eoghan gave him the edge of his tongue – said he was the seed, breed and generation of *ceithearnachs*, which I suppose he was. Unknown to Eoghan some of Cronin's retainers were in the house. One word borrowed another until they came to blows. Now Eoghan could give as good an account of himself as any man in a fair fight but he didn't get a chance. One of Cronin's servants, a treacherous crew, picked up the tongs and cracked him on the head with it.

He was brought to Knocknagree, every care his friends could give they gave it, there was no medical attention at the time. It was heartbreaking for them to think that one so full of life should go. His friends couldn't accept it that there was any danger. They coaxed a young woman to go into the bed with him. It was no good. He fell into a fever and died. No one knows rightly where Eoghan is buried but the day of his funeral Father Ned Fitzgerald said that he was a fine Christian man.

The Golden Ball

Guirteen was living in the townland of Lyre. He was alone there in the house for he never married. He was too shy when he was young and too old when he got the courage. He had a greak liking for mushrooms, and he'd be out at the crack of dawn in late June walking barefoot through the dewy grass.

This morning as he went along his toe struck a bunch of growing rushes, and a little gold ball hopped out to him. He put it in his pocket and brought it home, and he was looking for some safe place to put it to keep, for it was a nice nest-egg to have!

Now for all the world that was the time he had the stonemason building the new chimney, and in all old-fashioned hearths you had a square hole left in the pier where the man of the house could keep his pipe, or the woman her tay canister.

'Do you know,' says Guirteen to the mason, 'that *cábúisín* is only a gathering place for dust, and my advice to you is to close it up.'

The mason was dressing down a square flag for the mouth of the cubbyhole, and when his back was turned Guirteen buried the gold ball in a lump of mortar and threw it into the hole, and the mason put the flag in position and plastered it over to 'match existing wall'.

In a while's time Guirteen went out to the haggard and what did he see there but a lovely young woman. He asked her who she was, and she said she was Mary O'Sullivan from the west of Kerry.

'You're a fair step from home so,' he said, and he wanted to know what message she was running in that part of the world.

'I'm going in service,' says she, 'to a big farmer in Shanagolden, but I'm afraid I'm gone a bit off my road.'

'You are,' says he. 'I'm very short-handed here, being alone and that, and if you'll come working to me I'll give you whatever wages you're expecting below in Shanagolden.'

There wasn't another word said, and no better servant ever came inside a man's door, to bake, to boil, to wash, or sew. She left the sign of her hand on the house – and indeed it needed it! But there was one thing. If Guirteen ever came in unexpected from the fields he'd always find her rummaging on the top of the dresser, along the thatch or behind the bin; and this day she was above in the loft with the tin trunk thrown sideways, and she going through the contents of it. Guirteen never tumbled to what she was searching for. How could he for he had something else on his mind.

She didn't go home at all for Christmas, and he didn't remark on it, not knowing how she was situated with regard to her people. Shrovetime came, and do you know it was younger Guirteen was getting, and no day went that he didn't throw on the collar and tie. This night the two of 'em were talking by the fire, and he said, 'Well now, Mary, you can't but know the extent of my farm and buildings and it isn't like another house, you'll have no relations to be playing with, so would you marry me?'

'Not at the moment,' says she, and placing her hand in his she said, 'You must have patience, that's what you must have.' He curbed his tongue, though 'twas hard for him, and reaching up for his fiddle he played her a tune:

Ar maidin inné sea do dhearchas an stuaire-cailín
Her limbs were complate and she nately clothed
   in green,
A malla ba chaol is a béilín ba ró-mhilis bhí,
And I knew by her gazing she'd play the hide-
   and-go-seek!

Faith! She remained on in the house with him after that, and as the days lengthened out into spring anyone living in the place and keeping his eyes open could see that she was still searching. She went from the house to the out-offices, and from the out-offices into the open and every loose stone she turned, even the rusty bucket with the dock leaf growing up through the broken bottom, she'd knock sideways to see what was under it. She tried every hole and corner and as time went by the colour left her cheeks and she pined away till she was only a bare shadow of the Mary O'Sullivan that stood in the haggard that June before.

Everything that could be done was done but in spite of all she died.

Guirteen waked her the same as if she was one of his own, and at that time the wake'd run three nights and the corpse'd be laid out on the kitchen table, and every night the house was full.

The first night coming up to twelve o'clock the horse's hooves came pounding into the yard. The door burst open and in came a strange man of pale appearance. He walked up and stood over the corpse and said, '*A bhfuairis an rud úd abhí á lorg agat?* Did you get that thing you were searching for?

And the girl said: 'I did not nor a sign of it,' and fell back on the table.

Cold sweat stood out on every forehead as the stranger went out the door and they heard the horse galloping out in the yard – I tell you no one went home after the rosary that night! They held on, and when day broke, they were so drowsy and upset that they thought it was how they dreamt it. But when the same thing happened the following night the men put their heads together, and one of 'em was for going with the first light to the presbytery.

'The wrong move,' says Guirteen, 'the only thing that'll come out of it is another sermon about drink at wakes.'

'What'll we do so?' says they. 'Here we have a riddle that we can't unravel.'

'Well,' says Guirteen, 'Malachi Dhónail is known to everyone of us and from his talks with the old people he can't but have an inkling into things. He was a long way on the road to ordination, and can light a candle on the altar by the dint of reading.'

Malachi Dhónail was seen in the morning and he said, 'I'll come along to that wake tonight.'

He was sitting among the men in the kitchen, when coming up to twelve o'clock the saddle horse galloped into the yard. The door burst open and in came the same man of the two nights before. He walked up and stood over the corpse and said, 'Did you get that thing you were searching for?'

'I did not nor a sign of it,' the girl said, and fell back on the table. The stranger moved to go.

'Now lads!' says Malachi and like lightning they were between the stranger and the door and holding up his hand Malachi said, 'I command you to give an account of the commotion you have created in this house for three nights running.'

'I was waiting for someone to ask me that,' says the stranger, and looking around the kitchen he said, 'I'm not one of ye! I'm from the other world. Our game there was hurling, and we played it under the full moon in that field below, but we've no game now, and all because of that girl lying there. Her job was to stand on the sideline and watch the ball going wide, but she neglected her duty and lost the golden ball and there'll be no peace in this house till we get it!'

'Where's the spawl hammer!' says Guirteen, racing around the kitchen. He found it and smashing the flag in front of the cubby-hole, he took out the golden ball and threw it to the stranger. He rubbed the mortar off it on his sleeve till it glittered.

'Ah ha,' says he, 'this is it, our hurling ball!' and motioning to the corpse he said, 'Come on! We'll be going!'

'You're going,' says Malachi, 'but she's not! Or do you mean to stand there and tell these people that any girl that lived so long in this house where she was every day in contact with the fire is one of ye! Isn't she a changling!'

'She is,' says the stranger, 'we have to have a go-between.'

'Well, I command you,' says Malachi, 'to clear the cloud from her mind and restore her to normal life.' The *joeyman's* face blackened with the dint of bad stuff, and muttering some words he filled the house with a whirling noise. There was a burst of light and like that the dead girl hopped off the table and stood there every bit as lovely as she was in the haggard the June before.

The man was gone for they heard the horse knocking sparks out of the paving stones in the yard. Guirteen was the first one over to the girl's side and taking her by the two hands he said, 'You're a free woman now, Mary, and I suppose you'll go back to your people. Why then, the two of us were happy in this house, and I made bold enough to ask you a certain question one time when you were under the spell.'

'Ask me again,' says Mary, 'and see what I'll say!'

He asked her again and she said she would, and what began as a wake ended up like a wedding!

> There was gaiety where grieving was,
> Music where mourning was,
> Singing where *caoining* was,
> And the rafters rung till the sun peeped in the
>   window.

The Station House

'In the name of the Father and of the Son and of the Holy Ghost.
Amen. The following are the stations for the coming week.
Tomorrow, Monday for the townland of Craughatusane in the
house of the representatives of the late Jeremiah Tagney. Tuesday,
for the townlands of Shrone and Meanageshaugh in the house
of Laurence . . . '

There was a station published for Larry one time. He
was a relation of my own, a man that lived to be nearly
ninety years of age and was only one week sick in his life
– that was the week he died of course! I don't remember
this too very well myself now. The old people I heard
talking about it, and what kept it so fresh in their memories
was something comical to take place the morning of the
station.

The station goes back to the penal times when people
of Larry's persuasion had to worship in holes and corners.
And the station, as we were often told from the altar, is the
morning when the kitchen becomes a sanctuary and the
room becomes a confessional. Indeed Larry's room wasn't
much bigger than a confession box. But the kitchen was
enormous. Paved floor, except that there was a big flag in
front of the fire, and buried under that you had two horse's
skulls to give it a nice drum effect for step dancing. Larry,
when the humour took him, could knot the ankles in a hornpipe.
Over the kitchen you had the loft, a recent renovation. There
were no grants in those days and the money ran out, so there
were only enough floorboards for what the bed stood on and

about two feet of a runway in front of it. You had to watch the way you circumnavigated in and out of the bed or you might come down the near way to the kitchen.

Sitting below you would not be aware of the deficiency above for Larry's wife had opened out flour bags and tacked them up underneath the joists. It looked all right except that it was 'Bee Brand' flour they used to get, it was a bob or two less than 'Purity' or 'Prosperity', and if you remember there was a picture of a big bee walking up the side of the bag. When the bags were opened out, God Almighty! all the bees!

Now Larry's wife did her best to get the bees out of the bags. She boiled 'em in the pot, she danced on 'em in the river. but whatever indelible ink was in the print, she couldn't get the bees out of the bags. And I wouldn't mind but it was lovely cloth in those flour bags, gave great wear. Women used to make sheets out of it and little garments for themselves with 'Purity' in front and 'Prosperity' behind.

Larry's son that was sleeping above, and the same young Larry the devil or Doctor Reilly would not get him out of bed in the morning. The schoolmaster said he'd never be confirmed only that the catechism was at twelve o'clock in the day. If you saw him facing out for Mass on Sunday you'd turn home for you'd know you'd only have the soldier's part of it. Indeed people were saying would he be up in time for Mass in his own house?

Larry and his wife were up with the cock. They had to milk the cows, feed the calves and let out the horse. Then they called Lar. He'd be down in a minute! They put down a big *béiltigheach* of a fire in the kitchen and another in the grate in the room where the priest would have his breakfast. Then they called Lar. He'd be down in a minute. The bottle of whisky had to be put away where the priest wouldn't see it. Larry and the wife had to dress up to welcome the people, and indeed looking out the window they could see 'em making for the house so they called Lar.

Now one thing you'd want to be very careful of the morning of a station is wet paint. In the house where there is a smokey chimney, and Larry had one, paint don't dry. The dresser was varnished and the settle, even the chairs. That varnish was like birdlime and if, having sat on a chair, you got up out of it, you'd bring the chair all round the house with you.

The people sauntered in, and the two Cahillanes put their backs to the dresser, and stuck to it the same as you'd put a stamp on a letter. They were big quiet men that could remain motionless for a century. Now the parish priest that was there at the time was a trifle hasty, a little impatient and stern of demeanor, and signs by innocent people were peppering in dread of him. Although to go to the house you couldn't meet a nicer man. Jeremiah Horgan that was telling me, he was there for a letter of freedom, he was marrying some bird from an outside community. He got the letter – as things turned out he'd be better off if he didn't.

Big and all as Larry's kitchen was, some of the neighbours waited in the yard. The morning turned out very dirty, but country people don't mind the rain – they say it never melted anyone. With that a son of Johnny Dan Thadhgeen's put his head around the corner of the cow house and said: 'He's coming!'

All the neighbours belted off into Larry's kitchen like lightning and left Larry there to welcome the parish priest. And Larry would rather any other job. He's rather be draining the Dead Sea with a silver spoon for he was a very shy, distant sort of an individual.

In the kitchen when they heard the shout that the priest was coming the two Cahillanes went to go on their knees and brought the dresser down on top of 'em. There was an almighty crash of breaking delph which woke young Lar in the loft. He jumped out of bed and in his excitement overshot the runway. There was a tearing of flour bags and a scattering of bees and young Lar came sailing down between two rafters and sat on Hannah Maroya Casey's lap . . . a big red-faced woman getting her breath back after walking against the hill.

There he sat my *fostúch* of nineteen years of age with only a skimpy little shirt on him. The woman had to turn her face away. As she said to someone after, 'Indeed, I had something else on my mind, preparing myself for confession.'

By the time the dresser was put back on its feet and the sound side of the cups turned out, and young Lar had his clothes on, Father Mac came sailing into the yard holding over his head a black round roof on top of a walking cane. This strange object left Larry speechless for that was the first umbrella that was seen in that quarter. Larry didn't say, 'Good morning' or 'Good day' or 'It was good of you to come', only took the horse and put him in the stable. Father Mac made off into the kitchen, and when those inside saw the doorway darkening all conversation faded like turning down the knob of the wireless. Every man turned his back, making himself small behind his neighbour in case any awkward question would be put to him.

When they turned around again, Father Mac had opened the umbrella at the bottom of the kitchen so as that the rain'd be running off it, and that it'd be nice and dry when he'd be going home by 'n' bye, that is when confessions'd be heard. Mass'd be said, breakfast'd be ate and dues'd be collected.

The morning wore on and all these things came to pass and the grace of God, glory be to Him, was in the house and Father Mac was in the room having his breakfast. The women were up and down to him, taking the legs off one another with excitement, and Larry's wife said and her face as red as a coal of fire, 'If you saw the look he gave me when he took the top off the egg!'

'Were they too done?' says Cáit.

'Bullets, girl! And I wouldn't mind, but I told that daughter of mine to watch 'em. But there you are the morning you'd want a thing to go right for you, that's the morning everything'd break the melt in you.'

The men were in the kitchen around the umbrella the same as if it was a German bomber. And they were saying that for such a simple thing, wasn't it a great wonder someone didn't think of it long 'go. And how handy it would be, they said, to prop it over the mouth of the barrel in the yard a wet day where you'd have a goose hatching. On the heel of that remark Father Mac came up from the room. They all backed toward the fire.

'Morning, men,' he said, 'what's the day doing?'

''Tis brightening, Father,' John Cronin said, a forward class of a man.

'I'll be going,' he said, 'there's many the thing I could be doing.'

'Good morning, Father,' they all said, and said it very loud and with great relief, for the bottle wouldn't be opened till he was gone.

Larry took the priest's horse from the stable and conveyed Father Mac down the passageway to the main road. They were nearly halfway down when Father Mac thought of his umbrella. 'Run up to the house,' he said to Larry, 'and bring me out my parasol.'

He didn't have to say this secondly. Larry ran up to the house and into the kitchen breathless. He took the umbrella by the leg, 'twas open, and brought it after him to the door, but it wouldn't go out. He came inside it and tried to shove it out before him, but the devil a out it'd go. He looked at those in the kitchen and they looked at him and they had pity on him. He took the door off the hinges – that'd give him an extra inch – but the umbrella wouldn't go out. Little beads of perspiration began to stand out on his forehead at the thought of Father Mac waiting in the passageway. He began muttering to himself saying, 'If it came in, it must go out.'

Well, there was a small man there and, wanting to be of help, he said, 'I wonder would it be any value if we kicked out the two sides of the door frame?' The two sides of the frame were driven out in the yard, but the umbrella remained inside. 'Well,' says Larry, 'there's nothing for it now only knock down the wall.' A sledge hammer was procured and when Father Mac heard all the pounding, he doubled back to the house. And when he saw what was happening, 'twas as good as a tonic to him. He roared out laughing. 'What are you at?' says he.

'Well, do you know now, Father,' says Larry, 'I think myself that if I got the corner-stone there down, the mushroom'd sail out – no trouble.'

'Move into the kitchen from me,' says he. They did. Father Mac took the umbrella by the leg – 'twas open always – and brought it to the door in front of him. He was a fierce big man, God bless him, overcoat and all on a wet day, and they couldn't see what was happening. When he came to the door, like lightening he shut the umbrella and opened it again outside and walked out the yard holding it over his head, leaving them there spellbound.

When he was gone, Larry turned to his neighbours and said, 'Say what ye like, *they* have the power!'

Con and Bridgie

There was this carpenter, and it would do your heart's good to see him working. Any sort of a fake-ah, no matter how complicated it was, if you could describe it to him he was able to make it, provided of course it was something in the building line. He couldn't make a clock or a mowing machine.

He was the first man around here to make a stand barrel-churn. It was described to him by a man that saw one of 'em below in the County Limerick. And by all accounts he improved on the original, for he put a glass peephole in front of it so that you could see the entire operation going on inside.

He built a new house for Johnny Pa Pad. He built it around the old one, so that business could go on as usual. Johnny used to sell fishing tackle to the tourists and according to some of the lads the right man for it, a fly boy. He built the new house around the old one and when the new house was finished he threw the old one out the window.

The man was a marvel! And people were coming to him from all directions with every sort of a complicated contraption to have it copied or repaired. He told me himself, as a great secret, that the strangest request was from a woman, and I know if I tell it here it won't go any further.

She came one day to the workshop and looking around to see if the walls had ears she said to him, 'Could you make a division for a double bed?'

'And what form would it take?' says he.

'I don't know,' she said. 'Aren't you the carpenter. I suppose like a gate. Isn't that right, Con?' says she putting her head out around the corner of the door. 'A gate?'

'I don't know, Bridgie,' the husband was outside, 'you have me out of my mind yourself and that bed! Don't be dragging me into it!'

The carpenter thought then it might be an old-fashioned camp bed they had. They were there when I was small, closed in on the three sides with a roof overhead. I don't know how people didn't smother inside in 'em. He thought maybe she wanted a gate to lock the children in. Children and all would be inside with the parents that time. If you looked down the room door you'd see all the little heads cocking out from under the quilt like chickens from under a hen's wing.

She said it was an ordinary wide double bed and she wanted a division in it. A gate.

'And where in the bed like!' he said. 'In the front?'

'No!' she said, 'in the middle.'

'Across?'

'No!' she said, 'up and down.' It would be very handy she explained to the carpenter if she could bring this thing into position before she'd go to sleep at night. But she wouldn't like it to be permanent. Could that be done?

He said it could, but that it would call for a lot of ingenuity!

She put her head around the corner of the door and said to her husband, 'It won't be permanent!'

The carpenter sat down, put on his thinking cap and began to draw lines on a piece of 11 x 1-inch deal board. He showed it to her saying, 'Maybe that'd do.'

She said it looked all right.

He made out a list of materials and told herself and the husband to go to Meagher's to get 'em and that he'd be over to the house Monday. Which he was.

He made a bench of the kitchen table and set to work. Three by one-and-a-quarter-inch scantlings he ordered. He thought they'd be strong enough, and he bridle-jointed the corners, 'twas the quickest, and in no time at all he had the gate made, six foot, six inches long by four foot high with a diagonal stiffening piece. He came then, and if you saw the clever way he put two grooves, one at the top and one at the bottom of the bed, so that the division could slide up and down, for all the world like the sluice gate on a canal.

But that was not the beauty of it. He put two pulleys above in the rafters, and he ran a piece of sash cord from the top and bottom of the gate through the pulleys and on to two weights, and kept adding bits of lead to the weights until he achieved a perfect balance. There was one rope and Bridgie could pull the gate up with it, and then before she went to sleep at night there was another rope that she could take, and turning to Con she could say, 'Goodbye old faithful,' and pulling the rope bring the gate down between 'em.

He called the two of 'em down to see it working.

Bridgie was diverted, and Con could not get over the mechanics of it. Nothing would persuade him but that it was running on ballbearings, for all he had to do was put his finger under the gate and it would go up and down like a zip fastener.

The carpenter was well paid for his trouble and when he was going home Con conveyed him down a bit talking about this and that, and then he said, 'I suppose you are wondering why Bridgie wanted that fake-ah put in the bed?'

'I am a small bit curious,' says the carpenter.

'Well,' he said, 'it is this way and it is hard to believe it, but I was breaking in a young filly. I put the car on her; I was going to the Christmas market with a butt of geese, a noisy cargo! Going up the road, whatever way it happened, a sheep to put his head around a gate pier, the horse bolted, went clean in over the ditch, and we fell ten feet into a field, myself and the geese and all. By the blessings of God we never capsized. The little mare did three rounds of the field, you'd swear it was Epsom and out the gap, but I got a great fright.

'When I came home that night I was telling the woman there. We went to bed anyway . . . Bridgie was between me and the wall . . . we were talking and then she fell asleep. I went to sleep too. What did I want awake for when there was no one to talk to? Out in the night I began to dream and this thing being in my mind about the fright I got that morning I dreamt that I was going with the young mare to bring a load of litter from the *muing*. Now, at the turn of the bridge there's a fierce declivity down into the *leaca* field. There were two dogs fighting and they rolled on to the road. The horse took fright and shot over the ditch and we fell down the declivity and were capsized. She was on the flat of her back, and you know she could kill herself kicking and she caught in the tackling. And the only thing to do in a case like that is to throw your whole weight down on her head.

'This I did and I caught her that way by the two ears. "Wee, hoa, hack, stand up, aisy, aisy girl, stand up there!" With that I woke up. It was Bridgie's screeching woke me.'

'What are you at?' she said, 'or will you take go of my ears. I'm smothered by you. I'll have to put a division in the bed if you don't give up your caffling!' And when it was the same thing the following night, Bridgie, as the man said, invoked the

1920 act and established partition.

Not long after, Pádraig Ó Tuama of Coolea that was telling me, Con was capsized coming with a load of litter from the *muing*. He threw himself down on the horse's head until help came. They disentangled the mare from under the car. She was all right but Con wasn't. He gave his leg the hell of a bad twist, and Dr Carey said he blunted the nerve in the cup of the hip. He had no control over the movements of the leg. It made Dr Carey nervous to look at it and he said Con'd have to go up to the Mercy Hospital in Cork.

Con missed the train out of Loo Bridge station. He had to wait till the following day. Delays are dangerous then. Anyway he was kept above, and he hated the hospital, his first time away from Bridgie. No privacy there. People in and out, confined to bed when he needn't, food or nothing agreeing with him. 'Tis then, as he wrote in a long letter home to Bridgie, 'tis then you miss your own *bothán* where you can go where you like and do what you like and he wound up the letter with, 'I miss you, Bridgie, and I miss the brown bread and the pot under the bed!'

Bridgie wrote back to him. 'You won't miss me long more for I'm going up to see you Friday and you won't miss the brown bread for I'm bringing two cakes of it with me, and as for the pot under the bed, well, Con, you always missed that.'

When Con was discharged from the hospital he missed the train home. He was in a pub late that night and the place was raided. They all cleared out the back way and into a graveyard, where Con fell into an open grave. He was wedged at the bottom, I suppose he had too much drink in to get up. It was the coldest night that ever came and it wasn't long until he began calling, 'Help, help! Lift me up, I'm perished. I'm dying with the cold!'

A drunk crept to the edge of the grave. The moon was

shining and when he saw Con on the flat of his back he said, 'No bloody wonder you'd be cold and you having all the clay kicked off yourself!'

The seagulls screaming in the morning woke Con. He stood up in the grave and people say that it was his first time ever seeing the dawn. The slanting sun shining through the headstones was a strange sight. When his eyes became accustomed to the light he saw many more open graves around him and lifting his eyes to heaven he said, 'Oh Lord, don't tell me it is the resurrection and I've missed that too.'

The Holy Well

I remember one time lining up for a drink at the holy well. The lame and the blind and the halt were there. I noticed that the man out before me had a sore face, his lips broken out and his mouth all to one side. I didn't know how I was going to drink out of the ponny after him. But faith, small and all as I was, when it came to my turn, taking the tin mug in my left hand, and dipping it down, I took a swig out of it. I looked up and there was the man with the sore face watching me, and he said, 'Ah ha, I see you are a *ciotóg* like myself!'

You could be cured of anything that time at the holy well. Different wells for different cures. Wether's Well for warts, Batt's Well for sore eyes, Brideswell for the colic and Ben's Well for the back. The old people swore by Ben's Well, anything to do with the bladder or the kidneys. They claimed if you drank a couple of saucepans of that for nine mornings running without a bite going inside your lips, it would dry you up no matter how quick your frequency!

But the holy well never dries up. The hottest day in the summer time, that's the day the holy well is bubbling over. A landlord one time objected to the people going through his fields the day of the pattern – look at that for venom! He filled in the holy well. But he was the sorry man. The spring cannot be repressed! That night the well came up through the hearth inside in his own house and put out the fire on him! The saints had power that time. There was Saint Laitíoran and she had two sisters, Saints Lasaire and Iníon Bhuí. You'd hardly ever hear of three saints in the one family now! Saint Lasaire was connected with the holy well in Cullen and her day is in July. It was said of Laitíoran that when the fire'd go out in the convent she'd cross the road to the forge and bring back the live coals in her apron, and such was her sanctity the coals wouldn't burn it.

One morning on lifting her apron a bit of her skirt came up with it, and the smith, so much wouldn't pass him, remarked on her dainty ankles, and for a split second she took pleasure in the remark. This was noticed above and the coals burned a hole down through her apron! She was so incensed at having incurred the wrath of heaven that she told the smith, 'A time will come when the sound of the anvil will not be heard in the village of Cullen!' And they tell me there's no forge there down to this day.

There's always a trout in the holy well. And a very mysterious fish. In penal times the people used get married in the houses and at night too, and the priest would remain on until after the supper. Now in one place the woman in charge of the cooking came and said that the pot she had hanging over the fire, and that should have come to the boil long ago, was as cold as when she put it down. The priest wanted to know where she got the water and she said: 'Mickeen brought it from the holy well.' And of course, that was a very wrong thing to do. To go to the holy well, to go to any well after dark, the old people held it wasn't right! The priest came up and lifted the lid of the pot and there was the trout swimming around inside. He told 'em to spill him out into a vessel and bring him back to the holy well. This they did and they had no trouble with their water after.

And before it goes out of my head I want to tell about this blackguard that took the trout out of the holy well and put him down on the griddle. Like Fionn Mac Cumhaill tasting the salmon of knowledge, he thought that sampling the little trout would improve all his faculties of body and mind. But there was a hop knocked out of him, before he had time to turn the trout it hopped off the griddle and went plop-ity, plop, plop, plop, plop-ity down the floor out the back door and into the well. And that trout bears the burnt marks of the griddle on one side down to this day, and when you are doing the rounds at that penitential place, and when you come to drink at the holy well, if it is your good fortune to see the burnt side of the trout you could be cured of anything from wind-gall to carbuncles!

The holy well is nearly always in a lonesome place. There is a ruin there, or a graveyard and in places it was part of the penitential round to say a prayer at the family grave. At the nearside of Carraig an Adhmaid, where some of my neighbours are buried, the rock is very near the skin of the ground, and if you are burying a man there it would tighten you to put him down four feet and indeed some of 'em are only gone down three. And we'll say now, if there was a lot of traffic to one grave in a short space of time, the people'd find it hard to put back the boards of the old coffins and the bones, for they wouldn't all fit. Over in Carraig an Adhmaid I remember there used to be a heap of skulls in the corner. And bloody frightening they were too for a small child to be looking at 'em, and they thrown this way and that and they grinning up at you!

At that time there was a tailor in the village and he had an apprentice, the devil's own airy card, and the two of 'em be sitting back to back up on the table every night sewing away, and the kitchen full of neighbours, for tailors have the name of being jolly. One night the conversation turned to things of the spirit and they were talking about the *bean sí* and the *bád sí* and the *ceol sí* and the *púcaí*. There was a great dread of the supernatural at the time but the tailor's apprentice was afraid of nothing. He said he was out all hours and never saw anything uglier than himself – and you'd think it'd be hard for him.

'All right, so,' says the tailor, 'would you go up to the graveyard this hour of the night?'

'I would,' says the apprentice.

'But,' says the tailor, 'would you bring me down a skull out of it?'

'I would,' says the apprentice, 'but I won't do it for nothing. I'll have to be paid for it. What will you give me?'

The tailor wanted to appear spunky in front of his neighbours so he said, 'All right. You have three of your five years apprenticeship done. I'll give the two years off. If you do what you say I'll give you your indentures in the morning and you can go away a journeyman!'

'A bargain,' says the apprentice, and he hopped off the table, stuck the two legs into the shoes and off out the door with him.

When he was gone the tailor got sorry. He said to himself that the apprentice was blackguard enough to do it. And if that same apprentice left him he'd be very short-handed. So he hopped off the table, stuck his legs into his shoes and made out the door after him.

The tailor, being a local man, knew all the near ways to the graveyard and he was there before the apprentice and ducked down behind a tombstone. And the sort of a night it was, you had clouds racing across the face of the moon, so that you had light moving across the graveyard, then darkness, and then light again showing the faces of the statues and the drunken crosses. The tailor thought they were moving and you wouldn't blame him for going bocketty at the knees, so that it was a great relief to him when the apprentice hopped in over the wall.

The clouds cleared from the face of the moon as the apprentice walked over to where the heap of skulls was. He picked up a skull, and if he did, the tailor, altering his voice, and he could do it, he'd get a medal for it, said, 'Leave down my head!'

The apprentice dropped the skull the same as if it was a hot coal. He looked around but when he couldn't see the owner of the voice he bent down and picked up another one.

And the tailor altering his voice again, said, 'Leave down my head!'

The apprentice was just about to drop the skull when he changed his mind, and looking in the direction of the voice, he said, 'Ah, back luck to it, you couldn't have two heads.'

Off with him out and over the wall and as he walked along between the trees he heard the twigs breaking on the ground behind him. Of course he didn't know it was the tailor was after him. He ran like hell back to the house and throwing the skull up on the table he went in to hide behind the press shouting, 'Bolt the door quick, the fellow that owns the head is after me.'

Doing the Rounds

From eight o'clock in the morning on the first of May at the City, the roads 'd be black with people going to the holy well. They'd be coming down the Slugadal and down the side of the mountain like a human waterfall, some men on horseback, their women up behind 'em riding cúlog. At that hour the beggars would have already taken up their positions. You'd see them sitting along the brow of the road, the blind with placards around their necks, the deformed displaying a withered hand, an undeveloped leg, an old shin wound or a running sore. They'd frighten the wits out of you as they shouted out to draw attention to their affliction, and God would have to be very deaf if he didn't hear 'em calling a blessing from Heaven on those who put a penny in a hat.

Tents 'd be set up around the City where women'd be selling cakes and candy, liquorice and lemonade, and there would be another tent in a secret place where you could get some of the home brew laced with goats' milk – that's the lad that'd put a gimp on you!

But no one'd touch the drink until the body was mortified, and it was mortification in those days. Usen't they do the rounds barefoot, and in some penitential places they'd walk on their knees and the men would have to fold up their trousers . . . like the man that was late for his wedding, the alarmer didn't go off, and when he woke and saw the cut of the clock, he got into the new suit, and ran across the nearway to the Chapel. Crossing a ploughed field the bottom of his trousers were getting all dirty so he folded the legs up above his knees. When he came out in front of the chapel they were all gone in and he got so excited he forgot to readjust the trousers, he ran up the chapel to the altar where herself was waiting, and the priest said, 'Leave down your trousers!'

He looked at his bride to be, and he looked at the people. He got as red as a turkey cock. The blackguards were ribbing him all the week, saying that there was a new rite now in matrimony and God only knows what they'd be asking him to do. The people were beginning to smile in the house of God, and the priest getting very impatient said to him again, 'Leave down your trousers!'

'If it is all the same to you father,' says he, 'I'd rather do it the old way!'

To walk on their knees the men had to fold up their trousers and the women had to take off their good skirts and put them on the wall of the City. Clever women would put their shoes down on the skirt, so that it wouldn't be blown away, for it can be very windy up there. Then the women blessing themselves would flounce out their flannel petticoats, down they'd go on their knees and they were off! At that time they used to talk about this man doing the rounds. He had two fat knees on him like a bullock you'd be stall feeding, and whatever he had done out of the way he had his head down and his eyes shut praying out loud as he walked with his muddy knees on a skirt that had blown down off the wall. A man nearby whispered to him, 'Lift up that skirt!'

'I will not,' he said, 'it is for doing that I'm doing this!'

Three rounds you gave outside the wall at the City, moving with the sun, praying as you went and talking to no one. Then you came through a breach in the wall and you did three more rounds inside, these rounds getting more complicated as you went along, but not as complicated as the rounds are over at Carraig an Adhmaid. You'd want to be a mathematician to do the rounds in Carraig an Adhmaid!

First there was the Confiteor, then the Apostles Creed, the Prayer to the Patron Saint, seven Our Fathers and seven Hail Marys, the prayers of the round, a decade of the Glorious, Joyful or Sorrowful Mystery as you began with four rounds outside the gate. Two in the big circle and two in the small circle, where Abbey's Hive was, since stolen out of it and brought back to Dingle, until you'd stoop under the flags to Abbey's kitchen. Here with the prayer pebble you'd make the sign of the Cross seven times in the stone and from doing this down the years the cross is worn deep into the pillar stone. That done you went inside the gate and you had seventeen stations in all to do before you finished the round by drinking at the holy well.

Then if you had a mind to go and have a drink at another well down the street, or if you didn't have the inclination to do another round – and the more rounds the more grace – at that time you could buy a round. There were women there for that purpose. Usen't they come from Millstreet to the City and from Macroom to Carraig an Adhmaid ... Nelly Grey, Hannie Dónailín Lynch and Molly Currans. Sure Molly'd do a round for you for a shilling – three rounds for half-a-crown. Molly claimed if you gave her enough money she'd get all belonging to you out of Purgatory, I don't know how it was that she didn't cause another Reformation!

Molly was a sort of *bean Chonnachtach*, a wise woman of the roads. She lived in a small cabin. She had nothing in the world only a goat for the colouring for the tea, and a few fowl for the fresh egg in the morning. You wouldn't give much at all for her if you saw her on the road, but the day of the pattern she was done up to the nines. She had a tartan jacket, navy skirt, button boots and a gingham apron with a big pocket for the book and the pencil to take down the rounds and another pocket for the money. Around her shoulders she had a damn fine fol-a-me-ding of a little shawl. And her hair, and she had a fine *mothal* of it, piled up on top of her head and held in position by a semi-circular comb like the arch of a bridge. And standing there on a mound over the holy well she made as big an impression on the people as if she were a bishop!

And a man told me, and a man I could believe, that the evening of the pattern she'd lump all the rounds in the book into one, and with the money she'd go down to the public house and get plastered. The following day according to him you wouldn't give tuppence for her. I saw her myself, and I a small lad, her hair flying in the wind, the brown stains of the porter on her mouth and she dancing barefoot around a bonfire that was lit below at the butt of the village the first time that De Valera went into power in 1932.

The sods of turf steeped in paraffin oil blazing on tops of three-prong pikes drove Molly out of her nut with excitement. She took off her black shawl and sent it flying through the air until it landed on top of the bonfire. There was a momentary eclipse while the flames worked their way up through the shawl. A shower of sparks went up to the elements bringing with it a mighty cheer. Wasn't that great grá for Dev! But Molly was the sorry woman the following morning and cold to boot, and no shawl came down from the Government.

One trouble never comes alone – didn't Molly's goat get killed on the railway and she cried as much after the goat as she did after the shawl, but relief wasn't far off. A farmer's wife that had been ailing for some time died in the district. The custom was at that time, that you'd give the clothes of the person who died to a poor man or woman to wear for three Sundays going to Mass and pray for the dear departed. Some widows'd find it hard enough to get even the poorest of men to wear the dead husband's clothes. Moreover, if you knew the husband! The Lord save us, maybe he died of galloping consumption. Then to get around the *piseóg* some poor widows'd make a bundle of the husband's clothes and hiding the bundles under their shawls they'd bring them for three Sundays to Mass, and say a prayer for the dead man's soul. Often those bundles would be forgotten on the church seat or left up on the baptismal font, where they'd be found by Father O'. You'd have pity for the priests that time and all they had to put up with. Father O' would be so incensed at the prevalence of pagan practices in his parish that he'd throw the clothes off the cliff down into the river.

After the funeral of the farmer's wife, Molly went to the house and she got the shawl, a lovely beige, Paisley shawl with a dark brown diamondy pattern around the bottom of it and an abundance of tassels. The first Sunday she wore it to Mass, Molly went up to the front seat. For all the world it was the opening of a mission, and the holy father who was giving the sermon had a beard, a damn fine chin wag. Oh, a lovely *meigeall* that used to go up and down as he was talking. Pausing for breath in the middle of the sermon he looked down and there was Molly in floods of tears below, and I suppose he was gratified in a way that his sermon was having an effect even on one person in the congregation – it was about sudden death and sin and the hot reception that's waiting for us all. The missioner was waiting outside at the chapel gate when the people were coming out. Of course he saw Molly, you couldn't miss her, her eyes were still red. He went over to her and said, 'Well, my good woman, what was it in my sermon you found so moving?'

And she said: 'All of it, father.'

'But,' says he, 'what was it that made you cry?'

'Oh, father,' says she, 'every time I looked up at you and saw your beard wagging it reminded me of my little goat that died last week!'

Seven Our Fathers and seven Hail Marys and we are inside the wall where we come to the mound, about the ninth station. You make the sign of the Cross here too, and on either side from the circular motion of the prayer pebble there are two hollows, like the inside of a basin, worn deep into the rock. There's a perfect circle cut into a flag over at the City. Whatever that signifies? You can be sure it wasn't ratified by the Council of Trent. On that mound you'd leave a token. A safety pin, a hairpin, a button off your clothes. It would have to be from your person, a nail you'd have in your pocket, a match, a piece of rosary beads, a holy medal or a wing-nut off your bicycle. You'd see every class of a thing there. I saw a sparking plug, a child's nipple, a man's tie, a woman's garter, a hurley stick and a crutch, all together in the one place!

The men and women'd tear strips out of the lining of their clothes, or pull a thread out of a ravelling *gansey,* and the girls'd take ribbons out of their hair and tie 'em to the branches of the tree at the holy well. When the pattern 'd be over that tree'd be festooned with *giobals,* pennies and ha'pennies driven into the bark, and a load of crutches there – if you broke 'em up they'd keep you in firing for a week. For there were cures!

Nell Casey

A man and a woman came by train and it was Hegarty brought them up in the jennet and car from the station to the City. And the woman was not good, the man was a pity by her, for she had no control of direction. Instead of moving with the people paying the rounds, she was more backing into 'em. Going down by Duggan's car-house coming up to the third round, she straightened a bit and went through the breach in the wall. She finished the rounds inside and drank at the holy well. Then all of a sudden like a greyhound that'd see a hare, a scatter came in her limbs, and she raced around inside the City as loose and as limber as any young girl there, throwing her hands to heaven and thanking God for being cured. She went over to the tent and bought an apron-full of cakes and candy and handed 'em around to the people, and she brought another apron-full down in the jennet and car to Hegarty's children. They were thanking God too. They thought it was another miracle. Christmas on the first of May.

But some people could be going to the holy well and rubbed with the relic every day in the week and they couldn't be cured. There was this man and his name was Casey and he had three daughters. Fine girls they were too. He needn't be one sign ashamed to be seen walking after 'em up the chapel any Sunday to Mass. And indeed he used to be a bit late so tht he would be seen walking after 'em. At that time all daughters was a bit of an encumbrance to a man. Where would he get fortunes and where would he get men for 'em.

Casey's house took fire of a Christmas night. The cat to

knock over the candle, they had straw inside after making the crib, and the place went up in flames. Casey and the wife and the three daughters were only barely outside the front door when the thatched roof crashed in sending a shower of sparks up to the elements. They were lucky. They came out of it without a scratch, except that the eldest daughter, Nell, by the dint of fright lost her power of speech. She was in a *balbhán* by him.

He brought her to this holy well and to that holy well; he brought her to the City the first of May and to Carraig an Adhmaid at Whitsun. It was no good. Then he brought her to the doctor. The doctor couldn't knock a *gíocs* out of her, so he brought her to the quack doctor near Scartaglin that had the name of licking a green lizard and was supposed to have the cure in his tongue. But the quack doctor explained to Casey that he couldn't do anything for her, for when Nell wasn't burned any place there was no place for him to lick.

In the heel of the hunt he brought her to a specialist in Cork and after paying the man a big fee, the price of a calf, do you know what the specialist told Casey – that Nell would never talk again unless she got a similar fright. Casey said he loved his daughter very much but it did not extend as far as burning another house over her!

The other two girls got married, he had no trouble getting rid of 'em, but there was no demand for Nell on account of she couldn't talk. And I thought that was funny! There was a huckster's shop at the side of the road, and a very knowledgeable woman at the head of it; she had the name of bringing many a happy couple together. Casey used to get the small things there. He'd get the big groceries in town. He was in the shop one day and he said to the little woman if she could at all to be on the look out for a suitable partner for Nell. She said she would. Who should call into the shop the following day but

Jeremiah O'Sullivan that lived a few miles up, and when she was papering up the few commands for him the little woman said, 'How long is your wife dead now, Jeremiah?'

'Three years, Hanna,' he said.

'And I suppose,' says she, 'you'll be taking in a young girl this spring. You have a fine farm of land and you are a young man yet, young enough anyway.'

'I woe not, Hanna,' he said.

'And why so?'

'I loved my last wife very much,' he said, 'but from the day I put the ring on her finger until the day she went out the door in the box from me, she talked twenty out of the twenty-four hours. I wouldn't be able to go through that any more. I had a reeling, a *méagram*, in my head from her.'

'Well, now,' says the woman, 'I have a proposition myself and you mightn't find any fault with it. Bend down your head.'

And she whispered to him for there were some people in the shop, and she told him about Nell Casey, and if you were there and watching his countenance you could see that he was taking the bait. When she finished he said, 'I'll be in again at the end of the week.'

He was in the following morning! An account of a match was sent to Casey's, and there was no trouble whatever in making it. Jeremiah bought a very expensive wedding ring for her. Indeed he was so delighted that Nell couldn't talk, if he could have afforded it at all he'd nearly have bought the lakes of Killarney and the hills of Connemara for her.

We'll skip now till the night of the wedding. No shortage of anything. Plenty of food and drink, and out in the night when they had enough of the Highland Fling and the Kerry Victoria, enough singing and reciting, a lot of the lads there had a good cargo on board, and one of them suggested why not play the game called 'Kick the Turnip', which was common in that quarter. And how the game was played was, you'd get a sizeable turnip and cut a channel around the equator. You'd tie a rope into that and at the other end of the rope you'd put a similar weight, maybe another turnip. You'd throw it over the collar-brace and then you could adjust the turnip up or down, a foot from the ground or whatever you wanted. And the man that'd win the game'd be the man that'd tip the turnip with the top of his toecap and it the highest from the ground.

They put it a few feet from the floor first, so as to give old lads a chance. There were some men there could kick the turnip and it on one level with their chins, and more couldn't touch it and it only up to their navels. Then someone said: 'What about Jeremiah O'Sullivan the man of the moment. Would he have a go!'

'Faith,' Jeremiah said, 'I will have a go. Why not!'

He was out to show off his agility in front of his young wife, and the people. He went down to the butt of the kitchen and buttoning his coat, he gave instructions to put the turnip five foot four from the floor, and running up he met the turnip with the father and mother of an almighty kick, and sent it spinning around the collar brace, but with the dint of exertion, the other leg was taken from under him and he came down with a slap on the floor, his poll hopped off the flag, making a loud report, and he went out like a light, his face as pale as the candle.

They began splashing water on him to revive him. His wife Nell was over at the fire preparing some grudles, and turning around, when she saw her husband that she only married that day out for the count, her mouth opened wide and a gush of speech came out. She ran over saying, 'Jeremiah, Jeremiah, Oh my darling Jeremiah, open your mouth, Jeremiah, and tell me you are not dead!'

Jeremiah opened one eye a small bit and said to the crowd, 'If that's my second wife talking, don't throw any more water on me, I'd rather be dead!'

He didn't die at all, and he got on fairly well with Nell. He was as happy with her as he was with the other one, for a while anyway. One in family is all they had. Yerra, the man was old. Eighteen or nineteen years older than the girl. For God's sake! Where would you be going without a bell on your bike! Nell was young and lively, she used to be going around to all the house dances, where she'd be out in the floor in every set. As time went by Jeremiah found he did not have the wherewithal to keep up the tally. Younger men'd ask her out dancing – you couldn't blame Nell for going out with 'em, and Jeremiah got jealous and jealousy is the worst thing that ever took a seat in the human heart.

Blackguards took advantage of this, and they were saying things in his hearing and Jeremiah was reading his own meaning into everything he heard. They'd say, 'Did you hear about the man that used be away from home. It would be three weeks before he'd get back to wind the clock. Well, himself and the wife went to confession. She was inside and he was outside waiting to go in, and in the middle of her story she opened the door of the box and said to the husband:

"Jim, when you were away from home last month, can you remember how many days did I say the carpenter was in making the press?"'

The thing about that story was that Jeremiah used to truck a bit in cattle, he'd often be away from home for three nights at a time, which gave the imagination plenty of scope to expand. One morning the children were gone to school, two he had, one by the first wife and one by the second, and Nell was gone binding to the Callaghan's. There alone in the kitchen jealousy got such a hold of him that he took a crock off the dresser, filled it with fresh cream and going down in the room positioned it centre ways under the bed. Then he took the pendulum off the clock, it was stopped anyway, and attached it underneath to the spring of the bed, adjusting it in such a way that the pendulum would not touch the cream with only Nell in the bed! And how he judged Nell's weights was with a half-sack of Reliable flour. Now that the trap was set he went off driving cattle down to Charleville.

When he came back in a few days' time he went straight down in the room and took the crook from under the bed. He looked into it. There was butter in it!

The way a man can be fooled. He was grinding his teeth with the dint of bad stuff. What he wouldn't say and what he wouldn't do to Nell. He ran out in the yard in a fit of temper and remained outside until the children came in from school; there was no trace of Nell. He had occasion to come in for the donkey's winkers, below in the room they used to keep the tackling, and when he went down there was his daughter by the first wife, a big mopsey of a one that should have sense, and his little girl by Nell and they dancing up and down on the bed.

> Taney tip and taney tow,
> Turn the ship and away we go?

The Effigy

Some people'd keep an all night vigil at the holy well. They'd pay the first round at nightfall and then sit by the well praying through the dark, or crowd inside the ruin, where they'd light a fire, until it was time to pay the second round at dawn. These'd mostly be the afflicted. You'd see a mother there with a sick child hoping for a cure and she calling out to the patron saint:

> *Is chugatsa a thánag ag gearán mo scéil leat,*
> *Is d'iarraidh mo leighis ar son Dé ort!'*

And in Kilfenora they'd keep a vigil for nine nights and the women'd bring their beds, and when the beds were set up around the holy well, with the hawkers' tents below and the fun of the fair at the side, you wouldn't see the like of it in Tibet. At nightfall the quilts'd be lifted up and tied to the four brass knobs to make a roof over the bed to keep out the dew, and around dawn you'd see these draperies being pulled aside and the women putting their heads out to see was there enough light to commence the first round.

And they tell of a woman that woke a bit late the ninth morning. She was so upset at having missed the round at dawn that in her excitement to get to her crutches, that were a bit away from her, she walked! She wasn't the only one. There was this man paralysed in the bones dragging himself from station to station and on the ninth morning he shouted out that someone touched him on the knee.

'Keep out from me,' he said, ''tis the sorest part of my

body!'

Jacko McGann, who was a witness to it, told me that no one went near him. Jacko said he heard something no louder than the flutter of a bird's wing and saw what he could only describe as a human outline bend down and touch the suffering man on the knee. And Jacko went over to him and said, 'Get up out of it!'

And he said the man got up and he walked!

At the twelfth station in Carraig an Adhmaid, which is the priest's tomb, you come to the effigy on the keystone so high up you'd pass it ten times a day without noticing it. To get to it you'd stand on the sill inside the ruin and reach out through the window and up and the figure is so small you'd cover it with the palm of your hand. Under your fingers you could make out the little monkey face and the neck. It had no clothes on, and the two hands came down to cover its nakedness. You rubbed your handkerchief to it making the sign of the Cross. You'd step down then into the ruin, where you'd see the sign of the fire after the vigil of the night before, and there'd be a travelling man there breaking a stone into small pieces and he'd give you a bit for a penny. You'd tie that scrap of slaty stone in a knot in your handkerchief and you'd keep it for luck.

But the naked figure reminds me of Ned Connor. Ned was a young lad of seventeen or eighteen years of age and he had a fierce row with his father. Ned wanted the price of a new suit of clothes, because he couldn't go outside the door in the old duds, and the father refused to give him the money. Ned lost his temper and said to his father, 'Wouldn't you even give me the price of a new cap, so that I can put my head out the window itself?'

The father wouldn't part with the money and God

knows Ned was working hard enough for him.

'All right so,' the son said, 'you'll never again lay an eye on me.' He ran away into the middle of the night in the general direction of America, and in the morning he came to Cromane pier and jumping into a small boat he hit the fisherman on the back and said, 'Boston, a *bhuachaill*!'

When it was explained to him that Boston was three thousand miles away and that no one had made the journey in a small boat since Saint Brendan discovered America, he said, 'What'll I do so? I promised my father last night that he'd never see me again.'

'Go away into Tralee,' says the fisherman, 'and join the Munster Fusiliers and if you do, ten chances to one but he'll never see you again.'

Ned Connor went into Tralee and joined the Munster Fusiliers. He was put into a new uniform and when he got his first week's pay he went down the town and into a public house, and even though he had no experience of drink, yet he lowered pint for pint with hardened old campaigners back from Khartoum. And when at closing time he came out in the street and hit the fresh air he was legless, stocious! He went down through the town singing and missed the turn to Ballymullen Barracks, and kept on taking the two sides of the road out into the country towards Castleisland. When the pins got tired under him he sat on a mossy bank at the side of the road, and he was so befuddled in his mind that he thought he was sitting on the edge of his bed in the barracks, so he kicked off the shoes; took off his little military hat; took off every single stitch, and folding up his tunic and trousers like he was shown to do by the officer, he put them, as he thought, under the bed! Where did he shove 'em only down a gullet

at the side of the road, and standing there in his pelt he gave
a blast of one of the Munsters' songs:

Tell my brothers when you go home
How nobly I fought and died.
With a bayonet hanging by my breast
And a small sword by my side,
Tell them at home that I'll n'er more roam
As I did in my boyhood days,
Where the grass never fades
In the pleasant cool shades
Of old Ireland far away!

He lay down then on the mossy bank and went to sleep, but there
is one thing I must tell ye, no matter how high the alcoholic
content in the blood, the frost will overcome it! The cold went
into the marrow of his bones, and he woke up and walked away
rubbing his eyes. He didn't even know that he was naked! A call
of nature that drew his attention to it! He had to keep walking
for he was frozen to a frazzle. As he came round a turn he saw
a light a bit in from the road. He went into the yard and threw
a stone at the door. 'Twas as near as he could go to it in his
condition. A young woman appeared so he ducked down behind
the hedge, nothing up but the head, that was all right, and she
said, 'Won't you come in!'

'I can't go in,' he said, 'I am standing here as naked as
when I came into the world.'

'Well,' says she, 'there's a suit of clothes here that'll
never be used again.' And she went into the house and
threw him out the clothes and shut the door – very
considerate. He went up and he got into the trousers first.
And even though that trousers was too big for him, he

could put two more into it with himself, it was like heaven to be inside in it for every limb of his body was in an icicle. He put on the shirt, waistcoat and coat, the socks, shoes and hat, and he went into the house. She put him sitting at the fire and filled him out a full cup of poteen, and went off up in the room with the bottle.

When you come into a house like that out of the dark it takes a bit of time for you to get accustomed to the light. He was taking stock of his surroundings and looking over towards the dresser – the Lord save us, he saw a corpse laid out on the settle. An old man, his hands joined and the rosary beads entwined around his knuckes, and the butt of a blessed candle lighting on the shelf above him.

Ned got an awful fright and he ran up in the room, and God knows he got a bigger fright when he went up. There was the young woman of the house above, sitting on another man's knee and she pouring drink into him, whatever was the meaning of it. He came back down and said, 'I must have some bit of religion in me.'

He knelt down to say his prayers. And like at a wake when you are praying you are looking at the corpse's face, and after a while a tiny spider came down on his rope, had a look at the lie of the land, and then alighted on the cheek bone. Wasn't it narrow the world was on him! The little spider rubbed some of his legs together and after another bit of fidgeting, skirted a turf of hair that was growing there and walked into the furrow below the eye towards the bridge of the dead man's nose. Then Ned's heart came up in his mouth for he saw the eye twitching. He made a dart to go, but if he did the corpse put out his hand and caught him, saying, 'Don't move, or if you do, *corp'on diabhal*, I'll kill you. I had to do this,' he said, 'I am an old man married to a young wife, I had to let on to be dead to catch her out. I've caught her out now. You go down to the *cúl-lochta* and bring me up the three-prong pike!'

Ned went down, brought up the pike and lifting the sheet put it by the 'corpse' in the bed.

'Go up now in the room,' says the old man, 'and turn down my wife and Jack the Cuckoo!'

The soldier went up to the door and said, 'Ye're wanting!'

The two came down and as they crossed the kitchen the 'corpse' hopped out of the bed, and as they went through the front door Jack the Cuckoo got a damn fine dart of the three prongs of the pike in the backside. That knocked the gimp off him! He wasn't able to sit down until Christmas!

'Take that going!' says the old man, and says he to his wife, 'never let me see your face again!' And he slapped out the door and said to the soldier, 'You can stay the night and keep the clothes. If I was dead in earnest she'd have given 'em to some poor man to wear three Sundays to Mass.'

In the morning the soldier didn't know how he was going to face the barracks in Tralee in those old clothes. He made another sally back to see if he could find the place he slept the night before. No. No good, there was no trace of the uniform, and as the morning was going he decided to cut across the nearway to Tralee. There were horny sheep in the field alongside the road, and as Ned walked by, a ram feeding there lifted his head, and when he saw the loose backside to Ned's trousers, a sure sign of a blackguard, the ram shook himself and like a bullet out of a gun he charged after the soldier giving him a dunt that threw him out on his face and eyes.

Ned Connor got up only to find that the ram was

settling himself for another charge. Well there was nothing for it, only catch him by the horns, and he did and knocked the ram back on his rump. Then the thought struck him, looking at the distance between him and the ditch, that he couldn't afford to let the ram go anymore, he was sore enough!

Well, as luck 'd have it who came down the road but an RIC man and Ned asked him to hold the ram while he was going over the ditch for a rope to tie him. The policeman came in and as he caught the ram by the horns, he said, 'Is he cross?'

And Ned said, 'Like a lamb, eroo!'

The soldier went off, by the way to get the rope, and when he got over the ditch he ducked down and ran like hell for Tralee. The policeman was left there so-hoing the ram, and every now and then he'd call over the ditch to see if Ned was coming back with the rope. Finally he got sick of it saying: 'Ah! Here he's poor enough to be his own servant.' He let the ram go and walked away. Merciful hour! The dunt he got! That was another man that didn't sit down until Christmas!

In the barrack square in Tralee the sergeant major was drilling a squad of the Munster Fusiliers and giving 'em dog's abuse.

> 'Left, left! ye're in the army now,
> Lift 'em up! ye're not behind the plough,
> Ye're not going to get rich digging a ditch,
> Ye're in the army now!'

He numbered them off, formed 'em into fours and gave them their marching orders., 'By the left quick march!'

They went off and just then the sergeant major looked and who was coming in the gate but Ned Connor in the big suit.

The sleeves down over his hands and the hat down over his eyes. The sergeant major when he saw the geatch of him got such a hearty fit of laughing he forgot to halt the soldiers! They were half way up to the County Limerick before an officer on horseback got up to 'em.

Ned got thirty days CB for losing the Queen's uniform – Queen Victoria that was there at the time, she'd look sweet in it! And he was only barely out of quad when he was put on board ship for South Africa. The Boer War had broken out. Ned used to write home to the mother, he never forgave the father for not giving him the suit. The mother used to read the letters for the post boy because the post boy was in the same book as Ned going to school, and he'd like to know how he was getting on in Africa. In one letter Ned said, 'Well, Mam, we're up to our eyes in it now, last night we made another shift for Ladysmith!'

'Look at that' says the mother, 'isn't the army great training for 'em, when he was at home he couldn't sew in a button!'

They used to say that time that one of the Munsters in a letter home to his father said: 'The army is a hoor!' Sell the pig and buy me out!' And that the father wrote back saying, 'Sorry for your trouble son. We killed the pig, soldier on!'

Ned didn't see much service in South Africa. He was invalided out of it. He got kicked by a mule in the Transvaal – a bloody sore thing too! He came home on a small pension and I'll never forget years after hearing Ned one night at a pattern at Carraig an Adhmaid. Now, my neighbours, who were there, could spend the whole night talking about animals, and the ways of animals . . . the fox with the sweet tooth and the clever way he goes about robbing a wild honey bee's nest. They were curious about the four-footed inhabitants of South Africa, and asked Ned what they were like. Well, Ned described the animals he saw to us, and I don't think the like of 'em were ever on the face of the earth! He said the biggest quadruped he saw there, it must be the elephant he was talking about, was a huge, bulging affair, like a gutterperka bull, picking up grass with his tail and shoving it up in his arse!

And he told us that himself and Danielo Moran, he was from Áthnablátha, were on scout patrol along the edge of the jungle on the look out for Boers. They came to a hole in an embankment and Danielo, who was of a curious turn of mind, went in, and where was he but in a lion's den. He came out and told Ned that there were lovely cubs inside, and that he'd love to catch two of 'em, and bring back to the bivouac and maybe when the war'd be over he could bring 'em home to Ireland.

'Dammit,' he said, 'when they'd grow up you could put 'em ploughing!'

He told Ned to watch out for the big lion in case he came back while Danielo was in the den. Ned, standing on sentry outside, put a bit in the pipe, and when he went to light it there was a breeze blowing, so he turned sideways and when he turned back the lion was half way in the hole! He had to do something quick, so he caught him by the tail, and as Ned explained to us, if we knew anything about zoology, there's a fierce knob at the end of a lion's tail. This gave him a great grip and he held on for all he was worth, putting his two shoes at either side of the hole. Danielo, the man inside, noticed that something was wrong and he shouted out, 'Ned, what's darkening the hole?'

'By jamonies,' says Ned, 'if the tail breaks you'll soon know what's darkening it!'

To save the man's life inside, Ned, with great presence of

mind, drew his revolver and shot the lion. I'm too much of a gentleman to tell ye where he shot him. Mercy of god, he didn't shoot the other man in the head coming out. Danielo managed to commandeer two cubs and brought 'em to the place where they were bivouaced. Himself and Ned put 'em on the bottle like two neddy bonavs. Well, they were the talk of South Africa with the two cubs walking around after 'em. When Queen Victoria got a wrinkle of it she sent out her special man for the cubs and they were the first lions to come to the London Zoo!

Abbey's Bowl

There were curing stones that time at the holy well, you'd see 'em glistening in the sun after a shower of rain. They'd be about as big as a goose egg, and you could rub one of them into yourself wherever you felt the greatest need for it, or you could rub your rosary beads, or a holy medal to it, and continue the treatment when you came home. In one place in Ireland there was a relic. I heard a man describe it as something in the nature of a knuckle-bone, or an ankle bone. It was a human bone, I suppose a saint's bone, and it was kept at arm's length in a secret place in the wall, and if you were so bad in bed that you couldn't get up, that relic could be brought to the house to you. There was such great faith in these healing objects at the time that a young girl over in America, and not getting a day of her health there, expressed a wish to have the relic brought out to her. It was her own cousin Thade Nóin brought out the relic baked inside in a cake of bread. She applied it for nine mornings running, without a bite going inside her lips, and she was game ball after it! She married a fine handsome man. He wasn't from Ireland now he was from Italy. Then it was her brother John, coming home on a trip, that brought the relic back to Ireland concealed inside a victrolla, what the returning Yanks called the first gramophones that came to Ireland. The ones with the funnel out at the side. They used to have these records that were there at the time:

> Shake hands with your Uncle Dan, me boys,
> And this is your cousin Kate,

She's the girl you used to swing
Down by the Garden gate.
Shake hands with all the neighbours
And kiss the colleens all!
You're as welcome as the flowers in May
If you never came at all!

John's concern was not how he was going to bring the relic
into Ireland, but how would he tell his mother that her
daughter had married an Italian in New York. At that time,
I don't know what they are like now, certain old ladies
would take a poor view of that message. This is the tune
you'd hear from 'em, 'What did you say his name was
again?'

'Lord save us! What's wrong with Irish boys!'

So when the welcoming was over in the kitchen, John
decided to take the bull by the horns and he said, 'Say,
Mam, I suppose you heard that Mary got buckled?'

And the mother said, 'We got a wrinkle of it. What's the
boy like?'

'A fine handsome man!'

'Where's he from?' says Mother.

And the son to knock the sting out of it said, 'He's from
the Pope's place!'

That was all right.

Some of those curing stones you would not bring 'em to
America unless you wanted to rub 'em to a buffalo, for they were
for curing animals. And such a thing was Abbey's Bowl so called
because it was similar in shape and size to the thing they have
for bowl playing. There was also Abbey's cord and if your mother
wore that around herself the night before you were born, your
first journey, as dangerous as any one you'll ever undertake again,

could prove an uneventful passage! You'll find Abbey's Bowl at arms length in a square hole in the wall over at Carraig an Adhmaid and when I was small I was told that it was in suspense, not touching the wall anywhere, and you could take it out and bring it to the house if a cow had timber tongue, dry murrain or black quarter. One man was going for it so often, when he finished rubbing it to the cow he threw it on top of the dresser and forgot all about it. The wife whitewashing for the stations found the holy object and made him put it back in its proper place. Then the next time he went for it he couldn't bring it out over the stream. There was like an invisible wall in front of him. Cold sweat came out through him as he tried to push his way across the bridge. There was a donkey grazing there and he went spread legs on him, but when the animal came up his head went skeeting along the 'glass' wall. Then he put the bowl up on the parapet of the bridge. It was the time the penny-farthing bicycle was invented, and he went down to the village, borrowed a bike, put the bowl in his pocket, hopped on the bike and came flying out over the bridge with it. The saints have no power over machinery! That curing stone is cemented into the wall now, and I think that's because two of the boys on the run the time of the trouble took it out and went bowl playing with it. Didn't the same two take the water out of the holy well and bring it to a house and put it down boiling in the kettle and made tea with it!

A Ruminating Animal

Talking about curing animals, there was a time in Ireland when those living in the congested districts knew as much about a horse as a dog knows about a holiday. At that time the country was teeming with people. They got married young and to give 'em a living the farms had to be divided and sub-divided until before the famine a whole family'd be existing on less than an acre of ground. They'd turn the sod with the spade, stick the *skiollawns* and bring out the dung in a *cliabh* on their back from the yard. What did they want a horse for! He'd be only coming in their way. Another mouth to feed! If they went away down to the main road they might see a landlord passing with a horse and some of those had more than one.

At that time there were these two brothers and they fell in for an *ábhar* of money and nothing in the wide world'd do 'em but to get a horse, *éirí in airde gan cur leis*! They made off Cahirmee fair and they bought a tried animal and they brought him home. When they were coming near their own place the people were taking the legs of one another running to the door when they saw the horse passing. They were shouting after the brothers and saying, 'What do he ate and do he bellow?'

They brought the horse into their own yard, they had no stable. Yerra, there was next to nothing in the line of out offices going with houses at that time, for the more out offices you had the more rent you'd pay to the landlord. So they brought the horse into the kitchen and down in the room, indeed they thought so highly of him, if they could have managed it at all, they'd nearly have put him into the bed! The kitchen was full of people, only very near neighbours and relations left in to view the horse at close quarters. And when they got an eyeful of him they were all put out for it was near his feeding time. The brothers had their instructions from the man they bought the horse from in Cahirmee, and the first item on the horse's memo was a tub of water tepid, followed up with a few *dorns* of oats in the bottom of a pan.

They knew about putting the bag on his head but they didn't want to do this the first night in case the mother'd think they were going playing blind man's buff with him. And the final course was a gabhal of Italian ryegrass. Then the two brothers put their shoulders to the jambs of the room door watching every single bite that went into the horse's mouth. You'd think they were eating it themselves, the way their jaws'd move in time with the horse's chewing, until finally the father sitting by the fire said, 'Can't ye close down the door and give the animal some privacy!' They came and sat by the fire and in a while's time one of the brothers went down to see how the horse was getting on and the father shouted down after him, 'Did he finish what was in front of him?'

The son said, 'He did.'

'What's he doing now?'

And the son said, 'Nothing.'

'Did he lie down?'

'No!'

Oh this was bad. The old man came running down and the horse was standing firm on three legs, the right hind leg half drawn up to him with the toe of the hoof on the ground, for all the world like a step dancer waiting for a hole in the music! The horse was nodding and his eyes were half shut. Of course what those poor people didn't know was, a horse can sleep standing up like a civil servant!

The old man felt the tops of his ears. If they are cold it's a good sign, and he ran his hand over the horse's nose to see would he feel the little *drúcteens* of sweat – a wet nose and dry somewhere else is a healthy sign for an animal. *Mo léir cráite*, the horse had a moustache on him like a drum-major! They get that from munching furze, which can be taken as a hint if there's anyone having difficulty in growing a moustache. Nothing would convince those people but that the horse was sick. They were looking at his loose mouth and when he'd go 'brrrrah' they thought he was trying to throw up!

'Maybe he was overlooked,! the mother said, 'and it wouldn't put a blister on anyone's tongue to say "God bless the animal!"'

They sat around the fire and at six o'clock in the morning when the horse wasn't lying down or acting in a normal fashion according to their lights, one of the sons was sent for the curing stone to the holy well. On his way home he met that little ex-soldier that was stopping at Dinny's at the time – he used to be in charge of horses at Lord Headley's – and he said to the son, 'Why are you out so early?'

'We've sickness in the house,' he said.

'Is it your father?'

'No,' the son said, 'it is the horse.'

The ex-soldier came up to the house and went down in the room and opened the horse's mouth and looked into it, lifted the lid to see was the eye bloodshot, he looked in his frog and examined every detail; he lifted up his tail fairly high to see how it would fall. Then he slapped him on the rump saying:

"Wee hoa, hack, stand up, stand up there!'

This woke the animal and he shook his head showing the white of his eye, which is a healthy sign of a horse or a woman. The ex-soldier began to laugh.

'There's nothing wrong with him,' he said, 'he's as healthy as myself.'

'Are you blind?' says the father, 'or what sort of an expert are you? Can't you see he is not chewing the cud!'

The Mermaid

As ye all know I'm a stonemason by trade and it is behind in Ballinskelligs I was one time building a pier. Tough enough work too, and you'd want to be well paid for it. And in a job like that, down on the brink of the tide, there are times when the shoes'd have to come off. Well, one day I noticed that the man tending me had webbed toes and of course I remarked on it. But it wasn't until that night above in Main's pub that I came by the whole story.

'You remarked on a certain thing down at the pier today, Ned,' says the man sitting beside me in the snug.

'That I did,' says I, 'if you are alluding to the lad of the webbed   toes.'

'The very man,' says he, 'a boy of the Shea's. Did you ever hear, Ned, that the Shea's are descended from the mermaid?'

'Never!' says I. 'Have you the running of it?'

'I have,' says he, 'and it isn't belittling anyone of the name I am for I'm a Shea man myself. The old stock and rooted in this quarter since before history began.'

'You're losing track of the mermaids,' says I.

'I'm not,' he said, and I knew by the way he settled himself that we were in for a night of it.

'The first Shea man,' says he, 'that came to this quarter had no wife, and it is said that he was taking the air down by the sea this day when the mermaids came up out of the ocean, and after a time they went back into the ocean, all except one. And what did this one do but come out of the black thing they have covering theirself from the elbows down. It is like a one-legged trousers with a fish tail at the end of it. And there she stood as lovely a young girl as you could wish to see!

She threw the fish tail up on the black rock and went for a canter down along the strand. Back she came again, got into the fish tail and hit off out into the ocean. The Shea man didn't sleep a wink that night only thinking of her, and the sun wasn't far up in the heavens the next day when he was down by the sea again. He waited and the mermaids came and she came and the performance was the same as the day before.

Well, the more he saw her the more he felt she was the only woman for him, for to give her only her due she was pure beautiful. He watched her antics for a week and then he hit on a plan, for as the man said: "Faint heart never won fair lady".

So this day he hid near the black rock and when she was gone for her canter down along the strand he whipped the fish tail and made off. She went after him and implored of him to give it back to her, that without the fish tail she could not make her way back through the sea to her own people. He told her of his fine farm of land and a house all to himself.

"And don't you think," says he, "that you'd be a lot better off sitting down in front of a roaring fire in my place than to be getting your death in a damp oul cave!"

He kept before her to the house and when he had her in the kitchen he shut the door on her and kept her inside. They were married in a few days – letters of freedom and all this coming and going that's in the world today was not necessary in those days. They were happy out together and in time the children were rising to 'em, and even though they had no secrets from one another in the style of all true lovers, there was one thing she never found out, and that was where he hid the fish tail. Times she would ask him for it, and those times he would pretend to be deaf, for he knew that if he got it she'd go back to the sea to her own people and they'd keep her from him.

As I said the children were rising to 'em and they were no more than able to crawl when the mother would bring 'em every day down to the black rock where she'd sit looking out to sea. When the eldest lad was crabbed enough she told him to keep an eye on his father, and if he ever saw him with a black thing like a fish tail to come and tell her.

Faith, she put her commission in the right hands, for that little lad was so sharp he'd nearly see a midge winking on top of a tall chimney. That was in the fall of the year and the Shea man had the oats in the haggard waiting to be threshed. And far back as that time was they had threshing machines. Engines were not invented, but the drum was turned by having a horse running around in a circle. If my memory serves me hadn't they the same plan for making butter. Now, when the oats was threshed there were three things you could do with it that time; you could bag it, put it in the loft or put it in a *sheegogue*. And what was that? Well, I'll tell you – it was a straw granary. You'd make a *sugawn*, three to six inches thick. Begin by making a circle, say eight feet in diameter on a stone platform in the haggard. Keep coiling the straw rope on that circle and throwing the grain into the middle as you went along, until you ended up with what looked like an enormous straw barrel, the sides splaying out so that it was much wider at the top. When the sheegogue was a little over the height of a man and filled with grain, you'd put a cone-shaped roof of straw on it. Thatch that roof with rushes, leaving a good eve all round, and your grain was secure for the winter.

The men were in Shea's haggard threshing and the Shea man was in one corner putting the grain in the *sheegogue*. The eldest son was there too, his eyes on *kippens*, and after a time he ran in and told his mother that he saw his father putting a black thing like a fish tail under the grain in the new *sheegogue*. The mother didn't say, "yes", "aye" or "no", but went on preparing the supper for the men that would be coming in from the haggard bye and bye. After the supper the neighbouring girls came to the house and there was a dance, and the Shea woman was as happy as anyone there, out on the floor in every set. She was only known to laugh three times since she came to this life, she laughed the night of her wedding, she laughed when her first child spoke and she was laughing tonight.

Around eleven o'clock the dance broke up and everyone went home satisfied after a most enjoyable night. Came the morning and the Shea man nudged his elbow out from him.

"Hop out woman! The day'll be gone!"

Mo léir, he was alone in the hammock. He got up then and he called her, and he called the children to go out there looking for their mother. He went out himself and the fowl house door was open but the fowl were not in the yard. It was the geese gave the game away for he heard them noising in the haggard. He ran up that way, and there was the bottom *sugawn* pulled out from under the *sheegogue* with the grain spilling out and the geese gobbling it up.

He knew then what had happened. He knew then that she was gone from him, back to the sea and to her own people and that he'd never lay an eye on her again. And he threw himself against the side of the *sheegogue* for the weight of the world was on him.

It was there the children found him. And those children missed their mother, but as was their custom, when she was with 'em, they'd go every day to the black rock, where they'd find every sort of fish left out for 'em. She never saw 'em short and they grew up to be fine handsome men and women, and they had the webbed toes you'll find on their descendents down to this present day. That's the story now as I heard it that night in the snug of Main's public house in Ballinskelligs.

Minding the House

Oh Carrig an Adhmaid! Oh Cathair Crobh Dhearg! If you fell in with the right company in either place the night of the pattern you would hear talk!

There was this woman and her husband was always finding fault with her work around the house. A snout on him looking into pots and pans watching what she was doing.

Finally she lost her patience. 'Look, we'll change places tomorrow,' says she, 'let you remain inside minding the house and I'll go setting *skillawns*.' It was in the springtime. In the morning after milking the cows she took the spade and hit for the field, not before she specified her husband's duties for the day. He was to turn out the braddy cow for a drink around eleven; he was to feed the calves and to feed the fowl; he was to bake a cake; he was to iron his shirt; make the churn, and go to the well. And most important of all he was to keep his eye on the goose hatching in the big box below the dresser. I think it's twenty-eight days for a goose! The goslings were due out any minute and it would be calamity if the goose got off the eggs. And he was to have her dinner on the table for her when she'd come in at one o'clock on the dot.

She went off and left him inside and there was no more awkward man from here to Kildimo, but isn't it the likes of him that'd criticise. The first thing he did was to sit down, and map out a plan of campaign, for as he said that's what was wrong with women – no plan!

'Now,' he said, 'so as to have the fire free later on for to cook the dinner, I'll bake the cake now, and at the same time heat the iron to iron my shirt.'

He put the iron to the fire and spilled the makings of the cake into the *lasaid*, added salt, and bread soda and began tossing it up and down. He was flour to the eyebrows. From rubbing his hands to his face and searching his pockets for his pipe, he finished up as white as if you pulled him through a lime kiln! He made a hole in the middle of the flour and poured in sour milk, mixing the whole thing and kneading it into dough. And of course he made it too wet; there was more dough on his hands than there was in the *lasaid*. Then he got the oven. He didn't bother putting it over the fire to heat it, or he didn't shake a dust of flour on the bottom or around the sides to keep the cake from tying to it. No. He just got the dough off his hands and lobbed it in one big lump into the oven. He never put the sign of the cross or anything on it with the knife; hung the oven over the fire; put on the lid, and put the live coals on top of it. That was one job done.

He took up the iron now and to see if it was hot he put it to his cheek. It isn't hot it was but red. He proceeded to iron the shirt, and for this operation he had a huge audience. Hens along the half door, calves looking in through the window, all with their mouths open complaining, for he had forgotten to feed 'em.

The noise was deafening and he went to prepare a collation for 'em, forgetting of course to put the iron on an upside-down saucer, when he came back there was a fine black triangle burned down through the shirt and half way through the table! He had to throw his hat with that for a bad job.

He decided now to make the churn, and go to the well.

It was a timber churn, what was known as a dash-churn, and the churn was made by hitting a staff up and down inside it. He took the staff out, that was a bit old fashioned for him. Then he spilled a tub of cream into the churn and put on the cover, and so as to be able to do two jobs at the one time – make the churn and go for water – he took the reins off the donkey's winkers and tied the churn on his back. That left his two hands free to pick up two buckets, and he said, with the movement of his body while he was walking to the well, the churn'd be making! What woman'd think of that!

Now, the well was deep and when he bent down to fill the bucket the end of the churn went up, the cover fell off and the cream shot out over his head and ran down inside his shirt like lava down the side of Vesuvius. As he walked back with the buckets he was kicking cream out of the legs of his trousers. But that was nothing to the confusion that was in the house before him.

He left the doors open going out. The calves were above in the room, the hens up on the dresser, the cock inside in the press, the dog making love to the bacon, and the cat with his head down to the two shoulders inside in the jug of milk. The cat couldn't get his head out of the jug. 'A chait, out of that,' the man said. And the cat hopped off the table and made flitters of the jug on the floor, giving himself such a fright that he went out the door spitting! The man had to go then and turn the calves down out of the room and the cock and the hens out of the press, 'Out blast ye, out! hurrish! Suck out of that!'

He turned 'em all out into the yard but before he could do another thing, he was so uncomfortable with the cream down inside his shirt, he had to take all his clothes off and go out and roll in the grass to dry himself. He came in then, sops hanging out of him. The burned shirt was nearest to his hand so he put that on, but before he had time to go in the room to put on his trousers he noticed that in his excitement, when he was turning out the other animals, he turned out the goose as well.

'If the goose got off the eggs it would be a calamity!' the wife had warned him. He went over and put his hand on the eggs and they were cold. He went to the door and called the goose.

'*Badaoi, badaoi, badaoi!*'

There was no trace of badaoi.

"What will I do now,' he said, 'the goslings could be dying in the shells at this moment. What will she say to me when she comes in!' He thought to himself that the heat of his own body might approximate that of the goose, so he went down and sat over the eggs. He couldn't put his weight on 'em, the weight had to be transferred to the two shins. And there he was when Moll Simon, a neighbouring girl, put her head in the door.

Moll was well into years, a girl that never settled down, and when she saw him sitting on the box she said, 'Jacos Jack how short your shirt is! What are you at?'

He explained to her that the goose had gone off the eggs and that he was trying to keep the temperature up until she'd come back.

'Damn it, Moll' he said, 'I have *codladh grífín* in my two shins, and would you ever come up and put down your hand and see is there anything happening!'

Moll came up, an innocent creature, and put her hand down.

'No, Jack,' she said, 'there's no egg out yet. There's no shell broken. Oh wait!' she said all of a sudden. 'There's one out! And judging by the long neck on him I'd say he's a gander!'

At this moment the goose appeared at the door and when she saw who was sitting on her eggs, she began to flap her wings and with her neck stretched out in front of her she came hissing at him. He was lucky to get through the room door without missing a piece out of his *sawtawn*!

Moll gathered herself out of the place, she didn't want to be there when the wife came in. He put on his clothes in the room and now he said he would have to attend to the next item which was to see to the bread. Blessed hour tonight you could smell it. He took the cover off the oven and a *bocarum* of blue smoke came up. The cake was as black as the ace of spades inside. He was hammering the oven on the floor, no good, he had to go out in the yard and get the shovel to dig the cake out of the oven. That was another job gone wrong!

He said he'd get dinner for the working woman, when with that he heard the cow bellowing, he had forgotten to give her a drink. He took the reins off the churn, went out to the stall and put it on the cow's horns, she was a *bradaigh* cow, he couldn't let her loose. On his way to the stream, as he was passing the house, he looked up at the roof and there was a fine crop of grass corn growing on the thatch. It was on the thatch the likes of him would have it! He said to himself 'Waste not, want not!' And when he was coming back from the stream there was a *leaca* field at the back of the house sloping up almost on one level with the roof. He walked the cow up the field and jumped her on to the thatch! Yerra, she didn't go down through it at all, she was like a reindeer. The cow began to graze away delighted with herself. He was holding the rope and said, 'I can't remain here all the time minding her, I have to get the dinner for the wife.'

He thought of another plan. He walked up the barge of the gable and let his end of the rope down the chimney; then he came inside and took the rope, it was fine and long, and tied it around himself and put a knot on it. That was a great plan altogether, for he was minding the cow on the roof, and at the same time his hands were free to get the dinner for the working woman! Sometimes the cow, moving on the roof, would pull the rope up the chimney and draw him towards the fireplace. 'Yeoish!' he'd say to stop her. He put the spuds in the pan and he washed 'em, then he took the little skillet pot, the mouth of it no bigger than the mouth of my hat, and this was to be his cooking utensil. Things were going so well for him that he began to sing,

> When we got into London the police they were on
>   the quay,
> *Bhí na barántaisí scríte san* Telegraph News *ó inné.*
> (The warrants had been published in yesterday's
>   *Telegraph News.*)

With that the cow fell off the roof! The legs were taken from under him and he was swept feet first along the floor and up the chimney until he came to the narrow place, and he stuck there like a cork you'd try to pull with a cord out of a bottle. The cow was hanging down outside, and he was hanging down inside! And he had the pot in his hands all the time. If he let it fall it'd break – hadn't he enough damage done!

There he remained till his wife was coming in from the field and when she saw the cow hanging down – her two hind legs in the yard and her two front legs up against the gable of the house, for all the world like the lads used be long 'go when the Black and Tans would be searching 'em – she ran up with the spade and cut the rope. The cow fell down and ran away and when there was nothing to balance him the man fell down the chimney for she heard him shouting. She ran into the kitchen and there he was standing on his head in the pot!

She helped her husband out of the fireplace and put him sitting on a chair. But if she lost Kate and the child she couldn't get his head out of the pot. It was down over his ears. Now, it is a simple enough operation to break a pot, but it is a horse of a different colour if there's a man's head in it. It was in the village of Cullen it happened and the poor woman had to take him by the hand three miles to the forge. As she was going along the road people were running out to the doors, and when they saw this man with the strange headgear they thought he was the advance guard of an invading army! They were following after her, the young blackguards laughing, and saying, 'How did he get his head into the pot?'

She was so vexed that she said, 'He was trying to see was there a hole in the bottom of it.'

When she got him to the forge, the smith, and a very awkward man too, hit him a belt of a sledge hammer breaking the pot into flitters and turning his head sideways until his jaw rested on his left shoulder. Whatever damage was done to the vertebrae the poor man was landed with a permanent crick in his neck, and the woman was a bigger show coming home with him than she was going! And people wanted to know what it was he was looking back at? She brought him to the City for nine mornings running and each morning after the round he drank at the holy well. There was a small rubbing stone there at that time, no bigger than a pigeon's egg, and each morning when he had taken the sup at the well the woman used to rub the curing stone to the outside of his neck, and as far down as she could get it on the inside so that nothing'd be overlooked. Blast me if the *amadán* didn't close his mouth on her on the ninth morning and swallowed the relic! With the effort he had to make to get it down past his Adam's apple he turned his neck and he was cured!

The Season of Light

As well as pattern day there is one other religious observance of long ago worth recalling. I'm thinking of Christmas. No word of a lie but it was something to write home about when I was small. Oh! the way we looked forward to twilight on Christmas Eve, for when darkness fell it was Christmas Night, the greatest night of all the year. We youngsters would be up with the crack of dawn that morning to have the house ready for the night.

Berry holly would have to be cut and brought in to deck out the windows, the top of the dresser, the back of the settle and the clevvy. We'd bring in ivy too and put a sprig of laurel behind the pictures, above the lintel of the door and around the fireplace. But we wouldn't overdo it, or if we did my mother would make us cut it down a bit, reminding us that she'd like to feel that she was in her own house for Christmas, and not in the middle of a wood!

Well, the transformation we could bring about in the kitchen with all that greenery! But we weren't finished yet. The Christmas candles had to be prepared; these were of white tallow as thick as the handle of a spade and nearly as tall. In some houses they'd scoop out a hole in a turnip and put the candle sitting in it. A big crock we'd use. We'd put the candle standing into that and pack it around with sand. If you hadn't sand, bran or pollard would do.

When the candle was firmly in position we'd spike sprigs of holly or laurel into the sand about the candle, and we had coloured paper too to put around the outside of the crock to take the bare look off it. With that same coloured paper, the girls in the family, if they were anyway handy, could make paper flowers to decorate the holly. Then what would cap it all, was a length of young ivy and spiral it up around the candle – it looked lovely! That done, we would go through the same manoeuvres until there was a candle in a crock for every window in the house.

Then we'd be praying for night to fall, for you couldn't see the right effect until the candles were lit. That honour would fall to the youngest in the house. My father would lift him up saying, 'In the name of the Father and of the Son . . . ' and when the child had blessed himself, he would put the lighting spill to the candle, and from that candle the other candles would be lit, and we'd be half daft with excitement, enjoying the great blaze of light, and running from the rooms to the kitchen and out into the yard to see what the effect was like from the outside. When we'd get tired of looking at the candles in our own windows, we'd turn and try to name the neighbours' houses as the bunches of lights came on, two windows here and three windows there, across the dark countryside and away up to the foot of the hills. And as sure as anything someone'd be late and we'd rush into my mother saying, 'Faith, then there's no light on yet in Rosacrew!'

'Go on yeer knees!' my mother would say. The time she'd pick for the Rosary, just as the salt ling was ready and the white onion sauce and the potatoes steaming over the fire. But I suppose there'd be no religion in the world only for the women. The Rosary in our house didn't end at five decades. Not at all.

After the Hail Holy Queen my mother would branch into the trimmings:

> Come Holy Ghost send down those beams,
> Which sweetly flow in silent streams.

She'd pray for everyone in sickness and in need: the poor souls and the sinful soul that was at that very moment trembling before the judgement seat above. She'd pray for the sailor on the seas: 'Protect him from the tempest, Oh Lord, and bring him safely home'. And the lone traveller on the highway and of course our emigrants and, last of all, the members of her own family, 'God bless and save us all.'

> St Patrick, Bridget and Colmcille
> Guard each wall.
> May the Queen of heaven
> And the angels bright
> Keep us and our house
> From all harm this night!'

Our knees'd be aching as we got up off the floor, and it would take my father a while to get the prayer arch out of his back. Well, we wouldn't be sitting down to the supper when my mother'd bless herself again, a preliminary to grace before meals, and you could hardly blame my father for losing his patience.

'Is it in a monastery we are?' he'd say. 'Haven't we done enough praying for one night?'

After the supper there was Christmas cake for anyone with a sweet tooth. My father'd never look at that. His eye'd be on the big earthenware jar below the dresser, and it would be a great relief to him when my mother'd say to us, 'Go out there, one of ye, and tell the neighbouring men to come in for a while.'

It was the custom that night, Nollaig Mhór, big Christmas, for the men to visit each other's houses. The women were too busy to be bothered. They had their own night, 'Nollaig na mBan,' small Christmas, for making tapes. In a while's time the men'd come, and at the first lag in the conversation my father'd take the cork off the jar and fill out a few cups of porter. The men, by the way, not noticing what was going on, and then when they'd get the cups, all surprise they'd say, 'What's this? What's this for?'

'Go on, take it,' my father'd say. 'It is Christmas night, neighbours, and more luck to us!'

Then the men's faces'd light up and lifting their cups they'd say, 'Happy Christmas, Ned. Happy Christmas, Hannie. Happy Christmas everyone!'

'And the same to ye men,' my father would answer. 'May we all be alive again this time twelve months.'

And my mother, who was never very happy in the presence of strong drink, would direct her gaze in the direction of the Christmas candle and say, 'The grace of God to us all!'

After sampling the beverage one of the men putting out his lower lip to suck in any stray particles of froth that had lodged in his moustache would enquire, 'Where did you get this, Ned?'

'Carthy Dannehy's,' my father'd say.

'He always keeps a good drop, I'll say that for him.'

'Sláinte, Ned,' from all the men.

> 'Sláinte chugat is cabhair
> Dealbh go deo ná rabhair,
> Is go bhfásfaidh gach ribín
> Ar do cheann chomh fade le meigeal ghabhair.'

(Health to you and suppost/May you never be destitute/ And may every rib [of hair] on your head grow to be as long as a goat's beard).

In every house on Christmas night there'd be a big log of elm or ash stretched behind the fire. It'd reach from the leg of the crane to the opposite pier with wet moss and strands of ivy still clinging to it. When the fire got going good, little jets of steam'd come hissing out of the log, and there'd be an occasional minor explosion which'd make the cat jump. He would eye the spot where the sound came from for a while, and then decide it might be safer back a piece. As time went on such would be the heat from the burning log that we'd all take a leaf out of the cat's book and move back.

The shuffling of the chairs'd bring about a pause in the conversation during which the men would remark on the quality of the Christmas log, some of them might remember the growing tree of which it formed part. The men would admire the decorations and compliment us young lads on our ingenuity. Then looking at the holly they'd say it was a sign of a mild winter when the blackbirds hadn't all the berries gone.

The men wouldn't stay all night in the one place. A neighbour getting to his feet'd say, 'Come on away down to our house until we sample what my woman brought from town. It'll have to be good to be up to this drop!'

Later on we'd have to go and collect my father so that he'd be in some shape for the chapel in the morning. We youngsters loved going to Mass in the dark and hearing the sound of the horses' hooves and the crack of the car axles if the morning was frosty, the loud greetings outside the chapel gate, people bumping into one another in the darkness.

'That you Mary? Happy Christmas to you!'

'Same to you!' Mary'd say. And then she'd add under her breath, 'The devil turn you. Will you watch what you are doing, or do you want to floor me!'

The Barefooted Gander

There were more people around the place at Christmas time. Boys and girls home from service strolling up and down the road at night or talking in bunches under the light spilling out from the windows.

The rambling house would be fuller too with maybe a visitor or two back from New York. Well I remember the year John Murphy came home. He handed out American cigarettes to everyone, which were accepted, as the man said, with avidity. I partly guessed from the way he was smiling that there was some trick to it. We all lit up and the next minute the fags began to explode! The men pulled them out of their mouths, but they exploded again in their hands, so they threw them on the floor, filling the kitchen with fireworks. The older men were palming their moustaches fearing they had been blown off! We laughed enough that night and as the smoke cleared the talk turned to America and the boat trip, which put our storyteller in mind of an attempt to fly the Atlantic long before the Wright brothers were born.

There was a man living one time not a hundred miles from where I'm sitting and his name was Timmie Warren. He was working for his day's hire drawing goods from the Railway Station for a big shopkeeper. He had good wages for the time it was, a house of his own, a nice wife and enough to ate, and wouldn't you think he'd be satisfied. He was not! For whatever little deficiency was in the top storey he never dreamt in his life. Whether he slept on his left side or on his right side, on his back or on his bread basket – 'twas all the one, he got up in the morning the same as he went to bed the night before, with no story to tell.

Now, this mightn't bother you or it mightn't bother me, but it did bother Timmie Warren, for in the place he was working, after the dinner every day the other workmen would be telling him about the grand dreams they had the night before. Places they visited, things they saw, the tall buildings and the different coloured people walking on painted flagstones, the banquets they were at, the wine, the food and the company . . . until they had Timmie Warren driven demented and he was losing the colour. So he went along and he spoke to 'Discount'. That was the shopkeeper's nickname, for his motto was, 'Take a pound's worth and I'll throw off a bob.' And as prime a boyo he was as you'd meet from here to the town of Tallow. So when he heard Timmie Warren's tale of woe about not being able to dream, he smiled and said, 'If every riddle was as easy unravelled as that life'd be heaven. All you have to do when you go home this evening is to put out the fire, bring the bed down out of the room and set it up inside in the fireplace. Retire there for the night, and if you aren't dreaming before morning, my name is not "Discount"!' When Timmie Warren heard that, 'twas like as if he was left a legacy. He went home delighted, but it took him from then until ten o'clock that night to convince his wife to fall in with his plan – *ní nach ionadh*!

'And,' says she, 'if the soot falls down on the bedclothes, is it you'll be dancing on 'em below in the *glaise*? And isn't it soft the wool grows on you, if you expect your wife to fall in with every daft notion that comes into your head.'

But if I didn't say it before, I'll say it now, there's great credit due to the wives of Ireland and the pains they'll go to to humour a cranky husband. Finally she fell in with his wishes. The fire was put out, the bed was brought down out of the room and set up inside in the fireplace, and the two retired for the night.

Timmie Warren was not too long asleep when he thought he heard a knock at the door and a voice saying, 'Get up, Timmie Warren and take this letter to America.'

'Hah,' says Timmie, 'what's that?'

'Get up,' says the voice, 'and take this letter to America.'

'Who's there?' says Timmie.

''Tis me, "Discount". Get up and take this letter to America.'

Timmie got up into his Sunday clothes and his velour hat, stuck his legs into his shoes, took the letter and ran off in the direction of America. He kept going, the tips on his heels knocking fire out of the road until he came to the broad Atlantic ocean. And there he saw this big white gander with his shoes off paddling.

'Hello, Timmie Warren,' says the gander. Ganders could talk then. "Where are you off to?'

'I'm going to America,' says Timmie, 'with this letter for "Discount", but the trouble is how am I going to get over?'

'Well,' says the gander, 'if every riddle was as easy unravelled as that life'd be heaven, hop up on my back and I'll fly you over.'

'I'm not too heavy for you,' says Timmie when he had himself settled.

'You're heavy enough, then,' says the gander. 'But we'll chance it now.'

And he flapped his wings and craned his neck, made one bounce and up he soared and away he flew. No more bother! And the lovely soft seat Timmie Warren had, and the view! He was in his element looking down on the world, and 'twasn't long until he was singing:

When I was young and in my bloom,
My mind was ill at ease;

  I was dreaming of Amerikay
  And gold beyond the seas.

Everything went smack smooth till they were half way across the Atlantic, when the gander said, 'Hop down off my back, Timmie Warren.'

'Hah,' says Timmie, 'what's that your saying to me?'

'Hop down off my back. I'm winded!'

'Hop down where?' says Timmie. 'Have you any *splink*? Where can I hop down to?'

'Hop down off my back,' says the gander, 'I can't fly another peg.'

'I will not,' says Timmie.

And a fierce argument cropped up between them, and the result of it was that the gander flew out from under Timmie Warren and left him falling down through the air. He was in a nice pucker now, the poor man!

Well, as luck should have it, it so happened that the Clare team were flying out to America to play New York, at a lower level of course! And where did Timmie Warren fall but down into the middle of 'em, and grabbed on to the goalie's hurley.

'Take go now,' says the goalie, 'or I'll give you a tap.' And he would in a minute!

'Ah, let me hold on for a small piece till the gander gets his second wind,' says Timmie.

'Take go,' says the goalie, 'you're only holding us up and we'll be late for the line-out. Do you want us to lose the match?'

'I do not,' says Timmie.

And he looked down to see how far he'd have to fall and wasn't there a ship nearly under him in the ocean.

'Throw yourself down,' says the captain of the ship, 'and we'll catch you.'

'How do I know,' says Timmie, 'but 'tis into the waves I'll fall and be drowned.'

'Can't you throw down one of your shoes,' says the captain, 'and we'll see where it will land.'

Timmie kicked off one of his shoes and with that there was an unmerciful yell from his wife.

'Is that you, Síle,' says Timmie.

'What's left of me,' says she. 'Where are you?'

'Wherever I am,' says Timmie, 'I can't lead or drive. Strike a light!'

She lit a candle, and where was Timmie? Half way up the chimney, with one shoe off and one shoe on! She knew then what hit her.

'Come down,' says she, 'you cracked *criceálaí*. What a dreamer I have in you.'

He came down, and by the time he had the soot out of himself, out of the suit, and out of the bedclothes he didn't care if he never dreamt again and he to live to be as old as Methuselah!

Small Christmas Eve the women'd get together for a party. They might come into our place for a bit and then my mother'd go off with 'em to another house. One night it was awful late when my mother came in, and my father said to her, 'Where were you?'

'Out there,' she said. She didn't say anymore.

The decorations weren't taken down until the morning after small Christmas Day. Any small lads who hadn't yet seen the crib, the mothers would take 'em in to the Friars' chapel that day. There was a brother from Belgium in the Friary then, and he was a pure dinger when it came to setting up a crib. The stable was very well brought out by him, with the Infant there and His mother and Saint Joseph of course. He had it nice and bright so that you could see half the town of Bethlehem sloping away from you. And all the animals that were there wherever he got 'em! Cows, very nearly as big as you'd see in the field, and sheep and the ass. You'd see angels flying overhead, shepherds below and the wise kings making their way in at the side. After saying a prayer the people'd pitch money into the stable as near as they could get it to the cradle. And by the time the crib was taken down the Infant'd be lying on a copper bed speckled with silver. That was how highly the people thought of the brother's work. You'd see nothing like it now anywhere.

The Dear Departed

Two priests home on holidays from the Jesuit College called into Hopper Dan's. Hopper's wife having nothing inside for the dinner – it was like her – killed two young cocks – they had hardly the red combs up on them – and put them down in the pot. She gave a bit of cold bacon to Hopper. After the dinner when Hopper was conveying the two clergymen out of the yard, the old cock, stretching himself to his full height and flapping his wings, began to crow on the gate pier.

'That's a very proud rooster you have there!' says one of the priests to Hopper.

'No bloody wonder he would,' says Hopper, 'and he having two sons in the Jesuits!'

If you look out that window and up the rising ground towards the foot of the hills you'll see a house, and when I was a small boy there were two brothers living there. Fine storytellers they were, for what one'd leave out the other one'd put in. And signs by it was a great rambling house, with not enough chairs in the kitchen for the crowd every night. A place where the affairs of the day were debated, where entertainment mingled with education, and where what you heard was genuine, for those two brothers knew their history. A man said to me there on that floor, 'Look, Ned Kelly, there are professors above in the University of Cork and if they had half their knowledge the devil in hell wouldn't stand them!'

But the wise are sometimes foolish. The younger brother got married when he was about thirty, but whatever he did or didn't do the wife stayed with him only one night. She ran away and if he shook gold under her feet she wouldn't come back to him. The subject was never mentioned between the two brothers until about fifty years later. The older man that never got married was complaining of a pain in his back, and the matrimonial brother, getting tired of listening to him said, 'What cnavshawling have you? Hadn't you your day?'

'I had,' says the older man, 'and you had your night!'

The people living up there are still talking about the row this remark gave rise to. The two brothers could be heard shouting in the *Domhan Thoir*! When things subsided there was silence, a long silence, for they never spoke to each other after, nor did one ever again mention the other by name. When they were high over eighty and very crotchety, two men were coming home from work in Kenmare's Demesne, and when they were passing the house the younger brother came to the door and said, 'Lads, if yeer coming over rambling tonight bring a few chairs. There's one of us dead!'

That was Saturday, and an awful awkward day to die at that time, for you couldn't open a grave on Monday. Nothing but bad luck would come out of it. Of course you can get round the *piseóg* by turning one sod of the grave on Sunday. And that is what was done. Only those closely connected with the dead man's family would open the grave, or be in any position of prominance during the wake or funeral. It would be considered highly disrespectful to the dead for a stranger to have hand, act or part in the proceedings.

Molly Donovan that used to lay them out when I was small. She was also the midwife. I remember seeing her up in the middle gallery of the chapel when she was old and doting, and looking down on the people coming into Mass she said, 'God made ye but it was I brought ye into the world!'

She did, and helped them out of it. The poor man that died was hardly inside the Golden Gates above when Molly was in the door and, fortified with whiskey, she'd wash the corpse, put on the habit, put the pennies on the eyelids, the prayerbook under the jaw and fold the arms with the rosary beads entwined around the fingers. The only case where she might look for assistance was the shaving. And a fellow helping her out one time had a ferocious shake in his hand. He was full of apologies after for not having the corpse look his best.

'Yerra,' says Molly dusting the badly shaven face with flour, 'he's all right. He'll do. It isn't to America he's going.'

Give Molly Donovan her due she carried out everything according to custom. The clock was stopped and the looking glass turned to the wall. The sad news was told to the bees, and in some places a crape was hung on the hive. Bees were considered part of the family that time and they should be told what was going on – not every fiddle-faddle, important things like the first day the child'd go to school. That morning the father'd go out and knock on the hive and say, 'Michael is gone to school today, bees.'

When Molly Donovan had the bed draped with starched linen, brought up over the foot and the head of the bed, a couple of boards under the corpse to keep him well *os cionn cláir*, his Third Order habit on him with the white cord, and he nicely groomed and serene for himself, no Pope that was ever laid out in the Vatican would look half as well. Of course we didn't have the custom here of tapping him on the head with a hammer to see if he was dead!

There was a woman died east here the road, Ah she was no great loss. She made her husband's life a misery – they say she was years older than him. And when she died he spared no money on whiskey and porter for the wake. He expected to get married soon again! The drink flowed and the carpenter was so spifflicated when he came to measure the corpse he made the coffin too short. The people, when they saw the coffin going into the house the morning of the funeral knew it was too short.

'You'd want to be blind,' they said, 'not to see that she wouldn't go into it.'

Well the carpenter brought the coffin into the wake room, and he wanted three chairs to lay it on while he was putting the corpse into it. Of course all the chairs were below in the kitchen where the hilarity was. And the carpenter putting his head down the room door said, 'Three chairs for the corpse!'

And one blackguard below said, 'Hip! Hip!'

The carpenter laid the coffin on the three chairs and took off the lid but the corpse would not go into it! He was in an awful way now and he got very red in the face. What was he going to do? The yard full of people waiting for the funeral, the parish priest and all there. He had to act quick, so he got a locksaw and he cut two holes at the narrow end of the coffin. The corpse went into it then all right, but her two feet were cocking out from the ankles down! The dead woman's two sisters when they saw that burst out crying, 'Poor Minnie,' they said, 'bad and all as she was she didn't deserve to have that done to her! You wouldn't do it,' they said, 'to a black Russian.'

And they wanted the husband to postpone the funeral until a proper coffin was made. The husband said, 'No! Delays are dangerous. There's no time like the present!'

So they put the lid on the coffin and brought it to the door. The chief mourners crowded round the front of it, and once outside the coffin was raised on the bearers' shoulders. And the front right-hand man under the coffin, Doherty was his name, took off his hat and held it over the feet. The funeral moved on with dignity and no one was the wiser. Even the parish priest didn't notice anything.

'All right,' he whispered to the men, 'I'll be moving ahead of ye to the cemetery.'

The people fell in behind the coffin. Then the sidecars, common cars and saddle horses. After a time Doherty's hand, from being in the same position, developed *codladh grifín* and was going to sleep on him, so he took his hand away and left the hat handing on the feet. People coming against the funeral halted in the middle of blessing themselves when they saw the hat. And you couldn't blame them for thinking they were at the wrong funeral . . . that this must be some great military hero and his hat was being buried with him. At what is called the changing of the bearers, Doherty, forgetting himself when he was going, took the hat and left the feet exposed. Lord save us! What an embarrassment this was for the next of kin.

They decided to take the short-cut, although the rule is the longest way round to the burial place. It is considered most disrespectful to be in the slightest hurry to get shut of the corpse! Even when the funeral procession gets inside the gate the wrongest thing in the world would be to make a bee-line for the grave. While they were rounding a bend on uneven ground and taking the corner too short, the legs were taken from under the front bearers and the corpse's feet rubbed against a blackthorn bush. There was an almighty shout from the inside of the coffin. 'Twas Minnie.

'What's itching my feet?' she said.

When the bearers heard that they dropped the coffin. The lid hopped off and Minnie sat up inside the picture of health – two red cheeks on her. The bulk of the people scattered, hid in the wood. Minnie stood up and walked out of the coffin and she was the first one home. It was three years to the day before she got her walking papers again, and I can tell you that this time the husband took great care that the coffin was long enough!

Poor Minnie! No tears for her. But if the person burying was a big loss, like the father of young family, the scenes of grief at the graveside would crack the heart in a stone. Instead of bottling up the grief inside in them that time people believed in giving full vent to their sorrow. Didn't certain women – the *caoiners* – make a trade of going to wakes and funerals to soften the hearts in the relations. I saw one of these women moisten the corner of her apron in her mouth and rub it to her cheeks to give the impression of sorrow. Oh, the loud wail of lamentation she made! In no time she had the women by the graveside sobbing and striking their hands together, and calling out the name of the dear departed. And when the young man's coffin was being lowered into the narrow grave his brothers, overcome with sorrow, surged forward to prevent it from doing down. And as the first shovelfuls of earth fell, with a hollow sound, on the coffin, oh, my God, a great cry arose, only fading down as earth falling on earth made hardly any sound at all!

Wing-nuts were all the go at the time. They were like thumb screws, and very handy they were too, because you could undo them quickly and the lid was off in a jiffy. It was the custom then when the coffin was laid at the bottom of the grave that one man would go down and unscrew all the wing-nuts and lay them on the lid. This was a nod to heaven that the door was being left on the latch for the resurrection. What great faith!

Now it so happened that a local man died somewhere foreign. This man in his youth had been connected with 'the Movement' and there'd be an outcry if his body wasn't brought home. It was, and when the coffin, foreign-made of course, was lowered into the grave a man went down to undo the wing-nuts, only to find that the lid was screwed down for ever! There he was below and couldn't loosen the lid, so he beckoned to those near him. They went on one knee and stuck their heads into the grave and began a whispered consultation with the man below. The question was, would they turn their backs on the old law and fill in the grave, or would they bow to custom? I don't have to tell you what was decided: one of the party got on a saddle horse and, after scouring the countryside, came back with an assortment of screwdrivers, which were handed down to the man in the grave.

In the end the screws were undone and placed in the shape of a cross on the lid, the grave was filled in down to the last shovelful of earth, and the green sods patted into place on the grave mound with the poll of the spade. It took a bit of time but the people didn't mind once the job was done right. There was only one person who seemed upset by the carry-on and that was the archdeacon. He was muttering to himself about *piseógs*, but he led the final decade of the rosary. That over, old comrades of the soldier that was gone came forward to fire a volley over the grave. Some of these men were so old and crotchety that it was tightening them to direct the guns into the air. So that people, dreading mortal injury, ducked down and moved back, with the result that Eugene Casey, who was craning his neck to get a view of the shooting was pushed and he fell, bringing three or four more with him, into an open grave and broke his leg! And as a reporter said in the paper the following week, 'Needless to mention this sad occurrence cast a gloom over the entire proceedings!'

The light of heaven to all that's gone and may they never come back to haunt us!

Washing the Cock's Feet

The pooka is a malicious spirit but not deadly. He can turn himself into any shape, but from what I hear he nearly always appears in the form of a pony. If you are coming home late at night from card-playing or any other carry-on you wouldn't like your missus or the parish priest to know about, ah ha! faith, you can meet him! He has the power to coax you up on his back, and then the same as if you put red pepper under his tail, he's off over hedges and ditches, through bogs, brakes and quagmires, from *Poul a' Phúca* to *Gleann a' Phúca*, and from *Carraig a' Phúca* to *Moing a' Phúca*, until finally with the living daylights frightened out of you and your clothes in tatters, just as the cock crows, he'll come to a sudden halt, and you'll go flying out over his head and maybe land up to your neck in a pool of *múnlach*. I'd rather meet Jackie the Lantern than him!

But look at the power of the cock – a small bit of goods. When the cock crows in the morning all things supernatural melt into thin air! The cock is a crabbed bucko. Oh, a fine specimen! And the proud gait of him strutting across the yard on his orange legs! And the plumage of his turned down tail. Did you ever notice the way he'd look at you? First with one eye and then with the other, and when he blinks his eyelid goes from below up! And the red comb like a crown on his head and the chest sticking out! He'd remind you of Henry VIII – another blackguard!

In our place long ago, cocks were suspected of having the power of prophecy. According to the place or the time they crowed, except at dawn, a visitor was expected or someone was about to die in the townland. Whatever was in them they were held in such high regard that they were never killed when they got too old for the caper! They were let go in Merry's Wood, and there were so many old cocks there one time, it was referred to as *Parlaimint na gCoileach.* And a very noisy House of Commons it was too, with the principal motion debated around dawn in the morning!

At that time people used to wash their feet going to bed at night, a custom that is fading away since they got shoes. It seems a big ceremony was made out of the washing of the feet. The biggest pot would be placed in the middle of the kitchen floor and to do it right the youngest male child should wash his feet first. Now the man that had only daughters in the family. What would he do? I'll tell you, he'd take the cock off his perch over the coop, and wash his feet first. Wasn't that a fine healthy piece of paganism!

The Cock and the Coop

I remember when I was small they used to keep the fowl in a coop in the kitchen. There was very little in the way of outbuildings at the time, and the more out-offices you had the more rent you paid the landlord, so the hens had to be kept in a coop in the kitchen. They were safe there from the fox. But not the cock . . . his majesty wasn't cooped up. He'd sit on a perch over the door or on the collar-brace – an alarm clock that needed no winding!

The coop made a nice companion piece to the dresser and the settle. It stood, not as high as the dresser, and in outline it would remind you a little of the chiffonier. At the bottom of the coop you had two big compartments. One with nests for the hens to lay in, and the other where the hens could hatch. Then overhead you had the living quarters. Three or four rows with sliding shutters in front. The shutters were made of vertical laths spaced a few inches apart so that when the hens retired in the evening they could put their head out between the laths and take an interest in what was going on, and in that position they'd remind you of nothing in this world only idle women looking out hotel windows in the summer time in Ballybunion!

Hens seem to be forever engaged in conversation. I don't think their musings have ever been recorded. A pity. For there's no end to the variety of sounds they can make from the sad clucks of complaint when they are hungry to the nice satisfied tone they make when they are fed, which can change all of a sudden if a dog rushes into the yard. Standing in a bunch together watching the cock they seem to be talking out of the sides of their beaks and for all we know indulging in a bit of calumny and detraction. Hens have a special tone when they are looking for a place to lay, which bears no relation to the commotion they kick up when they have laid. And of course the hatching hen has a lingo all her own, not very musical, like two stones hitting together – cloch cloch – but she can substitute a more appealing call to the chickens when she finds some out of the way piece of food. I think she picks this sound up from the cock, for you'd hear him going on with it when he has a little tit-bit for his favourite wife.

The mother hen has a system of sounds to suit every degree of danger threatening her young. One of these sounds she raises to a frightening note when she sees the hawk overhead. As soon ever as the chickens hear the alarm they disappear or freeze under a leaf or a chaney, and when the mother hen sounds the all clear they come out again as perky as you like. But nothing in the fowl world can equal the lunatic sounds that comes from a hatching hen when her 'chickens' turn out to be little ducks and take to the water. You have then, judging by speech and appearance, a very demented hen!

In many places these articles of furniture, the coop, the dresser and the settle were made of bog oak and that was very hard timber to work. But the people had to use it, for the landlords wouldn't let them cut the trees in the demesne woods. A man explained to me once how the local people got the black oak up from the depths of the bog. They would go to the uncut bog early in the morning when the frost was on the ground. And it seems where the log of oak would be reposing, maybe seven feet under the turf, there would be very little frost on the grass over it up.

You could see the outline of the log like a shadow on the ground. The men had, as part of their equipment, two long rods of iron. One of these rods was driven down at one end until it met the wood. By driving it down a few times the men were able to determine the width of the log. That done they would leave that rod in position touching the wood, and go off and drive the other rod down through the soft bog to find the length of the log. Then a man would place the end of one rod against his teeth while the other rod would be tapped with a sledge, good and hard, and if the first man felt the vibrations in his teeth that log was all one piece and worth digging up.

Then with a hay-knife they'd cut around the shadow in the frost – they had to work quick before the sun'd rise. The grassy top-sod was removed, and with the *sleán* they cut the turf spreading the sods to dry. The trench deepened and when they reached the log they'd free around it. Because there was no outlet from that trench, in a short time it filled with water and the log floated to the top. All they had to do now was tackle a horse to the end of the log and haul it home. When it was dry it was cut with a fake-ah called a whipsaw into boards and planks for the carpenter, who'd come to the house and make the settle, dresser and coop.

And I could not give down on the amount of ingenuity that went into the making of these articles of furniture. Raised panels in the settle with the rails stop-champhered and shaped arm-rests. But it was the dresser that took the cake! A lovely cornice at the top, ogee-moulded with dentils, shelves double-beaded throughout, side and top face-boards with pierced or sunken centres, and two or maybe three overlap drawers in the lower section. If you made it yourself you'd stay up all night looking at it!

They're all thrown out now! Daughters coming back

from England or America, not seeing the like over, got rid of 'em. A man told me that he saw a field full of dressers thrown out in the County Clare. And he blamed the women too. He said that they went into town and bought plywood furniture with glass fronts to keep the bees off the butter!

The Blacksmith's Wife

Ní phósfhainnse an gabha dubh – Ye all know what the lady in the song is saying: I wouldn't marry the blacksmith! Why then I heard of a woman that married a blacksmith, and what's more she came all the way back from America to marry him. He was a good mark for as well as the forge he had a nice bit of land with a good house on it. There was no out and out great love between them, just that he had an empty house and she was tired of America. They got married, a made match, and they made history for they were the first couple from that part of the world to go away on a honeymoon. When they got off the train above in Glanmire station in Cork she says to him, 'They are all looking at us. They know very well that we are fresh from the altar! Is there anything I could do,' says she, 'to make it appear as if we are a couple of years married?'

'Of course there is,' he said. 'Catch hold of the bag and walk on in front of me!'

When they came back from the honeymoon she got in the carpenters and the masons and renovated the outside and the inside of the house. I can tell you that the dresser and the settle walked out the door fairly quick! She put into effect ideas she saw foreign. She made a lovely job of it, concrete paths – you wouldn't see them at all at that time – all around the house outside and a steep concrete path running all the way down to the wicket. With a monkey tree here and a monkey tree there – she was used to the good thing in America, where she was a lady's companion, wintering it in New York and summering it in Spring Falls!

She was full of airs and graces which she tried to transfer to the blacksmith! The poor man! She was always correcting his speech, which might sound all right to you or me, for it was the speech of the locality, full of 'fhots' and 'fhoys' and 'fhuichs' and 'fhayers my woman!' The man's grammar was putrid! Always saying things like 'she have' and 'he have'. Well, she gave him such a drilling about saying 'he have' and 'she have' that in the wind up, would you blame him, the blacksmith thought that 'have' was a word that shouldn't be said in front of children. And I remember distinctly the blackguards waiting to go into Mass – 'twas the fall of the year – and when they saw the blacksmith coming they said to him, 'Have they the hay cut, up yeer quarter!'

'Oh, they has,' he said. 'Indeed they has, sure if they hasn't it cut now they'll never has!'

There was a station published for the blacksmith that year. Things were going a bit late because there was a change of parish priest. The way it was, the smith didn't mind whether it came or not, but his wife was delighted to have the station in the house, as it would give her an opportunity of showing the priests and the people the improvements she had made, and it would also be a chance to show them all the curiefibbles she had brought back in the trunk from New York. She made up her mind that the day of the station was to be a big day and she wasn't going to have such an important occasion ruined by her husband's awkwardness, so training was the answer.

For weeks before the station the poor blacksmith hated to see the sun going down in the evening, for it meant home to night-school! And when he got inside the door of the lovely new house he had to get out of his old duds that were dirty from the forge, scrub himself from head to foot, and get into what he called his conversation clothes. She put a lot of stress on speech: 'Yes, father' and 'No, father' and 'I beg your pardon, father'. Being the man of the house he would have to have his breakfast in the room with the priest after the station Mass. So she showed him how, in smiling fashion, to fix the chair at the head of the table for the priest, and for God's sake not to pull it from under him as he was going to sit down!

'Have your manners,' she told him. 'Make sure everything is up to the knocker. Pass the sugar and pass the milk, and no coarse conversation,' she said, 'in the presence of the priest.'

She didn't want him saying things like, 'Excuse me, dear father, the butter is hairy; the dog and the cat slept in the dairy!'

'None of that,' she said to him. 'And use your serviette and don't have drops of tea falling from your moustache! And take the spoon out of your cup while you are drinking, and don't have it going into your eye while you are talking to the priest!'

Being the man of the house he would have to go down the steep path to the gate the morning of the station to greet the PP when he got off the sidecar. Before he'd go to work in the forge his wife brought him down a few times to show him how to do it properly. He was to stand there showing no agitation and when the priest got off the sidecar to extend his hand and say, 'Good morning, dear Father!' Then he was to look around and with a controlled laugh add, 'Fall already. We won't feel it now to Christmas!'

He didn't want to say 'Fall already' because he hadn't heard it around. It was a proper term, she told him, and used in New York to describe the autumnal part of the year. It was the coming thing, she persuaded him, and that he could put his bottom dollar on it. He was doubtful. He didn't think it a homely expression, and he used to be saying it to himself to get used to it. 'Fall already. Fall already!' When he got up in the morning before his prayers he'd say 'Fall already!' Even when the forge was full of customers all of a sudden he'd stop hammering the hot iron on the anvil and looking up at the roof he'd say 'Fall already!' until the people thought he was going out of his nut!

Every evening when he came home from the forge the table would have a new cloth on it, and each evening she would introduce him to a different item of cutlery, spoons for this and that, a little silver tongs for the loaf sugar, knives crooked and straight and pieces of tableware, glassy salt cellars and a butter cooler with a roof on it!

The night before the station he washed the footpaths all around the house. And the steep path down to the gate . . . bucket after bucket of water he sloshed it down. Then as he was at the gate and there was no one looking he extended his hand. This would be the final practice,

'Good morning, dear Father.' Then he looked around and laughed as directed. 'Fall already! We won't feel it now to Christmas.'

He went back up to the house. They went to bed, himself and the returned Yank, and whatever happened that night, maybe the clock didn't go off in the morning or the cock didn't crow, whatever it was they were only barely down in the kitchen and when they looked out the window there was the parish priest's sidecar drawing up below at the wicket gate. The blacksmith stuck his legs into his shoes and ran out the front door. Lord save us! There was a fierce fall of frost the night before and the minute he hit the icy path the two legs were taken from under him and he came down with a crash on his backside and went skeeting down to the gate! From the sitting position he extended his hand and said, 'Good father, dear morning. What a day you came! God, I broke my bum in the fall. I'll feel it now till Christmas!'

It Snowed That Night

There were these two poets and they used to go every year to the winter fair in Kenmare to buy two cows for the tub. When the deal was done they'd tie the two cows to the lamp post and go into the pub, where they'd spend the day and portion of the night arguing, insulting people they didn't like and exchanging verses. When they'd come out by an' by they wouldn't be cold but the two cows would be perished. When they'd rip the ropes off their horns the cows'd gallop off to get the blood back into circulation.

Now it so happened one year that the poets bought two black cows and when they got out of the light of the town, the night was so dark and the cows so black that the poets couldn't see a splink. There they were with two ash plants running up and down, hether and over, in gaps and out gates after the cows. They could only go by the sound, so when they heard anything they'd draw with the ash plants and were hitting one another as often as not.

They spent the night on the road, up bohereens and into fields, and when it brightened in the morning they were driving two animals before them! Not their own I'm afraid. Two rangy bullocks belonging to some farmer in the Roughty Valley. By the time they had the bullocks restored to their rightful owners, by the time they had gone around to all the schools and made public the fact that the cows had strayed, and by the time they had found them they swore they would never again get into such a mix-up of an adventure if they could at all avoid it.

Time moved on and the winter fair in Kenmare came round again, and neighbours were surprised to see the two poets late at night in a public house and they *maith go leor*!

'It is none of our business,' the neighbours remarked among themselves, remembering the fools the poets made of themselves in the dark the year before. 'Yerra, let 'em at it!'

Drink or no drink you couldn't be ikey enough for poets. They got an inkling they were being talked about so one of 'em got up and sang:

We don't give a *tráithnín* about darkness,
Be it blacker than nature allows.
We're prepared for it this time, my buckos,
We've purchased two handsome white cows.

It snowed that night!

May Morning

I often heard it said that on May morning before the sun would rise people used to go out to the wood and bring in branches of greenery, hazel, holly, elder and rowan, and they'd come chanting through the fields:

> *Samhradh, samhradh, bainne na ngamhna,*
> *Thugamair féin an samhradh linn!*
> *Thugamair linn é is cé bhainfeadh dínn é,*
> *Is thugamair féin an samhradh linn!*
> (Summer, summer, milk for the calves/we brought the summer with us/we brought it with us and who'd take it from us/we brought the summer with us.)

They'd bring the green branches into the house, hanging a big one maybe on the outside of the door, and then when the rising sun'd light up the kitchen they'd greet the summer with:

> Come sit you down on a chair of silver,
> Come sit you down on a chair of gold!
> You are welcome, my brother with us to linger,
> It is long since we saw you and we are tired
> > of the cold!

If people were seen doing that now, they'd be committed, we have got so Anglicised!

We used love to be sent out that morning to pick flowers for the May altar. You'd see the young calves calling for their breakfast. They'd give only a small bellow first so as to let people know they were in the receiving line. Then if no notice was taken of that, they'd increase the volume until you could hardly hear the hens clucking, the cock crowing or the dogs barking turning home the cows from the *macha*! Looking over a ditch that morning you might see a hare sitting in a field, and even though you ducked down, he'd have a sort of notion you were watching him, and rising on his haunches and craning his neck he'd take stock of his situation. No need to turn his head, for he can see behind as well as before, and his hearing is so acute that at the breaking of a withered kippen he's off like the *sí gaoithe*. Like Balor of the Evil Eye the hare is often connected with the superstitions of May morning.

There was a certain man and even though he had a big bane of cows he had nothing worthwhile in his churn. He couldn't make out what neighbour was doing the damage until he was told to watch his herd on May morning before the sun would rise. He rode down at break of day, a couple of dogs at his heels, and concealed himself. Nothing unusual, only that he had a bit of trouble keeping the dogs quiet for there was a hare in the *macha* moving around among the cattle, and he couldn't believe his eyes when he saw the hare sit down on his little corrighiob and milk a cow!

He let the dogs go and galloped after 'em. Talk of a chase and many is the turn the dogs knocked out of that hare. One of 'em got so close to the hare he took a piece out of his shank. Even so they lost the hare but they didn't lose the scent for it brought 'em to the front door of a house. The man got off the horse and looked in the window and there was an old woman inside and she bandaging her leg where the dog had taken a skelp out of it! The Lord save us!

She had to be read over. I forget what priest was there at the time, but they said when he went into the house smoke was seen coming out of it. I can tell you the Latin cured her and the man's profit came back to him and he had no trouble making his churn after.

Butter-making, like everything else connected with farming, was a risky operation, and you could never be sure that it was going to turn out right until the cream would crack and looking down you saw a fine lump of gold sitting in the bottom of the churn. The churn was made once a week and anyone passing by was expected to pause, bless the work and lend a hand to show that there was no ill-will. In other words put the size of his head in the churn, for that was the amount of profit he could take with him if he didn't give a hand.

You couldn't take fire out of a house on May morning. And another time you couldn't take fire out was during the churning. There was a grand-uncle of mine, often I heard it, and he was going the road east to Knocknagree and he came to a place where they were making the churn. Well, how was he to know that! He went into the house to light his pipe – he had no matches. As he was going out the door the son of the house came before him and wanted to take the pipe out of his mouth and spill the reddened tobaccy on the floor. Now my grand-uncle might have to walk two miles before he'd get another pipeful so he hit the son a clatter and knocked him against the dresser. Then the father came with the tongs, and as true as heaven he'd have opened my grand-uncle with it only at that very minute the woman of the house came out of the dairy and clapping her hands she said, 'The churn is made!'

So full of apologies they let my grand-uncle go.

As far as we know dairy farming was ever the way of living in this barony, and the return from the sale of home-made butter was the principle income of the people in those days, so if anything went wrong with the cattle they were in a bad way. There were no vets or department help or advice when animals got sick. There was no one to turn to but the cow doctor, a man born with the 'gift', the likes of Johnny Con. And another thing, you see, there was a wide-spread belief in remote places that disease was a result of some evil influence, and one way to get rid of it was to give it to someone else! So that if a man's cows slung and continued to sling, to be clear of the misfortune that man might go at dead of night and bury the lost calf or the cow's 'cleaning' in the neighbour's land!

Was it any wonder that people, frightened by the paganism of bad neighbours, used to resort to driving their cattle between bonfires on Saint John's Eve, and was it any wonder that they had to shake holy water on the young crops during days of rogation. One man described that to me as Christian paganism.

Archdeacon Godfrey went a long way towards ridding our parish of such superstitions. Before he came no man would cut his hair on Monday. There was no luck in Monday's work, and the old people'd go out of their minds if they saw you throwing the hair cut off your head into the fire. Every rib of it had to be gathered up and put outside in a hole in the ditch to await the resurrection. Don't you think but there will be some hairy old lads knocking around that day!

Archdeacon Godfrey was death down on the *piseóg*. No incantations or spells, supernatural observances, *dúirt sé dáirt sé* or pagan *cogar mogar* as far as he was concerned. You'd have to tell it in confession if you turned back from a journey because you met a redheaded woman on the road, or if you made a *snaidhm na péiste* over a cow with a colic, or if you passed a child under a donkey's belly as you recited the Lord's prayer, and then put him sitting on the cross on the ass's back to cure him of whooping cough! When the archdeacon heard of such carry-on he used to say, 'Why are we sending missionaries to the swamps of New Guinea when paganism is rampant at home?'

And it was! Not in our part of the country where the people were a little more enlightened. But this way to the north of me towards the Shannon evil abounded! Usedn't they put eggs in hay! It seems you could do great damage with a *glugger*! I heard from a man's very own lips. Twelve winds of hay they had, he said, and when they drew the hay into the shed, they found two eggs three feet down from the top in every wind. He said his father nearly went out of his nut. They made a fire in the haggard and they boiled the eggs, and he said it was the devil to boil 'em. Then he said they perforated the eggs, steeped 'em in paraffin oil, burned 'em and buried the ashes. It was all to no avail. Everything went wrong that year. The cows slung, the cock got the croup and a litter of bonavs they had never grew! They drove black hair out through 'em as long as your finger. They were more like badgers than bonavs. The little pigs began to bark and turned very vicious until they had to be destroyed. I tell you the egg is something of a mystery!

But to go back to Johnny Con. He was in great demand when I was young for curing people and animals. He was said to be the seventh son of a seventh son, born on Good Friday and baptised on Easter Sunday, so where would it go from him?

'How would you stop a cut bleeding, doctor?' says the archdeacon to him with *searbhas* the morning of a station.

'I'd put a cobweb to it,' says Johnny.

'And what, might I enquire, are the curative properties of the cobweb?' says the archdeacon.

'Isn't it well known, Father,' says Johnny, 'that the spider was ever highly thought of. Didn't he spin a web around the manger so that Herod's soldiers couldn't get into our Lord when he was small!'

Johnny had an answer for everything. Although the Holy Ghost didn't descend on him until fairly late – he was shaving before he was confirmed! And the bishop, questioning the confirmation class, couldn't help noticing the size and the rakish appearance of Johnny, so he asked him did he know what was forbidden by the ninth commandment. Johnny said he did. The bishop was doubtful so putting it in very plain language he said, 'Would it be all right for you now to make love to your neighbour's wife?'

'*T'anam* on *diabhal*, my Lord,' says Johnny. 'Why would I do a terrible thing like that and the country full of young, lovely   girls!'

But what made Johnny the talk of the parish was one Sunday during a sermon on company-keeping. The archdeacon was very vexed, and when he came to the part about the young couples going up the lonely bohereens, he raised his voice to a shout and a young girl that was leaning over the gallery fell down, only, mercy of God, to be caught by the legs by her aunts above, but they weren't quick enough. Her clothes fell down over the girl's head. A gasp went up from the congregation, and the archdeacon looking at the people said, 'Any man who turns his head and gazes at this woman in her nakedness will be struck blind!'

And Johnny, covering the left side of his face, said, 'I'll chance one eye!'

Daniel O'Connell
and the Colonel from Battersea

That was one story about Johnny, but a story he used to tell himself was in great demand when weather was bad and people were down-and-out.

The Cork butter market, in its heyday, was the biggest in the world and it was said to grease the axel of the entire British army. You'd go up Shandon Street to it. It was like a beehive, well a *cruiceog* for it was round, with all the activity of buying and sampling and weighing and grading and testing. There was a man then with a fake-ah like an auger which he'd drive into the firkin and when he pulled it up, he had a cross section of what was inside. He'd run it across his nose tasting it with his tongue – what a job to have! – to see if it was all of equal quality and that there was nothing rancid at the bottom, and you were paid according to his pronouncement. The butter market made Cork, gave plenty of work and made the merchants rich. And one of those merchants went up for election one time; the opposition said he wouldn't get in, but his followers said he would,

'For,' says they, 'we'll graze his arse with butter and we'll skeet him to the top of the poll!'

It wasn't a landslide but he slipped in!

Butter was going to Cork from every corner of Munster on horseback long before the roads were made. Squads of men would set out from as far south as Cahirciveen, and one horse would be loaded down with food for the journey. Later on when the coach roads were developed the car-men came. They were a hardy breed of lads, and my own great-grandfather was one. And they'd take as much as a horse and cart could carry of butter to the city and they'd bring back goods to be sold in the local shops when they were coming.

All that long journey could not be done in a day, so the butter men had special houses, in places like Carriganime, where horses and men could rest the night. These were houses where stories of the past and the present were exchanged, and every man would bring home a headful of news about the heroes of the day.

Daniel O'Connell was over in London at the time and he was staying in this hotel called the Royal Victoria. He was having his dinner one day surrounded by a lot of rich people. They didn't think very highly of Dan, for it was well known that Daniel O'Connell was on the side of the poor. Wasn't it the poor people that put him into parliament the first day. And another thing, at the time Dan used to defend people in court that broke the English law, and because of that, I can tell you, he had very few friends in the city of London. During the course of the meal Dan, maybe he had a sup in, had occasion to go out the back. And while he was outside what did this fellow that was sitting alongside him do but spill the contents of a packet of white powder into Daniel O'Connell's cup! The servant girl was there and spotted it, and when Daniel O'Connell came back she said:

'A Dhónail Uí Chonaill,
A dtuigeann tú Gaoluinn?'
'Tuigim go maith,' duirt sé,
'A chailín ó Éirinn.'
Agus ar sise, 'Tá nimh id chupán a leagadh na céadta!'
'Más fíor san, a chailín,' duirt sé, 'is mór é do spré-sa!'

('O, Daniel O'Connell/do you understand Irish?'/
'I do, and well,' he said,/'O, girl from Ireland.'/And
she said, 'There's (enough) poison in your cup to
stretch hundreds.'/'If that's true,' said he, 'your
dowry will be great.')

And she told him then in Irish – Irish is handy abroad –
she told him that she saw this fellow, *seanachornal ó
Bhattersea a bhí ann*, putting white powder into his cup.
With that there was a great commotion outside in the
street, shouting and cheering. Queen Victoria that was
passing down, so all the quality ran over to look out the
window. When there was no one watching him what did
Daniel O'Connell do but exchange the cups so when this
old lad from Battersea came back he took the cup with the
poison in it and drank it down. He died on the spot!
Thanks be to God that Dan came safe out of it. Daniel
O'Connell wiped his mouth and wrote out a cheque for the
servant girl. He went out then taking the air for himself.
He was going along when this *gioghlachán* came after him
jeering him and singing a disparaging *rócán:*

A Dhónail Uí Chonaill MP mar eadh!
Taoi i bhfad ó do mhuintir san áit seo.
Téir ar ais go hUíbh Ráthach,
Dos na prátaí is bláthach,
Is fág an áit seo do na huaisle!
(O Daniel O'Connell MP/you're a long way from
your people in this place/go back to Ivearagh/to
the spuds and the buttermilk/ and leave this place
to the nobles.)

Daniel O'Connell eyed the singer and enquired,

'*An Ciarraíoch tusa?*'

'*Ó sea,*' he said.

'*Duine de mhuintir Coffey?*' says Dan. The Coffeys were of the travelling class.

'*Ó sea,*' he said. '*Is mise Dydeo.*'

('Are you a Kerryman?'/ 'I am,' he said./ 'One of the Coffey's?' says Dan./ 'Yes,' says he, 'I'm Dydeo!')

'I know your clann very well,' says Dan. 'I know ye all. Often I saw ye on the road from Castleisland down to Cahirciveen. Tell me this, Dydeo. Who put you up to sing that piece of *ráiméis* for me?'

''Twas the owner of that hotel over there, the Royal Victoria. "Sing anything you have handy in Irish for Daniel O'Connell," says he, "and you'll get money from him!"'

'Oh, you'll get money all right,' says Dan, 'but it won't all come from me! Come over here!'

And he brought Dydeo into a barber's shop where he got the man to give him a good clip and a shave and to powder him up. Then he took Dydeo into a haberdashery – 'Formal Wear' was written over the door – where Daniel O'Connell fitted Dydeo from the skin out in what was the height of fashion at the time. A tall silk hat, a cravat, a cutaway coat, patent leather shoes and when he came out carrying a walking cane and wearing a 'glass eye' Dydeo looked a real gentleman!

Then Daniel O'Connell says to him, 'There's a fistful of money for you now, and go back, down to the hotel, find the owner and rent a room from him for the space of a week. Be sure to bring me back a document signed by the owner to show that all is legal. And come here,' says Dan to Dydeo, tutoring him up and showing him how to walk with a nice measured pace. 'Be very careful of your speech. Don't open your mouth over-big when you're talking and keep the tone a little bit down out of your head! Say you are from Siam and that your wives are coming this evening!'

Aren't they broad-minded in London! Imagine bringing a squad of wives into a hotel in Tralee.

Off with Dydeo, and do you know, when you're in the right clothes it is easy enough to fool people. Dydeo came back in no time with the document signed and the room ready for occupation. Dan ran his eye over the paper.

'That's fine,' he said. 'Keep it safe. Where's the rest of the clann? I don't see them around.'

'There's only the one place they'd be now,' says Dydeo, 'and that's above in Dirty Dick's in Cricklewood.'

'Off with you up so,' says Dan, 'and get all your friends, men, women and children to come down to the hotel and take over that room you are entitled to.'

Away with Dydeo up to Cricklewood and when he went into the public house above of course he thought no one would know him in the fine clothes. *Mo léir,* when he walked in the door they all stood up and burst out laughing.

'Come out from under the hat,' they said, 'we know your legs.'

He told them of the plan and they collected up the pots and pans, the canteens and the tin, the clippers and the timber hammers, and men, women and children came down in a body, down to the hotel. They went in the door and up the stairs and into the room, and they weren't a second inside when they began clouting tin, and the like of it for a *clismirt* was never heard before or since in the city of London.

The quality were having their dinner downstairs and the noise knocked such a start out of them that the food went down the wrong passage. The owner ran up the steps when he heard the cliotar, and when he beheld the state of the room and saw what was happening inside, he rushed over to the window and called a squad of police that was passing outside. Now, it was a man called Sullivan, one of the black Sullivans from between Listry and Lisaphooka, that was over the police in London at the time. The minute he walked into the room and saw the Coffeys he knew who he had, and going over to Dydeo he said to him in a very threatening tone, 'You'll g'out of it!'

'I wo' not,' said Dydeo, 'g'out of it!'

And Sullivan shoving his jaw into Dydeo's face said to him again, 'You'll g'out of it now!'

'I wo' not,' Dydeo told him, 'g'out of it now or any other time. I've this room rented for a week, as I have a contract to make saucepans for the British army. Take a look at that paper,' giving the agreement signed by the owner to Sullivan. The policeman ran his eye down the paper and as he read it his face fell. Then turning to the owner he said, 'This document is pure legal. They can't be evacuated for a week!'

The owner went into a reel and began kicking the wall with the dint of bad temper.

'I'll be ruined,' he said, 'by that time. The quality are moving out already!'

'Well,' says Sullivan, a man well up in the matter of bribery, 'if you want the custom of your lords and ladies gay you know what to do,' and he winked at him and gave him the nod, so the owner drew Dydeo aside and asked him would he evacuate for a consideration and Dydeo answered that that depended on the size of the consideration! The bargaining began and they went from a pound to two pounds to four pounds and Dydeo and the clann didn't put a foot outside the door until everyone got a fistful of notes. Then they gathered up the pots and the pans, the canteens and the tin, the clippers and the timber hammers and went down the stairs and out into the street. There was Daniel O'Connell outside on the flags waiting for them and a big *clab* on him laughing!

Dydeo looked at the money and then at the heavens saying, 'God direct us where will we go, Cricklewood or Castleisland?'

'There's a better kick,' says Dan, 'off the stuff in Castleisland.'

The Biddy Boys

There was another custom at the time called going out in the biddy! We young people used to go in parties from house to house on St Bridget's Eve collecting money, and in return we'd sing and dance in the kitchens. With the proceeds we used to buy shop bread and jam, and if we could rise to it a half-tierce of porter for an all-night dance which would be held before Lent began.

All the fun was in the dressing up for the biddy and we went to great extremes to conceal our identity. Women used to dress up as men, and many is the sedate old farmer, sitting in a neighbour's kitchen, spotted his Sunday suit dancing around in a set. His daughter Mary that'd have it on! She'd hear about it after. A very forward young lady might get into her father's long johns, and if there were a few family heirlooms like a cutaway coat and a caroline hat to go with it she would look something going around in the hornpipe figure of the set dance.

A lot of straw was used in the disguise. You'd see biddy boys in straw capes and straw puttees, and back around Beaufort they had specially made mitre-shaped straw hats to wear over the capes and puttees. When they'd burst into a house on Bridget's Eve you'd swear they came up out of *Lois an Phúca*!

We used to wear high fiddles – hallowe'en masks which were coming into the shops at the time – or we'd cover our faces with the screen off the window.

You could see out and breath in through this lacy fabric, and the alteration it made to the physiognomy was truly remarkable.

Every party had a *brídeog*. There is some doubt as to who this effigy was supposed to represent. We thought it was St Bridget and the priest thought it was St Bridget, but then again you'll hear another person say that the custom of lugging the *brídeog* around was in the world long before St Bridget saw the light of day.

To make a *brídeog* you'd put straw around the handle of a brush bulging it out below and above. Doll it up then with a skirt and a blouse, and with a carved turnip for the face set in a head shawl and fixed to the top of the handle. What would give a damn nice effect would be to scoop out the inside of the turnip and put the butt of a lighting candle into it. Every party going along would have a musical instrument, or maybe two, but if they couldn't rise to that they'd dyddle or they'd play on the comb.

When we came to a house, and if we were admitted, we'd take over the kitchen. The person with the biddy – the *brídeog* – would stand by the fireplace, the musicians by the dresser and the rest would crowd on to the floor. As the music struck up we'd take a partner saying, 'Come on, shake a leg!'

Mhuire Mháithair, the pounding the flagged floor'd get, and if any pots or saucepans came in the way they went flying under the settle. When the set was over, order would be called for a step dance or a song. Then the biddy boy would collect whatever money the household was inclined to give. Not a great lot, but by setting out at nightfall and covering a fair bit of ground we'd get a good few bob together for the ball night.

Local people who became a bit enlightened, or should I say Anglicised, were always ashamed of those customs, and the clergy considered the *brídeog* a mockery, an insult to St Bridget. They discouraged the practice and put an end to the porter nights. And the young people had only themselves to blame for that for those biddy balls, as they were known, were often held in houses without proper supervision. As a man said to me, 'With all the drink and everything, Ned, the thing could develop into an orgy.'

And he was right, partly right anyway, for you had fellows there half-plastered and couples *mouzing* up along the stairs, in the room and in the linny! Then you'd have a modicum of men who can't get women and they'd be up to some other devilment. They might go out and tie the door from the outside, put a coarse bag over the chimney, and as the house filled with smoke shove red pepper under the door. Pendemonium would follow, sneezing, coughing, cursing, swearing and as the music came to a halt the stairs would become alive, and the room and the linny, for as we all know there is no vexation in the world to equal that of men interrupted in love-making. They would swear vengeance on those responsible and by shoving a small fellow out through the window to untie the door, they'd rush out and it would be open war with the crowd outside. And I remember one night one section took cover behind the rick of turf and the opposing party behind a pit of turnips. Sods and swedes came flying through the air. It was like Dunkirk, which gave Archdeacon Godfrey any God's amount of ammunition for the following Sunday's sermon. As if the man hadn't enough to contend with already!

Mary O'Shea's Story

Every year in the springtime a woman used to come to our house to give my mother a hand cutting the *siolláns*. A worn table knife she'd use with a rag around the handle to give it a nice comfortable grip. And whatever knack she had she'd knock as many *siolláns* out of a twenty-stone bag of spuds as another woman wouldn't knock out of a buttful.

Myself and the other small lads in the family had the job of keeping the *cliabh* at her left hand side full of potatoes, and then to draw away the *siolláns* and the *sceamhacháns* as they came from the knife. A *siollán* is a wedge of potato having at least one good eye from which the young plant will grow, and a *sceamhachán* is what's left of the spud when the *siolláns* are cut from it. There'd be a box of lime handy and we'd have to put a shake of that on the *siolláns* to keep them from bleeding. Another job we had was to keep the different varieties apart. You had a fair share of varieties in those days, some of which you wouldn't hear of at all now. You had the 'Puritan', an airly, the 'Champion', the 'White Rock', the 'Up-to-date', semi-airlies, the 'Irish Queen', the 'May Queen', the 'Epicure', the 'Flounder' and the 'Blue Ball'.

But to get back to my story, the woman's name was Norrie. A tidy, compact little *dailc* of a woman, fresh for her age, well dressed, no finery and with a very correct form of speech, if she found herself in the right company, keeping the words a degree or two down in the throat to give the effect of politeness, but when she was cutting *siolláns* she spoke like the rest of us.

She was a good hand to put a face on any story she heard in her travels. When the tea'd be wet by and by, operations would come to a halt, and as often as not the conversation between Norrie and my mother'd turn to whatever those subjects are that women don't consider suitable for broadcasting. Norrie's eye would roll in our direction and my mother would tell us to, 'Go out there and see is the cow in the cabbage and don't be watching every word that comes out of our mouths!'

Small and all as we were we wouldn't be natural if this order didn't make us all the more eager to know what was being said. So by diving under the settle or running above the room door we'd often hear what wasn't meant for pen or paper. And I remember the same as if it was yesterday Norrie saying to my mother on one occasion, '*Cogar i leith chugham, a stór*, and I'll tell you something that'll put the cap entirely on what you were hinting to me a while ago. We went to Wether's Well one time, we used to go there paying rounds when my husband got the rheumatics. We used to go to Lady's Well in Ballyheigue too but he found Wether's Well more beneficial. We used to stay with a man whose name I forget, I think he was from Clare and his job was giving out the back milk in the creamery. He was married to a local woman, as big a talker as himself, and when there'd be a crowd in the night of the rounds the place'd be like a university.

One night the talk turned to *piseógs* and the capacity certain people had in the old days for doing evil. According to the man's wife there were two women and they had a fight. Neighbouring women can fall out over many a thing. Fowl trespassing, geese and ducks wandering, it is easy enough to put a match to the powder where this type of livestock is concerned, and the fight developed into a black feud. Now, one of the women was expecting an increase in the family. Her time came but if it did nothing happened. She went here and she went there but doctors couldn't do anything for her. Don't you think but hadn't she a nice story of it!

'At that time there were very knowledgeable individuals going from place to place. They were known as the Connacht women. One of them bowled the way and she hadn't her leg inside the door when the woman of the house gave her a full account of her trouble.

'"And it baffled the world," she said to the Connacht woman, "for it should be here long 'go whatever is keeping it."

'"Tell me," says the Connacht woman, 'have you an enemy?"

'"I have," she said. "Myself and my neighbour are no friends."

'"I'll go into her now," says the Connacht woman, "and she will ask me if I have any news."

'"I'll give you money if you can do anything for me," says the woman who was expecting.

'"I won't take any money from you," the Connacht woman said. "Not for a while anyway."

'She went to the neighhour's house not pretending a bit and the neighbour's first question was, "Have you any news?"

'"I haven't then," the Connacht woman said. "I haven't any news, only that I was into this house over and there is a fine baby there after the night."

'"Are you telling me the truth?" says the neighbour turning very tetchy.

'"I am, eroo," says the Connacht woman. "They have a great time over. They'd give me whiskey if I'd drink it but I didn't. A big belter of a baby that's there, God bless it."

'The neighbour's face went every colour and going up under

the chimney she brought down a *leithéide*, like some sort of effigy with a shawl around it.

"'*T'anam 'on riach*," says she. "What did I want this thing above here for if what you say is true. No child could be born to her while that was up the chimney. Bad luck to it, I mustn't have put the right spell on it!"

'And she took the rag doll and threw it into the fire, Well, it blazed up like carbide and when the last shred of it was burned the child was born to the woman over! And a fine boy he was too, with his front teeth up and down to him.'

There was a knot out of one of the boards of the room door. I put my eye to the hole to see how my mother was taking it. I think she believed every word of it, for lifting her eyes to heaven she said to Norrie, 'Isn't there an awful lot of badness in the world!'

And of course there is too!

The Archdeacon,
His Clerk and His Curate

The old people held that you should talk about a priest for only as long as you could hold your finger in the fire.

In Victorian times Archdeacon Godfrey would never lift his eyes from his book if you met him on the road. He was a fine block of a man and never wore an overcoat or had a fire in his room, and signs on it, he lived to be nearly ninety years of age. He was an arch-Tory and so well in with the powers that be in London at the time that he could save a man from the gallows if he wanted to. He thought the sun, moon and stars shone out of the royal family, and no Sunday would pass that some time wasn't given over to praying for one of the crowned heads of Europe. He was kept busy, for at that time, kings were so plentiful you could hardly throw out the feet water at night without wetting one of them.

Archdeacon Godfrey was a cut above the commonality, coming as he did from big people. You'd nearly want a permit to talk to him, and when he came to the stations he'd always have his breakfast on his own in the parlour. Even the curate wouldn't venture down, and if he did the archdeacon wouldn't throw a word to him. No one was allowed down only his retriever. He was as standoffish as his master. If you looked at the dog he'd turn his head and look at the ceiling. He sat there by the table waiting for the occasional morsel which the archdeacon dropped into his open mouth.

The archdeacon wore a full beard, a tall silk hat and a

swallow-tail coat with two buttons at the back as big as the cover of a teapot. And sitting up on the wing of the sidecar going into town with a watch chain glistening across his middle, if he didn't look the picture of grandeur call me Davey! Patey Barry, the parish clerk that used to drive the archdeacon, Patey would take a drink when he was out, but he wouldn't go too far seeing the responsible position he had. One day in town he ran into a wedding party from Gortamikeerie. Barry's mother was from there, and the Gortamikeeries brought him into Washout's and treated him to plenty of porter. When he came out he was staving, legless; he was so full that if he leant sideways, he'd spill!

He made his way to the courthouse where he had left the sidecar with the horse tied to the railings. The archdeacon was there before him, his wing of the sidecar down and he sitting up reading his breviary. He never turned his head, being a bit sulky at the delay he had waiting for the parish clerk. Patey Barry ripped the horse and leaving down his wing of the sidecar sat up and drove away. Everything went fine and when they came to the bottom of the Pike Hill the horse slowed down to a walk going against the rising ground. Then with the nice even sway of the sidecar, and the fumes of the drink rising to his brain, Barry nodded off thinking of his mother's people, and the horse, when there was no one urging him on, his pace got slower and slower, and his head sank lower and lower; even the archdeacon nodded a little bit as his eyes got weary of reading the holy scripture.

Up the hill they went like that until they got to the top and then Barry woke up, and noticing the slow pace of the horse he did a thing no human being should do, he drew a lash of the whip. And the horse in dreamland, and not expecting it, made one bounce forward so that Archdeacon Godfrey was catapulted off the wing of the sidecar and describing what one eye witness called a parabolic curve, landed on his head in the gutter of the dyke. Barry drove on, never missed his passenger, and when he arrived outside the chapel there were people there waiting to go in to early confession, and they wondered what could have happened to their good priest. The next car on the road picked up the archdeacon and when he arrived he was in a ferocious temper and facing over the parish clerk he said, 'Barry, you are drunk!'

Barry looked at the archdeacon's silk hat made into a concertina on top of his head, he looked at the side of the swallow-tail coat caked in mud and winking at the crowd he said, 'Tis aisy to see who's drunk, Father!'

Of course the archdeacon never touched a sup in his life. Even so, age overtook him and in the end it was the curate was running the parish; and when I was young the people were never done talking about the difference between the two men. The curate was only a couple of weeks in the parish when it got out that he was an easy man in the confessional. His only comment on the most hyronious of misdemeanours was 'Three Hail Marys and say a prayer for me, my child!'

One Saturday night the archdeacon and the curate were hearing . . . their two boxes facing each other across the floor of the chapel. There was a huge crowd for confession the same night, the last chance of making the Easter duty. Three quarters of an hour went by and no one had darkened the door of the archdeacon's box. He got a bit curious and getting to his feet he parted the purple curtains and looked out, and there he saw half the parish around the curate's box. He uttered an 'Ahem,' for attention and said, 'Is there a slope in the floor or what!'

Unlike the archdeacon the curate was never out of the

people's houses, drinking tea and playing cards. Royalty wasn't bothering him. Not at all. He'd be down to the inch every Sunday evening his coat and collar off kicking football. When the men were busy during the week and he had no one to practice with he trained the archdeacon's retriever to bring back the ball to him. In time he built up a great team, and the Sunday they were in the final, that's the Sunday you'd have a short Mass! He'd scorch through the Latin, no sermon, only a tight warning to the congregation to be sure and be down at the field. This message would be given when he had rattled off the announcements. Then picking up a sheet of paper from the corner of the altar the dead would be prayed for in a hurry, 'Your prayers are requested for the repose of the souls of Hannah Finn, Johnny Deegan, Jimmy Connolly and Lizzie Horgan whose anniversaries occur at this time.'

Then as he rolled the sheet of paper into a ball he would continue, 'May their souls and the souls of all the faithful departed rest in peace!'

And as he came to the final word, he'd toss up the piece of paper and meeting it with a flying kick put it out between the two pillars of the gallery!

The King of the Lies

The three sure things that show a man is falling into old age are: one, a fondness for money, two forgetfulness . . . and I forget now what the third one is! Oh, yes, itchiness.

> Where I slept last night
> There was commotion there.
> With ducks and geese
> And a gander there.
> The yella drop down
> It fell on my crown,
> And I slept ne'r a wink
> With the fleas, my boy.

They've no fleas now in Sweden! A professor there is mad looking to lay his hands on a few. He wants them for some experiment. But who'll admit they have them? No one! A Gortnabrochus woman said to a Raynasup woman one day, 'You'll always know those with fleas. Fleas always follow people with big mouths!' And the Raynasup woman making her mouth into a little roundy 'O' said, 'Is that so!'

The first fine day in spring, my grandmother'd carry the bedclothes out in the yard and spread them abroad on the hedge, and there she'd be belting the feather tick with the stave of a barrel, and dust flying out of it! This day a tramp was passing and seeing her flaking the tick, 'The right way to get rid of 'em!' says he.

My grandmother was mortified. A very respectable

woman, one of the Buckleys of Glounacoppel that always wore a dandy cap. To think that she'd have the like! So the tramp seeing her blushing said, 'You needn't be one sign ashamed, Ma'am, the queen of England have 'em!'

It was said Queen Victoria was peppering in dread of fleas, so she must know they were there. When she visited Killarney in 1884, Lord Kenmare's gamekeeper had to sit on his *grug* outside her room door, at the ready in case of an attack! The Killarney fleas were outrageous. They could hop as high as the cathedral and bred with such rapidity that every little crab-jaw of them coming into the world was a grandfather inside of twenty-four hours.

The Swedish professor'd be in his element that time for the world was full of fleas. Two hundred years ago Dublin had a very vicious brand of them. They came in in the turf from the Bog of Allen. Oh, they were a terror altogether. Worse than the flying fleas of Italy that bit Peter Shea to death on his way home from Rome after getting forgiveness for striking his father! A man told me that the Dublin fleas were the cause of the Act of Union, for the members of the Old Irish Parliament, who were a bit classy in themselves, refused to sit in the chamber, for he said they couldn't sit in the chamber, always on the move, so no motion could be carried. 'Twas worse than the entertainment house in Cork they used to call 'Lourdes', because if you went in a cripple you came out 'walking'!

A fox one time was 'walking', so what did he do? He put a ball of wool in his mouth and sunk his tail into the lake. Bit by bit, ever so gradual so as not to create a panic. Then as it became dampish and uncomfortable for them, the passengers moved up in the bus. And the fox, taking his time, let his tailboard into the lake, *diaidh ar ndiaidh síos le fánaigh* until the water was up to his ears, and when he was full sure and certain the fleas had collected into the wool in his mouth he let the ball go and diving down he said, 'If that ship'll sink it won't be for the want of a crew!'

My uncle's father-in-law, a mine of information, told me he was one day out fowling. A muzzle loader he had. 'And after tamping down the powder,' he said, 'I forgot to take the ramrod out of it! I fired at a batch of geese, and they must be flying one over the other in formation, for the ramrod went up through three of 'em. They fell down and spiked a salmon that was rising for a fly – the surprise he got! I waded into the river and when I was backing out with my three geese and my salmon, damnit if I didn't trip and fall down on a hare that was passing and killed him!'

That is if you could believe him!

There was a king one time in the eastern world and he had no family only one daughter, as fine a girl as ever looked out on air or land. The king himself was falling into years and the way he'd like to pass the time was listening to stories – the bigger the lie, the better he liked it, and the nickname for him was, 'The King of the Lies'! In time he got tired of his own storytellers as the lies they told him brought him no comfort, so he let it be known far and wide that he would give his daughter in marriage and half of his kingdom to any young man that could tell him a story so outlandish and tell it so well that it would make the king forget himself and say, 'You're a liar. That never happened!'

At that time there was a widow woman living in Ireland and she had a son whose name was Timmy. A fine boy! If he had any fault at all it was that he was a liar, but a gracious liar for he spoke like a bishop. Timmy heard of the king's pronouncement so he said to his mother, 'I suppose I'll have to get married sometime so I might as well marry where money is. Throw a few things together for me I'm going on a journey.'

So she washed his shirt, baked a cake and killed a cock and he hit the road a *welt* for the eastern world, and going up he knocked at the door, and the king came out. 'What brought you?' the king said.

'My two legs,' says Timmy, 'that won't take me to the grave!'

'Come on away in!' the king said, and he put Timmy sitting that way by the side of the fire and the king sat here. The king's wife was there at the table preparing the dinner and the king said to her, 'There should be a couple o' bottles of stout below there in the room. Throw us up a one!'

She brought up two. The king took the caps off them, and handed one to Timmy. They had a few slugs out of them, and looking then towards the table where the wife was working, the king said, 'I'll bet you anything now you never saw turnips as big as them in all your life before!'

'I didn't too,' says Timmy, 'my mother had turnips sat in Páirc na bPoll last year and do you know how big they were? Well, we had a young sow, she was a while back after being with the gentleman, and she went astray. High up or low down, we couldn't find her. What was it, you *diggle*, but she broke into the garden and ate her way into a turnip and that turnip was so enormous that she had a litter of *banbhs* inside in it. The *banbhs* were six weeks old and fit for the market before she tunnelled her way out the other side!'

The king finished the bottle of stout and put in on the hob.

'Come on away out here!' he said. And he brought Timmy

out in the haggard. 'I'll bet you now,' says he, 'you never saw so many beehives in the one place before!'

'I didn't so,' says Timmy, 'we have a hive for every day in the year. And it is my job to stand at the gate of the haggard every morning and count the bees going out, and be there again in the evening to count 'em coming home in case any one of 'em be dodging the column. One evening I was a bee short! I went looking for her, and made off the hill behind the house where I had a good view of the countryside. There was a horse there and I jumped on his back, that lifted me another few feet, and looking around me what should I see away over from me at the edge of Merry's Wood but my bee. I galloped down on the horse and there was the bee so full of honey that she couldn't lift a wing.

With my penknife, I cut a whole lot of sally rods to make two baskets – you know like *sráthar fhadas* – and filled 'em up with honey, not a bad day's work for a bee! When I loaded the honey on to the horse, a big hollow came in his back from the weight, and when I clapped the bee down between the two baskets, if the horse's back didn't break! I caught a long spar that was there and I said to the horse, 'Open your mouth!' and I ran the spar back through him and out behind to reinforce the backbone. I took him by the head then and brought him up to the house. We had so much honey that year we were giving it to the pigs!'

'Come on away down here,' says the king and he opened the gate into the orchard and looked at a lofty cherry tree, you'd know he was very proud of it. 'I'll bet you now,' says the king, 'you never saw a tree as tall as that before.'

'I didn't so,' says Timmy. 'There's a cherry tree growing in my mother's orchard at home with branches reaching up into the clouds, and that tree is so tall isn't it up through the middle of it I go to heaven to Mass every Sunday for we're living a bit away for the chapel. Well, I was this Sunday above in heaven and a storm broke and knocked the cherry tree. Wasn't that a nice pucker to be in. When I was walking around heaven after the breakfast in the morning, I saw three women winnowing oats and I said to myself, "Wherever there's grain, there's straw". I got a couple of loads of it, and began to make a *súgán* rope and as I twisted it I added to it and let it fall down from me until I thought it was long enough to go to the ground, then I hitched my own end of it to the gate of heaven and down with me hand under hand. Well the view I had, and everything went fine until the *súgán* broke and looking down, I saw that I had another good mile to go before I'd settle. With great presence of mind, I took an apple out of my pocket and threw it down our chimney. My mother ran out opening her apron and I fell into it, but whatever rotten material was in the apron, I went down through it like a pillaloo through a country, rolled over and fell into the river and sank to the bottom of the pool. When I opened my eyes, there was this big laverick of a salmon passing. I put my hands around him and waltzed him out on the bank. I brought him in home and throwing him that way on the table, I said to my mother, "We'll have a bit of him for the dinner." She opened the salmon and what fell out of his belly but this big book. And there printed in the very first page, was that your father worked for my father for one and fourpence a day with his shoes off on soft ground shaving gooseberries!'

'You're a liar,' says the king, 'that never happened!'

'That's the daughter gone now!' says Timmy.

Timmy married the daughter and got half the kingdom and when he came home here on holidays after, he was so rich, a pound note he'd light the pipe with!

The Jennet

It is often you'll hear the question asked what is the difference between a mule and a jennet. A mule is a cross between a donkey and horse and so is a jennet. In the mule's case, the mare horse is the mother and the gentleman ass is the father, and it is the other way around for the jennet, the horse is the father. Mickeen Callaghan called the offspring of that partnership a 'hybred'. Now those offspring don't breed any more, which is just as well, for there are enough queer things in the world! And people will tell you that it is the lack of breeding in the lives of these hybrids which makes them very vicious. You'd want to take cover when a mule gets going with the hind legs. There is a monument put up to a mule in South Africa – they were in great demand for pulling small cannon in the Boer War. And down on this monument is written in capital letters –

> *This mule kicked fifty privates, thirty corporals, twenty sergeants, ten majors five captains, two generals and one mills bomb* – full stop!

In olden times, a man with a small way of living could carry an extra cow or a few more sheep if, instead of a horse, he kept a mule or a jennet; next to nothing would feed them, they were great workers and would live to be as old as Methuselah's cat.

There was this man, I won't mention his name here now, he was near enough to me, I danced at his wedding. And by the same token it was a love match too, *an rud is annamh is iontach!* The girl he married, Nell Connor, because she carried no fortune in, his sister couldn't go out. Poor thing, she had to go to America after and earn it hard, and the last we heard of her was that she struck up with a Mayo lad, rotten with money, so she was lucky the creature!

But to come back to Nell Connor and the husband. They weren't too long married when they had good news, so he put a cradle making. At that time there'd be no talk of going for doctors, 'twas all home industry. Máire Bhán was the woman around here, the nurse, the *bean chabhair*. It was she was everywhere, and if you didn't have whiskey inside the night she came, you'd hear about it!

On this particular occasion complications arose and Máire Bhán got panicky, which was unusual for her, and said to the husband, 'If I was in your shoes, I'd have Nell anointed!'

In that case what'd happen is that the man'd saddle his horse and ride off to the presbytery and the parish priest or the curate'd hop in the saddle – the clergy were expert horsemen at the time – gallop back to the house and the man'd wait at the presbytery until he returned, which was a very quick operation, except in this case Nell Connor's husband had no horse: 'twas a jennet he had and he'd be there as quick walking on his knees. I suppose he was too proud to ask a neighbour for a horse, but who was visiting at the time but his nephew, a little *garsún* God help him, only about seven or eight years of age. The uncle said to him, 'Here, go on now you're the youngest and the soonest to get married. Run off to the presbytery and tell the parish priest or the curate to come over as quick as they can that Nell is bad!'

The little lad was too shy to refuse and set off through

strange country he had never seen before. He was given the directions. Well, the heart was being put crossways in the poor lad. Big dogs scattering fowl out of the yard when they saw him coming and ferocious boyos of ganders with their necks stretched out before them trying to take a bite out of his *collops* at the corner of every car house – 'twas in the springtime, everyone with his own trouble!

Finally, with the life barely in him, he got to the presbytery and the housekeeper told him that the parish priest was away on a month's mind, and the curate was off on the other side of the hill on a sick call.

'But the minute he'll come,' says she, 'I'll send him back. I know where the house is; and let you be trotting off now and don't let the night overtake you on the road!'

She gave him a cut of buttered bread with sugar sprinkled on top. He ran home as hard ever as he could. He was there before the curate, and going in the yard it was a different atmosphere altogether, everyone talking and laughing. He met the cracked carpenter out against him going to Eugen's with a canteen for porter. When he went in he heard the good news: the child was born – a big beater of a baby boy, and Nell Connor sitting up in the bed drinking tea! And they were saying if the curate came now into this scene of hilarity he'd be vexed, and no wonder, bringing him on a fool's errand. So the uncle says to the garsún, 'Look, as your legs are on the ground run back along the road and tell the curate not to come at all, that everything is all right.'

The youngster turned around, and now it was dark and going between the high hedges, he was seeing all manners of frightening objects – *Spiorad an Tobac* and the spirit of Balnadeega – in the bushes against the sky, and he was half crying to himself as he said, 'If my uncle had only a horse . . . *dá mbeadh capall aig e siúd is istigh cois tine anois a bheinn ag ól té!*'

With that he heard the horse galloping and the curate came flying round the turn. He ran out in the road and putting up his hand he shouted, 'You needn't come at all now, father, everything is all right.'

The curate was relieved, and swinging the horse on his hind legs he was about to go home, when he thought of the baptismal ceremony that'd be there in a few days' time, and maybe a pound or two coming out of it. He decided that it might be polite to make some enquiry, so he said to the young lad, 'What have they?'

And the answer he got was, 'A jennet!'

Spiorad an Tobac

An old woman used to appear at the dead of night, sitting under the eye of a bridge smoking a pipe and she was known as *Spiorad an Tobac*. No one'd go near the place after nightfall, they were so frightened of her, until, because of some big dust-up in the world, tobacco got scarce. The smith was so bad for the want of a smoke – he claimed he was running blind – that he decided to approach *Spiorad an Tobac* for a couple of pulls. After a few *smatháns* of the hard tack to give him courage, he went under the eye of the bridge in the middle of the night. She handed him the pipe and he took a few draws out of it, oh the relief, and handed it back to her, saying, 'May the Lord have mercy on your soul, good woman, and on all the souls that are waiting for a glimpse of the beatific vision!'

She gave him the pipe again and he had another blast out of it and handed it back to her, praying again for her soul, even more fervently this time. She had a few draws herself before she gave it to him again and when he prayed for her a third time, she said, 'That's my purgatory over! I was made to sit here smoking – that was my punishment – until such time as someone would pray three times for my soul. I'm off to heaven,' says she, giving him a nudge and like that, she was gone up!

And it was held that it was that occurrence that gave rise to smoking at wakes! Around here the mourners took a few draws of the pipe to lighten the burden on the soul that was gone. It was at a wake I smoked my first pipeful of tobacco, and it was at the same wake I had my first taste of strong drink. I was only thirteen years of age at the time, and not being accustomed to the pipe the fumes of the tobacco smoke going down into my breadbasket were meeting the fumes of the alcohol coming up to my brain. I got very dizzy and the kitchen began to wheel about me. As I was about to faint someone said, 'Why don't you go out in the fresh air!'

'I will,' I said, 'when the door comes around again!'

Clever Dogs

Well, I was one night at a wake. A wake to my mind was an ideal place for storytelling, for you could suit the story to the occasion and if the man was no great loss, a little hilarity wouldn't be out of place.

A Galvin man that was dead and they were waking him at his sister's. After the visit to the room – the prayers and the condolences, 'I'm sorry for yeer trouble. He wasn't long going in the end!' A man that had been threatening to die since he was confirmed! – I came up then and I found myself with as prime a bunch of heelers as you'd meet in a day's walk sitting below at the butt of the kitchen. Our seat was a board down on the rungs of a ladder resting on two keelers. We were out of view of the room and near the half-tierce that was sitting that way on a side table with a white bucket under the tap.

As well as basins of porter there used be snuff and clay pipes going around that time. As each man or woman accepted one of these offerings he or she intoned a prayer, 'The light of heaven to us all!' or 'The Lord have mercy on his soul!' '*Amen a Thiarna!*' was the usual reply to these prayers. After we had downed the second basin of porter, the conversation turned to clever dogs – you were never caught short for a topic at a wake. There was this man near me on my right. No . . . 'tis on my other side he was. A swarthy individual with a big *mothal* of black hair cocking down all round under his cap. Such a fleece . . . covering his ears. Tufts of hair on his cheek bones like grass on a *turtóg*. A big beard and two enormous bushy eyebrows that you could put fencing cows out of cabbage. Only for the whites of his eyes, you wouldn't know whether it was his face or his poll you were looking at. Sure, the time he was measured for false teeth, when he went back for the fitting, the dentist didn't know where to shove them! He was like a Kerry Blue he was so hairy!

When it came to his turn to talk about man's best friend, he took a slug out of the basin, settled himself and said, 'I had a very clever dog myself and his name was Bun. And I was never fonder of any dog than I was of him. I was one night above in our kitchen and I was telling about Peter Shea. There was a crowd in and my dog, Bun, was sitting there, his head on my knee, opening and closing and rolling his eyes with every twist and turn of the story, giving me as much attention as I would get from a Christian, and a lot more than I would get from some of 'em, for people can allow the mind to wander. And that night I was just at the part in the story where I had Peter Shea coming back from Rome where he went for forgiveness for striking his father and everyone had his ear cocked for I'm coming to the place where he's devoured by the locusts, when, with that, one woman turns to another and in a loud voice says, "Do you hear from Hain?" I can tell you she heard from Bun! I never saw an animal so vexed! The story was ruined on him. He rounded her up and turned her out. He was used to driving sheep out on the mountain!

'That dog was as good as an extra man around the place. One morning I was driving the cattle up to the long inch. I had a little dexter cow, a breed of short-horn cattle first bred in County Kerry, and she was on the point of calving. But you couldn't time her. One year she'd carry three days and another year she'd carry four. I decided that morning I'd drive her up to the inch with the rest of the cattle. I did. I left Bun above in charge. I came down to the house only to find the kitchen full of people – the Toornóineachs, the wife's relations. We were talking and after a while the dog came barking into the yard. I went to the door and here was Bun outside making every motion for me to come on away with him. How could I go and the kitchen full of people? What would the wife say if I went away from the relations?

'I came in and sat down and Bun followed me in and caught me by the leg of the trousers and kept pulling me till he brought me to the door. Then when he saw that I had no notion of going with him the look of disgust that came into that dog's face. In desperation he ran down to the dairy and dipped his tail into a tub of cream and off with him the cream dripping off it. The Toornóineachs when they saw him said, "That dog is out of his mind. He's in the reels."

'We came in from the door and sat down, and for all the world it was exactly the time that Mussolini invaded Abyssinia and De Valeria was over at the League of Nations trying to stop him! Well, in the middle of this discourse I heard the dog barking a second time. I ran out to the door and here was Bun coming along and a lovely little dropped calf sucking his tail and the mother of the calf walking after it.

'Such an intelligent dog. When I'd have him standing to cattle the morning of a fair I'd be lazy to go aside with myself in case he'd have 'em sold when I'd come back. But that isn't all. If I'm out working in the field and I forget my matches I have only to tell Bun go into the house and bring me out a coal of fire. Away he'd go and it is often the wife told me, "If you saw the nice handy way he'd get a hold of the sod, the red portion away from him and walk out the door with it."

'Well, I was one day ploughing the *leaca* and I forgot to get matches the night before at the shop. And I said to Bun, he'd be always lying in the headland when I'd be working, "Go in," I said, "and bring me out a coal of fire."

'He went in and he was a long time away, and it wasn't like him to delay when you'd send him on a message. I went up to the mouth of the *poursheen* to see what was keeping him. And what was it but the wind was blowing towards the house and here was Bun coming, and he backing after his tail to keep the smoke out of his eyes!

'When Bun died my wife said to me, "you ought to be ashamed of yourself, a big *fostúch* of a grown man crying after an old dog!"

'I couldn't help it. You know the way you get attached to an animal, moreover a clever animal like a dog or a horse. Poor Bun! He was killed by a car below there at the turn of the bridge, and before he lost consciousness, with his paw, he scratched out the number of the car in the dust of the road!'

The Woman That Went to Hell

In my father's time, when a young woman was getting married, the other women of around her own age would come to her house one night, bringing with them materials to make a patchwork quilt, and this quilt when it was made was a present for the young wife to bring to her new home.

They had a quilting frame that time on which to stretch the base and cover of the new quilt. Then one clever lady with an eye for design would take a splinter from the fire, let the burnt end cool, and with this draw out the shapes on the cover. Each woman was given a section to work at, and she'd take out the odds and ends of coloured materials cutting them in various shapes according to fancy while the supervising lady moved the pieces around to get a nice balance of colour and so on.

As the women sewed up and down, they'd put a lot of packing between the base and the cover, bits and scraps of worn garments, a piece of an old woollen drawers, anything there was heat in. And when they were finished, some of those quilts were so heavy you'd nearly want to get artificial respiration after coming out from under them.

There would be great jollity among the women as they worked and talked of comical and strange happenings, and talk of courting and talk of love, for it was Shrovetime and matrimony was in the air. You'd hear talk of the man that went to hell for the flail. The journey was made possible by three things which he got from a knowledgeable woman. One was a piece of leather no longer than a haime's strap, which when he'd squeeze on it, would lift him up and take him in whatever direction it was pointed, and so as to be able to withstand the high temperature below, the second thing she gave him was ointment in a round, tin car-grease box. This ointment he was to rub into himself all over, but there was one spot between the shoulder blades which he couldn't reach, so he threw a dollop of it at the wall and rubbed his back to it. The third thing she gave him was a flute which when he'd play it the devils couldn't stop dancing. The only tune he knew was, 'If I Had a Wife that I Didn't Like'. He struck it up as soon ever as he got inside the gate below, and all the devils fell in to knocking sparks out of the flagstones of hell. He took the flail, a miraculous weapon that could do the work of ten men. He brought it home where in time he made a fortune hiring himself out to big farmers threshing oats in the fall of the year.

The night before Dydeo Moriarty got married his wife-to-be came to the house. She wanted him to promise that he'd support her mother as well as herself. Dydeo Moriarty was not a very generous individual but this young woman was the only woman he wanted as a wife, and, even though it went against the grain in him to do it, he made the promise. He lived to regret his promise. Very soon he got sick of the wife's mother. His house wasn't his own; from the time she put her leg inside the door she was ordering and bossing him, and at the table she had as big a stroke as a man that'd be mowing! So he said to the wife that the mother would have to go.

'All right,' the wife said, 'I knew it would come to this. But I can't turn her out now the weather is so cold. I'll make some warm clothes for her and then she can go.'

They agreed to that. At that time you wouldn't walk into the shop and order a rig-out. No. The wife had a few sheep shorn and the wool washed and carded and spun on the old spinning-wheel near the fire, and warped on the warping-frame and the thread taken to the weaver to be woven into cloth. Then the material was brought home and cut and sewn so that an enormous length of time had gone by before the mother was finally togged out.

'Is she going now?' says Dydeo.

'She's going now,' the wife said, 'and I'm going with her!'

'Don't you go at all,' says Dydeo. ''Tis how I couldn't support the two of ye!'

'How could you support a family so?' says the wife, pulling the shawl out over her head, and herself and her mother went off down the road.

'You are well rid of him,' the mother said to the daughter as they went along. 'A *padhsán*. I never liked the *táthaire*.'

They kept going, the two of them, a bite here and a sup there, until after about a week, they struck into a big farmer's house. They stayed the night there and the following morning it was lashing out of the heavens – you wouldn't put out a dog.

'Can't you stay where you are!' the farmer said to the young woman. 'Yourself and your mother. I am short of servants anyway to work in the kitchen.'

So they remained on. The farmer had another big house at the other side of the farm, and from what was known, anyone that spent the night there was found dead in the morning. Because of some evil occurrence there was a curse on the place. The farmer didn't let on about this but he asked the young woman would she spend a night in the house and she, thinking that there must be something at the back of it, said she would if he gave her enough money and crossed her palm with silver. That was all right, the bargain was made and she went alone to the house. She put down a fine fire and sat up beside it and good enough, about two o'clock in the morning there was a knock at the door. She wanted to know who was outside.

'You don't know me at all,' the voice said. 'Open the door!'

She opened the door and there was a young man there and he drove a cow into the kitchen before him, and taking a vessel he told her to milk the cow and drink the first of the milk and to go out then and throw the rest of it against the wind. She milked the cow, drank the first of it and walked out and threw the rest of it against the wind. He didn't say another word, only drove the cow out of the kitchen and was gone, and there was no more commotion for the rest of the night. When she went back to the farmer in the morning, she could see by the stand in his eyes that he was very anxious to know what transpired. And there and then she made up her mind that she'd keep what she saw to herself for a while anyway.

'Are you all right?' he said.

'I am,' says she.

'Did you see anything?'

'No,' says she. 'I didn't see anything – I didn't see anything unusual.'

'Would you go there again tonight?' he said.

'I will,' says she, 'if you double the money.'

The money was doubled and she spent the second night there and the same thing happened. When she said to the farmer in the morning that she didn't see anything he seemed to be disappointed. He asked her would she go the third night. She said she would if the amount of money was doubled again. She got all the money into her hand, and at dusk that evening when the crows were noising overhead, she set out for the strange house. She put a fine fire down. She was so used to the place now that she went to bed and sure enough, on the stroke of two, the knock came to the door. She didn't ask at all who was there this time, she let him in, milked the cow, drank the first of the milk and threw the rest of it against the wind. He drove the cow out and as he was turning on his heel to go, she said, 'What hurry are you in? There's a fine fire here!'

He put his hand to the door and closing it out he came in and sat down. In the morning, when the young woman came to the farmer, she asked him if she could stay at the house now altogether and bring her mother too. This was agreed and herself and her mother lived there except that the young woman came each day and worked in the kitchen for the farmer. This went on, as the old storytellers used to say for three spaces of time, *trí ráithe*, until one morning the young woman did not come to work for the farmer.

'As sure as anything 'tis dead she is,' the farmer said to his wife, so the two set out for the strange house only to find the young woman, propped up in the bed and a big *poltóg* of a young child dancing on her lap and there at the head of the bed was the cowboy! The farmer and his wife went white with terror. They knew him well, and why wouldn't they for he was their dead son that had been brought back from the grave by some power, the working of which we are better off not to know.

There was a belief in the old religion that the dead came back for a favourite animal and I was given the man's name that came back for his horse. The two men that saw him were standing inside by the manger late at night when the dead man's spirit came in the door – they knew him as well as I know you – and walking up the spirit laid his hand on the horse's mane and ran it down along his spine. The horse rolled over and died and two white objects sailed out the door. That incident was told to me by Timmy Callaghan, a man that's dead himself now, and I would not belie him.

But to get back to the farmer. When he and his wife got over the shock of seeing their dead son they said to him, 'Where were you since?' and he said he was in hell.

'Now that you are restored to life,' the farmer said, 'and able to do things!' looking at the child, 'you'll remain with us!'

'I can't, I've seven years more to do in hell,' the son told them. 'If I don't go they'll come for me!'

'Don't go from us!' they said to him.

'Look,' the farmer said, 'I'm an old man now, my race is run. I'll go for the seven years in your place!'

It was arranged as things could be arranged that time and that old man went straight down to hell, but it wasn't long until he was back screeching and roaring and they had to throw buckets of water on him to quench him. The mother said she'd go. 'The men have no bearing of the heat anyway!' she said. She stuck it for a few days. Then the young woman said, 'It's up to me. I'll go!'

God help us! That young girl wanted most of all to be with her small child, but she went down into the black pit of hell. A dark valley with high burning buildings, red windows and devils looking out of every window. For seven years she suffered in the fires of hell and when the seven years were up the authorities came to her and said, 'If you remain on here for three more years any amount of souls will be set free the day you are going!'

Her inclination was to go home and see her child but

then she asked herself the question – was there any other woman anywhere in a position to do the same amount of good that she could do? And knowing what the suffering in hell was like she decided, for the sake of the souls that would be freed, to remain on. Every minute was an hour, every hour was a day, every day was a week and every week was a year. But the time came and she was set free and so many souls were let out of hell that you could hardly draw a leg the traffic was so thick coming up the stairs. On the second landing who should she meet coming down against her but her first husband Dydeo Moriarty and it came to the tip of her tongue to shout down to the devils, 'Shove him into the blackest hole below!'

But she curbed her tongue. She came back to this world and went straight away to the farmer's house. When she went in the door the farmer and his wife were dressing up as if for a journey. They didn't know her at all.

'Where are ye going?' she said.

'Well, 'tis this way,' says the farmer, 'I've another house at the other end of the farm and my son is getting married there tonight.'

Oh Dia linn! This was something she didn't expect and she didn't know what to do!

'Can I go over with ye?' she said.

They didn't raise any objection, and when they got over to the other house, the crowds were collecting for the wedding . . . the priest's horse coming into the yard. The minute she went inside the kitchen door, she looked around to see would she see her child that was only a few days old when she went away. There was a young lad of about ten years of age playing with a castle top on the flag of the hearth, and she was wondering could this be her son. When she sat down, the little boy came over to her and they were talking and this was unusual for at that time children were uncommonly shy. She looked up to see the father of the child watching her. He had changed like she had, ten years is a long time, so that for a while they were doubtful of each other. When he realised who she was, he ran over and put his two hands around her. The father and mother of the bride-to-be, when they saw that, had pusses on them from here down to the door and wanted an explanation.

'There'll be no marriage now,' he said, 'because the woman I thought I'd never see again, the woman that restored me to life and the mother of my child, has come back to me! But as the food is prepared, it would be a pity to waste it! So let what began as a wedding party, end up as a hauling home!'

Tóg Bog É!

When I was a young lad there was a man living here. The devil, I never heard any other name for him only *Tóg Bog É*. Not that he was lazy or disinclined to work, for he was not, only that he kept his private affairs very much to himself, and if you were to press him for information about domestic occurrences, he'd say, 'Ah, *Tóg bog é anois!*' To give you an example of the man: he was coming from the fair one day after selling a cow and he met a neighbour on the road and the neighbour said to him, 'What class of a fair was it?'

'Only a middling fair, then.'

'I see you sold the cow.'

'I did.'

'What did you get for her?'

'O . . . h! *Tóg bog é anois!*'

'Well, did you get what you expected?'

'No then,' he said, 'or I didn't expect I would.'

Wouldn't he make a star witness at a murder trial! He didn't get married until late in life. He was too shy when he was young and nearly too old when he got the courage. And he'd be left there altogether, and die wondering as many did in those days, only that his relations came together and made it up between himself and Tidy Womaneen. She was called that because when she was young she was a lovely pudgy, small, fat little lump of a baby, and her grandmother used to be bouncing her up and down on her knee and singing to her:

Tidy womaneen, tidy womaneen
Tidy womaneen *sásta*,
Milked the cow in the tail of her gown
and left it there until morning.

Throw her up and up and up,
Throw her up in the sky,
Throw her up and up and up,
And she'll come down bye 'n' bye.

She didn't dance and dance,
She didn't dance all day . . .

and I don't know any more of it! And I never laughed so
many, as the fellow said, and you would laugh if all
belonging to you were laid out in front of you, the night
that Tóg Bog É went over to look at Tidy Womaneen. He
had a couple of the neighbours with him to give him
courage. There was Jer Gorman and a few more and they
were walking up and down outside her house – 'twas dark.
Tóg Bog É was talking very loud – whistling passing the
graveyard! – referring to the blight on the potatoes and
how many times the crop should be sprayed. And that was
the time the knapsack sprayer came in, and the improvement it
was on the bunch of heather, spattering it on the stalks like holy
water: and they were arguing about how many pounds of
bluestone you should put to so many pounds of washing soda
to get the right spraying stuff, and no two of them on the same
word. And Jer Gorman in the middle of all this said to Tóg Bog
É, 'did you see the woman yet?' Of course this'd be the last
consideration!

'No then,' says Tóg Bog É, 'I didn't.'

'Maybe,' says Jer, 'she'd be in this bunch coming down.'

There was a bunch of girls the breadth of the road coming down against them.

'We'll stop 'em,' he said. And they did.

'There she is,' says he, 'the one in the middle.'

Tóg Bog É only cracked a match like that, and held it up in front of her face, and then turning to Jer Gorman, he said, 'Why then you can overdo the bluestone!'

Wouldn't you think that that was the wrong approach to matrimony. 'Twas not, for there's no understanding women. Whatever she saw in his eye in the light of the match, she fell head over heels in love with him! And he responded – took to courtship like an ass to clover. They got married and he brought her home where everything in the garden was velvet. Well, not everything. There were two flies in the ointment. Tóg Bog É's mother and Tóg Bog É's eldest sister Eily that never settled down – she was always there in the house. And the two of them were tall and thin, long, lanky and lonesome as the man said. For all the world the same as if you put a petticoat on the tongs!

And do you know, it galled them to have a strange woman inside on their floor and it killed them down dead to see her hand inside in their tea canister. They were watching every single thing that she did and criticising everything she did. She was of a very quiet disposition, poor Tidy Womaneen – a nice, *nacoss*, friendly, accommodating, small, little lump of humanity – and she didn't say anything. Another woman'd be dug out of the two of them. Or she didn't even say a word about it to Tóg Bog É. How did she know but that he might take sides with them – as if it didn't often happen.

Things went from bad to worse and Tidy Womaneen couldn't stick life any longer with these two frowning viragos, so Tóg Bog É woke up one morning to find himself alone in the hammock

– the bird had flown! And then the thing was, because of the secretive nature of the man, to keep the disgrace from the neighbours. And if you went into that house the following day or the day after, Tóg Bog É would be inside wetting tea and shouting up in the room, 'Would you like a bit of toast with it?'

You'd know, by the way, she was above!

But the neighbours know what's going on – you couldn't take out the pot unknown to them. This was brought home to Tóg Bog É in a very comical fashion. He was at the fair. He was buying a springer and he was a very tough man to make a bargain, too. Maybe ye don't know what I'm talking about? A springer is not a thing for putting off a rocket, 'tis a thing you'd milk, a cow about to calf.

'Twas about eleven o'clock in the morning and he hadn't the little cow bought; then he saw Jer of the Hill and Jer of the Hill had a small black cow that'd suit Tóg Bog É's place down to the ground. She'd be able to fend for herself among the rocks. He asked Jer how much was he looking for for the cow.

'Sixteen pounds,' he said. Tóg Bog É offered him ten, and Jereen, oh an awful man with the tongue, said, 'Suffering duck, I wouldn't wake her out of her sleep for that!'

Tóg Bog É went up a pound, two pounds and three pounds, but Jer of the Hill would not come down! Finally, after an awful bout of words in which they threw every *asacán* at one another, Tóg Bog É offered him thirteen pounds ten. But Jer wouldn't take it. And Tóg Bog É, his face blackening with bad temper, for he fancied the cow, said, 'You can take her home so!'

'I will,' says Jer of the Hill, 'and what's more, she'll stay with me too!'

I can tell you that knocked a hop out of Tóg Bog É and he said to himself, 'If it is known on the hill, it is known in the hollow. I won't deny it any more!'

That evening over a few drinks, he asked the advice of a long-headed man about getting back Tidy Womaneen, for he was miserable without her, and what he was told was to drive the mother and the sister, Eily, down in the room, wall up the door and break out another door in the gable for them. This he did and when Tidy Womaneen heard that she was going to be queen of her own section of the palace, she came back to him. And there was no more devoted pair! If you saw them back there in town linking arms! So much so that strangers were asking who they were, and they were told. Tóg and Mrs Bog É!

The Golauns

My great-grandfather, Seana-Neid, in his young days knew no English only what he'd use for a fair or market day. He was up before the court one time, and when he came home, the neighbours wanted to know how he got on.

'I took the stand,' he said, 'and cased my state!'

Seana-Neid seemed to like the court for often when he had a few drinks in, he used abuse the peelers and he used to be hauled up for using language likely to lead to a breach of the peace. So his English must be improving!

He was called one time as a witness in a will case. Seemingly the relations that didn't benefit from the will wanted to make out that the dead man was of unsound mind when he made it. Seana Neid was called by the beneficiaries and the attorney for the non-beneficiaries turning to my great-grandfather, when he took the stand, said, 'Is it not a fact that the deceased was given to soliloquising!'

Seana-Neid said nothing. Smiled at the judge. Although he remarked to someone in private after, it was well known the man died sudden!

'I'm afraid,' the judge said to the attorney, 'you'll have to simplify your question for the witness.'

And the attorney, who, no doubt became a judge himself after, put it another way. 'Is it not a fact,' he said to Seana-Neid, 'that the dead man talked to himself when alone?'

'I don't know,' Seana-Neid said. 'I was never with him when he was alone!'

The Golauns, that's where he came from, were very lazy to use Irish in town for the crowd inside, the townies'd be only making fun of them. Although it was said that in the lanes, up Bóthairín Caol and over Bóthairín Dennehy, the very poor people knew Irish. But you can be sure the man with the polished boot was making fun of those too.

'Give over your *cadrawling* in Irish,' a shopkeeper said to Seana-Neid one day. 'We all talks the best of the king's English here.'

'Why then, if the king walked in the door now,' says Seana-Neid, 'I don't think he'd understand what you are saying!'

It was amazing the rapidity with which the people picked up English that time. They had to. To get away to America. Some of them learned their English over, and they didn't pine away for want of someone to talk to in their own lingo while they were learning it, for there was as much Irish spoken in New York then as there was in the province of Munster. But they never let on to the foreigner that their people at home spoke Irish. And my uncle's father-in-law's father was telling me that there was this girl and she married an Englishman with a top-notch position and in time they had a little *bonóicín* – a baby girl. God help us, what the grandparents at home wouldn't give to see the child so they decided to take a trip home. But the daughter wrote to the mother beforehand, saying, 'Tell Dada and the lads not to have any Irish in the house during the visit.'

So, *duirt sí le Dada and the lads gan aon Ghaolainn a labhairt ós chomhair an tSasanaigh. Bhí go maith agus bhí go holc leis.* They arrived and everything was fine and civilised – no Irish until the old woman, who had been to the spout for water, got a glimpse of the baby. All the good resolutions not to talk Irish went by the board and hugging the child she said: '*O mo chircín! Mo chircín circ! A stór mo chroí istigh. Dia do bheannachta a laogh, a leanbhín gleoite!*'

Then seeing the look of consternation on her daughter's face, she knew the fat was in the fire and drawing English to herself in a hurry the old lady proclaimed, 'You're nate, Nate out. God blast you!'

Of course the big argument to get people to give up talking Irish that time was, 'What good is it to you when you'll g'out? I don't know. There were these two brothers and they were walking from Birmingham down to London and when they got to Dunstable that's there near Luton, they spent the last few bob they had on a bite of dinner. They were broke then, if you could describe people as broke who had nothing starting. They fooled around the town until they came to a place where there was a side-show, and a big prize being offered to the person that could eat the most chickens at the one sitting.

Now one of the brothers was so huge, a fine ball of a man, that he could hardly come in the door and the other fellow was so small he could nearly come in through the keyhole. Two chickens was the most devoured by any man entering for the prize so far. They put in for the competition, the big fellow to eat the chickens and the small fellow to act as his second and to see that the big man'd get fair play.

They took their place on the platform and the first chicken was handed up to the big man. He began to wire into it, and when he was half-way through he turned and said to the brother in Irish, '*Nac é an trua go deo é go raibh an dinnéar againn!*' bemoaning the fact that they had the dinner!

'What did he say?' says the judge to the small fellow.

'As nice a chicken as he ever tasted, sir!'

He finished that chicken and the second one was handed up to him. He began with the legs, then the wings and he was getting encouragement now from the crowd, and do you know that encouragement is as good a sauce as anything. He finished the second chicken. A big cheer from the crowd as the third chicken was handed up. If he finished this one he'd be the winner. But the small lad knew by the look on the big man's face, and he knew from the way he was chewing, and the lazy way he was swallowing that the edge had gone off his appetite. And with a good three-quarters of the chicken to go the big man turned to his brother and said, '*Is baolach ná deanfad an gnó!*'

'What did he say?' says the judge.

'That he could do for three more!' says the small fellow.

'Ah give him the money,' says the judge. 'That fellow'd ate us out of house and home!'

Dean Swift and His Serving Man

When Dean Swift was going round Ireland on horseback, from what we hear the food he got in the lodging-houses did not agree with him! No knowing the amount of bread soda the poor man consumed to alleviate the effects of bad cooking. So the Dean decided to bring his serving man with him the next time he was going around Ireland comforting the people. He was more in need of comforting himself! It so happened that they were passing through Cork and they put up in a lodging house in Washington Street. Dean Swift had always the name of having a great eye for the women, *agus bhí cara mná tí aige an oiche seo in Sráid Bhaisinton*, and this lady, when they were parting company in the small hours, gave him the present of a fat goose. What you might call a happy woman!

The Dean gave the goose to the serving man next morning to prepare her for the dinner. The serving man plucked the goose and cleaned out the goose and stuffed the goose and clapped her down in the big bastible oven over the fire – they used to have the use of the kitchen in any house they'd be staying in.

This way up in the parlour the Dean was, reading and writing and taking it easy after the night. Now, the serving man was so taken up with the goose, turning her in the bastible and spooning the gravy over her, and putting strips of bacon, like saddle pieces on her back to add to the flavour, that the goose was nearly done before he thought of putting down the spuds. So he put the bastible to the side, and he washed the spuds and put them down. It took the potatoes an awful long time to do, and the serving man's belly was nearly back to his spine with the hunger as he gave every second glance at the goose, and the lovely smell, and the little bubbles winking in the gravy all round her. In the end, his patience gave out and taking hold of the goose, he broke off one of the legs and made a mouth organ of it. And then looking at the goose, and the cut of her with only one leg, he got guilty but what was the good, the harm was done now.

Finally when the spuds boiled, he strained them and brought the pot down in the parlour and turned them all out on a bageen cloth, and himself or Dean Swift couldn't see one another across the table with the steam rising out of them! He came then and he knocked the goose on the flat of her back on a big plate and landed her that way o'er right the Dean out, and the two of them sat in to the table.

The Dean, noticing that the goose had only one leg said, 'Explain this to me!'

'Ah,' says the serving man, 'that's the kind of geese they have here in Cork. They never have but the one leg under 'em!'

The Dean, a knowledgeable man, didn't say any more. The two of them fell in and finished every morsel of what was on the table before them. Well, the appetites men had at that time!

The following morning they were on their way back to Dublin. A frosty morning it was too, you could hear the echoing of the horses' hoofs going up Glanmire. There was a pond covered with ice at the side of the road with a squad of geese on it. And as is their habit in the cold, the geese were standing on one leg, the other one tucked up inside the wing warming. The horsemen pulled up.

'There you are now,' says the serving man, 'do you see the comrades of the goose on the plate last night. Only one-legged geese in Cork!'

The Dean shoved over near them and striking his two hands together, he said, 'Coosh!'

With that every goose there put her second leg under her.

'Now!' says the Dean with great glee, 'are they all one-legged?'

'Ah but,' says the serving man, 'you didn't say "coosh" to the goose on the plate!'

I am a Young Fellow

I met a man from Clydagh once and he told me he was the youngest of a family of twenty. I remember him telling me that when his eldest brother started to talk it was all Irish that was in the house, and when he began to talk himself English was the everyday speech. That man didn't know a single word of Irish. He was scuffling mangolds in the field as I came down the road and I shouted into him, '*Dia's Muire dhuit!*'

'Straight on,' he said, 'You can't miss it!'

And how can you account for the fact that his family slid from Irish to English in the time between the births of the first and twentieth child? The Clydagh man explained it to me.

'The desire,' he said, 'to get on in the world outside is strong in people of no property, and after the establishment of the national schools many parents that were able to string a few words of English together didn't speak any more Irish to their children. They'd as soon give them the itch as give them Irish. Although when the neighbours came visiting they spoke Irish among themselves around the fire, but they'd hunt the children out of earshot in case they'd pick it up. "Rise! Get up," the parents'd say. "G'out! Go abroad. There's no rain on it!"

'The only time they'd ever turn to Irish in front of the children was when they had some local gossip or scandal to hide. And people like those, caught in a gap between two languages, could sound awful funny to the Irish speakers they were trying to run away from, as well as the English speakers they were trying to catch up to.

I asked the Clydagh man if he had ever heard of Jack and Jer *Balbh*. He had of course, everyone heard of the Balbhs. Brothers they were and Jack had some schooling. He claimed to have gone as far as, 'Can a snail walk?' in the second book. Naturally a man of his learning spoke only English. At suppertime in the winter he was often heard to say to the brother, 'Scarce the milk, Jer, the cow is going thirsty!'

Jack and Jer had only a small way of living, one cow, but they weren't altogether depending on her as they had an income from the services of a gentleman goat. And to make these services more widely known and therefore more lucrative they decided to make out a notice and hang it on the chapel gate. This they did, and when the parish priest read the notice he nearly lost his cork leg, for what they had written down was –

Us have puck. Us charge sixpence for the pucking,
But if the goat comes second rutting,
Us will puck that goat for nothing!

Eoghan Rua Ó Súilleabháin Finds an English-speaking Son-in-law for a Wealthy Farmer

Eoghan Rua Ó Súilleabháin, the poet, was out walking one day and he called into a rich farmer's house. An only daughter was all the farmer had and he was on the look-out for a *cliamhain isteach* for her. But the farmer would not be satisfied with any son-in-law, only a young man that could talk English.

That was a stiff enough proposition at the time, two hundred years ago. But even then, English was thought to be a leg-up for the man that wanted to rise and be well thought of in the world. The farmer told Eoghan, and he told the right man, that he was having trouble getting an English-speaker for the daughter, and did Eoghan know of anyone.

Eoghan said he did – *go raibh aithne aige ar gharsún mín macánta*, but the pity of it was he could not come into such a fine house, having no fortune.

'Don't mind about the fortune,' says the farmer, 'if he can talk English won't we all be learning from him.'

'The way it is,' says Eoghan, 'the English isn't good by him, but if you look at it another way, the English isn't bad by him.'

'Can't you bring him here to the house,' says the farmer, 'and we'll see!'

Eoghan went off and he never drew rein until he met a fine strapping young man that had neither land nor means nor English. Eoghan brought him along to his own house, put a good suit of clothes on him and gave him a few days tutoring him up on how to give a perfect answer in English to a question Eoghan was going to ask him.

When the young man had mastered the piece of English, the two, Eoghan and the young man, set out for the farmer's house. There was a big crowd there that night. All talking away in Irish. The young lad, when he went in, made off the farmer's daughter, a nice little mallet of a one, and in no time the two of them were whispering and canoodling in the corner.

Out in the night, as was pre-arranged, Eoghan gave the young man the nod and he went out in the yard. When he was gone, Eoghan said to the farmer in Irish, 'I suppose you're anxious to hear this young man talking in English?'

'Isn't that what we are here for,' says the farmer.

'He is gone out there now,' says Eoghan. 'I'll put some talk on him when he comes in.'

When the young man had done whatever it was he went out to do, he turned back and when he was noising at the door Eoghan says to him, 'Well, friend, and what are the climatic conditions abroad?'

On hearing this, the young man straightened himself, and clapping one eye on the farmer's daughter he said, 'From my astronomical observations, from my reckoning and my calculations, from the widespread fermentation of the atmosphere, the constant rolling of the firmament and the dismal aspect of the stars, I prognosticate a heavy discharge from clouds!'

'Good,' says Eoghan. 'I find your peregrinations most pertinent to behold!'

Well, the farmer was there and his mouth opened back to his two ears, you could put a turnip into it. Anything foreign impresses the Irish!

'Ó,' ar seisean, 'nach iontach go deo an t-urlabhra an Béarla.

D'fhanfainn ag eisteacht leis an gcainnt sin go lá an Luain!'

The young man's English was so good no one had the courage to engage him in conversation. The farmer thought he was a professor out of Trinity Hall. There was no trouble in making the match but they weren't too long married when the farmer found out that that was all the English he had. The farmer had a pain in his head from 'the widespread fermentation of the atmosphere.'

Came the big fair at Knocknagree and the farmer and the daughter were there standing to a cow, when who should come down the street but the poet Eoghan Rua, singing one of his new compositions. The farmer ran out in front of him and caught him by the two lapels of the coat and gave him a good shaking. 'You blackguard of the world,' says he, 'and the way you codded me!'

'Take it easy now,' says Eoghan, 'don't be running away with yourself! What's wrong?'

'Didn't you tell me,' says the farmer, 'that that *bodach* of a son-in-law knew English!'

'I told you no such thing,' says Eoghan. 'Recollect yourself! Didn't I say to you that the English wasn't good by him?'

'You did,' says the farmer.

'And didn't I say to you the English wasn't bad by him?' says Eoghan.

'You did,' says the farmer.

'And didn't I say to you so that he had no English good nor bad!'

Turning to the daughter, Eoghan said to her: 'Do you find any fault with him?'

'No,' says she. 'But of course 'tisn't for English I want him!'

The Man That Never Slept

When my Auntie Nora came home from America ... I don't know now was that the first or the second trip. Anyway, her husband was with her and they stayed here. We did up the room below, broadened the window and put in a boarded floor, for the stone flags are cold to put your bare feet on when you get out of the bed in the morning. We put down a blazing fire for it is common knowledge that the yanks do complain about the damp.

Nora's husband was mad to be off sightseeing every day in the pony and trap. He was American-born and as the country was new to him, he couldn't see enough of it. We went one day to the seaside and for the bite to eat we dined in a house on the knob of a hill. There was an old man by the fire and I knew by the glint in his eye that he had any amount of talk if he could be tapped.

There was a ruin of what looked like a mansion between us and the strand, you could see it through the open door. When Nora and the husband went out to see the sights, I said that there must be some story attached to the mansion. The old man said there was. He told me the name of the man who built it.

'An only son is all he had and when the house was finished the father went to great trouble to get a nice young woman for the son. She was from the country up, all belonging to her very respectable it seems. She came to live in that house below, and while she was there she never wet her fingers, or she had no need to, for she had plenty of servants.

'No day passed that she didn't go swimming alone in the sunny cove beside the house. You can't see it from here now. It is well cut off from view. The only place you'd see it right is if you were in a boat out on the waves. Every day, as I said, she went in swimming by herself. According to the servants and those who had recourse to the house, the young couple were happy out. Plenty of money anyway, no complaints in that line. The only thing was, the years were going by on wings and they had no family. They must be about ten years married when one evening she came in from the sea, and when she stood in the door the servants knew that something had happened to her, for as the storyteller put it: *Bhí aiteas agus scannra uirthi* – she was strange and frightened. She was put to bed and she got all the attention they could give her and nine months after a child was born to her. The old women that were there that night said he was a remarkable child, very beautiful. A boy it was and the parents, and indeed the grandparents, were delighted with him. Every day and every night that went by, the child improved until he was as fine a young man as ever walked down that road outside.

'But there was one thing and it was a strange thing, he never slept. He'd go to bed the same as you or me but since the day he was born, he never closed an eye.

'Now it happened one fine summer's evening, his father and grandparents were dead by this time, a travelling scholar came to the house looking for lodgings.

'"Come in, poor scholar," the young man said.

'The scholar did and he put his books down. The supper was going and he was invited to sit into the table. "*Cabáiste Scotch*" they had: they'd put down a head of white cabbage and when it was done, they had an affair to squeeze the water out of it. Then they'd cut it up small, mix

in chopped onions, add some cream you had left go sour, pepper
and salt and put it outside on the wall to cool – it was no damn
good unless it was cold. Then peel a big floury spud and with
a little pat of butter on it, plank it down in the middle and with
a mug of buttermilk you did have a supper!

'When everyone had enough, the young man of the house
told the servants to go away to bed now and himself and the
scholar remained up, well into the night, putting the world to
and fro.

'"You'd be asleep long ago only for me," says the
scholar, making a move to rise.

'"You wouldn't say that if you knew me," the young
man said. "I don't know what it is like to sleep, for I never
slept in my life."

'"There's something very mysterious about that," says
the scholar. "I never heard anything like it!"

'"You are a man of great knowledge," the young man
said to him, "so why don't you open your books and see
if there's any class of people on this earth who never slept."

The scholar drew his books to him and many is the hour he
spent over them and finally he said to the young man, "In all
I've read, I can find only a bare reference to a people of that
nature, but they no longer live on the surface of the earth for
their land was swallowed by the sea!"

'"I'll pay you well for your trouble," the young man
said, "go to bed now, 'tis late!"

'The bed for the poor was near the fire, so the scholar
lay down and closed his eyes and the young man watched
him until his breathing was even and he was sound asleep.
He went up then to where his mother slept.

'"What's troubling you, son?" she said, waking up when he
came into the room.

'"There's something I want to ask you!" he said, talking very quiet so that he wouldn't wake anyone.

'"I'll answer it if I can," she said.

'"How long were you and my father married before I was born?"

'"I thought I often told you, son. It was ten years," she said.

'"And you had nothing to do with any other man only my father? Tell me the truth!" he said, when she wasn't answering him.

'"I was never with another man," she said. "But I have something to tell you, which I could never bring myself to tell before. I was one day swimming in that cove below. I was so accustomed to the sea at the time that I could swim for a good spell under the wave as well as on it. I knew every little cave along by *Faill na nGabhar*, and often I dived down to bring a fancy shell up from the sea bed. The day I'm telling you about, as I swam I thought there was someone by my side. I looked and there was no one there; the water was clear all round but I had the feeling that there was someone near me. Imagine the fear that came over me when on looking down to where the sun threw my shadow on the bed of the sea, I saw a second shadow that moved with mine which ever way I turned. The two shadows came together as I swam in to the strand, where I dropped down at the brink of the tide so tired that I fell asleep. When I came up to the house after, everyone was worried about me I was out so long. I was put to bed, three spaces of time passed and you were born."

'He left the room and in the morning when they all had broken their fast together, he went to where he kept his money and he paid the scholar for the information. The land he divided up among his servants, and left the mansion and plenty to do his mother while she'd live. He parted with her then, and it broke her heart to see him take his coat and make for the door.

"'I'm sorry to go," he said, "but I have to go to my own people."

'A big crowd followed him down to the strand, where he went into the sea and swam out. And the people there saw a man rise up out of the waves and embrace the young man and together they swam left by the black rock until they were out of sight.'

And that is the story as I heard it, without adding to it or taking from it, the day I went to the seaside in the pony and trap with my Auntie Nora and her husband when they were home on their second trip from Springfield, Mass.

After a night's talk in this house long ago when the visitors'd rise to go, my father'd see them to the door. If the night was bright they'd stand a while looking up the rising countryside wondering what sort of weather tomorrow would bring. Every field up there had a name at the time, and some little story of its own to make it different from any other field. So had every prominent rock and every stream. Up there you'll find *Loch an Dá Bhó Dhéag* – the Twelve Cow Lake, which got its name from *an Ghlas Ghaibhneach*, a very beautiful and mysterious cow that gave a never-ending supply of milk for the poor. She was highly productive! The old people used to say that the field in which she grazed and slept and manured remained fertile forever more.

But some prime boyo, we are told, sold her milk to line his own pocket! This was sacrilege as far as the cow was concerned. So she called together her eleven daughters ranging in ages from eleven years to a yearling heifer and cocking their tails they put the hill up out of them, and jumped into the lake leaving a greedy world behind them.

Show *Loch an Dá Bhó Dhéag* to any young lad living here now and ask him the name of it and he'll tell you that's 'the lake'. Show him *Páirc a' tSasanaigh*, and he'll tell you that's 'the field'. *Cnoc an Áir* is 'the hill' and the *glaise* that runs down to the *Abhann Uí Chriadha* is 'the stream' that flows into 'the river'. The changing world has left them without a name and without a story, like my ancestor, Tadhg Ó Cíosáin

If you walk up there in the daytime you'll find remnants of houses under the briars and ferns. You can trace the room and the kitchen, the yard, the *cróitín* where they kept the cow, and the ridges of a potato garden that once bloomed. Only traces are left, like old words in everyday speech to remind us of the people that lived there once and the language they spoke.

The Hiring Fairs

Go deo, deo arís ní raghad go Caiseal,
Ag díol is ag reic no shláinte;
Ag margadh na saoirse im' shuí cois balla
Im' scaoinse ar leath taoibh sráide.
Bodairí na tíre ag teacht ar a gcapall,
Ag iarraidh a bhfuilim hyreálta.
O teanam chun suibháil tá an cúrsa fada,
Seo ar siúl an spailpín fánach!

Bhí na cursaí fada go leor ag na spailpíní fadó. Servants walked
a long way to the hiring fairs. In later years these fairs used to
be held on Sunday after late Mass in places like Tralee, Mallow,
Ennis and Galway. The men'd be lined up there. They'd have
spades if they were going on harvest work, digging potatoes; or
pikes or scythes if they were going saving hay or cutting the corn.
But in January or February they'd have only the Sunday suit and
a bundle with their working clothes on their backs. *An puc ar
a dhrom aige agus é ag imeacht mar a dúirt na sean daoine.*

Looking back, in many ways those fairs were like the slave
markets you'd hear about out foreign. And 'sclábhaí', which is
our word for labourer, means slave. The farmers'd vet the men,
you'd think they were buying an animal.

'Walk up there now! Can you milk? Can you plough?
Can you mow? . . . can you follow horses at all? Answer
me this and answer me no more. When is it too late for me
to put down seed potatoes?'

'It is too late, sir, when you can no longer see out

through the branches of an ash tree!'

'Good, good! A very good answer!'

Then the bargaining would start and there would be great rivalry between the rich farmers for a big loose-limbed man, or a fine scopy woman. Those servants would get anything from nine to twelve pounds . . . a year! They'd be fed and found for that, and of course the girls wouldn't get near as much. After the First World War wages went up to twenty and twenty-five pounds, and one man told me that he got thirty-one pounds the year of the Eucharistic Congress – whenever that was? But like all the servants at the time, he had to give two weeks, when the year was up, working for nothing. This was known as a *tuille*. And he told me too that the woman of that house was related to his mother, and that it was the hardest house he ever worked in.

'And God knows, Ned Kelly,' he said, 'I worked in hard houses in my time. I slept in the stall under the cow's head, and I was glad of her breath to keep me warm in the frost! But that woman was so tight she nearly starved me. Often, late at night, I'd come into the kitchen in my stockinged feet and look for a cake of bread. If there was a piece taken off it I'd take another piece. I'd bring it out to the *cúl lochta* over the dairy where I was sleeping, and with my head under the clothes I'd eat it. And even though I was a grown man at the time, I'm ashamed to say it now, many is the time the hot tears came into my eyes at the hardness of that woman. And do you know what I'm going to tell you. She found the bread crumbs in the bed and I never found the cake after, wherever she hid it!

Isn't greed a fright! And what good did it do 'em. Look at Damer the miser. Damer wore out the backside of his trousers sitting on a chair admiring his gold. He was too miserly to buy a new trousers so he sent out for the tailor to put a new seat in his pants. Of course Damer had to go up to bed while the tailor was at it. When the job was done the tailor threw the trousers up to Damer. He put it on and came down and said to the tailor, "What do I owe you?"

"Yerra, nothing at all," says the tailor, "if you'll let me look at your gold for a while."

The door was unlocked and a chair brought into the treasury and the tailor sat down admiring the gold. After a while he got up to go.

"Well," says Damer, "what good did that do you looking at it?"

"The same good as it is doing you," says the tailor.

"Sure all you are doing is looking at it!"

But before you can look at the gold you must make it first. There was a farmer from near Cloundrohid and he hired a servant in the city of Cork thinking that he might be a better bargain than a country lad. It was late at night when they left the city. The darkest and the coldest night that ever came. The two of them sat into the horse car and drove out into the country. The young lad from the city never saw so much darkness before. On they went, mile after mile, around turn after turn, over humpy bridge after humpy bridge, so that you couldn't blame the young lad from the city for saying in his own mind, 'Isn't it a long way from home some people live!'

When they got to the farmer's house, late and all as it was, the young lad was put to work right away, choring around the kitchen and the yard. After about an hour he was given a cup of cold milk and sent up in the loft to bed. He had hardly the impression of his body made in the feather tick when he was called again to go out and tackle the horse. The farmer was going to Macroom fair to buy a bull calf. He came down and he was given the horse's winkers, and out he went slipping and falling all over the icy yard. His fingers were so numb he couldn't get the bridle on the animal. And the farmer impatient in the kitchen called out, 'What's delaying you?'

'I can't,' he said, 'I can't get that thing back over his head. His ears are frozen!'

He was tackling the bull!

The Young Woman's Denial

There was this young woman and she was going with a young man. After a time they made up their minds to make a match of it, and she swore by all the mysteries of creation since the first star began to shine that she wouldn't marry any other man but him. That was fine until another young man began to take notice of her. They talked and they walked and in no time they were going together strong, for she found that she had more meas on him than she had on the first one.

Everything was being settled up for their marriage, but when her first lover heard this, he came to her in the night, just as she was going to bed, and he said, come what will, he would spend that night with her anyway. She said fine, but would he let her be for a short space; that she had forgotten to rake the fire and that she'd run down and do it, as it would be a fright if there was no seed in the morning! He said, all right.

When she went down, instead of raking the fire, she took a shawl or whatever was next to her hand, and went out into the night. She ran, for she knew that before long he'd be after her. I don't know why she didn't go towards the man she was going to marry but she didn't. She kept going until she lost all sense of direction. At last she saw a house and she went in. There was a very respectable man sitting inside by the fire. He was surprised to see her at that hour of the night, shivering with cold and terror. She explained to him what happened.

'You'll be safe here,' he said, 'and you can remain as long as you want. Why don't you come in service to me and I'll pay you well.'

She put up there and did everything that had to be done. He was always in the house during the day, but as soon ever as the night would come, he'd straighten out. She never heard him coming back, and she thought it must be late for he was never in any hurry out of the bed in the morning. He was like this, going out every night and she got it into her head that she'd like to find out where he was going and what it was he was doing.

This moonlight night she followed him and he never suspected that she was behind him. She often wished after that she had never done it, for where did he go but into the graveyard. He went over the stile, and she thought to herself that maybe it was a near way he was taking, but on looking in through the bars of the gate, she saw him remove a stone flag and disappear into the inside of a tomb! The Lord save us! When she saw this she got very frightened and she ran as hard as she could to the house. In her hurry she lost one of her shoes and when he was coming home after he found it. She heard him coming in that night for he came to where she was, but she let on to be asleep. In the morning, he asked her, 'Where's that other shoe I saw you wearing yesterday?'

'I lost it,' she said, 'when I was giving the milk to the calves.'

'Get that shoe,' he said, 'for your own good get it. Have it here for me tomorrow!'

He went out again that night, whatever time he came home, and in the morning he wanted to know whether she had found the shoe.

'I lost it the day before yesterday,' she told him 'when I was feeding the calves in the haggard behind the house.'

'It would be better for you now,' he said, 'to tell me the exact place you lost that shoe. Have it there for me tomorrow morning or it'll be the price of you. I'll knock the head off you!'

When night came he went out but when he came home she wasn't there before him. She was too frightened to stay in that house any longer. She said she'd look for some place to go in service, some place where he'd never find her. She walked all through the night and in the morning when the sun began to shine, she came to a fine house in an opening between the trees, and she settled there in service, and if she did she was well thought of there, for she was a willing worker. She was a young woman who could turn her hand to any sort of a job she'd be called on to do within the four walls of a house. She was pleasant and witty too and the young man of the house was very taken with her, and he swore that she was the only one for him. When she heard that, she spoke to the priest that was living near them. All the arrangements were made. They were married and in three spaces of time she had a young son.

About twelve o'clock that night, when the old women who were supposed to be minding her fell asleep, the door opened and in came her former master and without raising his voice in case he'd wake the women, he said, 'Where did you lose that shoe?'

'I told you before,' she said, 'I lost it when I was going feeding the calves.'

'If you don't tell me where you lost your shoe,' he said, 'I'll take the child from your side. Do you hear me?'

'But what can I do,' she said, 'that's where I lost it.'

He took the child and walked out and it was her crying, her loud crying, that woke the women. They found the child was gone and they called her husband. His first words were, 'Is she all right herself? We'll get over the loss of the child some way if she is all right!'

It so happened at the end of another year, there was a second child born to the young woman, and the same company of women was sitting up attending to herself and the child that night. And the man of the house was so divarted with his little son that he gave the women a *tomhaisín* or maybe two tomhaisíns to celebrate. In the night they fell asleep and again the dor opened and in walked the same man.

'You know the information I am looking for,' he said.

'Only too well,' she told him, 'and my answer is the same. I remember well losing that shoe when I was going to feed the calves!'

'Tell me this minute exactly where,' he said, 'or you'll lose your child!'

'*Ná tóg mo leanbh uaim!* Don't take my child from me. I'll tell you the exact place.'

But when she tried to say it the words wouldn't come to her, because the image of what she saw in the graveyard that night came into her mind, and all she could do was repeat what she had said before, 'I lost that shoe when I was bringing the milk down to feed the calves.'

He took her child and he went away.

The story went out that the child was gone, the husband was called and a lady that was in the house that night said to him, 'If you had married my daughter as everyone wanted you to do, you'd have a wife and a family now!'

'I can't believe,' he said, 'that the woman I married would do anything wrong. I'll pay no heed to what people are saying. I'll wait, and maybe time will tell.'

Time went on, and as happened before, another son was born to her, and as happened before, when the old women dozed off that night, the same man came in and when she didn't give him the answer he wanted, not alone did he take her child but he smeared . . . like chicken's blood he had brought with him on her face and hands and spilled it on the bed and went away.

God help her! She was finished now. Even her husband that was constant for so long had to give in. The law was put in motion and what chance did she have? Who was to give evidence on her behalf? She was tried for doing away with her children. Sentences were stiff at the time and the sentence in her case was the rope. The scaffold was erected outside as was the custom of the time and just when the hangman was about to put the blindfold over her head, a coach drew up and in it she saw the man who was the cause of all her misfortune.

'That woman is innocent!' he shouted out, 'and I'll prove it!'

He opened the door of the carriage and out came her two eldest sons. The small one he had in his arms. He came up and she could see that he was a different man now, the cloud had lifted from his face.

'I was under a spell,' he told her as he gave her the little child, 'a black curse. I was condemned to lie down with the dead every night of my life, and there was nothing could save me but an innocent person's denial even in the face of death. You did that for me and I'm a free man now.' And putting a purse of gold sovereigns into the child's lap, he went into his carriage and drove away.

When it was gone her husband came over to her side. 'I failed you,' he said, 'when you most needed the support of a comrade. I failed you!' And kicking the toe-cap of his shoe into the ground to keep down the *tulc* rising in his throat, he said, 'We'll only have to try and make the best of it.'

She didn't say anything. She took the three children and went into the house after him. What could she do only make the best of it!

Two Fierce Lies

Men coming home from service were every bit as good as the returned yanks for boasting. Nothing we had at home could match what they had up the country. The land in Limerick was so good, we were told, that if you dropped a spancel in the field after milking in the evening, you'd never find it in the morning the grass'd have grown so high overnight.

And we thought the midges were bad down here, but it seems you could be eaten alive by the breed of midges they had in Tipperary. There was a man there and he had a prize cow, a valuable animal. She had won several cups, and when she had her calf he kept them together in a wooded place near the river. And he put a bell on her so that the calf would know where his mother was if he strayed through the trees.

Now August is the worst month for midges, they'd eat you without salt if there's no puff blowing. And this way of a heavy evening the farmer heard the bell clanging as if the cow was in trouble. He sent down the servant boy and what was it? The midges had eaten the cow alive! Those midges were massive! And when they had her flesh picked to the bones, they were still so hungry that they took the bell off the cow's neck and rang it for the calf!

The biggest lie I ever heard used to be told to the tourists by the Killarney boatmen, when those visitors'd ask a contrary question like: 'How deep is the Punch Bowl?'

The Devil's Punch Bowl, as we all know from our geography lesson, is at the top of Mangerton, which overlooks the town and the lakes, and we were told by the master, the few days I was at school, that the Punch Bowl is an extinct volcano with the crater now filled up to the top with the purest of spring water. But how deep is it?

'Well,' the boatmen used to say, 'there was a Sweeney man up there on the verge of the crater looking for sheep and he fell into it. Down with him and the Lord save us, as it got dark he saw this enormous fish coming towards him, his eyes blazing like the headlamps of a train coming through a tunnel. The fish opened his mouth and Sweeney went down into his belly. That gave him a breathing space! He sat down and lit the pipe' – tourists'd lap that up! 'He looked around and there was the dog, Sooner! – he had followed him down! With that the fish turned tail and instead of going up towards Killarney and civilisation, he was going down into the bowels of the earth.

"'I'll have to get out!" says Sweeney. So he climbed up into the inside of the fish's neck. God knows then, that was a slippery enough track too! He had the strong shoes on, and between that and smoking the pipe and the dog barking and wagging his tail, the fish got very tickly in his throat, he began coughing and coughed them up, and as he came out, Sweeney blew the pipe smoke into the fish's eyes which delayed him. Sweeney kept going out before the fish, holding on to the dog's tail – and did that dog make speed! I don't know how many days and nights they were travelling when all of a sudden the water got roasting hot with bright light shining through it.

"'O God," says he, "we're facing into hell!"

'Not at all. The next thing was they were catapulted into the open air, landing up on mossy bank. Sweeney shook the water out of his eyes, looked around him, and there he saw this huge animal with a jennet's head on him, sitting on his bottom like a dog begging. He had two short lops for front legs and a young one looking out of his waistcoat pocket!

"'Ah, blast it," says Sweeney, "I know where I am now!"

'So he went down the road, got the bus into Sydney and wired home for a change of clothes! And the dog? That dog was crossed with a bush dingo and that's how sheepdogs came to Australia!'

Small Michael and the Major

On your way down from the county bounds, and before you come to Derrynafinna, you'll notice the remains of a house, that way, in to your left, and at one time there was a couple living there. An only son was all they had, Small Michael, and his father died when Small Michael was thirteen years of age and he was left with the mother to support.

This way coming up to the fall of the year, Small Michael got a spade and he told his mother that he was hitting for the harvest hiring fair in Mallow to try to get a few pounds together so that they could have some sort of a Christmas of it.

So he struck out by the side of the Paps, down the Slugedal and into Millstreet. For all the world it was a fair day there and a farmer seeing Michael with the spade on his shoulder, and he so young and so small, for the fun of it more than anything else, asked him what he'd charge for a week's work.

'Fifteen bob,' says Michael.

'All that money,' says the farmer, 'and you without a rib of hair on your face!'

'If it's hair you want,' says Michael, 'why don't you go and hire a goat!'

Michael met some of the local lads at the fair, they used to go from here to Millstreet at the time, and he knocked around with them for the day, so that he was carrying the night with him when he hit the road again for Mallow.

He was going along until he saw an old man leaning over a half door.

'Where's your journey?' says the old man.

Michael told him.

'Erra, leave that alone until morning,' he said, 'stick the spade there and come on away in!'

Michael went in. There wasn't any great *slacht* on the house. There was no fire down.

'I'm only in from the fair,' the old man said, and stooping under the bed he brought out two course bags and throwing one of them to Michael, he said, 'Here, we might as well bring in a night's firing!'

'Twas very dark now, and it struck Michael as strange that the rick of turf should be so far away from the house. He didn't say anything. They emptied the turf out.

'Bad manners to it for a story,' says the old man, 'I forgot to bring in enough potatoes to tide me over till Sunday. Come on!'

So they went off with the two sacks, and if the rick of turf was a good bit away from the house, the potato pit seemed to be in the next parish. The old man took the straw from the mouth of the pit and when his sack was full a dog began to bark.

'Lift this on my back,' he said to Michael. 'I'll be off! You can fill your own!'

Michael had the bag just about full when he was caught by the collar of the coat and lifted off the ground.

'I'm a long time watching to catch you!' says the farmer, frog-marching him up to the house. 'Hold him down there!' he said to one of his sons, 'while I'm tackling the horse to bring him into Millstreet.'

He was taken in to the old police station in Millstreet and he got free lodgings there until the court day. When the case was called, Michael told the bench the story as I have told it to you. Maybe times have changed since but at that time poor people were not believed in court, and he got a month in Cork jail. The food wasn't very good there then, and if Michael was small going in, the skin of a gooseberry would make a night-cap for him coming out.

Twenty-six days I think is all that's in a jail month so on the evening of the twenty-sixth day he was put outside the gate and late and all as it was, he belted out the Western Road. 'Twas dark by the time he got to Coachford. He travelled on until he got tired. Then he saw a light in from the road. He went up. There were two doors. He opened one of them and he was in the dairy. He felt around and found a pan of milk on the *stellan*. He put his head in that and when he had enough he lay down and went asleep.

He woke in the morning to hear a lot of activity in the yard and he said to himself, 'If I'm caught here now it'll be another free trip to Cork.' He looked around for some place to hide. There was a big dash-churn in the corner. He hopped into it and squeezed himself down. In came a woman and her son. What a day he picked to be coming from Cork jail – it was churning day! They lifted up an enormous tub of cream and spilled it in on top of Michael. She picked up the staff and with the first crack Michael got of it on the nut he rose up with a roar, knocked over the churn and ran out the door.

The woman and her son set two ferocious dogs on him and Michael knew by the cut of them that they'd tear him to pieces, so he threw them the cap and they began licking the cream off it. That didn't delay them long so he threw them the coat and in like manner the waistcoat and the shirt. In the latter end to save his life he had to throw them the trousers. A lot of cream had collected in the backside of the trousers which gave him enough time to cross a small river and throw the dogs off the scent. There he was now as naked as when he came into the world, only a lot whiter!

He crept along by the shade of the ditches until he came to a house where there was some washing out, and the hedge, thank God, was a good bit down from the front door. He didn't have much time to pick and choose. The first thing to his hand was a combination. The old men used to wear them long ago. They were a one-piece undersuit, long drawers and vest buttoned up to the chin. It was miles too big for him, but by rolling up the legs and the sleeves he was able to move around in it. Then on examining himself he saw that it was no uniform in which to face the public! So he went into a graveyard nearby to hide, hoping there would be no funeral that day, and waited for the night to go home.

It was barely dusk when he heard three men approaching and whatever came over him, he called out to them. If he had kept his mouth shut they'd have thought he'd just risen from the dead and ran away.

'God above!' they said, 'you put the heart crossways in us. We thought you were the Major!'

They explained to him that there was this Major in that locality that died a few days ago, a man that had spent years out foreign and picked up some strange religion in Mesapotamia. They said he had a special tomb built for himself . . . he wasn't going to get his feet wet! And he left an instruction that food and everything was to be put in with him, and enough money to get him across the Jordan.

'And as you know well,' they were all looking at him in the drawers, 'as you know well, that's a trip that'll never materalise. The money'll rot down there with him!'

There was only a small opening in the tomb. They undid the bolt and opened the little door and as they were all too big to go through it, they shoved Michael in and gave him a box of matches. He cracked a match and thunder and turf, there was the coffin on its end with a glass front, and the Major standing up inside in it, and a white coat on him and a white *figario* on his head.

He was so frightened he darted out through the hole, but they shoved him back in again for the money. He cracked another match and there was a table and chair there and he came to a box. There was some *ábhar* of money in it, so he handed it out to them, and the dirty ruffians, what did they do? Shut and bolted the door and left him inside!

Poor Michael! He was in a nice pucker now! The first thought that came into his head was how long would the matches hold? For he knew he would die with terror if he was left alone with the corpse in the dark. He cracked another match and dang it if he didn't find a candle. He lit it and sat down on the chair. There was food there, a cake of bread, 'twas all right too for a hungry man, and a bottle of Paddy with a map of Ireland on the label. When he examined the label he jumped out of the chair with fright. The whiskey was down as far as Athlone! Was the Major fond of his drop? Was he tippling?

He looked at the box again where he got the money and there written on it was: 'For the first part of the journey.'

That put him thinking and looking around he saw, in a *cabúis* in the wall, another box and written on that was, 'For the final stages!'

This was to put the Major into orbit! He opened that and there was any amount of money inside – notes of all denominations. He stuffed them down the leg of his combination, tying his shoelace at the bottom. With that he heard voices outside. He listened, a different crowd – the Major and his money were popular tonight! When they opened the door Michael shot out! And when they saw him in his white underwear!

'The Major,' they shouted. Two of them scattered and the small fellow fainted! Michael took the coat and trousers off him, put them on himself and hit for home, and when he landed into the mother at Derrynafinna, she said: 'Michael, how did you get on up the country?'

'Famous, mother,' he said, 'the men that hired me worked late but they paid me well!' And he threw the roll of notes on the table.

'Buy a bicycle,' she said.

He did. And himself and his mother had one whale of a Christmas of it! They had whiskey hot and cold, porter natural and mulled, ling and white sauce, jelly and tapioca and a roast pig running around with a big knife sticking out of his back and he shouting, 'Eat me! Eat me! Eat me! I'll be gone cold in a minute!'

The Bicycle

Before the scythe, corn was cut with a reaping hook, and God knows a slow-enough process it was too. You'd cut a handful and put it down and so on until you had the makings of a sheaf. But the straw to my mind was better for thatching . . . the blades weren't crushed or broken, moreover if you threshed, or as they said, scutched, the sheaf on the back of a chair sloped against the table, or on the rungs of a ladder, you had nice clean strands to make a *súgán* rope to seat a chair or tie down a meadow cock.

The first scythe to come into this corner of the universe was brought from Cork by a young man who was at the butter market. His father was cutting corn with the reaping hook when he arrived into the field with the scythe.

'Shove back there from me, Da,' he said, 'till you see this machine working! But first I'll have to edge her.'

And as we all know the edge is the secret of a good mower. So he took the scythe-board, with the carburundum at the two sides, off the scythe-tree. Then resting the tip of the blade on the ground, he began to rub the scythe-board with a nice circular motion to the two sides of the cutting edge singing as he worked:

> Some say the devil is dead,
> The devil is dead, the devil is dead,
> Some say the devil is dead,
> And buried in Killarney.

Then, putting his back to the scythe-tree, the blade forward over his left shoulder and with his left hand on the flange of the blade to firm it, with the same circular motion of the scythe-board he sharpened the tip:

> More say he rose again,
> Rose again, rose again,
> More say he rose again
> And listed in the army!

That done, he put the scythe-board back on the scythe-tree and taking a grip on the two handles, *duirníns* as he called them, he settled himself for mowing. The swish of the sharp blade through the corn stems made a sweet sound and he cut a swath the width of the track of a horse car through the field. And if you saw the nice way, with a small motion of the tip of the blade, he could throw all the ears of corn together. Then he halted and turning to his father he said, 'What do you think of that now, Da?'

The old man looked at the cut corn and then he looked at the scythe. 'No word of a lie,' he said, 'but it was an idle man that thought of it!'

And wasn't that old lad before his time! Look at all the idle men we have today because of inventions. After the scythe came the horse-drawn mowing machine. Then the tractor was invented so that even the horses were idle!

There was something new out every week that time and some people wouldn't hear of the new thing until it was standing in front of them! And did it cause some excitement! Jerry Con Rua was over here at the forge the day he saw his first bicycle. All the men were taking the legs off one another rushing out of the forge as the cyclist came down from Casey's Cross, hopping off the road on his solid tyres.

'What is it called?' says Jerry, 'what is that contraption called?'

'A bicycle!' he was told.

'A bicycle. Good!' says Jerry. 'That's the first question the woman'll ask me when I'll tell her about it, "What's it called, Jerry?" *Corp an Diabhail* but I have the answer for her now. A bicycle!'

He came home and Juiloo, 'the woman' as he called her, gave him a cup of beef tea on the backless chair sitting near the fire. The comfort some men had that time!

'Any news from the forge, Jerry?' says she.

'Juiloo!' he said, 'you missed it you weren't over at the forge today! A fellow came down the road from Casey's Cross, and as I own to God, he was like he'd be spread legs on the gate of the haggard outside! There were two wheels under it, and his legs were going around. He was going as fast as a galloping horse and his legs weren't even touching the ground!'

'And what was it called, Jerry?' she said.

'Ah ah, I knew that was the first question you'd ask me. And I have it here for you as round as a hoop. 'Tis called . . . There's a "b" in it!'

'Go out there and give a sop to the cows and it will come to you, Jerry!' she said, consoling him.

He went out and you could see him through the window crossing the yard, a pike of hay over his head, pausing every minute, sops falling down all round him, and he talking away to himself, 'And it wasn't a big word. There's a "b" in it! Whether the "b" is in the back of it or the front of it I don't know! There's a "b" in it. Bad luck to it, there's a "b" in it!'

He was like a bag of weasels all day. No word out of

him at the supper. The children had to shut up and the dog had to be put out as they were disturbing his train of thought!

The rosary was brought forward and the trimmings cut, the small lads put up to bed with a strict injunction to be silent. When there was utter quietness in the house he put Juiloo sitting down and implored of her to say all the strange names she heard in her geography lesson, the mountains of Greece and the rivers of China to see would anything give him an inkling. She went through as much *ráiméis* as she could – but it was no good. They went to bed. And Juiloo dropped off the second her head hit the bolster. What did she want awake for, and her man preoccupied!

And here was Jerry, his hands behind his head looking up into the darkness searching every nook and cranny of his head for the word wherever it had gone to!

About two o'clock in the morning he sat up and nudging Juiloo he began to shout, 'I have it! I have it!' Juiloo didn't know where she was.

'I have it!' he said.

'What have you, Jerry?' she said, all concern.

'I have it!' says he, 'Sickly boy!'

'*Mhuire Mháthair!*' says she, 'I hope it isn't contagious!'

The Singapore Policeman

One of the Túróineachs was coming home after spending ten years in the Singapore police, on a pension of a pound a day. This was at a time when a man'd bring home change out of a shilling after a day's carousing at Barraduv sports. The Singapore policeman had married an English lady while abroad, and she would have to be put up in the house too for a few nights anyway. The house, the ancestral home, was presentable enough and well kept when the mother was alive. The son, the policeman's brother, who was in it now, had the misfortune to marry Hannah Damery. She was pure easygoing. The clothes looked as if they had been thrown on her with a hayfork, she was sitting on the chair from morning till night chewing away and the children lapadawling around the floor! That kind of a woman!

Neighbours came in to help her put some *slacht* on the house. They whitewashed it inside and out and green rushes were cut and spread on the muddy approaches to the door. Grandma's bed was done up for the strangers, the tick put outside on the hedge to air it, dust rising out of it as it was beaten with the back of a grubber. The sheets were washed and bleached to knock the flour brand out of them! Crockery was borrowed for the table, and a big feast prepared for the homecoming night. 'Spare nothing,' Hannah said. Thinking of herself she was! All the neighbours were invited, and Hannah said they'd have some of that 'shaky' shivery stuff you'd ate with a spoon'. So jelly and trifle figured largely on the menu. They forgot the hundreds and thousands, little spheres of no consequence as Father Horgan called them at the stations, to shake on the trifle.

But early in the day, Hannah dispatched the husband to town for some, as she said the trifle wouldn't be the thing without them! And whether it was that she didn't give the husband the right description, we don't know, but in the shops in town they didn't seem to get the hang of what he was looking for, so he wound up in a bicycle shop where he purchased a large carton of ball bearings!

When the night came these were shaken on the trifle, and when people took a few spoons of it they found under their teeth what they couldn't chew. And they couldn't very well spit it out! How could they with the English lady and all there, though some did make off the yard to see what the weather was doing. Later in the night and the following morning people suffered dire pains in their lower regions and these two women met at the well out in the day.

'*Airiú*, tell me, Mary,' says one, 'did you try any of Hannah Damery's trifle yesterday evening?'

'I did,' says Mary, 'and it is I am the sorry woman. Up and down all night! Himself was going to go for the priest for me! Did it have any effect on you?'

'Effect! *Dia linn is Mhuire*! I thought it was "pintecitis" I was getting. An awful deadness in my right side! Like a lump of lead! And I thought then, with respects to you, I thought if I could break a little wind, that it would bring relief. Well, when I bend down to light the fire I did, and shot the cat.'

Padden

There was this couple, Paddy and Norrie Kirby, and they were twenty-one years married and they had no family. They were heart-broken because of it, no one to leave the place to, the grass of a cow and two goats is all they had, but to them that was wealth indeed.

One night on his way home from Killarney, Paddy was passing by the Seven Stoney Sisters – that's the druids' circle near Lissivigeen – and a grey man came out. He spoke to Paddy, 'Why are you so down and out?' he said. 'Why are you so mournful?'

'Well,' says Paddy, 'I'm hitting up to middle age . . . 'tis all downhill now to the grave, and I have neither chick nor child to cry after me! No son to put a shoulder to my coffin.'

'You mightn't be always like that!' says the grey man.

'Wisha, God help us!' says Paddy, 'I'm married now twenty-one years and there's no likelihood of anything yet!'

'You can take my word for it,' says the grey man, 'that in three spaces of time, your wife Norrie will present you with a son.'

Paddy went home.

'I'm afraid,' says Norrie when he told her what transpired, 'that that grey man is a bit of a rogue!'

'Only time can tell,' says Paddy. 'We might as well go to bed anyway!'

They went to bed, and six months after it was plain to anyone looking at Norrie that an event was expected. When her time came, Paddy was planting a tree in the field *oright* the house out, in honour of the occasion, when one of the women ran out to say his son was born! The poor man was so overcome with excitement that the heart gave out, and he died on the spot.

The son was called Padden, a variation of the father's name, and his mother promised him, as soon ever as he could follow what she was saying, that she'd keep him on the breast until he'd be big enough and strong enough to pull the tree from the roots that his father planted the day he was born.

When he was seven years old she put him out in the field and told him to pull the tree. And even though he had a pair of arms on him as big as a lad twice his age, he couldn't knock a shake out of the tree. The mother saw that there was nothing for it now but nurse him on for another seven years. This she did and at the end of that time, when he got up he was so big that his head went through the ceiling. He had to crawl on all fours to get out through the door. Once outside he spit on his hands and made for the tree and we must not forget, that all this time the tree was growing too! So he had his work cut out for him. He got a grip on it, and with the first heave the ground shook and cracked – for seven perches all round. He pulled again and you could hear the roots breaking below, and with the third heave, he brought the tree clear out of the ground, leaving a hole big enough to bury all the cows that died of foot-and-mouth disease since the first homing pigeons brought that malady in from the continent of Europe!

He got a saw then and a hatchet and lopped off the branches and the roots, and rounding the butt of it he made a walking cane out of the trunk of the tree.

'Mother,' says he – and she was proud of him! – 'You worked hard to keep me in sustenance for fourteen years. It is time for me now to do something for you. I'm going off to seek my fortune so that you can live in comfort in the remaining years of your life!'

He set out through the country as it was then – no roads or railways – and never drew rein till he came to the court of the King of Leinster. And when the King of Leinster saw this big *fostúch* of a man outside the front door, he came out. 'What are you looking for?' the king said.

'I'm looking for work,' says Padden.

'What can you do?' says the king.

'I can do anything,' says Padden.

'I'll make a bargain with you now,' says the king. 'I'll give you three jobs to do and if you succeed in doing them, I'll give you your weight in gold going home, but if you fail, what you'll get'll knock a hop out of you – cut the top of the ear down off me!'

'I'll chance my luck anyway,' says Padden. 'What'll I do first?'

'Go down,' says the king, 'and empty that lake below, and your dinner will be waiting on the table for you when you will come up.'

'And where will I put the contents?' says Padden.

'Empty it over that small hill and down into the glen!'

Padden went down and he ran his walking cane, the same as you'd run the handle of a shovel under a load of sand, under the hill and made a tunnel level with the lake shore. He went down then on his two knees and he sucked up the lake and shot it back through him and into the tunnel and down into the glen. A cloudburst is how the *Cork Examiner* described it, or whatever *Examiner* was there at the time. Only goes to show how wrong newspapers can be! A wall of water came down the valley. People saving hay in the inches ran for the high ground – didn't go back for their coats! Only a few men thatching houses is all that were saved. Even the local tailor that was crossing the stepping stones at Gortalick at the time was swept away and as he was borne off on the breast of the flood he was heard to shout, '*Tá rud amháin cinnte, beidh an gleann seo gan táilliúir!*'

When the king saw that Padden had the lake as dry as the palm of your hand, he said to himself, 'This fellow is not the fool I took him to be. If I don't get a harder job for him, I'll soon be parting with my gold.'

'What'll I do now?' says Padden.

'Don't do any more today,' the king said, 'go in and have your dinner!'

That same night, the king went to his adviser, the *Dall Glic*. He told him about Padden.

'You'll have to give me a hard job for him to do. Something that's next door to impossible or I'll soon be parting with my money!'

'Haven't you a brother in hell?' says the Dall Glic.

'I have,' the king said. 'There's hardly any other place that blackguard could be.'

'Send Padden down for him. Say that you want to see him!' says the Dall Glic.

The following day the king dispatched Padden down to hell for the brother.

'How'll I know him?' says Padden.

'He'll have only one tooth,' the king said, 'standing up like a *golaun* stone in the middle of his lower jaw!'

When Padden began hammering on the gate of hell with the trunk of the tree, the devils inside started shivering in their shoes. They thought it was the end of the world, so they opened the gate.

'I'm here,' says Padden, 'for the King of Leinster's brother!'

'How'll we know him?' says the devils.

'By a single tooth,' says Padden, 'standing up like a *golaun* stone in his lower jaw!'

Off with the devils and it isn't one fellow they brought back, but twenty single-toothed, ugly looking devils as look alike as guinea hens.

Padden had no notion of spending time in the hot, sweaty atmosphere of hell, finding out which of these was the king's brother, so he drove them all out before him back to Leinster and into the royal parlour. I can tell you the king got a fright when he saw smoke coming out of the boarded floor where they were standing. In no time at all they burned twenty holes through the floor and fell into the cellar.

'Get 'em out of it,' says the king in a rage, 'before they turn Ireland into an inferno. Drive 'em back down to hell!'

'What about your brother?' says Padden.

'The devil turn him,' says the king, 'if they are an example of what hell can do to a man, I don't want cut, shuffle or deal with him! Drive 'em down!'

While Padden was on his way to hell with the twenty toothless men, the king went again to his adviser. And the Dall Glic said, 'It seems nothing is impossible to Padden and you'll be without your gold!'

The Dall Glic gave the brain a bit of a shaking and then he said: 'Haven't you a deep shaft in the yard where you were mining for copper?'

'I have,' says the king.

'Send Padden down to dry up the bottom of it,' says the Dall Glic. 'And when he's below, get some of your hefty men to throw a heavy weight down on top of him!'

The following day, the king showed Padden the mine shaft. 'And if you can dry up the bottom of it,' says he, 'that'll be the third job done and I'll give you your weight in gold going home and a new hat into the bargain!'

Down with Padden and when he was below, the king got his men to throw a millstone down on top of him, but the hole in the centre of the millstone was the same size as Padden's head and when it landed on him it was such a nice fit he thought it was the new hat!

He dried up the bottom of the shaft, came up and when the king saw him emerging out of the shaft with the millstone on his head, he was man enough to admit defeat, so a huge weighing scales was procured and as Padden made for it the king said to him: 'Surely you're not going to stand on it with your new hat on!'

'Isn't it as natural for me,' says Padden, 'to stand on it with my hat on as with my trousers on!'

The king was done for again and he said, 'All right!' but of course he didn't have enough gold in his kingdom to weigh down Padden, but he gave him what he could afford.

Padden came home to his mother. He dined her and he wined her; he made her burn her old shawl and he bought her a nice navy coat, a big floppy hat, white gloves and the swankiest pair of 'lastic boots you ever clapped eyes on, and when the days lengthened out into spring, he brought her here and there to see the sights. They went everywhere together, to races and regattas, and the last place they were seen was at the hurdygurdies at Puck Fair, the two of 'em going around on the chairoplanes!

The Cat and the Splinter

'Tis only when you'd see the big blaze of electric light in the houses at the present time that you'd wonder how the people before us managed with the rush light and the splinter!

The rush was peeled – old people'll follow me here, for if they didn't see it they heard tell of it. The rush was peeled – not fully, a thin strip was left on at the back for reinforcing, otherewise the white core'd go in *brus*, in your hand. The peeled rush was dipped in goat's fat, or any other fat, and allowed to harden, and a *carn* of them'd be kept in the *cúilín* in the corner. Though to my mind the rush was not a permanent light. It didn't give the battle, but 'twas handy for *ootumawling* around the house, or showing the old couple to bed.

Then you had the bog deal splinter – a pure *dinger*! And that was the only form of illumination you had before the candle, the tilly lamp or Ardnacrusha were ever dreamt of. To select a splinter you'd select a straight-grained *creachaill* of bog deal and with the saw you'd run it off into lengths of, say, from one-and-a-half to two feet. Then with the hatchet you'd come at these lengths and cleave them down into thin strips 1 1/2" x 1/4" and put them up in the shoulder of the chimney to season for the winter. And at that time, up on the wall you had a bracket – a holder made by the smith, and when night'd come, lob a blazing splinter into the bracket and you'd have plenty of light for playing cards or any other caper.

Earthen or mud floors you had in houses then, except for the flag of the fire, and the *gáirdín na nóinín*'d be danced on that flag, or the door would be taken off the hinges to make a platform, and I often heard it said that every member of the company would light a splinter in the fire and ring the musician and the dancers with a ribbon of light. It was lovely! And how long would a splinter live? Half-an-hour, I suppose, maybe longer, according to the quality: but when it'll die, you could light another one, or two. They were plentiful and there was no fear of blowing a fuse!

Well, in the time of the splinters there was this carpenter and he was living alone in a small house. He had no apprentice or servant, only a butter-coloured cat called Bubble, for he was puffed out like a football. The carpenter was a first-class man, served his time, did journey work, and was in great demand for making commons cars, and all that goes with them – wheels, butt, rail, guards and seat across.

In the kitchen he used to function, for business was that brisk he had no time to put up a workshop. In the winter he'd be working at night. He'd have the body of a car, we'll say, together on the floor, and he'd be fitting the back set-lock down on the shafts and sidelaces – knacky work! and you'd want good light for it. A splinter is all he had, and 'twasn't the thing, for he'd want it at the car where he'd be fitting, and he'd want it at the bench where he'd be cutting, and he'd want it at the grindstone where he'd be edging, and a man has only two hands, so what did he do but train the cat to hold the light. And if all belonging to you were dead you'd weaken to see the cat holding the splinter out at arm's length, so as not to singe his whiskers!

In the beginning, the carpenter was saying to the cat, 'Down this way, Bubble. Slant it over. Right! A bit more to your left. That's the tack! Hold it there now, that's the real goat's toe!'

And so on till the cat got so well up that he knew the carpenter's next move and was there before him. All this was miraculous of course, though I'd say that the cat wasn't in with himself for the ears were only half-cocked and the tail was down flat. But there again I could be wrong, no man knows what goes on inside in an animal's head. That's one closed book to us anyway!

Well, news of Bubble and the splinter leaked out. The saddler told the master, the master told the scholars, the scholars told their mothers and the mothers told the parish! And when night fell you couldn't draw a leg in the carpenter's yard with the crowd gaping in the window all marvelling at Alladin. A tay-man came the way. In with him to the carpenter's and when he saw the cat supporting the blazing splinter he was spellbound. When he found his tongue he said to the carpenter, 'How do you account for the animal's perspicacity?'

'Training,' says the carpenter, 'it overcomes nature!'

'I doubt very much,' says the tay-man, 'if there's one atom of truth in that.'

The tay-man went away in his pony and car and when he came back in a week's time, the carpenter was having his supper and there was Bubble sitting on his *corragiob* at the top of the table holding the light. The carpenter invited the tay-man to sit over. He did. And the tay-man could see that the carpenter was full of admiration for Bubble, and hopping the ball, he said, 'Perspicacity my eye! No amount of drilling can overcome the natural bent in an animal!'

'There's an animal there now for you,' says the carpenter, 'and nothing will deflect him from his duty!'

'Would you like to bet on that?' says the tay-man.

The carpenter said he would and bets were put down, and the tay-man took out a Van Houeten cocoa tin and taking off the perforated cover he let a mouse go on the table!

The cat dropped the light – *Is treise dúchas ná oiliúint!* – and went after the mouse. He was the only one of the three of 'em that could see in the dark!

The Tay-Man

A tay-man put up one night with a man and his wife in a one-roomed house in which there was only one bed. You had a lot of those houses at that time – thatched huts built by the farmers for their workers. They cared about the comfort of their servant! The tay-man put his pony in the boarded shed outside. Indeed he wouldn't have stayed in such a poke of a place at all, only that the night was stormy and he couldn't get to his usual lodgings.

Before they went to bed the woman of the house took up a lovely cream cake . . . oh! the aroma that was from it, and put it standing that way – a wheel with four spokes – on the ledge of the dresser. Well, the tay-man's teeth were swimming inside in his mouth for a bite of the cake, and the wife noticing the hungry look on his face was about to break off a piece for him.

'No, no,' the husband said, 'you'll ruin the cake if you break it while it is hot! Can't he wait until morning like the rest of us?'

They went to bed. The wife next to the wall, the husband next to her, and the tay-man on the outside. God knows then that the bed was narrow enough too, so that they had to lie spoonways, and when one'd turn they'd all have to turn! In the course of the night when the husband had occasion to go out, which was often . . . he had a little frequency . . . that runs in families! . . . he made the wife go with him. He was slow to let her with the tay-man, and indeed she complained bitterly about having to go out in the yard, the breeze going through her! And as she said herself, moreover when she didn't have occasion to!

In the end she kicked against going out, and the husband, still nervous of leaving her alone with the tay-man, lifted up the cradle with the child in it, and put it between the two of them in the bed and went out. When he came in, after shedding the tear for Parnell, he lifted up the cradle and put it back on the floor – the busy night he had!

Around six in the morning, the storm got so bad it began to rip the boards off the shed, and the husband in his excitement to get out to tie it down, forgot all about the tay-man. When he was gone, the wife turned to the tay-man and said, 'Now is your chance!'

He got up and ate the cake!

The Connachtman's Story

According to Johnny Curtin, when his father was putting in for the pension, he couldn't find his age. What happened in a case like that was, you would go before the Old Age Pensioners' Committee. Father Horgan that was at the head of that at the time, and if a man could remember an event, an act of God or such like, that happened long ago, that would be taken as evidence of age, and an affidavit would be sworn to that effect.

Curtin's father, a man who couldn't stop talking once he started, was asked if he remembered the night of the big wind? A usual question when the pension came out in 1908. He said he did. He was sitting inside by the fire, he said, when the wind blew in the door and that gale was so strong it whipped the roof off the house. Even the pot of potatoes boiling over the fire was taken holus bolus up the chimney, and as it emerged at the top it was struck by lightning . . . you could see the stream rising out of it . . . and they were the first spuds to be boiled by electricity! The pot got as red as a coal of fire and went floating off through the air. The people running out of their houses and seeing the ball of fire in the sky thought it was one of the great astronomical tokens of disaster given down in the prophecies of Saints Moling and Colmcille, when Ireland will be invaded by Spaniards, Portuguese, Turks, French and rattle-snakes: when a clergyman wearing a black cloak will lead the men of the North into the valley of the Black Pig, and fighting men will be so scarce that old lads will be turned in their beds three times to see would they be fit to shoulder a gun! The young will forget what men looked like, and a daughter and her mother crossing Thomond

Bridge will see a figure. And the daughter will say, 'What is that?' And the mother will say, 'That's a man!' and the daughter will start laughing and that night the mother will kill the daughter so that she'll have the man for herself!

'Stop, stop, stop!' says Father Horgan, 'do you want to bring the flames of hell jumping up at me. Give him the pension,' says he, 'or we'll be here till doom's day!'

Of course it was in the prophecy too that the time would come in Ireland when we wouldn't know the women from the men ... the Lord save us! And that the wrapper would be worth more than the contents, though that is said to have come to pass during the Economic War with England when farmers couldn't sell their stock.

Calves were skinned, the hides were sold and the carcasses thrown away. Of course Bull gave in in the end but, like always, he waited until we were nearly all dead!

In bad times like that when the price of what you have to sell is falling and the price of what you have to buy is rising, a small farmer might have to go out in service himself, and leave the place to his wife to work it with whatever help she might get from a neighbour or a relation.

Now, it so happened, away far back, that there was this man living in the province of Connacht. He wasn't long married, a couple of months maybe, and he decided, so that they could keep body and soul together, that he would go out in service for twelve months. So he crossed the Shannon and into the rich land and after a long time travelling he was hired by a big landowner and he worked for him for twelve months.

He was treated well, the wages were good, he slept in the house and sat down to the same table as the family, and when a bullock was killed, looking into his plate, you'd see as much beef as turnips. He had time off to go to a football match or pitch and toss, and when Christmas Eve came round the farmer said to him, 'I'd take it as a great favour if you'd stay for another twelve months.'

'I would and willing,' he said, 'if I could get an account to Nora.' She was the wife. There were no roads or railways, no postmen or telegraph wires at the time. 'But Nora is a knowledgeable person,' he said, 'and maybe she'll understand.' So he remained on for another twelve months, and at the end of that time coming up to Christmas Eve the boss called him in.

'You are going now,' he said, 'and which will you take: three pieces of advice or your wages?'

'You were always fair in your dealings with me,' says the Connachtman. 'Which would you take yourself?'

'I'd take the three pieces of advice,' the farmer said. 'For the road now here are three oaten cakes herself made, a small one, one not so small and a big one, but on no account broach the big cake until you are landed at home!'

'All right,' the servant said as he went out the door.

'Come here. You are going now without the three pieces of advice. Never go the near-way when you are on the road at night. Never sleep in the same house where a young woman is married to an old man and, never make a judgement when you are in a temper!'

So the man from the west set out for home, taking a bite out of one of the small cakes when he got hungry and drinking a sup from a well. When night came he fell in with a group of men, who like himself were going home from service with their wages in their pockets. They came to a place where the men said they knew a short-cut through a wood, but he, remembering the advice, held to the public road. Times were as bad then as they are now; the men were waylaid and robbed of their money.

He went on another while and as he was tired when he came to a house he went in. He was given shelter and the young woman spilled him out a cup of milk. Looking around he could see that there was no other one in the house with her only an old man of perished appearance sitting by the fire. He asked the young woman, 'Is he your husband?' and she said, 'He is. God help me!' And remembering the second piece of advice, Never sleep in the same house where there is a young woman married to an old man, he got up and went out. 'Twas raining now, so he took shelter in a car house.

He wasn't long there when a young man came and tapped on the window. She put her head out. 'All right,' she said without lowering her voice – the old man must be deaf! She came out and he overheard them planning together... how to get rid of the old man. He said to himself that it was time to go, so as not to get implicated in that.

He walked on and when he got drowsy he put his back to a rick of hay or a stack of oats and slept for an hour. By the middle of the following day the two small oaten coates were finished and even though he was often hungry after, he never broached the big cake, and when he landed at his own house that night he put it on the table. Nora, his wife, had great welcome for him. Such a long time! But he said he was so tired after the journey, he'd throw himself on the bed for a while, and made for the room door.

'Oh,' she said, coming before him. 'You can't go up there. John is sleeping in that bed with me.'

'John.'

'Oh,' he said. '*Croi an Diabhail!* and flaring up he rushed over and caught hold of the tongs and just then he thought of the third piece of advice: Never make a judgement in a temper!

'What's wrong?' says Nora, going into the room. 'Look at John!' she said from inside, 'he hasn't his clothes on him yet!'

When he heard that he was going to go for the tongs in earnest! She came down the room door. 'Hold the child!' says she, 'I'll get the supper. We'll try a piece of the Kildare bread!'

'Twas his own child, a fine agreeable eighteen-month-old baby, teeth up and down on him, and called John after his own father!

'Cutcha! Cutcha! Cutcha!' he said, poking his finger at the laughing bundle.

And all the tiredness went out of his bones as he danced around the flag of the fire. Nora was singing as she laid the table. She broke the cake and what was inside in it? His two years' wages! So they put down the kettle and made the tay, and if they didn't live happy that we may!

Filling the Firkins

Farmers like to see their servants observing their religious duties, but they wouldn't give them a seat on the side-car going to Mass on Suday.. No! Nor no seat in the family pew the farmer owned in the chapel. No, nor no seat at the dinner table in the farmer's house on Sunday nor any other day!

'The servants always had their meals abroad,'Johnny Curtin told me, 'abroad in the back kitchen or the linny. In one place I worked, the farmer used to come out to the linny and sit with the servants. Then just as we were all reaching for our first mouthful, the farmer would rise to his feet and say: "Grace before meals. In the name of . . . and the Holy Ghost. Amen!"

'When we had blessed ourselves he'd move back from the table, and we were all so young and so innocent at the time, and God help us, so ill-equipped to fight for our rights, that we'd take our caps and go out the door half-hungry. The farmer then'd go into the house and sit down with his wife to his real dinner!

'And what was left of our meal, the potatoes, were broken up into a big tub, given a shake of Indian meal, and a dash of skimmed milk and taken out to the stall-fed animals that were being fattened up for the market.'

'But not all men you'd meet,' Johnny told me, 'were like that, but those that were, were bad, and the wives were worse. I was coming into my supper, such as it was, one night. I was in my stocking feet, and the woman of the house, whose back was to me, didn't know I was there, and she said to the husband: "Did you put out the servant boy's cup and did you thin the milk for him?"

'And you'd think the servant girls, that were more in the house with the food under their hands, would fare better than we did. They did not! And you didn't have to go up to Limerick or Tipperary at all to see it. It happened here inside in your own parish.

'When the farmers were joined in butter, you remember that, Ned? Well, their wives would all collect in one house once a week to pack the firkins for dispatch to Cork. The butter'd have to be washed and blended, the servant girl, the two arms dragged out of her, drawing water from the well a couple of fields away; lifting the heavy firkins – all the horse work was hers! When the job was finished there'd be a feast in the parlour. Indeed the servant girl might be sent down to the village for a drop of the foxy boyo. The kettle would be ready, on the boil when she came back to heat the glasses. Then the bottle of whiskey would be tilted into the glasses.

'"Oh, no, no, no," you'd hear the women saying. "That's enough for me! It travels to the head!"

'Boiling water was added, a couple of lumps of loaf sugar and a clove! Oh glory! The sound of the spoons in the glasses. Small bells tinkling!

'Like the parish priest that fell from grace! The bishop was discussing it with the canon at a month's mind. The canon was all concern, for as he remarked it is so seldom a thing like that happens. And he said to the bishop, lowering his voice, "Was it punch, my Lord?"

"Yes," the bishop said, "and Judy!"

'While the women were sipping the punch, the table in the parlour'd be laid by the servant girl. She'd bring in plates of this and that, cream cake and apple tart, and last of all the special chinaware teapot, and the tea-cosy! The women'd sit in – such a babble of talk after the punch. And if the servant girl lingered at the door looking longingly at the laden table, the woman of the house would say to her, "Go on away out there. You'll find something to do outside. Standing there, watching every bite that goes in our mouths!"

'The servant girl would go out and all the other ladies would agree with the woman of the house. All talking together, you could hardly make out what they were saying!

"You're right not to be giving her the habit of it!"

"She'd ate you out of house and home. The size of her!"

"Pamper 'em, I always say, pamper servant girls and they'll walk on you!"

"The next thing is they'll be throwing the glad eye at your son, or, the Lord save us, at your husband maybe!"

"Oh, the glad eye is no good to the man of this house. John has enough to do as it is. Eh, Hanna!"

"Cut 'em down on the food, that's the thing!"

"Then they won't have the *gimp* on 'em for it!"'

But there was nothing more calculated to drive a farmer and his wife off their rocker than for the servant boy to fall in love with the daughter. I tell you a match'd be made for her in double quick time with a man of substance.

The Apprenticed Doctor

Up the country where habitations are few and a knocker on every door, I don't know what servants did during the few hours they'd have off at night. Of course, they wouldn't be off in every house. They worked until they went to bed. Around here where farmers were big enough to afford hired help, the servant boy could knock into the rambling house at night in the winter time. Lift the latch and walk right in. This'd be the residence of some honest to God farmer that was pulling the devil by the tail, or the house of the postman, the carpenter or the tailor.

These rambling houses, as far as I remember, were a cross between the Dáil and the Cork Opera House! There you'd have debates, old 'statesmen' would answer questions and try to unravel the mysteries of the universe and the economy. You'd have stories and riddles, songs, music and an occasional dance. In the long summer evenings, the Dáil would adjourn! Go to the country! The company would sit on a mossy bank under a shaped hedge by the roadside, and passers-by could add a note to the general hilarity.

Another place of assembly in the fall of the year was around the mouth of a limekiln , the red glow from the fire lighting up the men's faces. At that time every well-to-do farmer had a limekiln on his property. It was built against a hill in a *leaca*. You'd cut an 'L' shape and clear out that triangle of earth. Then the stone-mason would build the kiln, circular inside, like an upside-down cone or the paper *tómhaisín* the old women used to get the snuff in long ago. Only a couple of feet wide at the bottom and widening out as it went up to about six or eight feet in diameter at the top. It would be twelve or fifteen feet high, and had to be built of good heat-resisting stone – the end grain to the fire. As the mason went up, like the Gobán Saor building the round tower, he built the front wall, the breast of the kiln, and the two returning walls. The removed earth he would now, return fill and ram, as they say, into the spaces in between.

In the front wall you had the eye of the kiln, arched . . . it would remind you of the eye of a bridge, or a fireplace with an opening at the bottom, to remove the burnt lime. Now to work it . . . you see, at the top level there was a gap or a gateway where you carried in the raw limestone and the turf with which to burn it. And at the lower level you could back in your horse and car and draw away the burnt lime – 'twas like a human being – in above and out below!

To work it you started off with a blazing fire, a good few feet of turf, and then a layer of limestone, broken small, another layer of turf and so on, limestone, turf, until it was filled to the top, and then you'd see the men jumping on it to pack it down. As it burned and the turf was reduced to ashes, the lime fell down and more layers were added at the top and this went on for days or weeks until the lime was burned.

There was a fierce draught in that chimney and when the kiln caught fire, in no time it developed such an intense heat that the grey limestone was burned through and whatever chemical was knocked out of it, it emerged below a creamy white and hardly half the weight it went in. Take up a small piece of it and let a few drops of rain fall on it, and it would crumble in your hand dissolving into a fluffy powder. That was used for making mortar and fertilising the land.

In the fall of the year that time, you might see five or six of these limekiln s burning, little volcanos, the white smoke rising up and drifting along in the breeze. The mothers of the locality, when they saw the smoke, they'd be along to the kiln the following day for an apron-full of the lime; it would be kept in a box below the dresser. Well, a lump of that would be put sizzling in a cup of water, or it might be put steeping in a crock the night before, and every small lad'd have to take a few sups of that before the breakfast. Often I drank it myself . . . it tasted like . . . Oh! . . . the clippings of horse hoofs! But the mothers swore by it, claiming that it killed all the microbes and germs lurking along the 'elementry' canal! You'd want to see no doctor after it; nor was there any living for doctors at that time.

They say the first doctor to come into this corner of the parish was during the 1918 flu. He wasn't seen again until the epidemic of appendicitis in the 1930s. Of course there was the occasional case of the man being sent to Dublin to the specialist. For many of those poor people that trip to Dublin was their first time seeing a train and I don't want to be too hard on the medical profession, but a lot of them went to heaven only seeing the train once!

One night I was at such a venue, the limekiln , and a brother's son of my own, Larry, came there for a load of lime. He had the contract of repairing Dr Collin's house – Board of Works job. That very day, he told us, he was putting in a new window, up and down sashes, ropes and brassfaced pulleys and so on.

'I had a crock of red lead paint, as specified for the priming,' he said, 'and with whiting and linseed oil, I was making the putty to glaze the sash, when along came Dr Collins. And when he saw the appurtenances of my trade he laughed. "Aha," he said, "I see putty and paint cover all your mistakes!"

'"That's right, Doctor!" I said, "And the spade and shovel cover all yours." He didn't like it at all!

Medical topics, like talk of love or small potatoes, once the subject comes down there's no knowing where it will end. And that night sitting on a clamp of turf, a few feet away from the mouth of the volcano, was a Tagney man – that's a son of his that's married in over there now in Tom Casey's place. Tagney *scrope* the inside of his pipe, a little smaller than the kiln, and knocking the ashes and *bruscar* of tobaccy into the cover, and putting it on a *ciarán* of turf, he settled himself and said: 'In ancient times in Ireland, if we can judge by what we hear, if you wanted to go on for the practice of medicine you wouldn't go to college at all like now. What'd happen is, you'd serve your time to the local dispensary man, the same as if you were going in for tailoring or stonemasoning.

At that time there was this rich couple and they had no family only the one son. God help us! as thick as the wall! The wife thought that it would be a great uplift for 'em in the community to have the name of having a son a doctor. And having the money and the influence they got the son bound down to one Dr Galvin that was operating at the time. So everywhere the doctor'd go Jack the apprentice'd be around after him, dressed up to the nines, and a little hard hat on him.

They were called out in the country this day where a man was sick. They went into the kitchen and up in the room, and Dr Galvin gave the patient a thorough examination, you may be sure, and put his finger on the complaint and prescribed for him. When they were going out of the room Dr Galvin, looking back, said to the patient, "Give up eating oranges. They don't agree with you constitutionally!"

Crossing out the yard, Jack the apprentice said to the doctor, 'How in the world did you know the man was eating oranges?'

'In our trade,' says the doctor, 'you must keep your eyes open. Didn't you see the skins under the bed?'

That was all right. About a week after, there was another call, very urgent, and the same day the doctor was away at a funeral – maybe he had a good right to be there! And as the call was urgent, Jack said he'd go. Off with him, with his little bag, into the kitchen bursting with importance and down in the room. He never looked at the patient, no more than I'm looking at the moon this minute, only lifted the quilt and looked under the bed. And there looking out at him was a set of harness! He turned to the patient and with his two thumbs he pushed down the lower eyelids, mercy of God that he didn't blind him with the pressure, and said, 'You'll die roaring if you don't give up eating horses!'

Now that Jack had his first success, according to himself, he decided that he would go off as a journeyman – an improver. His father, a saintly man, at the altar every morning, tried to persuade him to wait until he'd have more knowledge, but the mother gave Jack the money to get a doctor's bag and some instruments, a big knife and a saw in case of amputations!

Jack set out and he was going along but no one put any come hither on him until he met a man of very pale complexion. The pale man asked Jack what his trade was and Jack told him. The pale man said he was fairly well up in medicine himself.

'Hire me,' he said to Jack, 'and you won't be sorry!'

Having a servant, Jack thought, would make him appear more important, so he hired the pale man, and the bargain was that whatever money was made in each case would be divided between 'em. They shook hands on it, and the pale man's hand was as cold as ice.

It wasn't long until they heard that the son of the richest man in the country was down with some strange malady. His case had bamboozled all medical science, and his father was now offering five-hundred pounds to any doctor, home or foreign, that could cure his son. Jack and the pale man went up to the house and after explaining who they were, the rich man brought 'em up to the sick room, and there was the son lying on the bed and not a *gug* out of him.

The pale man felt his pulse and told Jack they'd want the sick room to themselves. 'What do these people want here for?' he said, 'they are only using up the air on the sick man. We'll want two pots brought in,' he said to Jack, 'one with hot water and one with cold.'

This was done, the room was cleared and the patient was now in what is known as intensive care!

'Where's the doctor's bag?' says the pale man.

Jack gave it to him. The pale man took out the saw and the knife and like that, in a jiffy, he had the head cut off the patient. He took an herb out of his pocket, the size of a head of *caisearbhán*, and rubbed it to the wound above and below, cauterising it. Not a drop of blood flowed. He then took the head by the two ears and ducked it into the hot water, gave it a swirl and then a *swee-gee* and like lighting ducked it into the cold skillet. He shook the water off it and landed it back on its place, lined up the wind-pipe, the jugular, the spinal and vocal cords, veins, arteries and blood vessels, gave the head a tap to firm it down, took out some powder, mixed it like Polyfilla and filled the crack all round!

'Are you all right now?' says the pale man to the patient.

'I'm fine,' says he. "Never felt better in all my life!"

And began to dance around.

The young man's father was delighted, paid the five-hundred pounds, no bother, and Jack and the pale man had to stay the night for a big party, polka sets and everything!

In the morning, when they got down to the gate of the road, the pale man said to Jack, 'What about our bargain? Half the proceeds, wasn't it?'

Jack took out the money and lazy enough he was about it too!

'Ah,' says he, 'a quarter of it is enough for you, after all I'm the doctor. You are only the servant.'

The pale man didn't say yes, aye or no, only turned on his heel and went off, and Jack was left alone. Well, it never rains but it pours. Jack was hardly into the county Limerick when he heard of another young man that was down with the same complaint. His father too was a very rich man, and was offering a reward of five-hundred pounds to any doctor that could cure his son. Jack went up to the house. The father came out and when Jack told him who he was and the success he had in treating such ailments the father was in the seventh heaven with delight.

'Come on away in!' he said to Jack.

But Jack made it plain to him that he would not put his foot inside the threshold, or lay a finger on his son down of seven-hundred pounds – Jack was learning his trade!

The father agreed; what can you do when your hand is in the dog's mouth.

Jack went into the house, cleared all the gapers out of the sick room, ordered two pots of water, one cold and one hot, took out the knife and the saw and cut the head off the patient. God – all the blood! Then taking the head by the two ears he plunged it into the pot, and when his knuckles met the hot water, he wasn't prepared for it, and damn it if he didn't let the head go. Blessed hour it was like snap-apple night with him trying to retrieve the head, and ages went by before he was able to lever it out with the tongs. Then he plunged it into the cold pot, shook it and put it back in its place, but if he did the head fell one way and the body fell the other. Jack knew now that the devil was done, and he was looking up to see was there a skylight he could get out through. He was shaking with terror and muttering to himself,

'Rocks hide me and mountains on me fall!' like sinners will on the last day when they'll see God's face in the heavens.

With that he heard some commotion outside. It was the pale man trying to get in.

'Where are you going?' the patient's father wanted to know.

'I'm the doctor's servant,' the pale man said. 'He sent me to the apothecary for medicine and I have it here for him.'

He was let in but would he be in time? He took the herb out of his pocket and rubbed it to the head and the body and whatever blood was left in the man was coagulated on the spot. Then he took the head by the two ears. Mercy of God that the ears didn't come away in his hands they were so long in the hot water. Nice and easy he ducked the head into the hot water, gave it a swirl and then a *swee-gee*, lifted it out and into the cold water. Another swirl and another *swee-gee*, dripped the water off it and landed it back in its place. He had to work like lightning because of the delay. He lined up the wind-pipe, the jugular, spinal and vocal cords, veins, arteries and blood vessels. He was so thorough that he ran his finger under the patient's tongue in case it was curled in his mouth. Then he gave the head a smart tap to firm it down, puttied the crack all round, and said to the patient:

'Are you all right?'

'I'm fine!' the patient said, 'but awful dizzy!'

The loss of blood, of course!

'Plenty of beef tea for the next three weeks running,' says Jack, 'and you'll be as fit as a fiddle.'

Jack and the pale man ordered a few bags of sawdust to shake on the blood, before they called the father in. When he saw his son able to move around, the father was delighted. He paid the money on the nail, and threw a big dinner for Jack and the pale man.

When they got down to the gate of the road in the morning, the pale man said, 'What about the bargain?'

'Look,' says Jack, 'I didn't earn a ha'penny of that money. Take it all, for without you I couldn't cure anyone. I know nothing.'

'That's all I wanted you to admit,' says the pale man.

'But the money is no good to me where I'm going. Sit down and I'll tell you a story.'

They sat down.

'On the day of my funeral,' said the pale man, 'my coffin was stopped at the entrance to the graveyard by a man I owed money to. He had a gang with him an they told the mourners that my body wouldn't be buried until my debt was paid. My debts weren't great, but my people were poor and they hadn't that amount of money between them. Now, who should be passing the way but your father, and on hearing the arguing he came up and when he found out what was wrong, he put his hand into his pocket and paid the money, and I got what every man is entitled to, a decent burial.

'Since you went on the road doctoring, your father has been praying to high heaven for you every morning at the altar. I was in his debt, I couldn't let him down, so that's why I came to save you from the rope! Give me the bag. You can keep the money but let it be the last farthing you'll ever earn at the trade of medicine. If you have to practice, go foreign, and don't be killing Irish people!'

They went the lower road, I came the high road, they crossed over the stepping stones and I came by the bridge, they were drowned and I was saved and all I ever got for my storytelling was shoes of brown paper and stockings of thick milk. I only know what I heard, I only heard what was said and a lot of what was said was made up to pass the night away!

Glossary of Irish (and Hiberno-English) Words and Phrases

a mhic ó	sonny
A Thiarna	Lord
a bhuachaill	boy
a leithéide	its like, the like of it
Abhann Uí Chriadha	Quagmire River
abhar	amount
airiú	aroo
amadán	fool
Amen, a Thiarna	Amen, O Lord
an buile tobac	tobacco madness
an domhan thoir	the eastern world
anois	now
áras	grand dwelling
asacán	insult
bacáns	hinges
bád sí	fairy boat
badaoi, badaoi, badaoi	idiom used to call geese
balbh	dumb
balbhán	dummy
ball seirce	love or beauty spot
bán	untilled field, bawn
banbh	piglet
bandle	a measure of twenty-one inches, in Irish *bannlámh*
bata scóir	tally rod
bean chabhair	help woman
bean Chonnachtach	Connacht woman
bean sí	fairy-woman
beart	bundle
béiltigheach	great fire
biddy boys	young people collecting money house-to-house on St Bridget's Eve
biddy	form of St Bridget
bocarum	puff
bodach	clown
bogán	a soft-shelled egg
bohereen(s) (bóthairíní)	little road(s)
bonóicín	new-born infant

bothán	little hut
braddy (bradaigh)	a thieving cow
brídeog	ceremonial image of St Brigid
brus	bits, crumbs, dust
bruscar	small, fine pieces
budógs (bodóga)	heifers
cabáiste Scotch	Scotch cabbage
cabúis	cubby-hole
cadrawling	Anglicised form of *cadaráil*=foolish chatter
cailín fionn	fair-haired girl
caipín	cap
caisearbhán	dandelion
caoiners	mourners
caoining	lamenting
carn	little heap
carraig	rock
Carraig an Phúca	The Pooka's Rock
ceannbhán	bog-cotton, cotton-grass
ceithearnach	local tyrant, or one who aped the English
ceol sí	fairy music
caorán	small sod of turf
ciotóg	left-handed person
circín	chicken
ciseán	basket
clab	open mouth
cliabh	basket, creel, pannier
cliamhain isteach	one who marries into a farm
clismirt	noise, din
cnavshawling (cnáimhseáil)	grumbling, complaining
Cnoc an Áir	Hill of Slaughter
cnocán	hillock
codladh grifín	'pins and needles'
cogar mogar	hugger-mugger
cois	shelter of turf bank
collops	calves (of legs)
corp an diabhail!	body of the devil!
corrighiob, ar a	on her hunkers
craicean is a luach	the skin and the price of it
cráinín	scythe sharpener
creachaill	gnarled piece of wood
Críost go deo!	Eternal Christ!
croí an diabhail	by the devil's heart
cróitín	byre
crónán	humming
cruiceog (coirceog)	beehive
Crymonás!	O crikey!

cúilín	a nook
cúis gháire chughainn	what a joke!
cúl-gháirdín	back garden
cúl lochta	back loft
cúlóg	one who rides behind another on horseback
cupóg	dockleaf
curie-fibbles	bric-à-brac
d'réir an sean-chultúr	according to custom
dailc	low sized, stout
dall glic	blind expert
Dia linn	God with us
Dia linn is Muire	God and Mary be with us
Dia's Muire dhuit	God and Mary be with you (Hello)
diggle	euphemism for devil
dinger	person outstanding in his/her field
donas	misfortune
dorns	fistfuls
dructeens (drúchtíní)	beads (of perspiration)
dúirt sé dúirt sé	gossip
dyddle	make port a' bhéil or gob-music
éirí in airde gan cur leis	unmitigated vanity
éist	listen
erra (arú)	yerra!
fág an bealach	make way

(This phrase is used in the sense of 'knocking sparks out of the flagstones'.)

faill na ngabhar	goat's cliff
fáilte romhat	welcome
figario	unusual item of dress
fionnán	coarse mountain grass
fol-a-me-ding	something that defies description
fostúch	hireling/grown lad (derogatory, a lump of a boy)
gabháil	armful
gadaí dubh	black thief
Gáirdín na Nóinín	Garden of Daisies
gaisce	great deed
ganseys	jerseys
garsún	young boy
geatch (geaits)	caper
glugger	addle-egg
gimp	urge
giobals (giobail)	rags
giobhlachán	ragged person
gíocs	sound

glaise	stream
Gleann an Phúca	The Pooka's Glen
go brónach	sorrowful
golaun (gallán)	pillar stone/standing stone
grá no chroí	lovingly
grá	love
grafán	grubber
gríosach	ashes containing small coals, embers
grug	haunches
gug	sound or stir
high figgles (aghaidh fidilí)	masks
hyronious	outlandish, outrageous
joeyman	fairy
keeler (cíléar)	tub used for cooling liquids
kippen (cipín)	little stick
lapadawling	crawling (*lapadáil*)
lasaid	wooden baking board
laverick	weighty, awkward
leabadh na mbocht	the poor bed
leaca	sloping field at base of hillside
linny	lean-to
Lios an Phúca	the rath of the Pooka
lipín báite	wet rag
lop (lapa)	paw
lúbán	bent thing
macha	field in which cattle slept at night in summertime
madra uisce	otter
maith go leor	(in drinking terms) nicely
mar eadh!	indeed!
méagram	headache
méaróg	thin hay rope, made by one person
meas	respect
meigeall	goat's beard
Mhuire Mháithair	Mother Mary
mo léir cráite	woeful sorrow
mo léir!	alas
mothal	mop of hair
mouzing	courting
muing	grassy swamp
Muing an Phúca	The Pooka's Marsh
múnlach	animal urine

nacoss	easygoing
ní nach ionadh	no wonder
nóiníns	daisies
olagón	lamenting
ootumawling	rummaging
oright/o'er right	opposite
ós cionn cláir	laid out (as of corpse)
padhsán	mean man (complainer)
Páirc a' tSasanaigh	Englishman's Field
Parlaimint na gCoileach	The Cocks' Parliament
pé in Éirinn é	however
peidhleachán	butterfly
pickey	high spirits
pillaloo	plague
pillamiloo	nonsense word
piseóg(a)	superstition(s)
poitín	poteen
poll	back
poltóg	fine walloper of a child
pooka (púca)	hobgoblin
Poul an Phúca	The Pooka's Hole
poursheen	boreen or passageway
put the cap entirely on	round it off
ráiméis	nonsense
réiteoir	pipe cleaner
rócán	old song
room	parlour
sásta	satisfied
sawtawn	bottom
sceamhacháns (sceamhacháin)	peelings of waste potato after seed eyes have been removed
sceón	terror
sciolláns (sciolláin)	potato set, small potato
scrat	stitch
scrope	scraped
sea	yes
seana	old
seanchaí	storyteller
sharoose (searbhas)	bitterness, sarcasm
sí gaoithe	fairy wind
skeeting	skating
skelp (sceilp)	a piece
slacht	neatness
slán mar a n-instear é	God bless the hearers

sleán	spade for cutting turf
smathán	a taste, a small measure of whiskey
smig	chin
snaidhm na péiste	serpent's knot
	(part of a charm to cure colic in cattle)
spág	a long flat foot
spailpín	a migratory farm labourer
spifflicated	confused with the weight of drink
splink (splanc)	spark (of sense)
spiorad an tobac	tobacco spirit
sráthair fhadas	pannier baskets
stellan	milk-pan stand
stór	love (term of endearment)
suarachy	small
súgán	a straw rope
súilíns	bubbles
swee gee	a turn, twist
tamall	while
taosc	to drain
taoscán	little drop
taoscing	pouring
táthaire	impudent fellow
teasbach	energy
teip	mark
tierce	barrel
tóg bog é	take it easy
tomhaisín	measure
tráithnín	dry grass-stalk, a wisp of straw
trí na céile	confused
trí ráithe	nine months
tuille	tilley - an added amount.
tulc	spasm, fit of laughter.
turtóg	lump or clump
welt	blow
whist (éist)	listen
yeoish!	steady!

Glossary of Irish Sentences

Agus ag trácht dúinn ar uisce
And talking about water

Agus do bhí cara mná tí aige an oíche seo in Sráid Bhaisinton.
And he had a lady friend that night in Washington Street.

Agus gan focal in a phluic aige
Without a word in his mouth

Aighneas an Pheacaigh is an Bháis
The argument between Death and the Sinner

An puc ar a dhrom aige agus é ag imeacht mar a dúirt na sean-daoine.
Going with his bag on his back as the old people said.

An rud is annamh is iontach.
What's rare is wonderful.

An Siota is a mháthair
The Siota and his mother

Bhí aithne aige ar gharsún mín macánta.
He knew a fine honest young man.

Bhí an Ghaelige go blasta aice siúd, agus is in nGaeilge a bheidís ag caint in gcónaí.
She had fluent Irish, and it was in Irish they always spoke.

Bhí na cúrsaí fada go leor ag na spailpíní fadó.
It was a long way for the itinerant farm workers long ago

Bí ciúin.
Be quiet.

Bíonn seacht n-insint ar gach scéal, a deirtear, agus bíodh cluas ghéar againn do na hinsintí is rogha le duinne de ríscéalaithe Chiarraí.
It is said that there are seven tellings to every story. Let us listen then to what the king of the Kerry storytellers has chosen for us.

Cogar i leith chugham a stór.
I'll whisper you this, dear.

Cogar i leith, a Cháit.
Whisper to me, Cáit.

Cuir uait an chaint.
Stop talking.

Dá mbeadh capall acu siúd is istigh cois tine anois a bheinn ag ól té.
If they had a horse it's inside by the fire I'd be now drinking tea.

Diaidh ar ndiadh síos le fánaigh
Little by little with the incline

Dúirt sí le . . . gan aon Ghaolainn a labhairt ós chomhair an tSasanaigh.
Bhí go maith agus bhí go holc leis.
She said to . . . not to speak any Irish in front of the Englishman. It
was good and bad as well.

Feoil agus cnámha ort, cosa agus crúba fút, is earbal taobh thiar.
Flesh and bones on you, legs and hoofs under you and a tail behind.

Gruaig ar do cheann, solus i do shúile agus fiacla id bheal.
Hair on your head, light in your eyes and teeth in your mouth.

Idir Clydagh agus Muckross
Between Clydagh and Muckross

I gcúntas Dé, a grá ghil.
In God's name, love.

Is tuísce deoch ná sceál.
A drink first and then a story.

Is baolach ná déanfad an gnó.
I'm afraid I won't do it.

Is treise dúchas ná oiliúint.
Nature beats training.

Nach é an trua go deo é go raibh an dinnéar againn.
Isn't it a terrible pity we had the dinner.

'O mo chircín, mo chircín circ, a stór mo chroí istigh. Dia do bheannachta
a laogh, a leanbhín gleoite.'
Oh my little hen, my heart's treasure. God bless you, my beautiful
child.

*'Ó,' ar seisean, 'nach iontach go deo an t-urlabhra an Béarla. D'fhanfainn
ag éisteacht leis an gcaint sin go Lá an Luain.'*
'Oh,' says he, 'what a wonderful language English is. I could listen to
that talk till doomsday.'

Seana-chornal ó Bhattersea a bhí ann.
He was an old colonel from Battersea.

Solus na bhflaitheas dúinn go léir.
The light of heaven on us all.

T'anam 'on diabhal.
Your soul to the devil.

T'anam 'on riach.
The devil take your soul.

T'anam an diúcs.
Your soul to the devil.

Tá rud amháin cinnte: beidh an gleann seo gan táilliúir.
One thing is sure: this glen will be without a tailor.

Trí lár mo chroí tá taithneamh duit.
In my heart there's affection for you.

Trí mo choir féin, trí mo choir féin, trí mo mhór-choir féin.
Through my fault, through my fault, through my most grevious fault.